# Intrigue at the Palace

## A Novel by Michael Murray

Cricket Cottage Publishing

For information about group sales and permission, contact Cricket Cottage Publishing, LLC, 4409 Hoffner Avenue, Suite 127, Orlando, Florida 32812 or call 407-255-7785.

Website address: www.thecricketpublishing.com

ISBN: 978-0692493120
ISBN-10: 0692493123

# Acknowledgments

First, to God be the glory! Without Him, nothing is possible.

I also acknowledge my ancestors, who paved the way; my parents, Melma and Ed, who raised me with unbounded love and encouragement; my wife, Maily, and children, Chloe and Michael, who've been by my side for all these years; Rob, my most steadfast and supportive friend of thirty-plus years; my family too numerous to list. It is said that God puts people in your life for a reason, a season, or a lifetime. I am eternally blessed that you've been all of these to me.

## Special Appreciation

I want to thank some very special people, who directly inspired me, who brainstormed with me, who helped me edit, and who otherwise lent me their energy and enthusiasm. Without them, this novel may yet dwell only in the eye of my imagination. I extend my grateful appreciation and thanks to my dear friend Yvette, who encouraged and supported me tremendously through this effort and others; my fabulous son, Michael, who lent me his acute ear and sharp mind as I typed and re-typed; my amazing Aunt Judy, who encouraged me and spent hours helping me edit; and last but certainly not least, my friends, colleagues, and fellow writers in the Port Orange Scribes, who advised, argued and laughed with, taught, cajoled, and pounded on me, and opened my eyes and ears—what a marvelous assembly of humanity!

And now, *Intrigue at the Palace*...

## Disclaimer

*Intrigue at the Palace* is a work of fiction. The names, characters, places and incidents contained in the story are products of the author's imagination or are used fictitiously. Any resemblance to actual events, locales or persons, living or dead, is entirely coincidental.

The man of character, sensitive to the meaning of what he is doing, will know how to discover the ethical paths in the maze of possible behavior.

-Earl Warren, 1891-1974
14th Chief Justice, United States Supreme Court

# Chapter 1

# Genesis

The G6 touched down at Seaside Beach International Airport and rolled to a stop at a private hangar opposite the public terminal. As soon as the aircraft stopped moving, its door opened and its occupants, minus the pilot, descended the stairs and began loading their gear in the back of the large black SUV awaiting them. The steamy night air was heavy and tinged with a hint of salt from the Atlantic only four miles east, and the early hour made the airport dark, quiet, and deserted. That suited the members of Field Team Six just fine since they weren't big on public attention anyway. As the team piled into the SUV, its leader exchanged brief remarks with the driver, and shortly thereafter, the car sped away from the jet toward the city streets. Five minutes later, it pulled into a traffic circle in front of the newest, largest, most ornate building in the county, and parked near four other black SUVs. A man in a dark suit hurried toward the vehicle, pulling open its front passenger door as the driver put it in *Park* and turned off the engine.

"Welcome to sunny Florida," the man greeted, extending his hand to the team's Chief. "Good to see you again, Grace."

Grace Tran paused to assure she had hold of the white lab-coat she'd dug out of her bag, and felt its front right pocket to assure the set of agency credentials she previously placed there were in fact still there. They were. She stepped out of the vehicle and grabbed the man's hand, shaking it firmly as she took in a long deep view of the headquarters of the Earhardt-Roane Avionics Corporation. The massive ultra-contemporary building was aglow with a golden hue cast from spotlights strategically placed to illuminate the feat of modern architecture built at the corner of the county's busiest intersection. Earhardt-Roane Avionics, or ERAC as it was commonly known, was a US defense contractor that provided cutting edge technology, research, and information to the Pentagon, which in turn deployed those items to important national security operations, including border patrol operations and the wars in Iraq and Afghanistan. The company occupied a sprawling campus full of modern new buildings near the airport, just a few miles from the town's beach destinations. They were also only a few hours from several substantial NASA facilities as well as important US Navy and Air Force bases. By most measures, ERAC was a very successful company, and its president and board wanted to embed that perception in the minds of the public by building a breathtaking headquarters facility.

"G'morning, Mark. Nice to see you too, and thanks for your help with all this."

"No worries," he said. "We had the building secured thirty minutes after your call and nobody but my Evidence Recovery Team has been in or out since. The only other person in the building is the security guard in the lobby there with my man," he said, pointing to two men standing inside the building at the security/reception desk. "And I think those gents over there want a word with you."

He motioned toward some dark figures standing just outside the building's main entrance about a hundred feet away. The bright light from the lobby silhouetted the three shadowy figures, so Tran couldn't make out their distinguishing features.

"The tall one is mine, but the other two are the company's Security Chief, and a local cop," he said.

"Oh great. This is the first thing I want to do the minute I get off the plane," Tran said sarcastically.

The FBI agent laughed lightly, knowing how federal agents enjoyed having to manage local sensitivities when more important federal issues demanded their attention. He patted her playfully on the back.

"That's why *you* get paid the big bucks, *Boss Lady*."

Despite the darkness, Special Agent Mark Allen could see his old friend roll her eyes at the obvious absurdity of his statement.

"*Yippie!*"

Tran motioned to the vehicle, signaling her team to disembark and get rolling. Four people quickly popped from the SUV, collected whatever gear they needed, and headed into the building. As they entered, they flashed their badges, paused to receive some initial information, and then walked briskly to the elevators behind the security/reception station. Outside, Allen watched the NSA agents disappear into the building, and turned back to Tran.

"Listen, 3:45 in the friggin' morning on a Saturday is prit-tee early, so unless you have any further need of our services, I'll get my team outta' here and take my ass back home to bed."

Tran smiled. "Thanks, Mark. You've been a great help."

"BUT WAIT! THERE'S MORE!" Allen said, feigning his best game-show announcer voice. "I'm gonna' leave my Evidence Recovery Team here to finish collecting evidence for you, and the driver, Thorsten, as your liaison. Use them however you need. When you're ready, Thorsten will bring you to our offices—we've got your team set up in work spaces, and of course, our whole facility is at your disposal. We have cars standing-by if you need them, and we arranged rooms for you at The Fly Inn there," he said, pointing at a five-story hotel situated on the edge of the airport property across a parking lot and an open expanse of grass. "Let me know if there's anything else you need."

"You're a life-saver, Mark," she said.

"Always happy to advance the cause of inter-agency cooperation," he replied.

With that, Allen turned slightly and softly barked instructions into his phone, directing his team to meet him back at the cars as soon as the NSA team was in place. He waved at his friend and started walking toward the traffic circle. He stopped after a few paces, turned, and walked back to Tran, speaking softly so only he and Tran could hear.

"Hey Grace," Allen said. "One more thing: in the years I've been down here, I've found the common folks around here are pretty nice, decent people just looking to make a decent living, raise their kids, go to church, maybe have a beer once in a while, and save some money to retire one day. But there's a power elite in this county—we call them *the poker club*. They pretty much control or heavily influence everything that goes on around here. They still talk about the *Yankees*, and they don't mean baseball, if you get me...They don't much like people who aren't members of *the club* messing with their way of doing things. They most likely wouldn't resort to violence, but subterfuge and anything short of violence is fair game. Don't be fooled by their uniforms, titles, or southern charm."

He paused in silent reflection for a moment.

"You probably know all that already. I don't know why I needed to say it."

"Never hurts just to be sure," Tran replied. "Thanks, now go home and get some sleep."

Grace Tran watched her friend disappear into the darkness, then turn and steadied herself to meet the men near the lobby door. As she walked toward them, she withdrew her standard-issue black leather ID wallet and flashed her credentials in front of their faces long enough for the men to inspect them as closely as they wanted. *National Security Agency, Joint Investigations Task Force* was emblazoned across the document positioned just beneath her imposing brass badge.

"Good morning, Gentlemen," she began.

"Ma'am," the FBI babysitter replied, immediately observing her badge and nodding.

With casual stealth, he stepped out of the picture and turned to rendezvous with his boss in the parking circle. The remaining two both began speaking at once, nearly yelling in excited tones.

"What the hell is going on here, and who the hell are you people?" one demanded.

"Yeah, I kinda need to know what's going on here," the other said.

The third was silent, tending to observe rather than speak.

"Gentlemen, gentlemen," Tran said, raising her voice above their excited utterances. "I'm Special Agent Grace Tran, NSA. I know you're Keithe Mantix," she said, shaking his hand, "but I haven't had the pleasure of meeting you," she prompted as she extended her hand to the second and third men.

"Detective-Lieutenant John Wardley, Seaside Beach PD," the more aggressive of the trio said, begrudgingly shaking Tran's hand.

Tran carefully observed them. Detective Wardley was a tall, lanky Caucasian man, probably in his late fifties or early sixties, and looked like he smoked and drank too much when he wasn't on duty. She knew it wasn't a reasonable presumption, but she got the sense that Wardley was a multiply divorced single guy, alienated from his 2 or 3 children, who lived alone in a rat-hole someplace where the glow of red neon signs shined through his windows at night. If this was New York or Chicago, she knew his apartment would have been near the el or subway tracks. The deep lines in his pallid face and the thinning tuft of salt-and-pepper hair, along with his semi-unpolished manner suggested he'd gained a lot of street smarts over the years, likely the hard way. He spoke with a slight drawl Tran found characteristic of many born-and-raised Floridians, but he lacked the slow, laid-back aura stereotypical of many US southerners. No, Wardley had a certain hurried seriousness about him, like one might find in a long-time resident of a heavily urbanized area. Nonetheless, she sensed he was an honest, competent cop.

His companion, Mantix, impressed Tran as a well-preserved fraternity boy of perhaps slightly younger age, who may not have realized he'd grown older. The designer glasses hanging from a cord around his neck suggested he'd nonetheless been forced to confront some aspect of his aging body, though begrudgingly. He wore a high-end custom-tailored suit and sported a Mont Blanc pen in the breast pocket of his dress shirt that matched the color and pattern of the silk tie he wore. His Bruno Magli footwear, the smart phone on his hip, the Movado on his wrist, and the I-Pad in his hand suggested the corporate security business was pretty good. Tran marveled at how snazzy Mantix was at this early hour on a Saturday, a day he didn't normally work.

"What the hell is going on here? Why is the NSA seizing a private building in my town?" Wardley demanded.

"I have to admit," Mantix added, calmly scratching the back of his head, "I'm equally as concerned that the NSA is in my building. I mean, whatever's going on here obviously involves Earhardt-Roane, and that's something I need to know, Agent Tran."

"I could tell you, gentlemen, but then I'd have to kill you," Tran joked.

Wardley found no humor in the moment, and Mantix had no reaction at all.

"Why are you here, Agent Tran?" Wardley said, more slowly and sternly.

Tran mentally debated how much information she should share with these guys and when she should do so. She sighed heavily and then unconsciously brought her right hand to the top of her head, rubbing firmly from there down the back of her head to the point where her neck and shoulder met. She craned her head to the right and slightly shrugged her shoulder to work out a small crick she felt developing.

"I will tell you as much as I can, when I can, gentlemen. For now, you should know there has been a very serious incident inside this building. NSA Field Team Six will be running the initial investigation under my supervision. Once we know exactly what we're dealing with, we'll make a determination whether we'll continue to handle the issue, or whether we'll turn it over to local authorities. Your teams will have roles to play in this matter, but until we hand this matter off to you, you'll have to take <u>my</u> lead on this unless you want to spark a national security incident, in which you'll be on the losing side."

"All right, Lady," the police officer barked. "You been talking for a few minutes now, but you haven't told us a goddamn thing. Now what the hell is going on? What kind of *incident* are you talking about?"

"We don't yet have all the facts we need to know, so I can't tell you everything right now. I will give you a bit more information about what we do know, but listen carefully, gentlemen, because I don't want there to be any misunderstanding. For now, this is a national security issue, and unless you two like wearing prison jumpsuits and making license plates for a hobby, you'll be damn sure you don't run afoul of my instructions."

She moved her hand on her side, almost imperceptibly pulling back one side of her jacket so the Glock-9 holstered to her side was in full view of her audience.

"Are we clear on this?" she asked.

"Yeah, yeah, yeah, I get it, Agent," Wardley snipped. "Top secret, 007 kind of stuff here, now can we just get to it?"

Tran smiled. "Psst, let me tell you something" she whispered, motioning Wardley into her personal space as she moved closer to his. He could feel the warmth of her breath and skin against the side of his face, and she was so close that he wondered whether she would kiss his ear or nibble his lobe.

"I'm not bullshitting you about this. If I find out that either of you or anyone else makes information releases I didn't pre-authorize about **any** aspect of this matter to ANYONE, somebody or some bodies are going to jail. You've heard about the secret CIA prisons?" she asked.

"Funny," Wardley answered, thinking she was selling her position way too hard.

"No it's not. I'm dead serious," Tran barked. There wasn't a wisp of levity about her. "Anyone making unauthorized disclosures about this matter will disappear in the middle of the night, and won't be heard from for a very, very long time. This isn't a joke because the stakes are far beyond whatever petty little politics you folks got going on around here. You get me?"

Wardley didn't know what to say. His nature compelled him to argue and probe whether the threatened consequences for leaking information were realistic possibilities, but the better part of his judgment warned against it. Tran didn't come across as a person to be toyed with, and Wardley knew nothing about her or her professional pedigree or the power she could wield. Finding out would become one of his first orders of business. He hated to be kicked around by anyone, much less a snooty, know-it-all bitch from Washington, but if Tran was even a small bit of what she seemed to be, he'd hate even more to disappear in the middle of the night. He'd heard of the Federal Joint Investigations Task Force back when the Patriot Act was implemented following 9-11, and he knew the secretive directorate had vast and expansive powers to do whatever it needed to do to keep the country safe. Making a few people disappear wouldn't be unheard of in those kinds of circles.

That wasn't the most pleasant thing Wardley had ever heard, but he nonetheless accepted it, for the moment. "I get you loud and clear, Tran," he replied, taking the safe route.

"Make sure you do." She turned to Mantix. "We got any issues?"

Mantix gave the question serious thought. "I'm gonna' need to talk to our President and probably a few other key people, including our General Counsel. There's just no way around that," Mantix explained.

Tran thought for a moment. The dead woman was a big fish in a small pond of a company headquartered in a small town with only a handful of major employers. It was likely that everyone in the company, if not in the entire town would hear about the murder, so Tran knew she'd not likely achieve one-hundred percent containment of information about it. That wasn't even her real goal. She really didn't want knowledge of the underlying investigation to get circulated, at least not until her team could find out what it was tasked to uncover. Since she couldn't contain all information about the case, her next best option was to effectively manage the message that got circulated. Corporate leadership and local authorities would need to be involved at some level, so Tran would start that process now, always remaining vigilant of local issues that might affect her team's work or taint the integrity of their product.

"All right," she conceded. She handed Mantix a business card. "Ms. Vivian Lawrence is my assistant, and this is her information. She'll contact you with arrangements for a meeting, probably tomorrow afternoon at the earliest. We can bring your brass up-to-speed at that time," she said. "For now, I'll tell you what we know, but you are sworn to secrecy on these details. You may tell your bosses that there's been a serious incident at this location, and they'll receive a full briefing tomorrow. Agreed?"

Reluctantly, both Mantix and Wardley assented to Tran's terms. If they wanted to know anything about what was going on inside, they had no other choice, and they knew it.

"All right then. A woman named Francine Ketcham was murdered tonight while sitting at her desk in her office."

"Oh my gosh," Mantix exclaimed, the air escaping his lungs *en mass*. "Murdered? Here in the building?"

"Yes. It happened a few hours ago."

"How? Why? What happened?" Mantix asked, obviously stunned at the news.

"I haven't even been to the scene yet, so I don't have all the answers," Tran said.

Mantix wiped his hand over his face, from top to bottom, and then covered his gaping mouth. "Oh my gosh, oh my gosh. Even *she* didn't deserve this."

That struck Tran as an odd thing to say. "Really?" she probed. "What did she deserve?"

"Not this," Mantix shook his head in utter disbelief. "Did you catch the perp?" he asked.

"No not yet," Tran said. "There doesn't appear to be anyone else in the building.

"Well what the hell have you people done?" Wardley yelled. "If we've got a murderer loose on the streets of Seaside, that's my job, Agent Tran, and no fed is coming down here from Washington to get in the way of my duties to the people of this county."

"The FBI has had an evidence recovery team in the building since shortly after the murder was reported, and we'll get all that information to whomever your department assigns as the case officer in due time, Detective."

Wardley crinkled his brow. "Reported? Who reported it and to whom did they report it? He asked. "We've not gotten any reports of a murder at SBPD, and by protocol, the Sheriff's office would have notified us immediately if they had. So that begs the question, Ms. Tran, who reported it and why did they evidently report it to you instead of us or 9-1-1?"

"*Special Agent* Tran," she corrected.

She didn't really give a rat's ass whether he called her Agent, Miss, or Ms., but she sternly corrected him to throw a stumbling block in the detective's line of questioning in an effort to derail it. After all, how she knew about the issue was irrelevant vis-à-vis the bigger issues.

"Apologies, *Special Agent* Tran," Wardley said, a quizzical expression on his face. "It's just, I can't quite understand how you folks knew of this, and my department didn't. Clearly, the company's own Security Chief didn't even know about this," he said, half asserting and half asking the man to his right.

Mantix shook his head. "I'd like to talk with my officer inside there," he nodded at the pudgy, white-haired man inside the building chatting with another federal agent. "But, I can say for sure, our dispatch desk has not gotten notice of anything wrong here, much less a crime of this magnitude."

"Well, gentleman, let's not stand here and ponder inane issues all night. There'll be plenty of time to discuss procedural matters later," Tran said, "but right now, I'd like to get inside and see what we've got. Maybe we'll start getting some answers."

Tran stepped to the side and started for the main entrance. Feeling the stares and unarticulated questions, she stopped and turned back.

"If we agree this is my crime scene, and you won't touch anything or say anything to anyone without permission, you're free to come up."

Without hesitation, the men acknowledged their agreement to Tran's terms, and matched steps with her. They passed through the revolving main entry, immediately garnering the attention of the men talking just inside. Tran walked to the FBI agent minding the private security officer, and engaged him in a whispered conversation the others couldn't hear. Mantix went to the security officer.

"Harry, what happened?" he asked.

"I really don't know, sir. I was sittin' here watching a re-run of *The Lieberman Show* when these federal fellas came through the door like a herd of elephants, but fast. They were flashing badges and guns, and firing off questions at me. I tried immediately to call *Dispatch*, but that fella there," he said, bobbing his head toward the agent he'd been talking to, "...stopped me and said I couldn't call no one or go nowhere. They said something bad had happened up in the executive suites, and the rest of them disappeared to upstairs I'm guessing. This gentleman asked me to gather all video footage from the night, and a bunch of other stuff too."

"You gave it to him?"

"Yessir. I should've, right? I mean, they had guns and badges."

"Yeah, Harry. You did well," Mantix said, patting the older man's arm.

Noticing the tenderness with which the Security Chief addressed the elderly security guard, Tran finished her briefing with the agent, asked him to summon the SUV driver, and dismissed him to join the rest of his team in the parking circle. Wheeling about, she politely introduced herself to the man with Mantix and Wardley, and displayed her NSA credentials. She requested the Security Chief's concurrence, and then asked the guard to assure nobody without a federal badge came into the building. The man looked first at his boss, and then acknowledged Tran's authoritative direction.

"Thank you very much for your assistance, Harry," Tran closed. She looked to Mantix and Wardley. "Come on."

Agent Thorsten fell in behind them as they walked past the security/reception desk into a short hall just behind it. They found the elevator banks, and Mantix pushed the button for the car at the far end of the alcove. They waited in silence for the penthouse express elevator to arrive.

"What can you tell me about her?" Tran finally asked.

Mantix was still quite flustered as he thought about the night's events so far. In his twenty-five years of corporate security work, he'd never had to deal with an issue like this. He'd handled angry former employees causing scenes, wandering homeless people seeking meals and handouts, and every now and again an Occupy Wall Street or other idealist protester spouting their anti-establishment propaganda, but a vicious murder was a whole new plane for him. His mind raced with a variety of concurrent thoughts about what he should do next, who he should notify, whether he could notify them in light of the instructions from the federal authorities now all around him, and what he should say. He contemplated whether there was a continuing danger to the company or its people, and how to minimize or eliminate that danger. He barely heard Tran utter some manner of sound, but he didn't recognize that she'd asked him a question.

"You were about to tell me about Ms. Ketcham," Tran prompted.

"Well, uh, uh, she's our CFO, or was, our CFO," Mantix finally answered. "She ran hot and cold, I guess."

Tran furled her brow, and that was enough to convey her question. *What do you mean?*

"She, uh, she, she could be sweet as apple pie to you if she wanted, but she also has a reputation for being real hard on people. They call her *The Ice Queen.*"

"Why is that?"

"Well," Mantix hesitated as he tried to phrase his next statement with the right blend of accuracy and respect. "There's a long line of bodies in her wake, if you know what I mean."

*Shit—probably a poor choice of words,* he mentally scolded himself as the words rolled off his tongue and hit his ears. The elevator arrived just at that moment. The men moved aside to let the lady enter the car, and then Mantix,

Wardley, and Thorsten followed. Chief Mantix pushed the button for the twelfth floor, and immediately, the car began ascending as the occupants' eyes turned up toward the digital indicator over the door. A soothing computer voice called out the number of each floor as they reached it, and a faint delayed *beep* sounded as though to punctuate the elevator voice's comment.

Tran leaned toward Mantix. "You were telling me about Ms. Ketcham."

"Oh, yeah, yeah," he recalled. "She was promoted to CFO about two weeks ago, and before that she was our Executive Director of Finance & Business. She's a decent enough person, maybe a little hard to some, but oh my gosh, my gosh."

"You mentioned bodies in her wake. I assume you were speaking figuratively of course, but do you think any of them would be capable of killing her?"

"I wouldn't have thought so," Mantix said. "But now?"

The elevator reached the penthouse and the doors opened. As they stepped out of the lift, Tran quickly surveyed the area, her eyes taking in as much information as they could. She'd learned early in her career to observe everything, for one might never know when a random fact or observation would become key to cracking a case. Immediately outside the elevator was a large, lavishly appointed reception area, replete with oversized tobacco brown, nail-head leather sofas, wood walls, and elaborate Florida wildlife paintings adorning the walls all around them. *Distinctly man in nature*, Tran thought. An attendant's desk lay straight ahead of the elevator door. Anyone coming from the elevator would see and be seen by the person manning that station, but at this hour and day, it was empty. Tran noticed security cameras at two locations in the reception area, but otherwise the area looked undisturbed to her eye. She turned to Mantix.

"You familiar with how this room normally appears?" she asked.

He nodded affirmatively.

"Anything look out of order to you?"

Mantix looked around the room. "Nope. It looks like it does pretty much all the time."

Tran nodded, and then pointed at one of the security cameras. "Are those active 24-7?"

"Yes," Mantix informed. "If anyone came out of this elevator, the cameras would have caught him or her. I'll make sure we get that to you if we haven't already."

Tran nodded in the direction of ambient noise down the hall, tacitly indicating that's the direction in which to walk. Obviously, that's where all the activity was occurring, which meant that's where the crime scene was. As the group moved down the wide corridor, they passed a bevy of nicely displayed artifacts from the early days of US aviation and space flight. Various members of the evidence recovery team passed them here and there as they went about their business, each of them greeting Agent Thorsten upon recognition, and Tran upon seeing the badge on her hip and surmising her identity. Tran paused every so often to observe the impressive wall displays, with complementary narration from Mantix about the items for which he knew the history. She gazed fondly at a black and white photo of the Wright Brothers standing beside the Wright Flyer. As she studied its detail, she draped the overcoat she carried on the knob of the nearest door. She told the small entourage with her that the photo made her think of her grandfather—a pilot in the 332nd Fighter Group during World War II—who'd kept a model of that same aircraft on the desk in his study. She remembered the many war stories her *Pop-Pop* used to tell about the Tuskegee Airmen. She smiled for a momentary stroll down memory lane before quickly snapping back to the reality of why she was here. The group moved a bit faster down the hall to the CFO suite.

A large, burly man with thinning gray hair stepped into the corridor from the CFO suite and walked purposefully toward them. The gun holstered under his arm, and the badge glistening from his hip signaled the SBPD officer and corporate security chief that he was a member of Tran's team. Special Agent Ian Lockwood was the oldest member of Tran's team, and had the most experience as an investigator at the federal level. He'd spent most of his career at the Federal Bureau of Investigation. He was a star agent there for a long time, but his career was self-derailed several years earlier after Lockwood shot and killed a twelve-year old boy while apprehending a known domestic terrorist. Given that the kid was pointing a loaded nine millimeter at him, Lockwood was cleared of any wrongdoing and no punitive action was taken against him, but Lockwood had never gotten over the fact that he killed a young boy. In his memory, the perpetrator's tender age overwhelmed the fact that the boy was trying to kill him at the time. When assembling her team, Tran had taken notice of Lockwood and saw something special in him, despite his past difficulties, and set about recruiting him as the first member of her NSA team. It was one of the best moves she could have made, for the older agent's experience had been invaluable.

The group stopped its forward movement as Lockwood closed the last few paces between them, and leaned in to whisper in Tran's ear.

"Gentlemen," she said to her escorts, "this is Special Agent Lockwood, senior agent on my team." To Lockwood, she said, "This is Corporate Chief of Security Keithe Mantix, Detective-Lieutenant John Wardley, SBPD, and Special Agent Thorsten, FBI."

Save for Lockwood and Thorsten, the men barely nodded in acknowledgement of one another.

"Excuse me a moment," Tran begged of the group.

She and Lockwood stepped a few feet away from the two non-feds, so Tran could get a pre-, pre-, pre-, preliminary report. Lockwood simply didn't want his boss to walk in blind, particularly because she had visitors with her. After a few brief moments, Tran broke off from Lockwood and turned back to Mantix, Wardley, and Thorsten.

"Okay, gentlemen, what you're about to see in there is pretty graphic, so prepare yourselves."

Both men were experienced cops—one former and one current—who'd seen a lot of nasty things over the years, so they didn't believe they'd need to steel themselves for anything they might see. Tran tried to prepare them nonetheless.

"When you go in there, remember that you're here only as observers, so don't touch anything—you'll interfere with the Bureau's Evidence Recovery Team. They're good, but they don't need any unnecessary complications. Also, remember that information on what you're about to see can't be released without my authorization."

"This ain't our first rodeo, Miss," Wardley condescended. "I'm pretty sure we can handle it."

Tran acquiesced to the detective's assurances, then turned and walked into the suite, expecting to see a hellacious bloody gore. They didn't. The room immediately off the executive corridor was an anteroom and small seating area that belonged to two executives and the administrative assistant they shared. It was as neat as a pin, the desk festooned with the things any proud grandma would keep around her—a collection of framed pictures of an adolescent boy in a soccer uniform fastidiously ordered on one side of the desk, a vase of fresh flowers on the other, and vacant *In* and *Out* baskets in the middle. It was as neat as a pin, as clean as a whistle, or whatever other adage best described the secretary's office. The door behind the desk in that area was ajar, and Tran could see and hear movement inside.

19

"The real show's in here," Lockwood said, leading the way. He paused and stepped to the side of the door so Tran and her group could see into the CFO's office proper.

Tran walked to the threshold, peered, and then stepped inside. Mantix, Wardley, and Lockwood followed, while Agent Thorsten stayed back in the anteroom. Despite the room's sophisticated femininity and the sumptuous appointments all around, this scene was more like what she expected.

Inside the office, a bluish-gray human female body sat slumped backward in a contemporary, top-grain leather chair behind an 18th century French neoclassical desk. Her face had been bashed in, clearly with great force, as the facial plates had collapsed into the rear of her skull, and gray matter oozed from both her ear canals and the remnants of what had once been nostrils. Deep lacerations had been opened across the neck as well as up and down the arms of the tortured corpse, and the woman's lavender silk blouse remained open enough to expose an abdomen that had been gutted, almost Hari-kari style, except this clearly wasn't self-inflicted.

A deep garnet-colored liquid splattered the walls, ceiling, desk, papers, floors, and everywhere else the eye could see, and the plush carpet beneath the desk and for several feet all around was saturated with blood having the texture of thick, viscous paint. The sheer volume of it reminded Tran of the last time Eagle Creek had flooded her basement, soaking the carpet so that each step upon it caused water to gush over the toes of her boots. Here, though, everyone was careful to avoid tracking blood or disturbing other evidence throughout the crime scene.

"Gee—zus," Tran uttered, walking into the room. "What the hell do we have here?"

"Boss, let me introduce you to Francine Ketcham, Senior Vice President and Chief Financial Officer of this company—thirty-nine year-old mother of two, employed here nearly ten years now, but recently promoted to the big chair there, following the untimely death of the previous CFO. I'm guessing she was working late crunching numbers on whatever that project is spread out on the desk beneath all her blood when the killer came in through the main door there to greet her. She probably knew the person and maybe even expected him or her because it doesn't look like she even moved out of her chair. Hell, given the position of her visitor chairs and the soda can on the floor," he pointed, "they may even have had a chat for a while."

Tran paused for a moment as she surveyed the scene from the entry door to the desk, the picture window behind, and all over the room. Ketcham's office was adorned with seemingly expensive original works of art, including paintings, large ornate Chinese vases, and antique furniture. Several gold Mont Blanc pens glistened in the pen/pencil holder, which sat beside the latest electronic notebook computer, cell phone, and gilt-edged coffee mug that said, *It's good to be the Queen.* A bloody but otherwise gorgeous Rolex clung to Ketcham's left wrist just a few inches above the enormous white gold-set rock on her left fourth finger. A ten-karat diamond tennis bracelet adorned the right wrist, with its matching necklace completing the bling ensemble at Ketcham's neck. A gold purse hook protruding from the back of Ketcham's chair held an open Louis Vuitton bag. A thick wallet was nestled comfortably inside, which Tran quickly reached over and removed. As she pawed through its contents, she saw a plethora of bank cards and a heavy wad of resident bills, which Tran didn't count but surmised it was more money than she'd earn in six months. Her cell phone was still there too. Everything seemed clean and untouched by bloody hands.

"So we're not talking robbery here," Tran concluded.

"Naw," Lockwood agreed. "No signs of forced entry, it doesn't appear there was a struggle, and it doesn't seem like anything is missing. We'll get confirmation but that's our operating theory right now."

"All this," Tran said, motioning around the room. "This was something personal. Any witnesses?"

"Of course not," Lockwood answered. "The place is covered by on-scene security and video surveillance but still we got nothing."

Tran shook her head and pursed her lips, disgusted by those facts. "That would be entirely too easy."

"Looks like the killer had an axe to grind against the vic,"Lockwood began.

"Yeah, right into her head, it seems," Tran added.

She turned and walked the few paces back to the door, where Mantix and Wardley stood, their mouths agape, observing the bevy of activity in the room.

"Gentlemen," she began. "As you see, this scene is a mess, and there's quite a lot of work left yet to do. I need to ask you to let us do our work here, and we'll brief you in a few hours. Chief Mantix, you may feel free to discuss this matter with your President, Vice President, General Counsel, and Public Relations officer. Detective, you may brief your Chief and Public Information officer. That's all for now, but we can revisit that if we need to do so later on."

"You're kicking us out of a murder scene investigation?" Wardley bellowed.

"Yes, Detective," Tran said. "That's precisely what I'm doing."

"Look, you've gone too far. It's fine for you to take charge of the investigation if there's some big secret federal government issue here, but you don't have the right to exclude us completely. We need to know what's going on here. I have duties to the citizens…"

Mantix interrupted him, patronizingly patting his arm, and imperceptibly pushing him aside. "Agent Tran, I think what the Detective is trying to say is that we have an important interest in this whole thing. That lady there was one of my co-workers and…"

Tran sighed heavily. "Do we really need to go over this again?" she asked. "Listen, your offices will have a role in this thing—of course. We simply need to assess the situation and get a handle on what we're dealing with before releasing the scene to you. So, if you don't mind," she said, suggesting they leave.

"I'm not going anywhere, Agent," Wardley barked.

A beefy young man with buzz-cut hair and a Glock-inspired bulge in his jacket walked briskly to the area where Tran stood speaking with the two civilians. Only with them for forty-three days now, Special Agent Stefan Kenison was the newest member of Field Team Six. With pecs and biceps that might make the Hulk feel inadequate, one might have thought the model-type bi-racial twenty-eight year-old Clemson grad was the team's muscle. But while he was indeed physically quite powerful, his real prowess was his wickedly high intellect along with his penchant for all things financial, mathematical, and complex. Known to follow something to complete resolution, he'd come highly recommended from the Agency's training supervisor, and Tran especially liked that he'd cut his teeth as an Army green beret who'd seen action in Iraq. And besides all that, he was simply a nice guy.

"Can I be of assistance here, Boss," he said, moving his hand toward his side.

Tran continued addressing Mantix and Wardley. "Gentlemen, I really don't have time for this right now. I'll tell you what, if you wish to remain here, you may take a seat in the anteroom there, or you may leave, keeping in mind my admonition about disseminating information. You decide what you want to do, but I need to get to work in here. Agent Thorsten can help you out there in the anteroom."

With that, Tran turned around and walked deeper into the CFO's office, immediately diving into the investigation. Kenison waited a moment for the gentlemen to return to the anteroom, and when they did, he handed them off to the FBI Agent, and conveyed Tran's instructions. Then he too returned to Ketcham's inner office.

# Chapter 2

# Torquing

Tran arched to stretch the kink forming in her low back, the result of prolonged sitting in a worn, uncomfortable chair, hunched over an unremarkable metal desk. The appointments of her temporary office were far from the lavishness of Earhardt-Roane's executive floor, where she'd spent most of the thirty-four hours since she arrived in Seaside. The ERT had all but finished its work collecting evidence at the crime scene and its members dispersed to wherever they'd normally be on a Sunday afternoon. At her insistence, Tran's team had taken some personal time to check-in to their rooms at the Fly Inn, rest, and freshen up a bit. Being whisked away from their lives in the middle of the night on short-notice, flying three hours from DC to Seaside, and then promptly immersing themselves in work for the succeeding twenty-eight hours took a toll on people, and Tran needed her team at its collective best to finish this assignment properly. She'd have preferred to ease into the investigation, but circumstances had thrust it upon them urgently, and it was important that they complete the evidence-gathering at the scene before Monday morning, when ERAC's employees reported for a new work week.

Tran took the opportunity to get in to the local FBI field office, housed in an obscure building in "downtown" Seaside. Her borrowed space at the end of a long, mostly vacant hallway in the back of the building wasn't at all fancy. It had a plain desk, plain visitor chairs, a phone, a lamp, a file cabinet, and a few other items one might store in an unused office rather than throw away, and it emitted a slightly musty aroma, also common to long-unused rooms. But, it was free, and her friend at the Bureau had lent it and other space and resources to her team based purely on a ten-minute call in the middle of the night. She wouldn't complain. It wasn't in her nature anyway.

24

The former Air Force officer was accustomed to achieving missions under less than ideal situations—adapt and overcome…it had been the motto of her flight at field training all those years ago, and stuck with her throughout her career. As she reviewed the beginnings of the case file on this issue, she knew she'd have to apply it here.

It was approaching 3 p.m., and the local officials and company big-wigs would arrive in roughly an hour. Anticipating they'd be territorial, hot-under-the-collar, and demanding, Tran wanted to be as familiar with all of them and the facts of the case as she possibly could be, and thus had dedicated a few hours in advance to thoroughly reviewing everything they knew so far. Even before she started, Tran knew this would be a difficult case. Everything about it seemed to be a spiraling mess. Each time she learned something about the company or one of its elite, something else popped up that deserved a look, which unearthed another lead that deserved a look, and then another, and another, and another. The murder of the company's CFO was another one of them. Tran had to determine whether the crime had national security implications for the NSA to deal with, or whether it was a run-of-the-mill murder belonging to local authorities. If the former, she wanted to deal with it and move on to her next assignment, but the seemingly unending discovery of new and potentially significant revelations prevented her from sewing this case up, *quick and neat* as her boss was prone to say. Whatever the case, she wouldn't be able to defend a huge commitment of costly resources to this matter forever, especially in light of the economy and the budget battles between the President and Congress, even threatening to shut down the federal government. She needed to find something to tilt the tables one way or the other.

Tran thumbed through a thick dossier on ERAC she and her team had assembled in the last few weeks. It and an insulated coffee mug had been her only companions for the last few hours as she learned and reviewed information about Earhardt-Roane.

ERAC provided a wide variety of training to military pilots, technicians, and mechanics, and performed a great deal of critical research for the Department of Defense and NASA. But its most significant product was an unmanned aerial vehicle, or UAV, called the Phantom, which the government considered *Classified Top Secret.* Using satellite and internet technology, the Phantom was controlled by pilots sitting at a console at the command base up to 5,000 miles away. It could deliver enough non-nuclear bombs and bullets to destroy a base, obliterate an air defense station, or crush a squad of moving tanks, or it could launch two nuclear warheads on target and survive the resulting blast, all without placing an actual person in danger of harm or death from enemy fire. Meeting most of the Air Force's requirements, the Phantom had performed reasonably well during its inaugural deployment, but ERAC was looking to win an even more lucrative defense contract with an improved version of Phantom called Casper. Casper could deliver even greater firepower than Phantom, but its real attraction was the new technology used to control it. Casper had a highly sophisticated cerebral linkage array, or CLA, that translated thoughts directly from the pilot's brain to a synthetic brain built into the drone, in effect giving it the ability to think and make decisions like a computer-enhanced person. It was an enticing concept, but CLA turned out to have some unintended and possibly lethal side effects, which ERAC had carefully tried to keep under wraps. ERAC's own studies had shown the hyper-sensitive CLA technology could cause severe brain damage to the pilots operating the equipment, or malfunction and cause the aircraft to ditch unexpectedly as though the drone itself had a stroke. Then, both the drone and its payload could fall into the hands of hostile elements and/or kill thousands of innocent people. Those were consequences far too serious for DoD's heavyweights to take lightly. Casper hadn't yet been pitched to Air Force or DoD officials, but ERAC's officials knew the administration's budget-cutting disposition didn't tolerate overly complex or problematic initiatives. If Casper got scuttled before it even had a chance to catch the fancy of an important defense department sponsor, ERAC would end up wasting hundreds of millions of dollars, mostly for nothing.

*That would provide someone with a motive for something,* Tran thought, *but how does this relate to the murder of its CFO? Where are the national security implications?* she wondered. *Perhaps ERAC was looking for a new buyer for Casper.* She flipped through some additional pages.

As CFO, the decedent was very involved in both the Phantom and Casper programs because she controlled ERAC's financial and accounting processes on all federally funded research. The Chief of Security's comments earlier this morning had corroborated the file's suggestion that Ketcham had a reputation as overly ambitious, cold, and hard-hearted—a *bitch-on-wheels* in common parlance. *The Ice Queen* came from a small southern town where high society meant Friday nights at the town mini-mart, drinking fresh moonshine and picking leftover road kill from one's teeth with the latest in fashion toothpicks. It was also the location of a farm used as the headquarters of a suspected hate-based militia group that had been on the FBI's watch-list for some time now.

Despite these inauspicious beginnings, the dead woman had managed to scrape and scrap her way through Hicksville community college, and then purportedly sexed her way into a four-year college. With a 1.9 grade-point average, she got a bachelor's degree in business administration, and worked her way into the mainstream where she seemingly lied and cheated her way to success. The psychological profile worked up on this woman suggested that despite her outer vestiges of success, she couldn't shake the insecurity that someone would one day discover she lacked any substance at all. To protect herself, she'd become a ruthless operator, going on the attack the moment she thought someone threatened her, threatened to discover or expose her secret, or if she was simply in a bad mood. Rumors were wide-spread in the company that she'd gotten her prior position as ERAC's Executive Director of Business Affairs because she had pictures of her boss in a compromising position, but it was clear that she'd recently ascended to the position of Senior Vice President and Chief Financial Officer because of the untimely death of her boss, Erich Day, two weeks earlier. The official police report indicated his new Mercedes inexplicably skidded off the road, slammed into a tree and burst into a ball of flame. Information from the Department of Justice suggested more dubious factors may have caused the death of Erich Day— the wreckage of simple car accidents didn't usually contain traces of military-grade high explosives and incendiary agents. That the explosive signature matched several found in the remnants of improvised explosive devices in Iraq was an especially alarming factor. Because it was legally prohibited from operating inside the USA, CIA had asked Tran's superiors for assistance in determining whether there was linkage between this car-accident explosion about which they'd learned purely on a lark, and MOIS—the Ministry of Intelligence and National Security of the Islamic Republic of Iran—which was known to provide IEDs to insurgents and radicals in Iraq. When coupled with the fact that one of Earhardt-Roane's most powerful board members was an Iranian national, red flags shot up in the minds of a lot of highly paid government employees.

"Hey, uhm, is this a good time?" a voice asked from the hall.

Tran looked up from her papers and files.

"Sure. Come on in and close the door," she said, leaning back in her chair. "Anyone see you come in?"

"Don't think so," the man answered, "except for the receptionist."

"No problem there. She's with the Bureau."

"Hey, thanks for the lab coat and badge," the man said, as he walked toward Tran's desk and seated himself in the chairs opposite her.

"I trust you had no problems?" she asked.

"None. With Agency credentials, I looked just like any of the other hundred agents scouring the place. It was a good plan," the man said, nodding and smiling wide. "Here."

He tossed a flash drive onto the desk. "This is why I was there. I didn't expect her or anyone to come in at that hour, so I was surprised to hear the ruckus coming from that suite. I tried to make my way over to Francine's office so I could see what was going on and who was making all that noise, but I got there only in time to see someone run down the stairs at the far end of the floor."

"Did you get a look at the person?"

He shook his head side to side. "I think it was a man, but I don't know that for sure. He was wearing an oversized hoodie that covered his head and body. Whoever it was, the person was agile and quick, and I'd guess he knew his way around the place."

"What were they talking about?"

"It wasn't really talking. It was arguing. I couldn't hear anything clearly, but more just very loud tones. First one yelled, then the other, then the other again, like that, back and forth for a few minutes, and then screaming and suddenly, silence."

"All right. I'm gonna have you give a statement to a woman on my team named Vivian Lawrence. She's back at headquarters, but I want you to talk to her and tell her your complete story in as much detail as you can possibly recall. You might've seen something that gives us usable information, and she has a keen ear for detail. And don't bullshit her. If you do, she might fly down here and kick your ass."

The man's eyes got wide, contemplating the thought of having his posterior seriously beaten by a woman. It was all the more concerning because it didn't seem like Tran was kidding.

"Seriously, she's been accused of being rough around the edges sometimes, but she gets things done, and she almost always right," Tran explained. "And she's good people too, a real straight-shooting, true-hearted person—very rare these days."

Tran heard noise in the hall outside her office, and knowing she was at the end of a long corridor, she guessed the noisemaker was destined for her office. Mindful that one of her anticipated visitors could have somehow passed undetected through security, she raised a finger to silence her visitor and then signaled him to get behind her door. When it opened, he'd be hidden from view unless the person came fully into the office and closed the door. She quickly returned her attention to the papers on her desk. There was a single solid rap on the door.

"Come." Tran yelled, loudly enough for whoever was outside to hear her.

She winked at the man behind the door, and motioned for him to just stand there and do nothing. The door opened slowly.

"Excuse me, boss," a voice interrupted.

It was Special Agent Deanna Starr, the second-newest member of Field Team Six. She was also a Ph.D. psychologist with an incredible reputation for accuracy in profiling based on available facts. From what Tran had seen of her, she could read people as easily as she could a large-print book, and often received praises and accolades from people she'd just tactfully insulted without them even perceiving the sleight. The tall, lanky Caucasian Iowan was thin, pale, and a bit on the quiet side, but her simple, innocent appearance belied the fact that she was a five-time national Judo champion. That's how Tran had come to know of Starr anyway—they'd both been honored as outstanding women Judoka by United States Judo Inc. Tran admired Starr's explanation during an interview about how she used her psychology background to help her anticipate what an opponent was likely to do with various types of provocations on the mat, and then she simply prepared for that likely reaction in advance. Her opponents often found themselves looking up at her from the ground, wondering how they'd been beaten so quickly. It was that sort of analysis Tran wanted on her team because, in her view, Judo held a great many parallels to life—both dealt with human behavior.

"The local authorities are arriving now," Starr reported, peeking her head into the room, but not entering. "I took the liberty of directing them into the conference room next door, and I've already had them execute *Classified Acknowledgement Forms*."

"Thanks," Tran said. "I'll be there momentarily, and I'd like you to join us there as well."

Starr nodded in acknowledgement of her boss's tactful dismissal of her, and backed out of the room, closing the door behind her. She waited long enough for Starr to move out of range of her normal speaking voice, and then stood, gathering and closing the file in front of her. She took a final gulp from the mug beside her.

"All right," she said to the man behind the door. "I'd like you to go in there," she said, ushering him to a spot on the far side of the room.

The man looked, but didn't see a particular place he might go. His puzzled expression rippled over his face. Tran maneuvered him to a spot along the wall a few paces further into her temporary office, and then applied pressure to what seemed a random spot on the wall. A well concealed doorway opened silently, leading to a darkened interior. The man could see nothing in the room, except the backs of a few leather office chairs that seemed to face more darkness.

"This is an observation room from which you can watch what happens in the next room. Please have a seat and remain absolutely quiet until I return for you. I want you to watch what goes on in there, and afterward, I'd appreciate the benefit of your observations," she explained.

"What am I looking for?" he asked.

"You've worked with these folks, and thus know them far better than we do. I want your read on them. Do they fidget when certain subjects come up? Do you notice any particular tells in their faces? Do they say anything that strikes you as odd, inaccurate, or untrue—that sort of stuff."

The man nodded his understanding, and Tran stepped back and gently closed the door as she went. She gathered her papers and portfolio, and straightened her clothing to assure she'd project a professional, in-command appearance when she stepped into the testosterone-filled room. As much as she'd deny it if asked, she'd harbored latent misgivings about the manner in which people perceived her. Tran needed all parties to this matter to understand the scorecard from the get-go. She was running this show until she decided she wasn't, and anyone who thought otherwise would quickly have reason to think again.

In high school, Tran had ranked in the bottom third of her class academically, and even though she'd already decided college wasn't the place for her, she took the SAT in deference to her loving parents who'd always wanted their baby to graduate from Harvard Medical. A slightly more than merely respectable SAT score of 2398 and all manner of scholarship offers from the full gamut of colleges and universities wasn't sufficient to change her mind. Tran had only determined to go to college when she finally got fed-up with taking orders from the managing-idiot-in-charge at The Burger Pit where she worked throughout high school. A full-ride at the US Air Force

Academy—which she'd ignored for a month by then—was the quickest, easiest route to a change-of-scenery, so she took it. Once there, the academic and physical rigor of the military academy became quite a turn-on to her, so she stayed, excelled, and enjoyed herself immensely for four years. After graduating first in her class and being commissioned as an officer in the Office of Special Investigations, she entered a challenging career that let her travel to exotic places and put her at the cusp of events often reported on the evening news, debated on the floors of the Congress, and decided in the Oval Office. She left active duty to attend Harvard Law school, and after graduating *Summa Cum Laude* there, she began her current career path at the invitation of a three-star general for whom she'd worked during active duty. She liked her job very much, but more importantly, she was good at what she did. But, despite her intelligence and competence as evidenced by the many notches in her belt, it often seemed people were most struck, and sometimes only struck, by her physical appearance.

The product of an African-American father and an Asian mother, Tran sported a dark, creamy complexion, long black hair that fell to her waist when allowed to, and high cheekbones carried on a thin, 5-foot, 11-inch frame. As a little girl, people always commented about her cuteness, and as she matured, so too did the terms people used to describe her—babe, hot, smokin', gorgeous, etcetera. Like most people, she got a stroke of the old ego when people said she was good-looking, provided they did so in a respectful manner, but after a while, the value of that sort of remark began to diminish for her, regardless of the physical prowess of its speaker. Rather than being ogled for her looks, she wanted more and more to be regarded for her professional skill, competence, and achievement. That seemed to be a tall order for many whose thoughts were more consistent with traditional stereotypes for working women, and her rejection of those views had on more than a few occasions earned her the label "bitch" during her ascent up the ladder of Air Force Special Investigations. *That's not my problem*, Tran had come to think. But it was a problem many professional women still faced in the workplace, especially in male-dominated fields like law enforcement and corporate America, and it was also a reason she was slow to heed rumors about the *Bitchy Ice Queen*, Francine Ketcham.

It was time. Tran exited her office and walked a few paces down the hall to a conference room, Lockwood and Starr awaiting her outside its door. She paused momentarily, and then entered authoritatively into the room. She went directly for the chair at the head of a long wooden table around which the

31

meeting attendees were already seated. Her team members took positions along the wall behind her, to the left and right flanks.

"Good afternoon, Gentlemen," Tran said, pulling out her chair.

All the principal people were there—from Earhardt-Roane, Don Johnston, President; Rick McCool, Executive Vice President; Chuck Matos, General Counsel; Dan Williams, Associate Vice President of Public Affairs, and; Keithe Mantix, Chief of Corporate Security. From local government: Dean Cuthbert, Mayor of Seaside Beach; Bill Lazlow, Chief of Seaside Beach Police; Anthony Datillo, Seaside Public Information Officer, and; Detective-Lieutenant John Wardley. Tran introduced herself and Agents Lockwood and Starr, and then greeted each attendee by name, in turn firmly shaking their hands. Afterward, she seated herself and quickly organized her papers, carefully observing the attendees as she prepared to begin the briefing.

"I'm sure Detective Wardley and Chief Mantix have given you some preliminary information about the matter that brings us together today, and I'll supplement that information to keep you as informed as possible as this matter progresses. I understand you've all already signed the *Classified Acknowledgement Forms?*"

She looked first at Starr who handled that particular administrative task, and then at each of the attendees. Invariably, all nodded their agreement.

"All right then," she began. "Let me make clear that this matter has been *Classified* by the federal government, and you are therefore <u>not</u> at liberty to discuss it with anyone outside this room unless I give you written clearance in advance. Pending further investigation, this matter is exclusively subject to federal jurisdiction, and your involvement at this time is purely a courtesy. Do you all understand?" Tran asked.

"Uh, yes Agent Tran, I understand what you're saying, but what is your legal authority for this?" the attorney asked.

"Yes, I'd like to know why the Florida Department of Law Enforcement is involved in this matter?" Johnston said. "I've not invited or informed them of this matter just yet, so what is your authority here?"

Tran looked blankly at the president. *FDLE?* she thought. *Where did that come from?* Without correcting his error, she addressed the lawyer.

"I'm simply the messenger, Counselor," Tran said. "I hope to spare you some trouble by letting you know what I know, but your argument isn't with me. This action has been cleared by the Foreign Intelligence Surveillance Act Court in Washington, the Honorable Michael Q. Murphy presiding."

"For purposes of this meeting," Johnston interrupted, an air of authority about him, "We'll move forward with what you have to tell us, but for the long term, my team will give me their recommendations, and I'll decide what our message will be on this matter later. Mr. Matos will keep you in the loop."

Tran debated whether to shut the president down hard in front of this crowd. His remarks and his demeanor indicated he thought he had authority to decide anything about this matter. He didn't. He didn't yet grasp that this wasn't purely an issue of corporate operations, but was instead a matter of national security. He didn't understand that a wrong move here could have dire consequences for him, his company, and its entire management team. She looked to the corporate lawyer, tacitly suggesting he get his client under control. When that didn't work, she moved to verbal cues.

"Counselor," she prompted.

"We understand, Agent Tran. If I may suggest, perhaps we can just get through this portion and then you and I can maybe talk offline about how we go forward?"

Adept at understanding legal speak, Tran perceived the lawyer was reluctant to contradict his boss in front of others, but neither did he want the Agent to ratchet up the potentially negative stakes for the company that were easily in her quiver. She decided to give him that leeway because her mission was getting to the bottom of the issue, not punishing little Napoleans.

"Yeah, yeah, I know how these things work, Ms. Tran," Johnston puffed. "But there's a little legal concept called prior restraint, you know, and that means you don't get to abridge our absolute constitutional right to say anything we want."

"Counselor?" Tran prompted again, her eyes insisting that he reel in his president.

"I just want to be clear so we're all on the same page," Johnston pressed. "We welcome your guidance and thoughts on handling this issue, Ms. Tran, but I'll have my PR people, in conjunction with our SBPD liaison, work up what we'll say about this event. As a courtesy to you, we'll happily run it by you to keep you in the loop."

Tran was surprised by the president's boldness. She sat there momentarily, waiting for the lawyer to intervene so she didn't have to. Matos remained silent and in his seat while Johnston continued to prattle.

"If you don't understand the reason for this approach, Ms. Tran, our very close legislative friends on Capitol Hill will be pleased to explain it to you."

*Oh no he didn't,* Tran thought. The man had a doctorate in art history or some other obscure subject, and he'd been adept at working his political connections to get him to the helm of Earhardt-Roane, but the rarified air around his position at the top of his silo, in addition to being his board's *little darling* had evidently gone to his head. Johnston seemed to think he had power to call the shots on this matter, and he wasn't at all fazed by the fact that an NSA agent was telling him otherwise. Tran knew she needed to make herself better understood.

"Mr. Johnston, you evidently place a high value on clarity, so let *me* be clear with *you*," she rebutted. "I recognize you need information and that you'll have some role to play in this matter, but until we determine how that can happen in a way that doesn't compromise the national security interests of the United States, you need to abide by my directions on this. If you or any your people act without my advanced approval to release information about this matter to anyone outside this room, the person or persons responsible will go directly to jail."

*Without passing go or collecting their $200,* she wanted to say but didn't because it might add levity to the moment, and she wasn't joking.

"The arrest will be instant, it will be public, and it will garner all sorts of bad press for you and this company for a very long time. Moreover, Earhardt-Roane's federal contracts will be immediately suspended and maybe terminated. This company, every member of its board, its executive management team, and any entities with which any of them are significantly involved will be disbarred from further federal funding of any kind, and you'll have a bevy of auditors and investigators crawling so far up your asses you'll be able to taste them. Now I don't know exactly what kind of money that represents for you, but I'm guessing it's more than you and your stakeholders care to piss away on a pointless ego game. Do I make myself clear?"

She waited a moment, staring dead into Johnston's eyes, but he offered no reply. She made eye contact with each person in the room, but her question and gaze were met with silence.

"All right then, gentlemen. These are the facts as we currently know them. Sometime between 11:00 p.m. Friday night and 4:00 a.m. Saturday morning, Earhardt-Roane's Chief Financial Officer, Francine Ketcham, was murdered inside her office at the corporate headquarters."

Gasps came from the mouths of the company employees assembled in the room. Tran continued.

"We're still gathering facts and analyzing evidence so we don't have all the answers, but there doesn't appear to be forcible entry, and none of the security footage so far has captured images of anything suspicious. We know Ms. Ketcham was working on some government-sensitive projects but we don't know if any of that information has been compromised."

"Why isn't my department running this investigation, Ms. Tran?" Chief Lazlow asked, an accusatory tone about him.

"We aren't quite sure what we're dealing with here, Chief. Once we determine what the situation is, I'll determine whether it should be turned over to your office in whole or in part, and if the latter, what parts you'll do and what parts we'll retain."

"I'm a bit confused," the lawyer asked. "Maybe I should start with a more basic question. For what entity do you work, Agent Tran?"

"I work for the NSA, Counselor."

"NSA, as in National Security Agency?"

"Exactly," Tran answered.

"You're not with FDLE?" Johnston asked, surprised.

Tran ignored the president and instead elaborated on her response to his lawyer. "Given Earhardt-Roane's extensive work on significant military projects of substantial national security interests, I'm sure you can appreciate the government's interest in understanding exactly what we are or aren't dealing with here."

"What kind of projects?" the mayor asked. "What national security interests?"

"I'm sorry but you don't have clearance to know that information, Mr. Mayor."

"Bullshit. I'm the damn mayor of this city, Ms. Tran, and if we're looking at some kind of 9-11-like threat that might put the lives of my citizens at risk, I better damn sure be informed of it as early as possible."

"I understand, Mr. Cuthbert. I really do. But at this time, we see no indication of that type of threat here. I assure you, if we spot anything suggestive of a risk of that nature, you'll be among the first to know."

"Tell me what the hell you're talking about. Your remarks concern me greatly."

"Sir, I wasn't joking when I said you don't have the clearance to know the details of the related issues. Maybe you can find comfort in the knowledge that President Johnston and a few officials of this company are fully aware of the federal interests in projects they're working on for us. He can't share the details with you either, but he can certainly validate the legitimacy of our interests here."

As if on cue, all eyes turned to the CEO at the other end of the table as they searched for confirmation, but Johnston remained stoic. Instead, he merely sat there staring back at Tran and the inquiring eyes of everyone else in the room. He didn't dispute Tran's statement. She looked to the city officials.

"Are we going to have an issue from your side of this? Tran asked. "Because I'd be happy to articulate the consequences for the City of Seaside Beach if I have to get the Department of Justice involved in this…"

Clearly unhappy, the mayor tossed his pen forcefully down to the table, yanked his head, and grimaced in disgust. "No damnit," he finally barked. "But I want you to know, I do this under protest. You put that on the record, Missy. You federal folks just breeze into town and do what you want without any coordination with state and local officials, but you don't have to live with the effects of your actions," Cuthbert ranted. "I'm pretty damn good friends with Ray Nagin and he told me about all the federal bullshit he had to deal with."

Tran didn't quite see the parallel between this matter and what happened after New Orleans was pounded by Hurricane Katrina a few years ago. The whole tragedy was bad for everyone, she agreed, but this was very different. But, she nonetheless understood the mayor of a small southern town was deeply bothered at being shut-out of one of the biggest gossip occurrences in the history of the town. This was one of those local sensitivities she and her fellow feds hated dealing with. But as Agent Allen had reminded her the day before, this was why she got paid the big bucks.

"Mr. Mayor, I truly am sorry I can't give you all the details you'd like to have at this point. I guess I'm just going to have to ask for your trust. We'll tell you what we can as soon as we can, but we've first got to establish some base-level things to know what we're dealing with."

"Ehhh," Cuthbert groaned, dismissively waving his hand at Tran.

"If we can go back just a moment," the police chief said. "I still don't understand how your folks became aware of this crime, got here, and began processing the scene before my department even knew about it," he pressed. "Why are we finding out about a local crime from a federal alphabet agency?"

*There it was,* Tran thought, *that annoying little question again.*

She shrugged her shoulders. "The federal government is a huge bureaucracy, Chief, and I don't know all its inner workings, of course. I just know this matter landed on my desk, the nature of which demanded I begin my inquiry before the crack of dawn yesterday…It could be that one of the security officers notified someone in the government." *Indeed it could be,* Tran knew, but that wasn't what really happened, and Tran wasn't about to explain the true facts of their discovery. "I could run that down for you and get back to you later if you like." *NOT!*

"I'm sorry," company counsel began, "but I too am still confused about something. Murder charges arise from state law, not federal, so are you suggesting our CFO's murder is related to one of our federal contracts?" he asked.

"That's kind of my point at this time, Mr. Matos. We simply don't yet know, and until we do, we're treating this as though there is a connection—yes," Tran replied.

Matos contemplated the answer for a moment, nodding his head, not so much that he agreed but more to show he was listening. "Well, can you tell us how she was killed?" he pressed. "I mean, we probably have some responsibility to other employees to keep them safe. Perhaps we should be doing something."

"At this point, we believe this was a targeted action and not a random crime of opportunity. There are plenty of valuable things around the scene, none of which appear to be bothered, including cash, credit cards, jewels, and other valuables belonging to the victim. The chairs appear as though someone may have been sitting in them and we located a pop can with prints on it. We believe Ms. Ketcham knew her assailant. I've got my lab techs looking at her computer for additional evidence."

"Hey," the president exclaimed, exploding from his seat. "That's got proprietary company information on it. You have no right to that information."

"Relax, Mr. Johnston," Tran suggested. "Your information is safe…we won't be spreading information around about a classified matter."

"What I think the president means is that we're just concerned about retaining the data on her computer," the lawyer offered. "Some of her work isn't duplicated anywhere else in the company, and losing it may hurt our ongoing projects."

Controlling clients who didn't understand legal and regulatory oddities was often the bane of a lawyer's existence, especially when the client thought he was much smarter or more knowledgeable than he really was. Tran had detected subtle cues that Matos was having that struggle here. He was trying to insert a breather in the increasingly combative dialogue between his president and a federal agency, no doubt hoping to prevent the immediate issue from escalating into a fight he knew the company really didn't want. Again, Tran gave him that space, knowing it would be to her own advantage to have effective insider help in taming a wildcard. Tran's mission, after all, was determining whether there were national security implications inside Earhardt-Roane, and not necessarily waging war on its people.

"Very well, Counselor. You may assign someone from your IT area to work with our lab techs so you get what you need, but we'll continue our investigation." She turned to the police officers. "Gentlemen, I need to know whether you've received any other reports of incidents of similar *modus operandi* in this area in the last twelve months?"

The Chief looked to his detective in charge of investigations for an answer, but Wardley clearly wasn't prepared to answer that question off-the-cuff. He merely shrugged.

"Understand, I'm speaking without having looked at anything to prepare, but I think the answer is *no*," the Chief finally answered. "We have the usual run-of-the mill petty crimes but nothing big like this for quite some time. Seaside Beach is generally a quiet, sleepy little beach community except during spring break and bike week, when it's usually a bunch of drunk kids or thawing aging cyclists getting into stupid mischief."

The mayor supplemented the answer. "We have the usual lot of drugs, robberies, prostitution, and murders in the bad part of town, but the riffraff that live there are incorrigible. It's in their nature to behave like that, and sending police in there is just pointless. They may kill one another, but they don't go usually venture out where decent people live. The blacks stay in their area and the whites stay in their area, and the students at the community college usually just stay on campus. We just don't have things like murder of prominent citizens in corporate office buildings."

Tran stared at the mayor in silent disbelief. He didn't even seem to realize his bias and racism, but that was often the case. It only caught Tran's particular notice because she hadn't actually seen it in reality in quite some time. But then again, this was a small southern town, she thought. Perhaps they'd not come as far since slavery as people might think.

Nonetheless, Tran explained as much as she could tell the group, and then articulated what she respectfully requested from each of them, including complete personnel files on a list of people, security recordings, criminal records checks, and a host of other items. They discussed and agreed for the time being that they'd only publicly release information that the CFO had unexpectedly passed away while working at her desk. If the situation demanded more of an explanation, they'd also indicate that authorities were performing a routine investigation into the circumstances surrounding the death, and leave it at that. The company could resume its normal operations, but no one was to use or access the office or anything in it. Tran agreed not to put up police tape around the office or seal it shut, but instead, the company allowed her agents to put monitored surveillance devices inside the crime scene so Tran would be alerted immediately if anyone entered the room. All agreed the goal was to turn the issue over to SBPD to handle and let the federal government step out of it as quickly as possible.

"Okay, gentlemen. My team will follow-up with you in more detail in the next day or so, and we'll also be looking to speak with some of your employees—at their homes if need be. I trust we'll have your full cooperation in getting necessary files, personnel information, surveillance video, and the other items. I don't anticipate there will be any issues, but if there are, please contact me at this number."

Tran passed out business type cards, blank except for her last name and a telephone number.

"I want daily updates of your progress throughout your investigation, Ms. Tran," the president stated. "This is my company and these are my people, so I need to know what's going on at every step. I trust there will be no problems with that?"

Tran checked her watch. Fifty minutes had elapsed since the meeting began, and that was more than sufficient. She stood from the table.

"We'll brief you when we have an appropriate amount of progress or a significant development in the investigation," Tran said to the group. She folded her portfolio. "If there are no other issues, then we're done here."

She nodded almost imperceptibly at Starr, who in turn walked to the door and opened it, holding it for their visitors to exit. Slowly, the assembled group stood, gathered what belongings they'd brought with them, and filed out of the room. They boarded a government-owned van driven by Agent Thorsten, who'd return them to the parking lot of the Earhardt-Roane Corporate Headquarters, only ten minutes away. When the last of them had exited the building, she called her entire team into the conference room and detailed their specific assignments, dismissed them, and then walked back to her borrowed office.

"Lockwood," she called down the hall. "I know you're planning to get back in the field this afternoon, so let's chat first thing tomorrow, before the Powwow?"

"Yes ma'am."

Tran returned to her office and closed the door. She found the spot on the wall, and opened the hidden door to the observation room.

"So what did you think?" she asked of its occupant.

"The President is nervous about something," the man answered. "Many of the top managers have whispered comments about him growing quite full of himself lately, and perhaps there's some of that, but he strikes me as being worried about something."

"You think he knows about the leaks and the fraudulent reports?"

"Can't tell for sure yet, but I wouldn't put it past him. He prides himself on being one of those southern gentlemen and even brags often about how he'll smile in someone's face while stabbing them in the back…so they never see it coming. And, he's quite the politician with the Board and other important people, so he's a skilled liar. He's pretty smart, and sometimes you don't think he knows something or isn't paying attention, and then he surprises you by doing something that shows he was paying attention all along. And, I know for a fact he's a big believer in plausible deniability."

"The old willful ignorance trick, eh?" Tran paraphrased.

"He's a slippery one—you gotta' watch him."

"And the lawyer?"

"He's a really good guy at heart, immensely book-smart, but afraid of his own shadow—jumps when little dogs yap. In the real world, he's maybe not totally confident in his own skin, and so he seems to operate in crisis mode all the time—you know, a little afraid he'll be fired if he looks at the wrong person the wrong way. It makes him walk a tight rope most of the time, and I think you witnessed that in there too. There's been tension between Legal and the CFO's group for a long time, largely due to *the Ice Queen's* influence over her boss, as far as I can tell. The problems only increased after I came to the company, because I'd report my findings to him and my other colleagues, only to learn that the senior officials of ERAC don't really want to know. Even though he's their lawyer and is supposed to help keep them out of trouble, our colleagues in the executive suite shut him down every time. It really pisses Matos off because he has legal and ethical obligations to do something about the issues I report, but he has to couch his words very carefully if he wants to keep his bosses happy."

"That's a hell of a way for a lawyer to do his job," Tran said.

"I know, and so does he. He's quite neutered and emasculated as far as being a real lawyer goes."

"Okay," Tran said, bringing their meeting to a close. "Why don't you slip out of here, and I'll be in touch. My team will be officially questioning you as part of our investigation at ERAC, but we'll protect your anonymity insofar as the other matter goes. This will look like a routine part of the investigation. "

"Later," the man replied as he departed Tran's office. He headed quickly to the door before any of the other agents saw him.

As he left, Tran withdrew the ERAC file from her desk drawer, and began to re-read every page. The answers were there, and in the evidence that continued to roll in with each passing minute.

# Chapter 3

# Crescendo

Morning had come early for Tran yet again. She awoke at 4:50 a.m., her norm as-of-late. She engaged her usual morning routine: a two-mile jog, followed by a dip in the hot tub, a long shower, and a nice hot breakfast, topped off with a mug of piping hot, fully caffeinated black coffee—the first of several she'd likely have through the day. Then, she hustled into the office so she arrived a good hour or so before anyone else. She liked to be early so she could get things on her own agenda done before her phone started ringing, emails started flying, and people started popping in her doorway. She'd been at it for a nearly fifty minutes before someone else arrived at the non-descript building.

"Morning Grace," Mark Allen greeted. "Hope you're still finding everything to your liking here, as far as accommodations."

"Hey Mark. Everything is great. Thanks for letting us crash your party while we're handling this thing."

"No problem. You know you can always count on me."

"Yeah I do," Tran agreed. She truly meant that.

With nearly thirteen hundred cadets in their class at the Academy and on very different career paths, Tran and Allen hadn't run across one another during the school year. They met the first day of summer break after a rigorous freshman year. That particular morning, both had awakened early and gone to the same running path through a park in the high desert mountains. Allen noticed Tran's shapely rear-end on the trail ahead of him, and increased his speed to get a better look. He liked what he saw, and thought it signaled the start of an interesting summer break. Allen had never considered himself particularly good-looking, but his long list of past and present girlfriends suggested otherwise. He hoped this beautiful prospect on

42

the trail ahead would find him as irresistible as the others. He matched her pace and ran beside her, staring for a few moments before introducing himself.

"Hi, I'm Mark, Mark Allen," he'd said to her.

Fully aware of him since long before he reached her side, she glanced quickly at his face, and then returned her gaze to the trail ahead. Unseen rocks, exposed roots, and depressions in the ground were constant hazards on a nature trail. "That sounds like a personal problem to me," she answered. She increased her speed and pulled ahead of him.

He sensed a challenge, and increased his speed to catch her once again.

"You have a name?" he asked when he again reached her side.

"Really?" she asked. "That's the best you can do? Of course I have a name."

Again, she ran faster, literally leaving him in her dust a second time. Once more, he ran faster to catch her.

"Well?" he asked.

"That's a deep subject," she replied.

"What? I don't get it?"

She rolled her eyes. "Clearly."

"Well?"

"That's a deep subject," she replied again.

He didn't say anything for a second as he contemplated why she offered that response. *Oh, I get it now,* he thought. *A well is a deep hole in the ground where water is found, hence that's a deep subject.*

"It's customary that when someone introduces himself, the other person introduces herself in return," he explained.

She didn't answer him, but increased her pace again, once more leaving him behind. Not to be undone, he ran faster, too.

"So?"

"…A needle pulling thread," she sang to the tune of a song from the musical *Sound of Music.*

He was quicker on that one, understanding her immediately.

Tran saw the parking lot a ways ahead, thus indicating she'd run the full squiggly circle-like route of the path and was nearly back to her car. She suddenly burst into an all-out sprint, trying to hit the burn at the end. Allen was prepared for her to try to outpace him as she had three times already, so when Tran began running faster, he immediately did likewise.

With two highly competitive personalities running side-by-side at a very fast clip, it instantly became a race. Neither liked losing, but Allen really didn't want to lose to a girl, especially one he was trying to impress. Tran wanted to show a little girl power to this dude who apparently thought he was cute and had game enough to hit on her while she was trying to exercise. Both put their all into the final leg of the run. They were neck and neck as they approached the last few feet of remaining trail, when suddenly Allen fell to the ground with a thud, punctuated by a series of rapid-fire curse words as he hit the ground and cradled his ankle.

Tran thought it was a ploy at first, and so she kept running with full gusto. But, when the young man remained on the ground in a messed-up heap, she suspected perhaps he wasn't joking. Not a hundred percent convinced of his sincerity, she was prepared to jump into action just in case this was his way of faking her out so he could suddenly get up, run to the finish line, and beat her there, or worse grab hold of her, wrestle her to the ground, and assault her. Whichever the case, she was ready. She stopped and went back to help him. "Are you okay?" she asked as she approached.

"Yeah, yeah, I think so," he stammered amid his swear words.

He tried to stand at least twice before Tran reached his side, but both times he collapsed as soon as he put weight on his left leg. Even as she approached, Tran could see the sub-cutaneous bruising already forming around his ankle. She guessed he had a very bad sprain or else it was broken. She reached his side and crouched down to have a closer look. Then, she palpated the circumference of his ankle, noting his veiled grimaces as he tried to hide the pain. "I think it's broken," Tran diagnosed.

"So now you're a doctor or something?" he said, joking. He winced each time she pressed down around his ankle, even though she did so gently.

Tran looked at him and smiled. "There's a reason my parents wanted me to go to Harvard Med."

Wow. He couldn't believe his luck. He'd been running with a gorgeous young female medical doctor, who just happened to be there when he needed one.

"Come on," Tran said. "I'll help you to your car." She put her arm around his waist, and he placed his around her neck. She lifted him and together they hobbled to the parking lot a hundred feet away. There were only two cars parked there, one of which was hers, so she presumed the other was his.

"Is the Camaro an auto or stick?" she asked.

Instantly, he realized the problem she was assessing. He'd never be able to operate his car in his current condition. His left leg and ankle couldn't bear the pressure needed to do so.

"Stick," he answered.

"You got some roomies you can call?"

"Yeah," he said, "but it won't do any good. He walked out of Sijan the same time I did, so he's probably through airport security by now or else he's 30,000 feet up already." He paused a second. "First day of summer break," he explained.

Tran nodded her understanding. With his last words, she just put together what she probably should have figured out when she first saw Mark Allen. He was a fellow Academy cadet. The haircut and general physique should have been a dead giveaway, but the fact that he was on his first day of summer vacation and lived in Sijan Hall helped complete the picture. Any lingering doubts she may have had would have been alleviated when they reached his car, where the AFA parking sticker on the window confirmed he was an active cadet.

"I guess I can drive you to the infirmary if you want —you can probably still make it to Sick Call."

"You're a cadet?" he asked.

"Sophomore."

"I thought you were a doctor."

"I never said that," Tran replied.

"You said you went to Harvard Medi—" he said as he recounted their conversation in his mind. "...oh, you said *'there's a reason your folks wanted you to go to Harvard Med.* I get it—you're one of those sneaky types."

"That's not quite what I said, but I guess that'll do."

"What do you mean?" Allen asked. "I quoted you verbatim."

"Not really," Tran rebutted. "What I said was *'there's a reason **my parents** wanted **me** to go to Harvard Med,'*" she said, emphasizing what was different between their two recitations of her comment.

Allen listened carefully, and realized his error. "Oh, a literalist I see."

"Not really. I just expect people to mean what they say and to be right if they're going to say something."

"You should be a damn lawyer or something," Allen said.

"Yeah, maybe, but for now, I guess you'll have to settle for me being a medic."

She helped him into the passenger seat of her classic GTO, then rounded the car, got inside, and fired up its powerful engine. They discussed school, people they both may have known, future career plans, and other matters until they reached the 10th Medical Group Clinic back at the Academy. She helped him into the building, and left him in the good hands of the professionals there. He thanked her, and they didn't see one another until a week later when he showed up at the running path again. He was waiting for her when she finished her run. Allen had borrowed his roommate's car with automatic transmission, and drove himself to the track, cast, crutches, and all. After a few witty jabs about him trying to drive the car or run the path, Allen talked her into letting him take her to breakfast. That was the moment their friendship was planted, and it grew closer and closer over the next few years. The relationship took on a slightly different hue in their fourth year, when celebrating his assignment as a fighter pilot and hers as an intelligence officer, she leaned over and kissed him lightly on the lips. She hadn't intended to do it, but in the exuberance of the moment, it just happened. After a momentary shock for both of them, he kissed her back, but more deeply and passionately, forever changing their friendship into something more. They were certain they'd be together for life.

But their plans changed over spring break, just months before graduation. Tran toured Europe with two girlfriends from high school, and Allen went with his friends to Cancun, Mexico. His friends locked him out of their party room on the hotel's fourth floor, but Allen was bound to beat them at their game. He convinced the girls in the next room to let him climb over their balcony to get to his own. In his haste, he lost his footing and fell forty feet to the ground below. Shattering both his legs and breaking his pelvis in four places, he spent the final semester of college in the hospital and rehab, while Tran finished her coursework, graduated, and received her commission. His condition left him medically disqualified for worldwide deployment, and as a result, he lost his pilot slot. Ashamed and humiliated by his own stupidity, he fell into a deep depression, during which he pushed Tran and most everyone else close to him further and further away. He told Tran he was incapable of loving her, and that she should move on without him. He refused her repeated phone calls and declined to open her letters. Eventually, he got what he asked for as Tran moved on with her life. Eighteen months after his injury, he returned to finish his final semester at the Academy and received his commission as a second lieutenant, but he was unable to pass the flight physical and thus couldn't become the fighter pilot he always wanted to be. His secondary choice was *Air Force Intelligence.*

They'd run across each other a few times on active duty, and of course were friendly and cordial, but their lives had gone in such different directions. Tran did well in the Air Force until she separated from active duty as a Major to attend Harvard Law School. Allen stayed on active duty until he retired as a Lieutenant Colonel in Air Force Intelligence. He left the Air Force for life in the Bureau, and had since worked his way into a supervisory position in the field office located in Seaside Beach. It was quiet and relatively peaceful, and Allen enjoyed life by the ocean. They exchanged Christmas cards every year, and kept abreast of one another's careers over the years, but their relationship never returned to the romantic realm. When Tran drew this case, she had a pretty clear idea where she would make her temporary base of operations. Not only could the pair cooperate and work well together, but she knew she could trust Allen implicitly and his Top Secret Security Clearance was still valid. Thus, if she needed to share aspects of her case with him, her superiors at NSA wouldn't have much heartburn about him knowing the details.

A booming voice recalled Tran from her brief reminiscence.

"So let me know if I can help you," Allen said, as he politely bowed out of her office. He had his own morning routines he liked to keep.

"Sure thing."

Tran watched him until he left her range of view, and then turned her attention to her agenda for the day. First thing was a debriefing with Lockwood, followed by a Powwow with the entire team. She wanted to assure all members of the team were fully abreast of where the case stood. She also made it a matter of routine to talk things over with Lockwood, so she could capitalize on his vast experience. It wasn't a good thing that a person had been murdered for any reason, but the truth be told, for Tran and her superiors, the real concern in this matter was the possible compromise of a vital national security edge held by the United States of America. That was her mission. She heard Lockwood's customary racket as he lumbered down the hallway. He was right on time.

"Morning boss," he said, stepping inside. "We still on for—" he checked his watch, "now?" He knew Tran hated to begin her meetings late.

"Good morning, Ian. Yeah, come on in," she said. "Grab the door behind you."

She waited for him to settle-in to her visitor's chair before she started.

"The others will be along shortly, Lockwood, so if you don't mind, I'd like to get right to it. I want to share with you some background about the case the others don't yet have. They'll probably become privy to it at some point, but right now, you'll be one of a small handful of people who know this information, including the President and Vice President of the United States."

"Of course." Lockwood's eyes grew wider with excitement, but he maintained his cool.

"All right then. I'm sure you're seeing by now that this Earhardt-Roane thing is really starting to get messy. It's got potentially long and disastrous legs," she said.

"I'll say."

"This whole case started with an anonymous tip to DoD's Fraud, Waste, and Abuse hotline alleging that Francine Ketcham and her bosses were reporting incorrect data about the Phantom and Casper programs to the project office at Air Force Materiel Command. The tip was anonymous, but it contained a number of details indicating the reporter was an insider who knew what he or she was talking about, and thus, it got into the system. DoD and FBI investigators eventually identified the reporter as a long-time employee of the company named Venita Renley, and approached her one day while she was shopping. She was shocked to say the least, and repeatedly denied being the anonymous tipster, but after receiving assurances that the government would protect her if she got fired, she eventually confessed to it, and provided even more information about the way the company was administering this research program. It was coincidental when they fired her on some lame, trumped-up charges only a few days after reporting the matter to us, but when her husband died in a fatal car accident while driving *her* car a few days after that, we became very suspicious. We still didn't have enough evidence to prove anything against anyone, but if we wanted to preserve our options down the road, we knew she'd be a critical source, and didn't want her dead. We assigned covert security to watch out for this woman."

"Okay. So I see why the Air Force and maybe the US Attorney would be interested in this case," Lockwood said, "but it doesn't explain why *we* have it."

Tran chuckled. "That's why you're a super-agent," she joked. "You're right, of course. There's more. The additional information Renley provided after we confronted her suggested the problem might be even bigger than a misreporting of numbers, Ian. Her comments suggest someone in the company may have been sharing money and information about these highly classified programs with agents of the Iranian Ministry of Intelligence and Security."

Lockwood's eyes opened wider with surprise. "Hence, the reason this got to your desk," he said.

Tran nodded. "Yeah, and there's more still. Ketcham wasn't the only loss Earhardt-Roane has suffered recently. As you know, the previous CFO, Erich Day, died in a car accident a couple weeks ago, leaving room for Ketcham's promotion to the Senior Vice President and CFO job. An agency contact in the state crime lab told us the wreckage of Day's accident tested positive for an explosives signature also found in IEDs in Iraq, which have been traced to Iranian Intelligence."

"I'm sure you knew one of the company's board members is an Iranian national."

"Indeed," Tran agreed. "I requested an analysis on the wreckage of Renley's car. Imagine our angst when the report showed the same chemical traces were present in the residue of her husband's accident."

"What made you suspect anything? Lockwood asked, wanting to learn Tran's ways.

She sighed and thought back a few months. "The reports of the first responders to the scene of Mr. Renley's accident described a peculiar odor and an intensity and color of flame I'd seen in after-actions reports on roadside bombs in Iraq and Afghanistan. That made me think about the report on the Day accident."

"Yeah, well I never really got why the state crime lab was looking for traces of explosives in that accident either. I mean, that's not normally something they'd do, especially when all the evidence points to a run-of-the-mill car crash."

"I have an answer for you: Marsha Day, widow of the dead CFO. Like most wives on getting such news, she was hysterical when she learned of the accident, but she just went off on the cops who notified her. She was repeatedly screaming that somebody had killed her husband and they needed to arrest somebody."

"Why did she think so?"

"She told them her husband had complained about people being after his job or after him, that they were all cut-throats who'd do anything to get to the top of Earhardt-Roane. She named names, including a Ph.D. named Bete'

French-Catin, a VP who heads their Research Division, Ms. Ketcham, and the Executive VP who runs their western sales division, a guy named Frank Grounds."

"Any evidence?"

"No, she had nothing to prove her allegations. Evidently, the closed-door chatter was that the hubby was the wife's whole life—she had no children, no career of her own, and no hobbies, social involvements, or outside interests of any kind. The local authorities did a cursory investigation of the accident, and tied the case up tight. She repeatedly pressed them, eventually becoming a nuisance, and they dismissed her repeated calls and complaints as the desperation of a forlorn woman whose entire existence had been her dead husband. She tried to get Earhardt-Roane's president to pressure local law enforcement to act, but after the company's memorial service for Day, she was evidently dead to him too—neither he nor his wife would take her calls or see her. Feeling herself out of options, Mrs. Day made public allegations that the locals weren't seeking justice for her husband or trying to find the truth of what happened because her husband was—and these are her words—*just an island nigger and this is still a small white southern town.*"

"Island?"

"Yeah, Day was from Cuba, or maybe the Bahamas."

"So what happened?"

"That was only a few weeks ago, so the fat lady hasn't yet sung, as they say."

Lockwood retraced what he'd learned about the history of the Day incident thus far, but still found something missing. "So what prompted the state lab to look for explosives in Day's accident?" Lockwood pressed. "I'm sure they don't act on the request of every hysterical wife who weaves a tale of espionage and murder to explain the untimely death of her husband."

"Mrs. Day is evidently a pretty determined and resourceful woman who doesn't like to be ignored… When the locals refused to act, she filed civil rights and corruption complaints with the Department of Justice. Something in her complaint caught the attention of a summer law clerk who evidently made a persuasive argument to someone in authority."

"And the Justice Department made the request for an explosives test?"

"Among other things," Tran explained. "I mentioned this murder wasn't the only mishap to befall this company's employees recently." Tran withdrew another file from her drawer and placed it on the desktop, laying it open wide. "That we have two dead CFOs and a dead spouse of a whistleblower is enough to raise suspicion, but it turns out that Frank Grounds—their Executive VP of Western Operations—is a pilot whose personal aircraft crashed in the Arizona desert a few months ago." Tran tossed some pictures of a gnarled, barely recognizable aircraft fuselage across the table. "Nobody died, but he lost some body parts most men would shudder to hear about, and his aircraft was a total loss. The NTSB pegged the cause of the crash as faulty maintenance, but Grounds swears the findings are wrong."

"Doesn't every pilot say that?" Lockwood asked.

"Yeah, but he's got records to back him up. Besides, he's a well-credentialed retired Air Force fighter pilot with an impeccable record. Maybe the conclusions were wrong and maybe they weren't, but the unusual events kept piling up. I asked NTSB to test the wreckage of his aircraft for an explosive signature as well…a much smaller amount, but there was a match. Also, the woman who heads their Research Division was in DC about a month ago to do some Congressional lobbying, and got mugged in her hotel room not far from the Hill. She was with a local hustler kid known to seek out the company of professional women in DC. The gunshot that took him down attracted a lot of attention, which probably saved the woman's life. Someone came upon them, after which the attacker fled the scene. The witness was pretty useless except for telling the cops the hooded attacker was young, white, and fast."

Tran flung pre- and post-beating photos of Bete "Betty" French-Catin across the desk to Lockwood, who snatched them up for comparison. The pre-attack photos showed a tall blonde, blue-eyed, pale white female whom some might have thought pretty, while the post-attack photos showed the aftermath of a brutal beating, concentrated mostly on the woman's face and head—not too different from what had happened to Ketcham.

Tran continued. "Looks like *Betty's* attacker beat her nearly to death. The prognosis for a return to her prior appearance isn't good, but she'll have essentially a full physical recovery. Mentally and emotionally—jury's still out on that."

Lockwood shrugged his shoulders, flexing his neck muscles as he winced while looking at the damage to Catin's face. "She should get her money back. The facelift didn't help one bit."

Tran frowned at the callous joke, and Lockwood felt her disapproval. Gallows humor was trademark of Ian Lockwood, but she knew he didn't really mean it. That and the fact that it was just the two of them present were the only things that spared him more of her castigation than her stern disapproving expression.

"All right then," Lockwood said, trying to break the awkwardness of the moment.

Tran shook her head, and then pressed on with the business at hand. "You know I'm not a big believer in coincidence. I thought the run of adverse incidents involving the top level of this group warranted a closer look, just to be sure there wasn't something there…"

"I'm not surprised," Lockwood answered.

"So, this Iranian board member you mentioned…"

"Iryana Hamidi, uh-huh."

"I did some checking. She's had a number of recent contacts with people the agency knows to have ties to the Iranian president. She traveled to New York a few weeks ago, when Ahmadinejad was here to address the UN. Of course, there was no direct meeting between Ms. Hamidi and Ahmadinejad himself, but she did have dinner with a clerical employee who came to the US with his entourage. Supposedly, their families have old, long-standing connections, but it's awfully convenient."

"Yeah and you're not a big believer in coincidence," Lockwood echoed. "We had her followed?"

"CIA tried but something interfered with the capture of conversation— another mystery. John Sedgwick's team is running that part of the investigation from New York. They'll keep us posted as things develop."

"I don't particularly like that guy—Sedgwick. His artificial southern charm and that stupid, shit-eating grin just rub me the wrong way," Lockwood said.

Tran nodded her understanding, if not agreement. "Yeah, he can come across as a bit full of himself sometimes, but deep down, he's *good people*, as they say."

"Yeah, deep, deep, deep, deep down, I guess."

"Yeah well, the Agency trusts him, and I haven't witnessed anything to suggest it shouldn't. So Sedgwick will run that to ground and keep me informed of anything big. Besides, all the twists and turns in this damn company are enough to keep us busy without anything else adding to it," Tran explained.

"'Scuse me, Boss," a voice called from the hall, it's owner knocking lightly. "You still planning for us to Powwow this morning?"

"Yeah sure, Deanna. Come on in." She simultaneously nodded with her head and pointed with her hand to a large plain conference table across from her desk.

Tran stood and walked to the head of the table as Special Agent Deanna Starr stepped inside and headed toward the table. She was followed closely by Special Agents Kenison and Ito, and then Mrs. Vivian Lawrence–in a manner of speaking. Lockwood spun his chair around to face the table, and adjusted himself to a more formal posture now that others were entering the meeting, and it was no longer just him and Tran. Dr. Starr seated herself in the chair beside Lockwood, and began organizing the files and papers she'd brought with her, as her teammates settled in for the early morning meeting. Kenison walked to the far side of the table and plopped unceremoniously into the chair beside Lockwood, and Ito took the one opposite him, next to Starr.

The thirty-five year-old Japanese-Mexican-American agent was officially the team's technical and science guru, but he was a man of many surprises and vast knowledge. Whatever the topic or issue of the moment was, it seemed he knew at least a little if not quite a bit about it. He frequently explained his knowledge of even obscure subjects by saying "I read that in a book once" or "I used to have a business doing that" where *that* happened to be whatever they were talking about. Ito's mother was a Mexican-American educator in Washington, DC and his father had served as the Japanese ambassador to the United States when he met and shortly thereafter married Ito's mother. Thus, from a very early age, he'd had a very cosmopolitan upbringing and had enjoyed many opportunities to travel the world and see a lot of things. He might have looked to some like the nerdiest of nerds, but he was formidable in every sense—mentally, physically, resiliency, everything. Ito was not someone to be underestimated, though many often did.

Ito carefully set on the table in upright posture a flat tablet computer-like device which he designed and built himself after witnessing the rash of copycat products rushed to market after Apple invented the I-Pad. His version had affectionately become known as the *Ito-pad*. Ito had rigged it to function as the eyes, ears, and avatar of the team's final member, Vivian Lawrence, who was too afraid to set foot on an airplane, and was thus condemned to work from the DC metropolitan area. The *Ito-pad* let Lawrence participate in the team's activities almost the same as if she were physically present. Tran didn't think it was as necessary for her administrative support to be physically present in the field like it was for the field agents, and more often than not it had actually been to the team's advantage for Lawrence to be back at headquarters when they were deployed. Thus, the arrangement served all their needs.

Tran held these Powwows every so often while the team was actively investigating a case so all members of the team could share and hear what they and other members were working on. One small piece of information that was seemingly insignificant to one member of the team might just be the missing puzzle piece to some other aspect of the case, and Powwows had proven effective in connecting these missing links, time and time again. The team settled in to the chairs, and spread their assembled papers over the tabletop in front of them. When it appeared everyone was reasonably organized, Tran opened the meeting.

"All right, this Powwow is officially opened," she began. "Let's start with forensics. We have a very preliminary report back from ERT, but it doesn't show much. They're still working on the autopsy, but it appears the body was cut sixteen times with a five-inch double-serrated blade. The face was bludgeoned with the base of a Tiffany lamp kept in the victim's office, and while it probably caused her a lot of pain, that's not what killed her. The preliminary cause of death is exsanguination incident to complete bilateral transection of the jugular veins and carotid arteries."

"The perpetrator probably harbored a great deal of rage for this woman," Dr. Starr offered. "These injuries were clearly designed to exact revenge for some perceived past wrong or indignity inflicted by her on the perpetrator or upon someone close to him. And yes, I mean *him*. For a number of reasons, these aren't injuries typically caused by a female assailant."

"Agreed, Doctor," Tran said. "There were no bodily fluids from anyone other than Ketcham in the room. The ERT did find some skin cells in dandruff left on one of Ketcham's visitor chairs, and a hair that doesn't belong to her on her clothes. They also lifted a partial set of prints from a can of Star Cola that was on her floor. We've got nothing on the hair or skin cells just yet, but the prints on the can belong to Ketcham and one of her sons."

"She had adult kids?" Lockwood asked.

"No. Her oldest is sixteen, a sophomore at the local high school. He's a Marine JROTC cadet who just received a scholarship, courtesy of our jarhead friends. As part of his scholarship processing, he was required to provide fingerprints, as are all military personnel, and for that reason, he happened to be in the system."

"Okay," Lockwood nodded. "That's not unusual—they may not be useful for many other good things, but most boys that age are quite capable of unloading and putting away groceries at home for their folks."

"I agree," Tran announced. "What is unusual is that there were no other prints in the room anywhere, and there were traces of bleach on the desk drawers. ERT found smudges of Ketcham's blood on files inside the drawers, and theorized they'd been rummaged, as though someone was looking for something in particular. We don't know what. That's about all we know at this point, forensically speaking. The FBI lab will continue its analysis of the evidence, and I'll apprise you as soon as I know more. So, let's go around the table and share what you've been working on thus far? Dr. Starr, please start."

"Well," Starr said, shaking her head as she reviewed her notes. "I've spent my time so far in this investigation reviewing personnel files and interviewing a few of the employees to try to assess the environment we're working with in this matter. I think there's no diplomatic way to summarize my initial impressions but the most delicate description is that this company could be a real *Peyton Place*."

That raised a few brows and fostered a few snickers from the team.

"I say this only somewhat in gest, colleagues, because if you recall, the term *Peyton Place* refers to a 1950's novel that dealt with hypocrisy, social inequity and privilege in a small community, and that's a pattern that seems to be emerging from my inquiry into the environment here. All external metrics may seem very good and desirable on the surface, but if you scratch a little, there is a recurring suggestion of a sordid foundation that's been allowed to fester for some length of time."

"That's quite a conclusion so early in the process, Dr. Starr," Tran observed.

"I wouldn't exactly classify it as a conclusion quite yet, Grace. My initial impression really speaks only to my sense of what the employees think of the environment here. The reality may be very different from my impression, but it's remarkable for the company and for our investigation because peoples' perception forms their reality."

"So what's that mean?" Agent Kenison bluntly asked.

"It means that regardless of the facts, people will act on their perceptions of the facts, whether accurate or not. In this case, there are wide-spread sentiments that the decedent blackmailed her boss—the former CFO—for promotions, raises, and free reign within the company to do as she pleased."

"Any truth to it?"

"Groupthink, or the tendency of groups of people to simply accept and act upon a mode of thinking, can be very powerful under the right or wrong circumstances," the doctor replied. "Recognizing that as a potential factor here, I am impressed by the consistency of these rumors across wide swaths of ERAC employees, including the executives."

"Lockwood?" Tran asked.

He nodded affirmatively as he sat forward. "Yeah, these folks feel as though Ketcham could get away with murder because her boss simply wouldn't do anything to her for any reason. The speculation runs generally to two theories: she was either blackmailing him with some deep, dark secret or, she was sleeping with him."

Tran seemed dubious. "Is this one of those situations where people just call an ambitious, perhaps less-than-tactful woman a *bitch* because they're unaccustomed to powerful women in a man's world?"

"It's possible," Starr agreed. "We have no concrete evidence of blackmail. But, it's certain that the opinion she brutally exercised her power is very widespread and deep-seated throughout the company. Her personnel file doesn't reflect any indication that official action was ever taken against her."

"Now that's a little weird," Stefan Kenison interrupted. "I got internal investigation files from their VP and Chief Compliance Officer that show numerous complaints against Ketcham. The company has an automated complaint system called *Ethics Plan* that lets people make anonymous complaints, which are then funneled directly to a select group of executives charged with taking action on them. The Compliance Officer's files show a bunch of allegations of abuses and misdeeds by Ketcham," Kenison explained. "Why would there be numerous official complaints, yet nothing in the dead chick's personnel jacket?"

"A little respect please, Agent Kenison," Tran admonished. "But you're right, that is odd."

"Is everybody happy in Toyland?" Lockwood asked.

"S'cuse me?"

"Are the execs all on the same page?"

"Oh, I get you," Kenison said. "No. Emails between the Chief Compliance Officer, Erich Day, and Eileen Reynolds, VP of Human Resources suggest tension between them over issues relating to Ketcham."

"Like?"

"The reports Stefan mentioned for one. One email from the Compliance Officer to Day urges him to take clear and decisive action in response to an anonymous report of illegal activity by Ketcham. There is no response from Day, which appears consistent with his pattern on things he really didn't like dealing with."

"We've seen that crap before," Lockwood opined. "A big-wig doesn't like certain facts of reality and just sticks his head in a hole like an ostrich, hoping the problem will just go away."

"That just leaves your ass end exposed," Kenison added.

Tran asked, "And so was there any response from HR?"

"Yes…She asked why he was pressing the issue so hard, and accused the Compliance Officer of bias against Ketcham. The Compliance Officer objected to the thought that he'd let his personal feelings interfere with his official responsibilities. He said taking corrective action was the right thing to do, and that the company was exposed if they didn't."

"And just what was the original complaint these folks were talking about?"

"There were several," Kenison answered, pulling several different pages from his pile of papers and notes. "I'll just pick a few here," he said. "One was about inappropriate charging of expenses to government contracts, one was about abusive behavior, and one was about a threat Ketcham made, supposedly as a joke."

"Please elaborate, Agent Kenison," Tran prompted.

"Well, Ketcham apparently told everyone at a staff meeting that she had friends in HR so if any of them said anything negative about her in a 360-degree evaluation they'd been asked to do the next day, she'd find out and would make them pay dearly. The complaint went on to say this was dangerous and illegal, especially in light of the—and I quote—*suspicious movement of money and accounting trickery apparently being used to doctor records.*"

"What records?"

Starr shrugged. "I don't know. The complaint wasn't specific."

Tran nodded slightly as she contemplated what she was hearing. Her curiosity was evidently piqued but she obviously wasn't fully convinced. "So what became of the complaint?"

"Nothing, so it appears," Starr answered. "That was an issue the Compliance Officer had with both Day and Reynolds. Saying they demonstrated poor governance practices, he complained bitterly about their lack of action to follow-up on the issue and inform the reporter."

"How does that square with their normal practices?"

"They apparently have a pretty regular pattern of follow-up on matters they find simple and unlikely to ruffle anyone's feathers, but for matters they seem to think will be more complicated or risky, they drag their feet, give incomplete responses, or simply take no action at all," explained Kenison. "Several complaints involving the dead lady fall in this category, according to the Compliance Officer's records."

"No action on Ketcham-related complaints?" Lockwood asked, thinking that was too obvious an error, even for amateurs.

"Nothing indicating findings, discipline, or substantive changes as a result of the complainant's report."

Lockwood hesitated a moment, glancing at Tran. She had no questions, so he asked one.

"Does this vary from how they treated other complaints in the system?"

"Significantly."

Lockwood nodded as he thought in silence.

"The Compliance Officer, Nichols, do anything else on the matter after two other execs ignored it?"

Starr sifted through her notes. "His desk file shows he briefed the president about the issues and noted his concerns about Day's and Reynolds' inaction. He warned that protecting an employee even from an investigation of allegations could expose the company to liability."

"And the president's response?"

"I've found nothing from the president himself, but Nichols made notes indicating he felt the president threatened him. A *CYA* memo in his papers says the president told him, and I quote, '*We have to be beyond mere 'he said, she said' on this matter, because peoples' jobs are on the line, including yours.*'

Nichols also noted that the president said if he found the allegations were true, he'd fire Ketcham and anyone else involved on the spot. Eighteen months later, Ketcham was still at the company and no substantive inquiry had been done into the allegations."

"Okay, so *nobody* in an official position responded to a formal allegation that the Executive Director of Business and Finance was cooking the books and issuing implied threats to her subordinates who reported improper, potentially criminal conduct?"

Starr shook her head side to side. "Nichols seems to be a pretty thorough guy, so I'm guessing there wasn't any response by anyone."

Tran sat back in her chair, incredulous at what she'd just heard. This was information her team had culled together from the company's own documents, and not merely hearsay from people who may have been jealous of Ketcham or had an axe to grind with her. This was harder to ignore than the rumors about Ketcham that freely floated around the company.

"What's Nichols' story?" Lockwood asked. "It seems like there's lots of tension between him and other muckety-mucks in this place. How did he manage to get so high up in the company if he was a pain in peoples' asses?"

"He's fairly new—hired from outside the company about two years ago," Starr reported. "The others have been at the company for quite a bit longer than he has, and so my working theory is that he hasn't yet developed the same company mentality as they have. They're more company-people, and he's more loyal to his sense of morals and professionalism."

"You're saying it's a *good ole' boy* network," Lockwood summarized.

Starr nodded. "An accurate description," she agreed.

"All right," Tran said, moving the meeting along. "Lockwood, what do you have?"

The senior agent sat up in his chair and cleared his throat.

"I'm focusing on the murder itself insofar as it may be indicative of a national security threat. Starting with the victim's direct reports, I've been screening employees for involvement in the murder. It's proving to be a monumental task, because there are a lot of folks in this company who have things they want to get off their chests. There are also a lot of folks with possible motives for the murder—so many that it's going to take a while for me to get through them all. Many of these folks are actually happy Ketcham's dead, and several were even—" He struggled for the right word. "—gratified at the *way* she died in light of the way she treated people. Frankly, people felt she was *a uniformly hated bitch*."

Lockwood instantly felt the tacit castigation of Tran's disapproving glance.

"Sorry boss," he said. "I'm just quoting what they said."

Not wanting to countenance such commentary, Tran pursed her lips and nodded. It was the best she could do to allow the man to continue his report without endorsing the comments or reproaching him for his choice of words.

Lockwood continued. "One of them—who by the way is pretty tight with the *anonymous* fraud reporter—said that a few years ago, the company's internal auditor found irregularities in several cash accounts. The information was initially reported to the Board's Audit Committee, but it wasn't reflected in the final report to the full Board and wasn't disclosed in the year-end financials."

"Those year-end financial reports are used in the company's annual tax disclosures, so if there's a falsity there, they've probably got a fraudulent tax issue looming out there," Tran mused. "Please tell me you got copies of the draft and final reports?" she pleaded.

"Of course, and all the auditor's working papers too," Lockwood said. "I got some crap from their pet lawyer about it. Like he did with you the other day, he told me those records were privileged under law and then challenged my authority to seize them. I told him I wasn't a panty-boy shyster who could quote all the relevant legal mumbo jumbo, but I was taking the records anyway and that if he interfered, I'd take him into custody too. I invited him to confer with our OGC at headquarters if he needed a better explanation than mine."

"Don't you think that's a little ironic, Agent Lockwood?" Kenison asked.

"Ironic? What the hell are you talking about, Kenison?" the older agent grumbled.

He laughed. "It's just, you said you couldn't quote all the legal jargon, and then you go and use words like *relevant* and *confer* in the same breath?"

The entire group chuckled lightly as Lockwood struggled for a response, and then gave in to his laughter.

"**An-y-way**," Lockwood continued, "I got the documents. Auditor Jackman used very delicate language to dance around making any direct allegations against her co-workers in writing, but what she said was enough to make me suspicious. Her working papers and draft versions were much stronger in their language, but it was severely edited before being submitted to the Audit Committee, so the final report is much less…accusatory than the drafts."

"Who did the editing?"

"Looks like the CFO and the President primarily, but the head of the Board's Audit Committee was involved as well."

Tran nodded in acknowledgment. "What was the gist of the report?"

"Essentially, the auditor thought she found skimming of money from the budgets of the individual cost centers."

"Yeah," Kenison added, "and from what I can tell based on the docs I reviewed so far, Ketcham impounded excess funds from various operating accounts in the company, and then transferred them into the UAV program accounts. Under that scheme, the end-of-year balances in the UAV accounts should have been far over budget, but they were exactly and I mean *exactly* on budget, down to the fourth decimal position."

"That's a red flag itself," Lockwood added.

"Precisely," Kenison agreed. "It's not unusual for accounts to be off by a few cents, maybe a few dollars, but these accounts were substantially off. She also used a lot of unusual accounting procedures and records of expenditures or transfers. The numbers on the reports to the Air Force program office, however, meet the expectations."

"So nobody noticed these issues?"

"The auditor apparently did, but was told by the CFO—Day at the time—to drop it, that it was just a normal accounting anomaly she wouldn't recognize because she wasn't a CPA. When the auditor reviewed her findings with the president, he told her *peoples' jobs were on the line, including hers*, and warned she had to be *way beyond mere he said/ she said allegations*."

"Familiar language, isn't it?" Tran noted. "How much we talking about?"

"As best I can figure right now, it looks like about $3 million to $4 million," Kenison replied. "With your permission, I'd like to ask the FBI's white collar techs to help me nail it down for sure."

Tran nodded her approval. "Who is the head of the Board Audit Committee?"

"Iriyana Hamidi," Lockwood added.

*That's it. The missing money just might be the missing link between whatever was going on at ERAC,* Tran thought. But, they still didn't have enough to be certain they were right or to make a successful national security case. Too many unanswered questions in the matter would leave room for crafty defense lawyers to land a 747 in the holes of any prosecution for anything just yet. Besides, the current information didn't really suggest a prosecution target. The most likely culpable people at this point seemed to be dead, but, they hadn't killed themselves. The identity of who did was what Tran wanted to know.

"Okay then," she said as she processed the information. "Let's move on. Rique?"

"Absolutely, boss," Ito began. "Of course, I started with the decedent's computer, and noticed something strange right away. This woman's computer is a different brand and model than everyone else in the company. That's a bit odd because big corporations like this usually buy the IT equipment in bulk because they get better prices, and because using the same equipment across the board reduces the risk of incompatibility and other problems caused by using different types of equipment on the same network."

"So they bought different equipment for Ketcham?" Starr asked.

"No," Ito replied. "Their IT folks said Ketcham bought her own laptop and had her own techie from outside the company who worked on it. They said she wouldn't allow anyone in the company's IT department to touch it for any reason. Apparently, it was an ordeal for them when they needed to run updates that required them to physically touch company computers. She *freaked out*—their words, not mine."

"Why would she do that? Even more, why would ERAC allow it?" Lockwood asked. "I'd think they'd have internal policy prohibiting something like this."

"Yeah, it's highly unusual for any company to let non-employees or un-contracted vendors access their internal networks, especially a company that has highly classified military research on their computers," Ito explained.

"They do have an Acceptable Use Policy for information technology that disallows that kind of compromise of the company's information networks," Kenison added.

"Their IT security guy apparently raised that issue too. He was particularly opposed to letting Ketcham's computer guy have access to the system for security reasons, but Ketcham was insistent. The issue lingered unaddressed until his boss warned him to just let it go and not make a big deal about it—the Chief IT officer reported to the same person as Ketcham at the time—the former CFO. Eventually, when Ketcham was promoted to CFO, she also became the boss of the IT department. Folks in the IT group just passed it off as another executive whim. They called them *primie* requests."

Lockwood wrinkled his brow. "*Prema*...as in *premature?*"

"*Prima,*" Ito answered. "As in *prima donna.*"

"I get it—the Ivory Tower Syndrome."

"And it's another indicator our victim here was allowed to do as she pleased, regardless of company policies and procedures," Tran observed.

Ito nodded affirmatively. "And there's more. In poking around on the hard drive, I found a number of encrypted files. I'm trying to break the coding, but whatever she used, it's pretty sophisticated because I haven't been able to get past it yet. I'm running an algorithm that hasn't ever failed me, but it looks like it's gonna' take some work. This is way beyond the simple little tricks people think they're being clever to use."

"Keep on it and let me know what you find. Anything else?" Tran asked.

"That's it for now, Boss."

"Thank you, Rique'," Tran said. She turned to the newest member of the team. "All right, Stefan. This should have been your first formal presentation to the Powwow, but you've been contributing pretty good stuff all along. Got anything we've not covered yet?"

"I think I've reported on most of my work already, but just so everyone knows, I'm still looking at the company's surveillance footage. There's a lot of it, but what I've seen so far doesn't show anything particularly noteworthy. Looks like the normal business traffic all day Wednesday, Thursday, and Friday before the murder. Through that night, there are a few folks coming and going but none of them are suspicious."

Tran glanced at her watch, and then to the opposite end of the table.

"Viv," Tran called. "You've been following the discussion so far. You have anything to add?"

The cocoa visage of Vivian Lawrence stared back at the Team from the *Ito-pad*. The jovial administrative assistant had been in the federal civil service for forty-three years, many of which had been working directly for Tran. She was Tran's first assistant when the latter entered the active duty military, and except for the time Tran was in law school, she'd supported Tran ever since. Raised in the church, Lawrence was a devout and principled woman who lived very much in accordance with the scripture. She didn't lie, cheat, or steal in any fashion, and she didn't brook those who did, regardless of their station or position in the world. Those who pushed her far enough would find her a cantankerous, fearless, intractable woman who made a point of saying exactly what was on her mind, whenever it was on her mind, and she—in her own words—didn't *give two shits about who did or didn't like it*. The cost of her disposition had been a fair number of confrontations with people, including previous supervisors, who weren't comfortable with her freely shared opinions and innate inability to cower from anyone for any reason. But, Lawrence and Tran had hit it off early on, and worked very well together. Tran liked the fact that Lawrence would say what was on her mind, because she never had to guess where she stood with her. The fact that Lawrence was also a very nice, warm-hearted person whose life stories could entertain the masses for hours on end was an added benefit, and it didn't hurt that she was almost always right about the things about which she pontificated. Tran could easily make a great many accommodations to keep talent like that on the bus.

"Yeah, I been listening," Lawrence said. "Y'all got to go through whatever steps your investigator manual says you got to do, but mark my words, at the end of the day, you'll see where there's smoke there's fire. My

*Self* is tellin' me that Ketcham woman was an evil woman who's right in the middle of this mess. Just follow the money."

"Words of wisdom," Tran said.

It may not have seemed like much to an outsider, but Tran found great comfort in Lawrence's remarks. They validated her gut hunch about the case, and Lawrence's *Self* and Tran's gut were rarely wrong, especially when they agreed with one another.

"All right, I've got to get going soon," Tran said, bringing the Powwow to a close. "Based on what we've learned so far, I think we're far from a valid conclusion that there's a national security issue in this…*Peyton Place*," she summarized. "But, it's clear there are a number of red flags here. I'm concerned that one of their employees reported something hinting at illegal activity but the senior leadership appears to have taken absolutely no action to confirm or refute it. I'm concerned about the missing money, and I'm concerned about the potential connection between a high official of this company and foreign intelligence elements. We've got work to do people. Dr. Starr and Agent Kenison, please interview that Chief Compliance officer and the auditor. Agent Kenison, you'll also need to follow-up on ERAC's contract and financial accounting arrangements. Viv can help you coordinate whatever resources in the Bureau or at Headquarters you may need. Rique', you take the IT issues, both inside and outside the company, and I need you to break the encryption on the files in Ketcham's computer. Agent Lockwood, I want you to say on the murder. Use your old police officer instincts, infused with your super-agent training and investigate it as a regular detective would any murder. I'm gonna follow-up on the potential ties to foreign intelligence, and Viv will stand-by for the assists for all of us. Follow your leads wherever they take you, people. We'll Powwow again in a few days. Anybody got anything else?" She waited but no one responded affirmatively. "Okay, then we're done."

As her team rose and filed out of the room, Tran leaned back in her chair and collected the notes she'd made, collating them into those she brought with her to the meeting. She stood and walked back to her desk, noting Lockwood loitering in her doorway.

"Close the door and spill, Lockwood," she said, not even looking him in the face. She knew he had something to say. He usually acted this way when he was about to say something he thought might be unwelcomed by those above him in the chain of command. "Obviously something's on your super-agent mind."

Lockwood closed the door as requested and returned to Tran's desk.

"How long have we worked together?" he asked.

Tran really had not appreciation for the set-up of a seemingly innocuous question that only served as a way to introduce what the person really wanted to say. She much preferred for people to just spit it out.

"Seven years, seven months, two weeks, four days, twelve hours, twenty-two minutes, and nine seconds," Tran joked, "but who's counting?"

"Seriously, Grace," he said. "We've worked together long enough that I know your *tells*. I've been around long enough to know not to ask questions that can't be answered, but just in case you're waiting for an indication I know something else is amiss here, you have it. I'll assume you'll let me in on whatever it is when the time is *ripe*, as you legal types say, or not."

"And just what do you think I'm hiding, Ian?"

"Not sure, but whatever it is, it has to do with the Chief Compliance Officer—Matt Nichols," Lockwood guessed.

Tran sat in her desk chair, staring at Lockwood without expression. Inside, she was surprised he could read her so easily and clearly. "What makes you think so?"

"You gave him a pass during the Powwow. Not once did you ask the sort of follow-up questions about him and his information you normally would. You didn't seem at all surprised that we got such juicy intel from him, so I'm guessing you already know something about him the rest of us don't."

Tran smiled. "I was going to discuss this with you soon anyway," she began. "Now seems as good a time as any."

She motioned for him to sit in one of her guest chairs.

"You're right. I do know something about Nichols I haven't shared with anyone else on the team. He's a confidential informant for us. He's been feeding us information about what's going on in this company for three months now. He was initially an asset to the DoD Inspector General on the Fraud, Waste, and Abuse complaint, but they turned him over to me when we started putting pieces of this puzzle together. We still don't know exactly what we're dealing with here, but we'll get further with him on the inside than not having an internal source. The Ketcham murder is regrettable, but it gives us clear cover for our national security investigation of possible ties to foreign elements. We can poke around in ERAC's affairs and nobody would be too taken aback by our presence. It also gives Nichols an official reason to talk to us without raising undue suspicion in the company. Here's another kicker.

Nichols was in the building at the time of the murder—he's the reason we knew of the murder before anyone else."

"Don't suppose he saw who did it?"

Tran shook her head. "He got to the scene just in time to see the perpetrator escape down the stairs at the far end of the executive hall."

"So he didn't see the person's face?"

"He didn't get a clear look, but said the person was hooded. He thinks it was a man who appeared to know his way around the building—an insider."

Tran could tell Lockwood wasn't completely buying into Nichols' story. The old cop in him was coming to the surface.

"What was he doing there at that hour?" Lockwood asked.

"At my request, he was downloading files from the company's computers. He went at that hour because he didn't think anyone would be there, and it was between the normal automated maintenance cycles the company routinely runs on its network."

Lockwood stared at his boss for a moment, and then voiced the thought running through his mind.

"I guess you want to trust this guy, but did you consider that maybe *he's* the perpetrator, and this whole *I-got-there-just-in-time-to-see-the-real-killer-run-away* thing is a ruse?"

Tran had been burned before by trusting people she shouldn't have, but she was sure this wasn't one of those times. Besides, even if Nichols was the killer, she still needed him on the inside of ERAC to get vital information for her national security mission. She realized there could be legal problems with warrantless searches and seizures of ERAC property if this matter ever reached the criminal prosecution phase, but she was more interested in protecting US national security and ensuring US troops weren't being harmed by possibly unscrupulous actions of someone in this company. The evidence to date suggested there were a lot of issues at the company, and that concerned her greatly.

"It did cross my mind, but I don't think he did it. He presented me with the flash drive of information from his covert mission, and its time stamps indicate he was obtaining the files at the time of the murder."

"All that means is he was copying files when the killer struck, but he could have been committing the crime while the files were downloading onto the drive," Lockwood insisted. "Besides, we don't know exactly when the murder took place."

Tran prepared to make another justification of her view of the matter, but then decided better. She knew it would be only another possibility. "My gut tells me he didn't do this, Lockwood."

"So you just don't want to believe it?" he summarized.

"I believe facts, Lockwood, and right now, they don't tell me Nichols did this."

"Okay. I get it," Lockwood said. "Would it matter if he was the killer?"

It was a good question, a version of an age-old question about ends justifying means. She needed Nichols' help to find answers to questions that were ultimately much more important than a single dead woman. If the only source of those answers was a violent criminal, well so be it. She paused to consider the answer.

"I'm sure it would matter to somebody. I'm just not sure who."

"It is what it is," Lockwood said, standing and heading for the door.

Tran withdrew a file on Nichols from her briefcase. "Here. Take a look," she said as she tossed it at him.

Lockwood caught it in mid-air, and then headed for his own temporary office down the hall. He had a few things to do before he got back into the field today.

# Chapter 4

# The Lair

It had been almost a week since John-Paul Ketcham had gotten news of his wife's brutal demise at work. After getting the boys off to bed, he sat on the back porch in the semi-darkness of the evening, drinking his seventh beer of the day. He didn't really like his sixteen year-old stepson, but the boy was easy insofar as taking care of him was concerned. His ten year-old son with Francine was an entirely different matter. He was a good natured boy but he was a sickly, injury-prone child who required a great deal of attention, and getting him off to bed was more than a notion. John-Paul hadn't yet returned to work since news of his wife's murder, but he still felt as though the day had been as brutal as any he'd had at the office in recent years. Rather than dealing with the demands of citizens seeking responsive service from a state employee, this day had been filled by phone calls from life insurance agents, lawyers, bankers, the mortuary, and a bunch of other people he never imagined having to deal with. A few family members had paid calls to the house over the last few days as well, but what he really wanted was to spend a little private time with Bete' French-Catin. They'd become *special friends* shortly after the first night that he and Francine had gone out for dinner and drinks with Bete' and her husband at the new and pretentious little café in town. The nicely appointed establishment was a bit too uppity for John-Paul's tastes, but Francine loved it. Just being in the place with its expensive Euro-reproduction appearance and its semi-wealthy clientele made her feel like she was somebody, a member of society's upper crust.

Francine loved to park her convertible BMW out front with all the other yuppie mobiles, and then prance into the high-end wine café wearing her newest Jimmy Choo heels and her diamond-studded Rolex Pearlmaster, which she inconspicuously—in her mind at least—flashed around the room to give everyone a chance to see it on her arm. She chatted with the other wannabe women of distinction, all of whom dragged their husbands to the stuffy place, cajoling them to pretend they liked it with veiled threats of hell-on-earth at home if they didn't acquiesce to their wives' whims. But that night, he happened to catch notice of Catin's not-so-tactful glances at him, and they weren't looking at his eyes. John-Paul didn't find Catin particularly attractive, but the thought of having a woman—any woman—that wasn't Francine was intoxicating to him. He'd be able to be a man again, instead of the emasculated puppy Francine had made him into over the ten years of their marriage. With his wife too caught up in the pageantry of her café, and Catin's husband so drunk he didn't care, John-Paul returned Catin's intense gaze, and soon thereafter, they found themselves hooking up in the by-the-hour motels throughout the seedy parts of town. That had gone on for nearly six years now, and though it too had become mundane at times, it had been a faithful escape from the harping, disapproving demands of his wife at home, and it was a comfort he needed now.

He wondered if that was why he wasn't more broken up about the fact that Francine would no longer be part of his, or anyone else's life anymore, forever. He felt he should be showing more distress about her passing, and particularly about the way she died, but when he was honest with himself, he wasn't distraught at all. Maybe, he was even relieved, hopeful. But he was careful not to let anyone see what he contemplated because it just wouldn't look right. He wasn't an unfeeling monster and didn't want anyone to get the sense he was. He had to try to show a much more mournful façade, but not tonight.

"Hey, Sailor," a voice called from the dark. "Going my way?"

Bete French-Catin opened the door of the porch's screen enclosure and stepped from the shadows. She made her way around the pool and walked to Ketcham's side, stopping long enough to remove her shoes before sitting as gently as a big-boned blonde could into his lap. She kissed him deeply on his mouth before realizing she hadn't assured the coast was clear. The lights on the back porch were off, but most of the lights inside the house were burning brightly, clearly illuminating a bunch of unwashed dishes, food containers, paper plates, and a lot of other clutter on the counters, table, and floor.

"Are we alone," she asked, quickly turning her head to look over her shoulder into the house through the large plate windows overlooking the patio.

"It's just you, me, and woody," John-Paul said, tilting his head to look into his lap. He kissed her deeply and began to fondle her breasts.

She stopped him. "Are you sure this is a good idea right now? What if somebody sees us?"

"All the family and friends have gone home, so it's just you and me. The boys are sound asleep for a couple hours now," he assured.

He kissed her, and began to tear at her blouse. She returned the gesture, and the temperature on the back porch of the Ketcham house began to rise precipitously. Had the doorbell not rung, it would have been the perfect end to a long day for John-Paul.

"Who's that?" Catin asked. "Oh god, I gotta' go."

"It's nobody," Ketcham assured. "Just ignore it, they'll go away."

"What if it's one of your in-laws or your family? What if it's—"

"What? Your husband?" Ketcham asked. "He doesn't care, and even if he did, he's too stupid to know anything about us."

The bell rang again. This time, they both jumped to their feet, re-zipping and re-buttoning parts of their clothing and staring nervously through the porch glass to the inside of Ketcham's front door and subconsciously holding their collective breath. Through the sidelights' privacy glass and that on the door proper, they could see the blurred profile of whomever stood there ringing the bell and waiting for someone to answer, but both Ketcham and Catin stood perfectly motionless, like deer in the headlights. After what seemed an eternity to them, the visitor stopped ringing the bell, turned, and walked away, his visage blurring even more with each step he took, and then fading completely from view. Neither of Ketcham's sons came from their rooms, so the couple presumed the children had slept through the noise, as kids so often can. They relaxed a bit, and then took one another in a deep celebratory embrace, followed by a passionate kiss.

"I was thinking," Ketcham began.

"Uh, excuse me," a voice called, again from the dark outside the screen enclosure.

Both Ketcham's and Catin's hearts concurrently leapt from their chests into their mouths at the sound of the soft vocal tones, and for a brief second Ketcham felt his body begin to bolt for the door. Catin would have done likewise had she not be clutching to her chest her loosened bra and lowered spaghetti straps of her blouse.

"I'm, I'm so sorry to scare you," the voice said. "I didn't mean to do that. I'm Special Agent Lockwood. I'm looking into your wife's death, Mr. Ketcham."

Lockwood opened the screen door and stepped up and into the radiant light shining from the house onto the patio. He instantly recognized Catin from her photograph in the investigation file, but Catin had never met Lockwood. The agent would use that to his advantage as he pretended he hadn't seen what the pair were doing when he interrupted them.

"Ma'am," he said, as he smiled and nodded to slightly bow his head to greet Catin whose name he pretended not to know. He turned to angle his posture toward John-Paul Ketcham. "I'm terribly sorry to bother you at this late hour, Mr. Ketcham. I was just driving past your house so I'd know where to come tomorrow, and I saw someone walk around the side of your house in the dark. With everything that's happened, I just wanted to make sure you were okay."

Catin spoke up. "Uh, oh, yes, that would have been me," she said, straightening her garb.

"Oh, uh, this is a friend of the family," Ketcham said, and then quickly shifted the conversation. "Yes, everything is fine here, Agent Lockwood. Thank you for checking on us, but we're all fine."

"Okay then. I guess I'll be on my way. I'll see you tomorrow."

"Yes, yes, thank you. That'll be fine," Ketcham answered. Then, after a split-second: "Uh, Detective." He called as Lockwood turned to leave. "Detective, you were preparing to come here tomorrow?" he asked.

"Yes."

"What for?"

"I've been out all day long talking to people who knew your wife, just to get a better handle on this case. I had a few questions to ask and things to follow-up on," he explained. "But since it was late, I was planning to come by tomorrow."

"Oh I get it," Ketcham said, "and the spouse is always Suspect Number One, right?"

Lockwood paused, smiled, and chuckled. "Well, not always, Mr. Ketcham. We're not making a Hollywood production here. You're not a suspect, sir. But we are looking into this case. I hadn't met you yet, and talking to the spouse is just one of the standard things we do to get some background on, uh, the victim, you know, to determine whether there was any reason someone would want to hurt the victim. I assure you, your wife's murderer will be caught."

"Thank you, Detective," Ketcham answered.

"Actually, it's *Agent*," Lockwood answered. "But you're welcome."

"Well, you're here now and so am I," Ketcham said. "You might as well just ask me whatever you were going to ask tomorrow."

"I'll, I'll just go back inside and finish straightening up," Catin said, manufacturing a reason to leave the area.

Ketcham fake-smiled and nodded his assent at Catin, and then turned to Lockwood. He motioned toward the wicker couch as he hastened to move the collection of beer bottles and other trash accumulated there.

"Please," he said, inviting Lockwood to sit down. "What can I tell you?"

"Well let's start with the question I mentioned. Do you know of anyone who'd want to hurt your wife?"

"No," he answered immediately. "No one."

"She hadn't had any spats with anyone, say at work, or old running feuds?"

"No, nothing like that."

"Have there been any strange phone calls, odd occurrences?"

"Nothing out of the ordinary."

"What do you mean by that?" Lockwood pressed.

"Well, Francine kept a lot of odd hours, like the night she was killed. Friday night/Saturday morning at that early hour? That's weird for normal people but not for Francine."

"How so?"

"She was a workaholic. She was always working late or going in early or on weekends and holidays. Even if she wasn't at the office or traveling somewhere, she was working out here on her laptop," Ketcham said.

"She traveled a lot? Where to?"

"Wherever the company has business."

"Anything overseas?"

"Sure, the UK, Singapore…"

"…Vietnam, China, the middle-east?"

"No, nothing exotic like that."

"How about phone calls? Odd phone calls?"

"Yes, some. Mostly from Erich before he…"

"Erich Day?"

"Yes, but—"

"Yes I know. He died a few weeks back."

"Yes."

"How about since then?"

"Don Johnston, the president of the company, and her colleagues in the executive wing."

"How did you know who she was talking to?"

Ketcham shrugged. "I guess I didn't know for sure. I just assumed. But whenever she had a business call, she'd walk out here or go a few feet away from the rest of us so she could tend to her business without bothering the rest of us with her conversation."

"Okay, good enough. You mentioned her executive colleagues. Any reason one of them might want to hurt her?"

"No. They were all really tight with each other." Ketcham glanced over his shoulder to the woman now cleaning his kitchen. "You might even want to ask." He paused and thought better of the idea and quickly snapped his gaze back to Lockwood, hoping the latter hadn't noticed.

"Ask who?" Lockwood pressed.

"Them—the other execs at the company. They'll tell you they were all pretty tight. They took a trip together each summer. We all went—execs and spouses together—Charleston, New York City, Charlotte, you know, nice places for executive retreats."

"Yes, talking to co-workers is another standard thing we do," Lockwood assured. "How about the members of the Board? Did your wife have any interaction with them?"

"Yeah, all the executives did."

"Hamidi?"

"Certainly. She's the Vice-Chairman of the Board and head of the Audit Committee, so Francine worked with her a lot."

"Any financial transactions between them?"

"Well, the company leases space from Hamidi's company, and they timeshare a private jet, so I'm sure there were payments made to Hamidi's company from ERAC."

"I see, and did they do any traveling together?"

"I guess just routine board meetings and stuff, nothing special that I know about," Ketcham said as he contemplated his reply.

"How about outside of work?"

"No, nothing I know of—just work-related social events and stuff."

"Okay. How was the relationship between you and your wife?"

"What are you implying, Mr. Lockwood?" Ketcham asked.

"I'm not implying anything, sir. I'm just asking what your relationship was like."

"We were married for God's sake."

"Yes, I know that, Mr. Ketcham, but what was your relationship like? Was it a good marriage? Were you both happy?"

"I didn't have anything to do with her murder, Mr. Lockwood," Ketcham said, indignantly.

"I didn't say you did. I just asked whether your marriage was good and whether you were happy."

"You implied that." Ketcham was obviously frustrated. "Yes. Yes, it was a good marriage and we were both ecstatic in our relationship."

"I see." Lockwood withdrew a pad of paper from his back pocket, and flipped through its pages. "So, please pardon me here, Mr. Ketcham, but you never said your wife was a controlling bitch?"

"Who said that?" Ketcham demanded, exploding from his chair and nearly lunging at Lockwood. Lockwood was an older man, but he wasn't a small guy who couldn't stand his own in an alley fight behind a redneck bar. Besides, the seasoned agent and expert marksman had a Glock strapped to his side.

"Who'd you say that to?" Lockwood calmly asked.

"Look, I loved my wife," Ketcham insisted. "She didn't control me okay. She made her wants and dislikes known, but she didn't control me."

"So, she didn't forbid you—a grown working man—from buying a motorcycle?" Lockwood asked.

Ketcham froze a little on the inside as the question was spoken into the air. That had been one of those occasions that nearly cost him his marriage, when he was still convinced he wanted to be married to his wife. The incident was humiliating to him because she treated him like a child. He'd mentioned in passing conversation with a friend that he wanted to buy a motorcycle and go for long rides when he had spare time, but when she heard the remark, Francine Ketcham told him, in front of his friend, that she wouldn't allow him to get a motorcycle. She went on and on about the dangers of motorcycles and that only men going through mid-life crises bought motorcycles to make themselves feel young and virile. With a condescending, dismissive cackle, she pronounced the notion ridiculous, and decreed that all discussion of the idea was done—period. His friend chided him, telling John-Paul he should *immediately go replace his tampon before she spanks you again and sends you to your room without supper.* His friend made the comment purely in jest, but it cut John-Paul deeply.

That wasn't the first time his wife had determined what he could and couldn't do, or dismissed his ideas out-of-pocket, and each time, the feeling of utter emasculation festered in him. This was even worse than the times she gave him hell, cut off the sex-tap, and made his life miserable because he hadn't planned a big enough surprise for her birthday or their anniversary, or hadn't planned it early enough in advance. All these things really bothered him, but he never tried to discuss them with her for fear of her reaction. But, the motorcycle was a different matter. He'd dreamt of one day getting a motorcycle since he was a teenager, and this time, she'd slapped him down in front of his childhood best friend. Over a period of weeks, he worked up the courage to broach the subject to his wife again, and she'd immediately slapped him down again, saying she didn't want to hear any more talk of it. So, John-Paul took her to heart. He didn't speak to her about the idea of buying a motorcycle, but instead went to the nearest dealer and spent $20,000 to buy a used one. When she found out what he'd done, Francine Ketcham was *pissed as hell*, as he described it to friends, and kicked him out of his own house for several days. She was so angry that she'd told people she was ready to file for divorce over this. He apologized profusely and kissed her ass for months afterward, and eventually, he kept his motorcycle and his marriage, but things were never quite the same. That was the week he and Francine had gone to dinner with Catin and her husband.

"All right, all right," Ketcham finally capitulated. "We had our issues, but every marriage does."

"You're telling me." Lockwood agreed. "I've been married and divorced three times."

"So you understand then."

"Sure do. I just wanted to be sure I was getting an accurate picture because…well, would it surprise you to know your wife had a reputation at the company as cold and callous?"

Ketcham stared at Lockwood without response.

"They called her the Ice Queen."

"Francine could seem a little harsh at times, but it was because she was so focused, you know. She wasn't a bad person," Ketcham said.

"No threats from disgruntled subordinates, then? I mean, looking at the list of people she fired, it's pretty impressive in terms of numbers."

Again, Ketcham had nothing to say.

75

"Okay then, how about your kids?"

"What about them?" the protective father snapped.

"You're really the step-father of the oldest boy, right—Dallas O'Brien?"

Ketcham nodded affirmatively.

"He's sixteen, right? Where's his dad? Is he still in the picture?"

"I'm Dallas' step-dad. His biological father is still alive but he's not a responsible father—Len's a surfer dude, just like a kid himself. He lives down the coast an hour or two. Hard telling where he is this week."

"So the blended family wasn't all smooth and easy going?"

Ketcham suddenly felt much better about this conversation because it identified another person who could take some of the suspicion he felt from Lockwood.

"Not really. He and Francine really got into it sometimes, especially about Dallas."

"So they fought."

"Bitterly," Ketcham agreed. "I don't know why the two of them ever got together in the first place because they were like oil and water. Francine lit into him about not paying child support, about not being strict enough with Dallas, about everything really."

"So I guess he was an involved father?"

"Yeah, but in a very irresponsible way."

"What was your relationship with him like?"

Ketcham paused. "Me? Nothing really. I didn't have that much to do with him. I'd see him on those rare times when there was a child drop-off or pick-up, and once in a blue moon, he'd come to one of Dallas' school functions."

"So your observations of him were all through your wife?"

"Yeah I guess. But I know they fought. They had a really bad argument a few months ago, and he told her she was a fucking bitch who'd die a lonely bitter woman."

"A lonely, bitter woman," Lockwood repeated as he took notes of Ketcham's statements. "So, he wasn't paying child support. Doesn't look like you guys were in any sort of financial straits because the guy didn't pay," Lockwood said, looking through the patio windows into the well-furnished home and remembering the dead CFO's office.

"No, we weren't. She makes in a month like ten times what Len earns in a year...We didn't need his money, but Francine wanted him to be responsible for paying support for his son. She said she was going to make him pay as much money as she could get out of him just because he needed to grow up and learn how to be responsible."

"I hear he runs a successful surf shop on the beach. She didn't think that was successful?" Lockwood asked.

"She thought that was child's play—a hobby. When they were married, she wanted him to go to college to get a business degree but he said he didn't like it and wouldn't do it. He opened that surf shop instead. Francine thought it was a ridiculous waste of time and effort. It was something teenagers did for fun, not something adults did for a living...and look, she was right. He can't even keep current on his child support. Francine said Len had treated her poorly when they were married and so she saw no reason to give him a break on anything now."

Lockwood nodded and took a few additional notes. "She was pretty hard on him, huh?"

"I guess, and he really hated it. I can't tell you how many times he said he hated her, and threatened her when she withheld visitation from him or his parents."

"In their history, was there ever any physical abuse?" Lockwood asked.

"Nothing official," Ketcham answered.

"So he hit her?"

Ketcham turned his eyes to the ground for a moment, and then spoke a little more softly. "You'll find out about it anyway if you look, so I might as well just tell you...There was an official report that Francine had hit Len a couple times...but he was drunk she said."

"Oh," Lockwood said, surprise in his tone. "So she beat him?"

"Yeah, it happened just once, not long before she left him. Never before and never after."

Lockwood nodded and wrote some more notes. "All right, and your other son—Michael is it?"

"Yes, my ten year-old with Francine. He's a good boy."

"Okay. No problems with the boys?"

"What do you mean?"

"They got along okay? No issues?"

"No, nothing unusual there," Ketcham agreed. "Michael is just an ideal kid...He's quiet and keeps to himself mostly. He's really smart—scary smart sometimes—and does well in school—likes to read a lot. The boys have the usual sibling rivalries, but nothing too serious."

"Adolescence can be a tough time for kids, and even worse on parents. How did you all get along as parents and teens?"

"Yeah okay I guess. They're boys and one is a teenager."

"Yeah," Lockwood chuckled. "I remember when mine started feeling his oats around that age."

Ketcham laughed slightly. "Yeah, Francine and Dallas had some pretty bad knock-down, drag-out arguments."

"Yeah, I heard she kicked Dallas out of the house?" Lockwood asked.

"I didn't mean literally, about the fights," Ketcham clarified, defending his dead wife. "She hasn't hit Dallas, not since he got his last spanking as a little boy. She loved Dallas a lot, but she sometimes got so pissed with his teenage antics that they couldn't be in the same space, or else he'd get so fed-up with Francine's *bullshit*, as he called it, that he'd run away for a few days. Eventually, things would cool down, and everything would be okay again."

Having barely survived his own kids' teens, Lockwood understood that, for sure. "What'd they fight about—a girlfriend, drugs, grades, anything in particular?"

"Yeah all that, I guess. Their worst arguments were about the Marines."

"The Marines?"

"Yeah. Dallas informed us he was gonna' be a Marine officer when he grew up, but Francine thought the military was for losers. She said people who did the military were those who couldn't cut it anywhere else or poor people with no other way out of the gutter."

"Most people regard military service as honorable," Lockwood said.

Ketcham bobbed his head this way and that, as though it would help remove the sharp edge from his wife's harsh view. "Ehhh, she just wanted him to become a top business mogul, a shark."

"Like her?"

Again, more head-bobbing. "Yeah, I guess. She wanted him to sit at the head of a boardroom one day and cut big deals that would reshape the way the world did business... Dallas wasn't really into it. He didn't give a shit about that at all—he didn't really give a shit about anything Francine cared about. He told her there wasn't a damn thing she could do about it because when he turned eighteen, he'd be a grown man and didn't need her permission for anything. That was his fallback whenever they fought about the Marines, which they did all the time. I was so tired of hearing it," Ketcham said, seeming to reminisce about it.

"They ever get physical with each other?"

Ketcham cast his eyes toward the ceiling as he thought for a moment. "Not really. There was a little pushing and shoving once when Dallas was trying to leave the house, but no hitting. He said he'd kill her once when she told him he couldn't have a girlfriend, but he didn't mean it. We laughed about it—said it was the testosterone overflowing his teenage balls."

"Uh-huh," Lockwood said. He switched his focus. "I understand Dallas had a history of trouble around town."

"What do you mean?" Ketcham asked, again feeling the need to defend his family, or perhaps his parenting skills.

"I heard Dallas got kicked out of school a couple times for fighting, poor grades, and truancy, and that he had some trouble with public intoxication, and for setting his dog on someone."

"He's had some troubles, okay, but he's basically a good kid. Every time he had a major issue, it was right after he returned from a visit with Len— what a loser," Ketcham retorted.

"So you thought it was the bio-dad's influence that caused Dallas to get into trouble?"

"Yeah, pretty much. All that was a while ago, though. He started doing better after he got into Marine JROTC. His grades are improving, his attendance is regular, and he's keeping his nose clean now."

"Okay, so that was just a rough patch, and they got over it, huh?"

"Yeah things were cool with them. Listen, I'm getting a little tired. Are we done?" Ketcham asked. "Think I'll turn in now, after I see my guest to the door of course."

"Of course," Lockwood repeated. "Just one more thing, Mr. Ketcham. Have you ever seen a knife like this?"

He reached into his breast pocket and withdrew the artist's rendering of the knife used on his wife. He unfolded the picture and held it in front of Ketcham's face. In consideration of the dim lighting on the porch, Lockwood activated the pin-light on his key-chain and shined it on the picture, closely watching Ketcham's face for any tell-tale signs or indications. He thought he saw perhaps a minute hint of something but he wasn't sure.

"Uh, that's what killed my wife? Ketcham asked.

"I'm sorry, Mr. Ketcham. Didn't mean to throw you for a loop like that. This is a rendering of what the knife we believe was used to cut your wife might look like. We're really only certain what the blade looked like, not the handle. We don't have the actual knife, and we don't know for sure that the knife wounds are what killed your wife," Lockwood explained.

Ketcham nodded his understanding. "Oh, uh, okay," he stammered. "I've never seen anything like that."

"Nothing like it? Take a good look."

"No, okay. I haven't seen that knife before," Ketcham retorted.

"Okay. I appreciate your time, Mr. Ketcham. Before I go, would you mind if I looked around your wife's office? I hear she's got a small office here at the house…"

"Oh, um, sure," Ketcham said. "It's this way." He walked across the patio and opened the sliding glass door. He pointed to a hallway just off the dining room. "Around the corner and then the first door on your left. Take whatever you need in there," he said.

"Thanks," Lockwood said. "I just want to have a look-around—see if there's anything that might point to who would want to do this and why. I'll just be a minute."

"I'm not going anywhere," Ketcham answered.

Lockwood nodded and then meandered in the direction Ketcham had indicated. As he passed through the kitchen, he paused momentarily to watch Catin clean up the mountain of accumulated paper plates, carry-out containers, empty pizza boxes, and cans of Diet Cola Blast soda.

"Uh, sorry it's a little messy," Ketcham said from behind him as he noticed the Agent looking into the kitchen.

"That's not messy, sir," Lockwood said. "You should see my place after a busy week."

Lockwood continued on his way through the house after a few seconds, and as soon as he rounded the corner, the grieving husband rushed to his kitchen helper's side, and engaged her in hushed whispers. In the hallway, Lockwood stood still and tight against the wall, straining to hear what he could from the kitchen.

"Do you think he saw us?" Catin quietly asked.

"I don't think so. It was dark and he didn't mention anything that suggested he did."

"I better get out of here, but I don't want to run off so fast. It'll look like we were hiding something."

"This is completely innocent. You were her friend and so that's why you'd be here, and even if he saw us, so what? It's only natural that you might comfort me…"

"By fucking the grief out of you?" Catin challenged. "That's all good and explainable for you, but I still have a husband and son to think about."

80

"I know. Let's just cross that bridge when we come to it. Right now, he doesn't know a thing. Just go, and I'll see you tomorrow."

Lockwood waited for cover from the noise of the closing front door before scurrying the rest of the way into the deceased's home office. Once inside, he scanned for anything worthy of closer examination. It looked like a normal home office, except that this one was extremely neat, clean, and organized. All the storage canisters were labeled for what they contained—paper clips, printer paper, pens/pencils, sticky pads, etc.—and the walls contained numerous photographs, certificates, and other memorabilia of Ketcham's accomplishments, significant events, and other occurrences in which she'd been the center of attention. There were also photographs from what appeared to be photo-sessions of Ketcham dressed in different outfits, sporting different hairstyles, or with different scenery, the kinds of scenes you'd get from one of those glamour make-up fantasy stores for little girls in a suburban mall.

"A classic obsessive compulsive control freak," Lockwood said aloud, shaking his head.

Other than the apparent compulsive order and neatness, nothing seemed unusual. Lockwood walked a few paces to the desk and began riffling around on the work surface, through the drawers, and the adjacent file cabinet. He found files of paid invoices, bank statements, leases and rent receipts from a rental property the couple owned, and old repair bills, but nothing meriting special attention. Lockwood plugged a special flash-drive into the slot on the home computer, and instantly, the entire contents of its hard drive began downloading onto Lockwood's personal device. He'd not know what to do with it himself, but Rique could decipher its contents in seconds. Once it completed its task, Lockwood then withdrew from his pocket a small scanner, and immediately activated it. A slight hum in the air told him the device was self-calibrating, and a few seconds later, its green *Ready* indicator flashed. Lockwood pressed the *Scan* button and waited for the device to do its job.

After a moment or two, the scanner's information screen told Lockwood there was a 14"x13" metallic cube beneath the floor of the closet ten feet to his left. He guessed it was a floor safe hiding the usual personal valuables—wills, jewelry, or other personal items—but it might also contain something relevant to the investigation. Lockwood hoped it wasn't one of the new electronic safes now widely available on the market these days, because he knew nothing about them. But, he could manipulate an old-fashioned rotary combination lock faster than Rique could break data from an encrypted hard drive. Lockwood entered the closet and moved the few boxes and oversized designer handbags strategically stored there, obviously to hide the cut carpet on the floor. Lifting the section of carpet, he pressed one side of the floorboards beneath, tilting the other side upward so he could grasp and pull it completely up from the floor. Shining his keychain pin-light into the closet floor, a smile creased his lips. Before him sat a rounded, lined and numbered dial atop a metal box amateurishly installed between the joists. This was something he could work with. He leaned over and rested his ear against the metal surface of the safe and began twisting its dial, annoyingly aware his backside was fully exposed. It wasn't that he was self-conscious about his chubby ass sticking up on display like one of those garden decorations laughed at by passers-by of suburban homes, but he was more concerned that someone could quietly come upon him and shank him, without affording him the slightest chance to defend himself. Through all his years in law enforcement, he'd seen too many friends leave this world because of stupid tactical errors, and now he was making the same kind of mistake. He was uncomfortable with what he was doing, but wanted, needed to get whatever was inside the safe. The whole investigation could turn on what he'd find.

As he slowly rotated the combination dial, Lockwood listened for the telltale clicks and knocks that revealed the order of the combination numbers to open the repository. He'd been a master at this in his early days, but had been quite some time since he'd last done it. Still, he was confident in his ability to break this safe—he'd never failed before, and this wasn't a very sophisticated device. *Click, click, thump.* He heard the final few sounds he waited to hear, and then sat up, turned the safe's handle, and pulled up the door. The box contained several neatly bound documents, two computer flash drives, and a few other random papers. Lockwood first removed all the papers, and began sifting through them—stock certificates, a car title, several written appraisals with attached pictures of high-end jewels, some certificates of deposit, and the *Last Will and Testament of Francine Ketcham.* They were the normal things one would expect to find in a home safe, and none were particularly relevant to the investigation. So, he set all papers back into the safe, and then pulled out the flash drives. He could tell nothing merely by looking at them without a computer, so he placed them in his pocket so he could take them back to Rique, who could do a more thorough examination of their contents. He got to his feet where he felt much more secure, and turned to check his six o'clock. He was surprised to find a small child standing there watching him. His instinctive fright response was to reach for his weapon, but he was quick to stop himself before terrorizing the boy too much. The child jumped at Lockwood's sudden movement, but otherwise stood motionless, without expression. Lockwood hadn't heard the boy enter the room and had no idea how long he'd been there. He wondered whether the boy had seen him take the flash drives from the safe.

"Oh, hello there. My name is Special Agent Lockwood. You must be Michael," he said. "Don't worry, Michael. I'm here to help."

The pajama-clad child stood silently staring at Lockwood for a moment, still without expression, but suddenly came alive with the same sort of precociousness of Lockwood's own children when they were young.

"That's not what's on your birth certificate. Your mom didn't name you *Special Agent Lockwood*," the boy said.

Lockwood chuckled. "You're right. She named me Ian, but when I'm at work, I tell people my title and last name, which is Special Agent Lockwood."

"Yeah, but you said your *name* was Special Agent Lockwood and it's not."

"You caught me, young man," Lockwood jokingly conceded.

A pause.

"Maybe we should let your daddy know you're awake, Michael," Lockwood said, suddenly feeling very uncomfortable being alone in the room at night with the minor child of a murder victim.

"Are you gonna' catch the guy who killed Francine?" the kid asked.

Lockwood was taken aback both by the bluntness of the unexpected question, and equally by the boy's use of his mother's first name. He turned back into the closet to put the floorboard, carpet square, boxes and handbags where he'd found them, and then backed out of the closet, gently closing the door. He turned back to Michael.

"Yeah, Michael. That guy will be caught and put in jail."

"Yeah, but are **you** gonna' catch him?" Michael pressed.

"There are a whole bunch of people working on finding out who hurt your mommy, Michael. One of us will get him. I'm real sorry about your mom, dude."

Michael shrugged and looked away, placing his hand on the wall and fiddling with a random chip in the paint there. He was silent and Lockwood didn't know what to say or do next.

"Okay," he said, trying to break the ice. "Why don't we go tell your daddy you're awake. I'm sure he'd want to know."

"Nah, John-Paul won't care, as long as I don't bug him," Michael replied.

Lockwood took one more quick look around the room, and then walked purposefully toward the door, gently guiding Michael into the hall in front of him. "All the same, I think we should let him know you're awake."

The pair moved a few paces down the hall, and nearly ran smack-dab into Ketcham as they rounded the corner.

"Oh, Mr. Ketcham," Lockwood said. "I'm all done. Your boy woke up and came in as I was leaving…" He looked down at little Michael. "Nice kid you got here… Anyway, it's late and I best be going."

He turned and bent slightly to put himself at eye-level with Michael Ketcham.

"It was nice to meet you Michael. You take care of yourself and maybe I'll see you around some time," he said, displaying his warmest smile. Then he stood to address the elder Ketcham. "Thanks for your time, Mr. Ketcham. Here's my card…please call if you think of anything that might help us solve this matter."

The grieving widower took the card and examined it. His head exploded upward until he locked eyes with Lockwood.

"NSA? Why is NSA investigating this case?" he asked. "I thought you were FDLE."

"Common mistake around here it seems," Lockwood replied. "I'm NSA. We're involved because of irregularities on one of ERAC's defense contracts, and it's possible whoever is responsible for those irregularities is also responsible for your wife's murder," he said, suddenly remembering the deceased's minor son was present.

"Okay," Ketcham answered, dazed. "Umm, did you finish up with whatever you needed?"

"Yes sir I did." He paused. "Uh, do you know the combination to the safe?"

"Excuse me?" Ketcham asked, his brow wrinkling.

"The safe. Do you know its combination? Or what's in it?"

"What are you talking about, Agent Lockwood? We don't have a safe."

"Sure you do," Lockwood replied. "You telling me you didn't know about it?"

"What safe?"

"I can show it to you if you want," Lockwood said.

"You mean Francine's box in the floor?" Michael asked.

"You know about a safe too?" Ketcham demanded of his son, a perplexed expression on his face.

Lockwood turned and walked back to the closet in the small office. He moved the boxes and handbags yet again, and kicked the small carpet square over the floorboards away from its position. With big toe pressure on one side of the floorboard, the other side tilted up, revealing the safe below. Lockwood shined his light into the hole for the second time that night.

"That safe." he said.

Ketcham gawked for a few seconds in stunned silence. The guy was either a really good actor, or he truly had been unaware that his wife kept a safe in their home. With nearly three decades of reading the body language of suspects and potential suspects under his belt, Lockwood guessed the latter. He stood and watched as Ketcham dropped to the floor and dialed in several different series of numbers. Lockwood caught bits and pieces of the different variations, but none of them seemed important to remember because none of them opened the thick floor vault.

"Any idea what's in there?" Lockwood asked.

"Shit," Ketcham exclaimed. "I didn't even know she had this thing."

"Okay, but do you have an idea what's in there?" Lockwood repeated.

"No," the widower yelled, clearly annoyed.

Lockwood shrugged. "Okay then. If you figure it out, let me know what you find, will you?" He didn't wait for an answer. "I'll show myself out."

He imperceptibly patted his pocket to assure the two flash drives from the safe were tucked securely where he'd last known them to be, and then headed briskly for the door. He retreated to his fed-mobile, anxious to know what was on the hidden flash drives. This could be the evidence they were looking for, to establish whether or not there was a national security leak at ERAC, via Francine Ketcham. Perhaps this would explain a coincidental rash of untimely deaths of people connected to ERAC. He'd soon have his answers.

He fired up his laptop and loaded the flash drives into its USB ports. Instantly, a security screen activated, asking the user to enter the correct password. *Another damn game.* Lockwood was pretty good at work puzzles and other brain teasers, but he knew many of these encrypted devices had failsafe mechanisms that would completely destroy their contents if bad security codes were entered more than the maximum allowable number of failed efforts. Some devices allowed three errors and some allowed as many as ten, but there was no way of knowing the limit on these. He decided not to take a chance. He lifted his cell phone and pressed a preset speed dial key that instantly connect him to Ito's line. It rang a few times before a voice answered.

"Rique?" Lockwood said.

"Yeah, what's up homey?" Ito joked.

"Where are you?"

"I'm sitting in my tub at the moment, if you must know, Lockwood," Ito said.

It had been a long day, and Ito had retired to his hotel room to freshen up before dinner, a little reading, and bed. The morning would come quickly, and he'd need to be as sharp as usual on this case. He didn't know his talents were already in immediate demand.

"I need to see you right away," Lockwood said.

"Easy, big boy," Ito joked. "I don't play for that team."

"You idiot," Lockwood snapped. "I have something I need to show you. I'll be at your door in a few minutes."

"I told you, I don't play for that team."

"Jackass," Lockwood snorted before disconnecting the call.

The night had been uncharacteristically restless for Lockwood, but only because his mind, conscious and otherwise, had been preoccupied with musing about what was on those computer disks. Like many other working types, Lockwood wanted to favorably distinguish himself in the eyes of his superiors, but he was also a civil servant motivated by true love of country and people. The mere possibility that someone—and especially another American—would do something, anything to endanger US security interests was abhorrent to him, and Lockwood would do nearly anything to prevent that from happening. Catching an industrial spy was precisely the type of thing that excited him every day, and doing so on this case at this time would give him the perfect career backdrop to retire after forty-five years of service. He'd not told anyone about those thoughts bumping around in his head, but he'd recently met a nice church-going woman whom he thought merited a jump over the broom, for the fourth time. They'd talked about moving to Hawaii and opening a bed-n-breakfast, but he had an important job to do first.

Lockwood got out of bed much earlier than normal that morning and hustled into the office to await Rique. He wanted to meet with the boss to let her know of the possible issue as well, and she was an early-riser. Tran and Starr were set to visit to Widow Day this morning, and since they had to drive to a town to the south of Seaside Beach to do it, he was sure Tran would be at the office even earlier than usual. He was right. He stuck his head in her office to assure she was there and not otherwise absorbed, and then went the rest of the way in to update her. They spoke for twenty or so minutes, ending with Lockwood relaying his plan to work with Rique to crack this new mystery.

"Keep me posted on what you find the minute you know it," Tran said when they concluded. "I'm headed with Starr to the home of Marsha Day to follow-up on her call to Washington and see if there's anything there. After you meet with Enrique, perhaps you can go have a chat with the president and General Counsel…to keep them in the loop. Give them a little peak at what we've learned already…maybe that'll shake something loose. Make sure we've first got surveillance in place on all executive computers, accounts, passports, and communication devices. If you rattle them, their panic behavior may be very telling."

Lockwood raised his brow. "A hunch?"

Tran shook her head. "A feeling. Something's just not right here. I'm not sure what we've got in this mess, but there are a lot of strange facts coming out. The employees all seem eager to talk but only if we assure their bosses and coworkers don't find out that they did."

"Secrecy—another red flag," Lockwood agreed.

"For the company, yes, but for us, it's an open door."

"Disgruntled employees are an investigator's wet dream," Lockwood chuckled.

Tran rolled her eyes at Lockwood's boorish characterization, but as unpolished as he was on occasion, he was right. Mistreated employees are a great source of information for those who might cause trouble for the bad actor, and in this case, Tran's team might just avail itself of the potential new resource.

"Yes, and in this case, an employee's wife may be of great use too. Keep on it, and I'll update you when we get back."

Lockwood nodded his understanding, and Tran left him standing in her office. Starr was waiting for her in the parking lot, ready for the thirty minute drive south. Lockwood hurried to the tech lab in the back of the building, eager to consult with Rique the Miraculous.

"You look like shit," he yelled as he pushed open a heavy glass, chrome-framed door and waltzed inside.

Enrique Ito was buried in a computer screen as his job so often required. His uncharacteristically disheveled hair poked high in the air in several directions, and a light layer of jet-black stubble covered his usually smooth face like moss spreading over the ground. His normal, fastidiously appointed appearance had given way to wrinkled, slightly stained clothing, and fast-food wrappers and Styrofoam cups were strewn about the work space around him, despite his nearly obsessive predilection for neatness and order.

"Nice to see you too, Lockwood," said the techie. "You really know how to charm a guy, don't you?"

"How long you been here anyway?" the senior agent asked.

"What time is it now?" Rique said, thinking aloud. "0745? I've been here four hours, fifteen minutes, and twenty seconds."

"Twenty *seconds*, Rique? Really?"

"Yep."

"You're bullshitting me again."

"Wish I was," he said. "I couldn't sleep after we talked last night, so after tossing and turning most of the night, I decided to just get up and get my ass in here to get to work."

"You're bullshitting me."

Rique chuckled. "Maybe, but you'd never know if I was." He stood. "Lucky for you, I'm just that good."

"You got something?"

"Don't I always?" Rique said.

"So are you gonna' tell me or am I gonna' have to beat it out of you?" Lockwood joked.

"As if you could, old man."

Enrique meant his retort playfully of course, but there was always some truth in a joke, he knew. Ito's mild manner, understated comportment, and casual garb effectively concealed the fact that he was as muscular, ripped, and strong as any of the body-builders at his gym, and had a sixth degree black belt in Jujitsu for which he'd won three national titles. Ito could kill even worthy opponents with little more difficulty than swatting a fly. In their long association, Ito had allowed Tran to know this about him, but he rarely shared details of his personal life with anyone, unless and until they had a need to know.

"Both these disks were protected with a very sophisticated encryption system, one that matches the encryption hardware on Ketcham's computer."

"But not too sophisticated for *Rique the Miraculous*," Lockwood celebrated.

"Nope…but it would have kept a lot ⌐
national intelligence services I imagine. T'
encryption technology."

"How fucking serious?" Lockwood pro
magnitude to Rique's report.

"It's really good—enough to keep most peopl
there's anything on the disk. If someone had broken the
have encountered several additional layers that wouldn't ev
them. It would look like the flash drive was a brand new, nev
device. You'd just have to know to enter a series of rolling securit)
the disk was inserted into a USB port. Then, the device performs ₁
the host device to make sure it's an authorized device before allowing ₁
to the next layer of security. It also records a lot of information from the h₁
device, so the user would be able to tell if anyone had attempted unauthorizeα
access to the device. If so, it implants a worm that will first upload an exact
copy of everything on the host device to a storage site in the cloud, and then
destroys everything on the host device. It'll work on a computer, a handheld,
any data device into which it can be inserted."

"That sounds like a pretty sophisticated encryption system to me,"
Lockwood acknowledged.

Rique nodded. "It didn't come from Best Buy or Office Depot, that's for
sure. This kind of system is designed to protect highly sensitive data, like
launch codes, identities of intelligence officers—that kind of serious stuff."

"You've seen this before?"

"Yeah. In tech circles, we got some news traffic that CIA had stolen this
from the Iranians. Especially for them, it's really good stuff—hard for people
to crack."

"I presume you did?"

"Yes, partially," Rique said. "As I mentioned, there are multiple security
layers on this device, and so we have to break the security layers for each file
on this device."

"So can you tell what's on the disk or not?"

"Yeah, but I need to make sure you understand what I'm getting at,"
Rique emphasized. "This level of data security suggests we're dealing with a
lot more than someone trying to prevent identity theft or looting of their
bank account. It raises my suspicion that someone is dealing in international
or corporate espionage—CIA, MI-5, the Mossad, FSB—these are the types of

.s typically capable of dealing in encryption of this magnitude, and rumor has it this one came from the Iranians."

IS?"

nodded affirmatively. "The Ministry of Intelligence and Security is the largest and most active intelligence agencies in the middle-east, and could do this...Probably also some of the big aerospace defense actors who want to snoop on their competitor's research."

Lockwood contemplated Ito's admonition for a few seconds. Then: Okay, so can you tell what's on the disk?"

Rique re-seated himself at his computer, and began working his keyboard like a concert pianist performing a concerto. He narrated as he worked.

"Disk One has a lot of video files on it. I'm still working on accessing them, but I've got a few of them opened."

"So what is it?"

"Have you eaten breakfast already?" Rique asked.

"What the hell does that have to do with anything?" Lockwood asked, his anticipation nearly bubbling over.

"Just wanting to make sure you really want to see this."

"What's on it, Rique?"

Ito depressed the *Enter* key, and seconds later, the movie player on his computer began to play. As the scene opened, it showed an interior view of the inside of a room that struck him as somewhat familiar but not wholly. It only took him a few seconds before he realized he was looking at the office of the Chief Financial Officer at Earhardt-Roane Aerospace Corporation, but its furnishings were different than what he'd seen the day Ketcham's body had been discovered. The date stamp in the lower right hand corner indicated the video had been recorded at 10:40 p.m. on a Friday evening nearly five years earlier. The late Erich Day was the corporate CFO then. The video continued showing what seemed like a static view of the office, but just as Lockwood was about to tire of watching nothing inside a boring office suite, the door in the far corner of the viewing area thrust open, sending the door crashing violently into the wall. Two people locked in what was clearly a passionate kiss seemed to fall first into the room and then onto a large, plush brown leather sofa just to the right of the door. The couple paused in their embracing and kissing long enough to begin unbuttoning one another's clothes.

*This is getting good*, Lockwood thought. He continued watching the video capture until it ended some twenty minutes later. When it did, he could hardly believe what he'd seen. He hardly had words to describe the value this brought and the insight this single video capture had lent to the investigation.

"I could just kiss you," Lockwood said.

"Funny, but not funny enough," Rique answered.

Lockwood chuckled at Rique's response, but even more so at his own initiating comment. "Okay, sweetie," he said, "you keep working on the other files and let me know the minute you get anything."

"Wait," Rique said as Lockwood rushed toward the door.

"I can't. Gotta' go."

"You might wanna' make some time for this, Lockwood," Rique warned.

"What is it?" Lockwood sensed something more serious was coming, and he was right.

"I also did some comparisons between this and the hard drive Agent Kenison took from the deceased's lap-top. The hard drive has this encryption system on it too, and based on my examination, I can conclude the laptop was used to access this particular file on several occasions. When we access the other files on the flash drive, we might be able to determine with certainty that this laptop was used for accessing all the files on this flash drive and the second one, which makes perfect sense. But, at the moment, we can only confirm the laptop was used to access the one file we've opened so far."

"Okay, that's nothing earth-shattering is it?" Lockwood asked.

Ito shrugged. "Perhaps not...It only makes perfect sense to me, but if we're going to build a case against somebody arising out of this, this will help establish all the elements of a criminal offense for each file and each violation. Depending on what else we uncover in the investigation, it might prove something else or lead us to something else."

"That's why you're so good at this, Ito. A sloppy investigation is no investigation at all, is it?"

"I've just seen way too many times when substandard inquiries and investigations torpedoed us...not anxious for that to happen on anything I'm part of. But that's not even the real big thing here, Lockwood."

"Go on."

"Having both the flash drive and the laptop, one other thing I can confirm is that one other computer was used to access this flash drive."

"Whose?"

"Did she have another computer at home?"

Lockwood shook his head. "No. She used this laptop at home and at work."

"Then I don't know. When we find that other data device, I can confirm that it was used to access this flash drive, based on the device's residual signature on the flash drive, but until we find it, I can only tell you that some other device than Ketcham's lap top was also used."

"That could be a motive or another problem," Lockwood said, thinking through the implications. "Get me into those other files ASAP."

With that, Lockwood jumped to his feet and headed for the door. Things were starting to gel. A short time later, he arrived at ERAC headquarters to follow-up on a lead. He parked in the Visitor's Parking area of the large ornate facility and meandered up the sidewalk into the main lobby. A very attractive, blond twenty-something with large breasts and the deepest blue eyes and reddest of lips greeted him without even looking up from the telephone she worked like an expert as the calls came in.

"Welcome to Earhardt-Roane Avionics. May I ask where you're headed?" she said, repeating a mantra she uttered a million times each day.

"You may ask," Lockwood said, not offering anything more.

"Do you have an appointment" the woman asked again.

"Nope."

The woman held up her left pointer finger without even looking at Lockwood as she depressed buttons on the phone console. "Thanks for calling Earhardt-Roane, how may I direct your call?" she asked. "Yes, just one moment please." She depressed two more buttons. "Hi Chantal. Call coming in for the president," she said, flipping a switch to connect the caller with the president's secretary."

The woman turned her attention back to the man standing in front of her, again without looking at him directly. "I'm sorry sir. Who are you here to see?" she asked.

"That's classified information, Sweetie," he answered. "If I told you, I'd have to kill you," Lockwood said.

That garnered the woman's full attention. In this day and age, all receptionists had to be weary of crazies making threats—they might actually mean them. Her hand reached for the silent alarm that would alert the facility's armed security service, and her head snapped up from the phone so she could get a good look at the possible lunatic standing before her.

Lockwood smiled his warmest, most seductive grin, trying to work the magic he worked as a fit, strapping young man thirty-five years earlier. Instantly, he could see the twinkle in his aging eyes wasn't up to the challenge of charming the magnificently beautiful young woman sitting in front of him, so he quickly whipped out his badge and credentials before she concluded he was just a creep.

"I was just, uh…joking around." He leaned in so he could see the woman's nametag. "Debbie. You know, *classified information,* like in the old spy days." His explanation wasn't working. "Sorry. I didn't mean that literally, but it's just… Never mind," he finally relented. "Is Dr. French-Catin in the building? I saw her car parked in its spot out front."

"Uh, yes officer. She just came back in a few minutes ago. Do you have an appointment?"

"Nope. I don't," he answered honestly.

"Well, what's this in regards to?"

He smiled. "Can't tell you, really, I can't."

"Well, if you don't have an appointment, I'm not sure she can see you today. She's pretty busy sometimes with all her meetings and stuff. Let me just call up to her office."

"Please don't do that, Debbie. It's better she doesn't know I'm coming."

"But, I have to—"

"I tell you what, Debbie. Why don't you just walk with me up to Dr. Catin's office?"

"I'm sorry officer, I just can't leave my post here," the lady answered.

Lockwood rounded the receptionist's desk and gently pulled the chair as though he would help the young lady stand up. "I insist," he said. "Please, show me the way."

Lockwood already knew the way to Catin's office, but he really didn't want the receptionist to call and alert the VP of Research that he was on his way up to see her. It just might give her time to leave, hide something, call someone, or do something else that might frustrate the investigation. Telling her that he was "letting her in on a secret investigator's trick," he politely explained all of this to Debbie as they walked. Debbie repeatedly checked over her shoulder to see whether anyone was watching her desk, or watching her and Lockwood, and wondering whether she was now in some kind of trouble. All the tips and processes she'd learned in mass shooter scenarios and other emergency training she'd attended quickly left her mind as the large man who flashed a badge and carried a gun gently but firmly held her arm, guiding her down the hall toward the elevator. Moments later, they reached the executive floor and stepped out of the lift, heading directly to a secretary sitting outside Catin's office. It was only a short distance—within easy eyesight—to the still-sealed scene of the crime.

Lockwood took the lead. "Dr. Catin?" he asked.

The secretary looked to her left into a glassed conference room, which housed several people, including Catin, engaged in deep conversation. Despite the glass walls, no one had noticed him.

"Thank you, my dear," Lockwood said to Debbie. "You can go now. I appreciate your kind assistance." He smiled at Catin's secretary. "Miss," he slightly nodded his head to thank and dismiss her.

Lockwood waltzed to the conference room and opened the door without knocking. The people inside quickly looked up to determine the source of the interruption, and Lockwood could see the annoyance on Catin's face.

"I'm terribly sorry to bother you folks," Lockwood skillfully lied, "but this is kind of an emergency, and I need to speak with you, Dr. Catin."

"Well, I'm kind of in the middle of something here, Mr. Lockwood," the VP chided. "You'll just need to wait until I'm finished here—about forty-five minutes."

Lockwood smiled. "I don't think so, Dr. Catin." He pulled his suit coat back to assure his badge hanging on his belt could be seen from across the room. It was purely incidental that the motion also displayed the Glock holstered to his hip. "We need to talk right now," he said sternly. "We can talk right here in front of your friends if you like, or we can talk privately in your office, or you can take a ride in the back of my car down to my office…your choice."

Catin stared daggers at the agent for a few minutes, but fearing exposure in front of her subordinates, she eventually relented, asking them to reassemble later that afternoon to complete their business. Begrudgingly, she escorted Lockwood a few feet from the conference room to her office, instructing her Secretary to call ERAC's corporate counsel to her office.

"Now what is it that's so urgent you rudely barged in here and interrupted my meeting?" she asked. She closed the door and pushed her way past Lockwood as she trekked to her plush desk chair and seated herself.

Lockwood half-expected some sort of invitation—verbal, a motion of the hand, something—to sit down in one of the visitor chairs facing Catin's desk, but no such invitation was forthcoming. Catin sat in her chair looking up at the Agent as she addressed him in sharp, short, crisp sentences.

"I'm just following up on a few leads, Dr. Catin," he explained.

"I've spoken briefly with one of the members of your team already, Mr. Lockwood, and there's really nothing more I can tell you. You have everything I have on the issue."

"Really?"

"Yes, really, now if you'll excuse me, I have quite a lot of work to do," she said, standing from her chair.

Lockwood seated himself. "How about you just let me decide when I have what I need from you, Dr. Catin. We can start with an easy one: have you ever seen a knife like this?"

He reached into his breast pocket and withdrew the artist's rendering of the knife used on Francine. He unfolded the picture and held it out for Catin's inspection, carefully observing her face for any telling signs or indications. He saw nothing even remotely related to recognition, but saw plenty relating to angst.

"No, Agent Lockwood. I've never seen that knife before in my life."

"How about something close to it?" he asked. "Doesn't have to be exactly the same."

She rolled her head and eyes. Sighing heavily, almost in juvenile fashion, she repeated herself. "I told you, Agent Lockwood, I have never seen that knife in my life."

"I know that, Dr. Catin. I was asking whether you'd seen something that *looked* like it. Check out the blade on it in particular…Go ahead, look again," Lockwood prompted.

She did.

"No, no, no, no, how many times must I say it? I've never seen that knife or anything that looks remotely like that knife?"

"Okay, doc. So let's talk about your relationship with John-Paul Ketcham."

Lockwood watched the woman's face for telltale signs of surprise, deception, discomfort and anything else that might help him. He saw it.

"Paul is…was Francine's husband and she was my best friend. My husband Stone and I would occasionally get together with them for drinks or dinner, but my friendship was primarily with Francine."

"Uh-huh," Lockwood agreed. "Is that the extent of your relationship with John-Paul Ketcham?"

"What are you trying to imply, Mr. Lockwood?" Catin demanded.

"I'm not trying to imply anything. I'm just asking a question."

Just then, the door to Catin's office swung open wide, and Chuck Matos walked briskly into the room, apparently on a mission or else putting on a show—for whose benefit, it wasn't clear.

"What's the meaning of this, Agent Lockwood?" the lawyer demanded.

"Oh Mr. Matos," Lockwood said. "Good to see you again, Counselor. I was just about to ask Dr. Catin some questions about her friendship with John-Paul Ketcham."

"I fail to see the relevance of that to an investigation of the death of one of our employees."

"You're a very creative lawyer, Mr. Matos. I imagine it's not a very long leap for your legal mind to come up with all kinds of scenarios as to how this might be relevant to our investigation."

"Why don't you spare us all the time and just tell me what you're looking for, Agent Lockwood."

"You know how this works, Counselor. First you pull all the pieces out of the box, and *then* you assemble the puzzle." He turned back to Catin. "So, tell me about your relationship with John-Paul Ketcham."

There it was again—the hesitation, the nervousness. Lockwood was sure he'd hit a nerve.

Catin turned to the lawyer. "It's all right, Chuck. I don't need you for this. I don't mind telling Mr. Lockwood about my and my husband's friendship with the Ketchams. No problem, and I'd hate to waste your time on something so trivial." She waited for Matos to depart the room, but the lawyer seemed to linger with uncertainty. "It's all right...I'll call you if I need you," she assured, trying to tactfully shoo him out of her office.

As the door closed behind Matos, Catin turned back to the Agent, her voice assuming a more aggressive posture. "I told you, Mr. Lockwood. John-Paul Ketcham was my best friend's husband."

"Yes, I know that's what you told me. I'm asking whether there was anything more to it than that?"

Catin was indignant at the question. "Even if there was, how is that any of your business?" she huffed.

"Look, lady, I don't particularly care who you're hiking your legs in the air for, but if you're doing it with the husband of a murder victim, then that just might be a reason for murder. So, I'm gonna' ask the question once more. Were you and John-Paul Ketcham just friends through his wife, or was there anything more intimate about it?"

Lockwood watched as Catin squirmed almost imperceptibly in her seat. She really didn't want to admit this and was doing what she could to deflect the question.

"Maybe we were flirting with each other but we weren't physically intimate," she finally growled.

Lockwood wrote her words down in his notebook, slowly repeating each word as he wrote it out. When he finished, he read it silently but conspicuously, and then looked up over the top of the note binder at Catin.

"You really gonna' stick with that?" he asked. "You know I've already spoken with your boyfriend at least the one time because you saw me and I saw you at his place last night while you were *helping him grieve*," Lockwood said, using air quotes to emphasize *helping him grieve*. "You do know people go to prison for obstructing federal investigations, don't you?"

"I'm well aware of that," Catin snapped.

"Okay, okay, Doc. Just making sure, because once I walk out this door, I file my official report of this interview, and then it's too late for you to avoid the natural penalties that flow from lies like the doozy you just told."

Catin squirmed, not knowing what to do next. Should she continue her misrepresentation of the facts, or should she come clean? It seemed liked the agent already knew the right answers, but had simply given her enough of a noose with which to hang herself. She had neither of her usual crutches—Ketcham and Day—to tell her what to think or do, and so she froze, like a robot stuck in a continuous programming loop. Lockwood amped up the pressure by offering her seemingly helpful options, but the reality was that they only added more considerations to Catin's tough deliberation.

"You want I should call your Mr. Matos back up here to give you some legal advice?"

Inside, Lockwood laughed to himself because he guessed Catin wouldn't want her husband, boss, the board, her priest, her neighbors, and quite possibly the entire community of Seaside Beach to know she'd been carrying on an illicit sexual affair with the husband of her recently murdered best friend. Besides the humiliation of having her dirty laundry washed in full public view, it was the sort of thing for which her colleagues and superiors would look askance at her, despite the fact of their own skeletons. Her unforgivable company sin would be letting her skeletons out of the closet, not that she had them. And then there was also the potential reaction of her husband. Stone was a cool, good-looking, moderately successful musician type whom Catin secretly felt she'd tricked into a relationship with her in the first place, cementing it with an ill-timed pregnancy. She feared he'd one day wake up from a drug-induced haze and realize he could have done much better. After that, he'd take their only child and leave her for a real woman. Those were consequences too great for Catin to bear, and trifling with this NSA agent might bring them crashing down upon her. Of course, admitting the affair might land her at ground zero of a murder investigation. She desperately needed someone to tell her what to do, but getting advice from the company lawyer meant telling him what really happened between her and Ketcham, and she didn't know who Matos might tell. Even if he didn't tell anyone else, he'd have something to hold over her head when the time came. That was the way of things in the Palace of ERAC. Still Catin sat in a nearly catatonic stare.

"Would it help you if I told you that your friend, Francine, also knew about the affair?" he asked, playing a hunch.

At this point, he didn't know for sure whether Francine Ketcham knew about the affair her husband and best friend were enjoying with one another, but he suspected she did. He'd not known her during her lifetime, but the picture he'd gained of her from the investigation thus far was of a woman hell-bent on manipulating people to extort from them what she wanted. Paranoid about everyone and everything, that sort typically kept closest watch on those closest to them for fear of being betrayed. Thus, it stood to reason she might have known about her husband and his mistress. Lockwood was now leveraging that possible truism for what he could learn from it.

Powered by shock and disbelief, Catin launched to her feet. "What do you mean, *she knew?* He promised me he'd not tell her," she said. "How could she have known?"

*There it was,* Lockwood thought. She'd admitted the affair because innocent people don't wonder *how someone could have known.* They might wonder how someone could think something in particular about them, but not *how could they know.* He smiled.

"I'm afraid I can't share that information with you just yet, Dr. Catin, but since I already know the truth, you should probably just answer my questions truthfully."

Catin sank into her chair, a pale, blank emptiness washing over her cheeks. She nodded her agreement.

"All right then," Lockwood said. "Let's try some more specific questions, shall we? When and how did your affair with Ketcham begin?"

# Chapter 5

# Burning Fog

The home of the late Erich Day was a magnificent McMansion located in a small bedroom community just on the outskirts of Seaside Beach. It had all the appearance of an antebellum style plantation, particularly during the heyday of American slavery, but smaller and built of modern construction materials. Still, it was clear that the home's builders and owners wanted to evoke the splendor of an era long past, except for the dark skin on the residents of this particular Big House. A *For Sale* sign from a popular local real estate agent was anchored in the ground at the base and to the left of a wide, grand stairway leading up to a long front porch, but it was an inconspicuous garden-toned sign that didn't clearly demand the attention of passers-by. Perhaps, Tran thought, that was because this sign wouldn't be easily visible to passers-by given the long winding driveway leading to the stairs, but the larger, more colorful sign near the roadway would be. Starr and Tran ascended the porch stairs and prepared to ring the doorbell, but someone inside opened the door before they could.

"Good morning, Ladies," an older black woman greeted. "Please come in."

The woman looked nothing like the picture Tran had seen in the dossier on Marsha Day, and for a moment, she wondered whether someone had made an error in assembling the file. Then, she wondered whether the woman might be a relative of the Days.

"Please, come into the parlor," the woman invited, holding open the double doors leading to a richly appointed receiving room. "Please make yourselves comfortable. I'll go get the Mrs. for you."

With an amazing alacrity, the woman backed out of the room and closed the doors behind her, leaving only the echo of her footsteps in the hall outside. Starr seated herself while awaiting the arrival of Mrs. Day, but Tran remained standing, taking the opportunity to peruse the room around them. Both the foyer and the parlor were nearly as grand as the outside approach, finely decorated with high-end furnishings, impressionist paintings, and rare sculptures. An oversized mahogany curio cabinet against the wall on Tran's side of the sofa housed a fairly extensive collection of expensive-looking porcelain vases, the likes of which Tran had seen somewhere, but she wasn't sure where or when. They were pretty, that was for sure. Tran noticed two unusually sized gaps in the arrangement of items inside the cabinet, and the lack of dust on the inside of the circular patterns in those spaces suggested at least two objects were missing from the cabinet. The simple, round clear area suggested the items had plain round bottoms to them, approximately ten inches in diameter. Tran scanned the area for anything else worthy of noting, but her inspection was interrupted.

A faint clicking from the hall garnered Tran's attention, telegraphing someone's approach—probably the *Mrs.* Tran wheeled about to meet its source, just as the door to the parlor swung wide, giving ingress to a short, distinguished, cocoa-skinned woman in her mid- to late sixties who moved with an aristocratic style, grace, and gait. She evidently dyed her hair on a regular basis, because not a hint of gray showed in the bun twirled onto the top of her head, keeping it far off the collar of her couture garb. Mrs. Day looked like she hailed from old pretentious money, but her demeanor was anything but.

"Good morning, Ladies," she said as she swept into the room, an enormous smile on her face. "I'm Marsha Day." She extended a firm but polite handshake first to Starr who was closest, and then to Tran.

The agents introduced themselves and shook Day's hand warmly in turn. The lady of the house ushered them to seats on the plush oversized linen sofa in the center of the room, while the older woman who'd greeted them at the door hovered nearby. Mrs. Day waited for her guests to seat themselves, and then took position in the chair opposite them.

"Thank you so much for meeting with us," Tran said, opening their visit.

"May I offer you some coffee or tea?" Day asked.

As a matter of routine, neither Tran nor Starr requested coffee, instead making excuses about how full they were or that they'd just finished their morning allotment of coffee. Although both agents would have loved to accept an offer of freshly brewed java, they observed their custom of not taking food or drink from people they didn't personally know, especially one

100

that might be a witness, suspect, or informant. After all, they couldn't really be sure the beverage wouldn't be adulterated when it was prepared outside of their sight and supervision.

"Nora, just coffee for me then," she said to the older woman at the doorway. "No cream or sugar."

The domestic employee disappeared into the bowels of the house, and Day turned her undivided attention to her visitors.

"You have a lovely home," Starr said, motioning slightly around the room.

Day waved her hand in polite acknowledgment of the compliment on her material belongings, but at the same time downplaying them.

"Oh, thanks," she said. "I guess it served its purpose." A somber look darkened her face as her eyes began to glisten. "I'm sorry, I'm sorry. I thought I was past all this," she explained. "This place, this stuff was so important to my husband."

"Mrs. Day, I'm very sorry about your loss," Tran offered.

"Thank you. May I call you Grace?" she asked, not really meaning it as a true request for permission. "On a cognitive level, I know death is one of those inevitable side-effects of life, but I just—"

"No worries, Mrs. Day. Take your time," Tran said.

Trying earnestly to avoid a full-on breakdown in front of other people, Day seemed to pull herself together and press onward.

"Please, call me Marsha," she said, strength returning to her tone.

"I saw you're putting your house on the market?" Starr asked.

"Point in fact, I've *already* put it on the market, dear," Day corrected.

"I'm surprised you'd want to sell such a fabulous home," Starr continued.

Day smiled, and leaned over to pat Starr's leg. "It's okay, dear. You won't offend me if you come right out and ask. I'm not selling this place because I can't afford it—I can. Besides the fact that we had plenty of insurance on Erich, I was quite a successful professional in New York before I retired to this *life of luxury*, so I'm not hurting financially. This place and all this expensive junk," she said, motioning around the room, "was very important to my husband more so than me. We both grew up on the Islands in very poor families, so we didn't have a lot of things at all, and certainly nothing like this grand little palace. We couldn't have children so it was just me and Erich—we didn't need a great big ole' place like this. Erich insisted on this place and all its flashy contents, he said so we could entertain and impress people for work purposes. We did have those backstabbers over a few times, but I think the real reason he wanted this so badly was that it made him feel like he'd finally become something and someone."

She paused for a moment as she silently reminisced, and then suddenly remembered she had company and they weren't inside her head.

"Oh child, you should have seen him with that damn Mercedes of his. He really loved that car...Sometimes I felt like he loved it more than me," she finally said aloud. "I told him he was crazy to pay $70,000 for a damn car, but he was convinced it would make his colleagues take notice of him and not take him for granted. Anyway, listen to me prattling on like an ol' fool. I'm sure you didn't come here to take a sentimental journey with me, but you're both very sweet to indulge me."

"It's quite all right, Mrs. Day," Tran said.

"I told you, call me Marsha."

"All right, Marsha," Tran continued. "We wanted to follow-up on your report to the Civil Rights Division."

"Thank you so much," Day said, a victorious smile warming her lips. "I was beginning to think the bastards were going to get away with it."

"You believe your husband was murdered, that someone at the company had something to do with it, and that local law enforcement is covering it up?"

The ladies sitting with her in the parlor seemed like nice women, but Marsha Day was very cognizant of the fact that they were also federal investigators. She feared they might be inclined to dismiss her as a hysterical widow just as the locals had, so she moved to pre-empt that perception.

"Listen, I'm not looking at things through rose-colored glasses, Grace. I know my husband was a flawed, far-from-perfect man, and I'm not trying to set myself up for a big lawsuit or anything. But Erich didn't deserve what they did to him. Those bastards are all alike—they think they can get away with treating people any ol' way they want because they're Earhardt-Roane. And the local authorities...well, they're okay as long as the *Queen of the County* is happy with what's going on here. If she's not, then the local authorities won't touch it with a ten-foot pole, regardless of law, regulation, or morality."

"Sounds like you didn't think too highly of your husband's colleagues?" Starr surmised.

"You're greatly skilled in the art of understatement, Deanna," Day snickered. "Perhaps one or two of them are decent people, but it's generally accepted and *never* acknowledged that the members of the ERAC elite don't give a damn about anyone else, until it adversely affects them. I'd even venture to say most of them wouldn't mind if their colleagues simply keeled over and—"

*Died*, she didn't say, stopping the second she realized the irony of her intended remark. The moment hung awkwardly in the air briefly as Starr and Tran joined their host in the realization.

"Uh, the investigation report indicated the collision was an accident. Why do you think they had anything to do with Mr. Day's death?" Tran asked

"First of all, Erich told me about two weeks before the accident that he felt someone was after his job. He worried that they'd do anything to make him look bad and embarrass him."

"All due respect, Marsha, doing something to make him look bad is a far cry from killing him."

"Yes, but you just don't know these people like I do."

"I'm sure, but if we're going to do anything with this in an official capacity, we need facts and evidence, Marsha, not supposition."

"Erich indicated that the VP of Research, the VP of HR, and the Executive Director of Finance and Business were out to get him."

"That would be Catin, Reynolds, and Ketcham?" Starr asked.

"Yes."

"All women," the agent noted.

"Yes, I guess so," Day replied. "He said they were doctoring the books to set him up for a fall."

"What books were they doctoring?" Tran pressed.

"Not sure, really. I know from Erich's past comments that Catin and Ketcham worked together a lot on research-related programs since Catin is in charge of research activities, and Ketcham handled the accounting for that area. I also know the two of them were very good friends. They lunched together, shopped together, vacationed together, and always had each others' backs at the office. Erich had grown very uncomfortable with the closeness between them. He worried about it."

"Didn't Ketcham work *for* your husband?"

"Yes, but Erich felt like he'd lost his ability to control her. He complained on more than one occasion that she was ambitious to a fault, but that he'd not seen it until it was way too late. He didn't think he could do anything to her without causing himself a lot of problems."

"Why is that?"

"I don't know," Day answered. "I suggested he just fire her, but he just didn't think he could do that. He said she was very connected politically—I know her husband is something in state government."

"Why would Catin want to do anything to hurt your husband?"

Day paused for a moment of thought. "Honestly, I think the woman is too stupid to independently formulate a desire or plan to do something to anyone else."

"Excuse me?" Tran asked incredulous of what she'd just heard. "Dr. Catin has a Ph.D. How stupid could she be?"

"Yes, I know it sounds a bit incongruous, but haven't you ever known people who were really book smart but didn't have the real-world brains of a gnat? Catin is one of those. She's really good at perceiving who around her has power, and then spreading her legs for them. She can also be led around by the nose fairly easily. She's very much into this girl-power idea of girls helping girls, and so she was very influenced by Ketcham."

"And how about Reynolds? Is she like Dr. Catin?" Tran asked.

Day chuckled slightly. "Have you seen her?" she asked, smiling. "She's a bit homely, like Abraham Lincoln in lipstick, so I'm pretty sure she wasn't spreading anything for anybody. She might be a decent person—deep, deep, deep, deep down inside, but she's fundamentally lazy at this stage of her career. She's only a few years from retiring, and therefore won't do anything to rock the boat. You might say she's the go-along-to-get-along type. If Ketcham and Catin involved her in something, then Reynolds would go along with it simply to avoid making waves. She freely ignores, belittles, or squashes people below her in the organization, but she'd never disagree with anyone in the executive hall, even if she truly thought something they were doing was flat wrong."

"And what would she do in a conflict *within* the executive hall?"

"Sit as still and quiet as possible until it blew over. If forced to take a side, she'd stick her finger in the wind and go whichever way it blew."

"If Catin is too stupid and Reynolds won't rock the boat, then you think Ketcham was behind whatever your husband perceived?"

"I do."

"But Ketcham is now dead, and definitely by murder."

"Couldn't have happened to a better person," Day said. "I know that's not very Christian of me, but that woman was a vile, disgusting wretch beneath her plumage."

"Any idea who might have done it?"

"None in particular, but the field of possibilities is probably pretty vast," Day said, "starting in her own home."

"Why would you suggest that?" Starr asked.

"I know how miserable she made the people at work. I can't imagine what it would be like to live with her."

"Let's talk evidence," Tran redirected.

"To be honest, I don't have much," Day admitted. "This state is an open records state, but I can't seem to get the local authorities to release any information about this case to me. They say it's part of an on-going investigation, so they don't have to release the records but at the same time, they've back-burnered it."

"So you just have suspicions," Tran summarized.

"No. I said I didn't have much evidence, not that I didn't have any," Day corrected. "When the locals stonewalled me, I snuck into the impound lot where they'd taken the wreckage of Erich's Mercedes."

"You did this?" Starr asked.

"Yep…I was a real *Jane Bond,* a super-spy," Day proudly answered. "I talked to a buddy of mine who's a private investigator in New York. He told me to take pictures and swab the wreckage, which I did. I sent it all to him, and he had some of his contacts test what I sent. Evidently, they found traces of incendiaries and accelerants. He told me he thought the stuff was military grade explosives."

"And what did you do then?"

"I sent a letter to the head of the state crime lab along with the extra samples I took, and asked them to get involved."

"And their response?"

"They told me that the crime lab wasn't available to members of the general public and that their services could only be engaged by official, duly sworn law enforcement agencies in the state….Whatever. I can recognize bureaucratic babble for what it really is, and in this case, it told me they weren't going to do a damn thing," Day said. "So my next step was the Department of Justice. I sent my evidence to the Civil Rights Division and, well, now you're here."

Tran raised her brows, and nodded affirmatively. "That's certainly something, but let me play devil's advocate for a moment. Your sub-division has a gate, guards, and security cameras, and you've got a four-car garage, which I assume your husband used for his $70,000 car. During the day, while your husband was at work, his car was parked in a patrolled lot on the grounds of Earhardt-Roane. When and where would anyone have had the opportunity to put military-grade explosives, incendiaries, or accelerants in your husband's car, and would they even have the expertise to do it?"

"I'm not an expert investigator, Grace, so I don't have all the answers," Day explained. "I can tell you that Erich routinely parked his car at the office in a reserved spot with his name on it, in a parking lot along the edge of a wooded area. Erich also traveled overnight a few days before the accident, and since the airport is so close to his office, he left his car parked at the office while he was gone."

She paused a moment to assess how well her story was sinking in to the minds of her guests, and then decided they needed even more convincing.

"I can also tell you that Ketcham was a *good ol' girl* from a backwoods town not far from here. It's called Rahain, and it's got lots of pick-up trucks with rebel flags and gun racks in the window, and no people with faces that look like ours, if you know what I mean. Those folks don't like outsiders, much less *uppity niggas* who drive cars that cost what some of them earn in ten years. They'd be happy to help one of their own take one of us down, and they know a lot about destroying things. The area is also home to some Aryan militia groups as I hear."

"So you think more people were involved?"

"Ketcham was a manipulative, ambitious bitch who controlled a lot of money at the company and who traded in secrets, information, and influence. She could have gotten a lot of people to do her dirty work, from anyone at the company susceptible to her domination to her husband's political flunkies to some hick from her hometown."

"And where is the company president in all of this?" Tran asked.

"Don...he's a wily little prick, pardon my French," Day said. "He'd smile in your face while shanking you in the back if it served his purposes."

"And what would his purpose be in murdering your husband or covering it up?"

"Money, popularity, and stability," Day explained. "Above all, Don Johnston values money like any other white-collar criminal, but he also wants to be liked by as many people as possible. He loves to hear his own name uttered in adoration, and loves for people to suck up to him. He was a different man once, but after officially becoming head of ERAC, he seemed to change. He started believing all the crap people filled his head with, and he'd do anything to keep it coming. This stuff with Erich, looking into something that's going wrong but doesn't directly harm him, seeking justice and doing the right thing…that's all too messy for Don. It would bring negative attention to the company and the town, and thus wouldn't be welcomed by him or the Queen of the County."

"You mentioned her before. Who is that?"

"Iryana Hamidi, a member of the company's board and a real behind-the-scenes operator whose hands are in everything that happens in this county. Her family owns several different businesses—restaurants, hotels, car rentals, a real estate development company…lots of stuff that depends on tourism and growth."

"And local law enforcement? Why would they cover it up?"

Besides the fact that the Hamidis regularly donate a lot of money to a lot of political campaigns around here, including the governor's, state legislators', and US senators', ERAC brings a lot of money and jobs to the local economy. If neither the Queen nor Johnston—in that order—want this issue to grow into a major investigation, the local authorities won't buck them unless their asses are on the line in a very serious way."

"Even for someone as important as your husband was to the company?" Starr asked.

"As far as they're concerned, Erich was only important in his own mind," Day said, resentment infusing her tone. "They paraded him around as a token black so they could show how much they valued diversity—like white folks who say '…*and I even have some black friends*' to prove they're not racists. As long as Erich towed the line, they tolerated the *island nigger's* presence among them. But the moment he crossed paths with a hometown white person, they put on their white pointy hats and gathered for a modern lynching."

"Do you know anything about irregularities on government contracts?" Tran asked.

"I don't know any details, Grace, but I know Erich was concerned about some Air Force research contract the company was working on. That's what he thought they might be doctoring the books on. He'd gotten some report from someone on the inside."

"All right. Might you have any of your husband's papers or records?"

"Yes. I gave a few to some yahoos from the company the day after Erich died. They said it was urgent to the continuity of what he was working on, so they came to the house to retrieve the papers. I made copies of everything I gave them, which wasn't much compared to what he kept at home."

She stood and walked first to the door and then into the foyer. Her footsteps echoed off the hard marble floors, but faded after a few moments.

Tran stood and walked back to the curio cabinet. The statuary and vases were pretty, but something more than that was whispering softly in her ear. She removed her phone from her pocket and photographed everything in the cabinet and the surrounding area. She meandered to the nearest window, pulling back the curtains there as she hunted for small shards of glass on the floor or in the window guides, new window caulking, or other indicators of a recent break-in, perhaps one even unknown to the residents. She saw none, and proceeded to the other side of the room to perform a similar inspection. Starr instantly recognized what her boss was doing, and went to assist. They found nothing that raised suspicion. After a few more minutes, they heard Day's footsteps out in the hall.

"I've packed up this box of items Erich was working on at the time of his murder," Day said, hauling in a heavy brown box. "Nora and I have copied everything in here, so you may keep all this," she announced.

"Thank you, Mrs., uh Marsha," Tran said, taking the box in her arms. She was surprised by its weight. It was much heavier than Tran anticipated based on the way the older woman was carrying it. Marsha Day was stronger than she looked.

Tran and Starr made a few last comments in polite banter before preparing to exit the Day home, but as they were leaving, Tran stopped and turned back to their hostess.

"Uh, one last thing, Marsha. Your art collection there in the cabinet."

Day looked in the direction in which Tran's head had bobbed, her eyes locking on the curio. "Oh yes, that's Erich's collection of some kind of antique Asian porcelain. I'm told they're pretty old."

"You're not the resident aficionado?" Tran asked.

"Not even a little. That was all Erich too. He loved to collect things—antique furniture, Lladro figurines, one-of-a-kind historical objects, all kinds of stuff. Don't get me wrong, I appreciate good art when I see it, but I prefer mine in a museum where it can be admired by and inspire all."

"May I ask what happened to the two missing items?"

"I beg your pardon?" Day asked.

"The missing pieces—what happened to them?"

"I wasn't aware anything was missing," Day said. She walked with purpose to the curio cabinet and peered inside to verify for herself what Tran had said. A quizzical expression creased her face. "I, I just don't know. This thing used to be full, and now I can see two things are indeed missing from these spaces here, but I couldn't begin to tell you what."

She hastened back to the parlor door, and called into the hallway. "Nora."

A split-second later, Nora Washington appeared in the doorway, drying her dishwater hands on her white apron. "Yes, Mrs. Day?"

"Nora, do you know what happened to the missing pieces in the curio cabinet," Day asked, pointing across the room.

Nora shrugged and simultaneously shook her head side to side. "I don't know, Mrs. I saw they weren't there 'bout a month or so ago. I pointed it out to Mr. Day at the time, and I think he said you'd moved them to someplace else."

"You *think* he said that?" Tran asked.

"Yes ma'am. I think that's what he said. He was in a terrible hurry that day, so he mumbled his answer at me, and then ran out to the car room. He weren't at all concerned about it so I weren't neither," Nora said.

"And nobody ever mentioned it again?" Tran asked, generally.

Neither lady said anything, and Nora just shook her head side to side.

"No break-ins or burglaries?" Starr asked.

"Now I'd know if that had happened," Day said. "The alarm company would have called me immediately and also dispatched the police here in a minute."

"Any strange people in the house?"

"We had those backstabbing bastards from the company over here about two months before Erich was killed, so of course we had strange people in the house. But, I watch those people like hawks when they're here, and if we'd caught one of them stealing, Erich would have used that to his advantage at the office. No doubt I'd know about that too," Day said.

"Okay. It's probably nothing anyway," Tran said, dismissing the moment. "I was just curious." She shifted her focus back to the box. "We'll look through all of this and we'll keep you posted on the status of our investigation as best we can, Mrs. Day."

"*Marsha*," Day emphasized.

"Sorry, old habits—Marsha," Tran said.

Tran and Starr said their good-byes and politely excused themselves from Day's home. They were quiet as they sat in the fed-mobile for the half-hour ride back to the office, both silently contemplating the value and meaning of what they'd learned at the home of Mrs. Day.

\* \* \*

Lockwood arrived fifteen minutes early for his meeting at the Earhardt-Roane Aerospace Corporation. The receptionist informed him the executive team was in the middle of an important operational meeting, and showed him to a receiving room adjacent to the Board Room where the executive team's meeting was taking place. The receptionist offered him coffee, and then retired to her work space to continue her duties while Lockwood patiently awaited an audience with the company's big-wigs and local law enforcement officials so he could brief them on the current status of the investigation. He waited until fifteen minutes beyond the appointed hour, and then stood. He walked purposefully to the receptionist, donning his most formal manner and tone.

"I beg your pardon, Madam," he began. "Would you please inform your president that if he would like a briefing today on the status of this matter involving his company, then I will need his immediate attention. Otherwise, I will take my leave of your company, and he can attempt to reschedule this matter for another time…sometime down the road."

"I'm so sorry, sir. I'm just doing as I'm told," the lady said.

Lockwood leaned in to get a closer look at the woman's nametag. "Chantal," he began. "I appreciate that you're just doing your job, and I am doing mine. Please convey the message, or I shall just leave now."

"I can't disturb them, sir. I'm sure if you just wait a few more minutes, they'll be with you as soon as they can."

"Thank you, Chantal. Have a good day," Lockwood said, turning about and heading for the door.

"Wait. Wait just a second, please. I'll go inside and tell them. Just a second, okay?"

The woman rushed into the Board Room, pausing momentarily to rap lightly on the heavy wooden door before opening it and stepping inside. She hadn't been gone long when she reappeared, chasing him down the hallway.

"Sir, Sir," she called to Lockwood's posterior. "The President will see you now."

All told, Lockwood had spent thirty minutes waiting in the reception area, while the folks with whom he was to meet were busy with an *internal operations* meeting. He reasoned that, even if he'd gone into the Board Room at the appointed time, he'd still be in there discussing the case at this point, so despite his annoyance, he'd meet with the folks who'd intentionally kept him waiting, and he'd stay at least until the time he would have left had they met with him on time. He knew he'd still have time enough to do what he really came to do.

The receptionist ushered him back into the room, and motioned to what looked like a simple student desk in the middle of a heavy burl wood, U-shaped table, around which sat the company president, all of its Vice Presidents, and its general counsel, in addition to the Mayor, the police chief, and Detective Wardley. Their seats were positioned on a slightly elevated dais that allowed them to look down upon the person seated in the center of the formation, and the symbolism wasn't lost on Lockwood. He politely waived off another offer of coffee from the receptionist as he waltzed confidently to the center of the room, and plopped his portfolio down on the table and chair set aside for him. He stood beside the table and prepared to begin. .

"You'll have to forgive us, Agent," the president explained, smiling. "Our meeting kept us a little longer than anticipated."

"When I was a young'un," Lockwood said, "I was part of a youth leadership development group called the *Center for Leadership Development and Growth.* Whenever one of us arrived late for a pre-arranged appointment, the whole group would stop whatever it was then doing and utter a phrase that went like this: *In time on time every time, except when a little bit ahead of time, and that's better time.* It taught us to be early, or at least not late."

The group seemed a bit stunned that the agent was lecturing them about their timeliness, although they knew they really deserved it. The delay had been intentional, and obviously, Lockwood knew it too.

"I only have a few minutes of time for you remaining, so let's get to it. I'll ask that you hold any questions and comments until I'm finished."

He shuffled some papers and pages as he quickly reviewed his notes.

"We last met on the day the body of your CFO, one Francine Ketcham, was discovered in her office down the hall at this location. The investigation was federalized, with local law enforcement providing support as requested. My boss, Special Agent-in-Charge Grace Tran, indicated we'd keep you reasonably informed, and that's why I'm here today."

"Have you made any substantive progress?" the company's general counsel asked.

"Our main focus isn't the murder, of course. Our main focus is whether events that may or may not be related to the murder represent a threat to the national security interests of the United States. If we find no threat, the murder investigation will be turned over to local authorities, but if national security interests are implicated, we'll remain involved until further notice. I remind you all that everything about this investigation is subject to gag-rule requirements of the USA Patriot Act. You may not disclose any information about this matter to any unauthorized party without the permission of the National Security Coordinator who in this case is Special Agent-in-Charge Grace Tran. Do you all understand that?" he said.

He wasn't really asking a question, but waited to see if there were hints of questions, objections or comments. They all stared blankly at him.

"All right then. We've pulled a lot of information, data, and records from a number of sources already, and while we've not reached any solid conclusions we're ready to announce at this time, we have found some indications that yield grounds for concern. To run down these concerns, we'll need complete access to your main database, the laptop and mobile devices of several of your employees, including all of you. We'll begin this process tomorrow."

"I'm afraid you'll need a court order for that, Agent Lockwood," the corporate lawyer confidently asserted.

Lockwood sighed deeply, primarily for effect. "Are you really gonna' go there, Mr. Johnston?" the agent asked of the president.

"Direct your questions and responses to me, Agent Lockwood," the attorney barked.

"All right then, Mr. Matos, if that's what it takes, we can make that happen."

"Unfortunately for you and your team, it's not going to happen tomorrow."

The lawyer opened his briefcase on the table, fished something from its bowels, and then stood to lean over the table. He pressed thumb and pointer finger along the document's outer edge to ensure it was closed, and then tossed it down at Agent Lockwood.

"This is an emergency order of court enjoining you from accessing our corporate databases," Matos explained. "It also temporarily enjoins anyone on your team from entering into any part of this building except the foyer, elevator and the halls leading to this chamber, as well as my office in case we need to meet to resolve issues."

Lockwood didn't even bother to touch the paper tossed at him by the anxious lawyer, much less read it. He looked over the smug faces staring back at him, the lot of them satisfied with themselves. Don Johnston was the most satisfied member of the group as he leaned back in his large executive chair and folded his arms sending a clear message of *So how do you like them apples?* Lockwood smiled and shook his head, hardly believing this is the manner in which a US defense contractor would choose to handle an issue like this.

Matos continued. "It's only a temporary injunction, of course. The court has set a further hearing on whether to continue this temporary order for two weeks from yesterday in order for you to retain counsel and get them up to speed on the issues. You can argue your case before the judge at that time."

Lockwood paused for a moment of contemplation as he pondered what ERAC hoped to achieve by these tactics. Perhaps that could create a few extra hoops for the feds to jump through, but surely they couldn't reasonably expect to win this fight. They'd gain some time by delaying the investigation's access to corporate databases, but time for what?

"Okay, if that's the way you want to play it," Lockwood said in as menacing a tone as he could muster. "It's not a smart thing to do."

"Is that a threat, Agent Lockwood?"

"As my kid says, Mr. Matos, *chillax, dude,*" Lockwood said. "If I was making a threat, you'd not need any clarification. What I'm trying to tell you is, we're going to access your databases tomorrow."

"I said that wasn't going to happen, Agent Lockwood," Matos reiterated, speaking slowly, deliberately, and sternly as if that would help Lockwood hear him better. "I'm sure you've not forgotten the court order. If you defy the court order and try to do this anyway, our local law enforcement officers will arrest any member of your team in defiance of the court's order."

"Really?"

"Really."

"Well, it just so happens that I too have an order of court, Mr. Matos," Lockwood said, pulling a document from his portfolio. "We were certainly hoping this matter wouldn't come up, but since it has, let me present this to you."

He closed the distance between his meager one-man table and the one hosting the senior executives of Earhardt-Roane and the Seaside Beach Police Department, and then tossed the document at Matos in the same manner as Matos had tossed the local court order at him. Then he retreated to his tableside, and stood there while Matos perused the document Lockwood had given him.

"*My* legal document is signed by The Honorable Michael Q. Murphy, Judge of the United States Foreign Intelligence Surveillance Court. His order indicates this case is a national security issue subject exclusively to the federal jurisdiction of the United States. If any of you—including the county judge who signed that piece of paper you threw at me—attempt to interfere with our investigation, agents of the US marshal service, FBI, and NSA will take you into custody and you'll face federal prosecution. The Department of Justice will give your police department some very close scrutiny, and everyone in this room will emerge with a federal criminal record. Now, since y'all got guns and we got guns, this could get messy. I hope you won't make that necessary," Lockwood said, looking at Chief Lazlow, "but the choice is yours.

He turned to Johnston. "As for you folks, your DoD contracts require your full cooperation with any investigation of related work. The failure to do so carries consequences previously explained by my boss, Agent Tran. Your actions clearly reflect your lack of cooperation with a federal investigation, and will be duly noted."

"Are you threatening us for asserting our legal rights?" Matos asked, indignantly. "We have a compelling legal interest in safeguarding the integrity of our proprietary and privacy-protected information, and even though you're the government, you don't have the right to run rough-shod over us."

Without expression, Lockwood momentarily paused before responding. "You said it aptly a few moments ago, Mr. Matos. *You can argue your case before the judge,*" Lockwood repeated. "The Justice Department and the Air Force will ultimately decide what they want to do with this."

An awkward silence hung in the air momentarily, as Lockwood's words sunk in. Then he continued.

"Let me just close today by saying that based on the information uncovered to this point, it doesn't appear we'll be ceding this investigation to anyone anytime soon."

"Exactly what are you people looking for, Mr. Lockwood?" someone asked.

"Yeah...I'm not sure I understand what kind of national security threat could be posed by the murder here?" another added.

Lockwood conspicuously checked his watch. "It appears our time is up, so that's all for now. Perhaps next time, we'll have enough time for a more in-depth discussion."

Lockwood snapped up his portfolio and then bounded for the door, listening to the room's occupants call after him, shouting questions he intentionally left unanswered. He was more interested in his own unanswered questions involving the two computer flash drives he'd left with Rique Ito.

* * *

While his teammates were handling other parts of the investigation, Kenison had been detailed to follow-up with ERAC's Vice President and Chief Compliance Officer as he investigated financial and compliance issues. Kenison had been sifting through volumes of internal files he'd previously obtained from Matt Nichols, and the next logical step was to validate what he thought he'd learned the last week against Nichols' first-hand knowledge. The pair met in a small dark office in the back of the local FBI office, which neither particularly liked, but Kenison knew it was temporary, and Nichols didn't care as long as he got to leave it at the end of the day. Kenison looked upon Nichols with much less suspicion and doubt after learning from Agent Tran that Nichols had already proven himself a reliable confidential informant. His days of dealing with Iraqi locals when he was deployed to the Gulf War had made him suspicious of a stranger who seemed to offer free and valuable help, but he would proceed with caution, careful about any assumptions he might make.

"So, it seems the company has been working a top-secret project, code named NexChem, but you don't know what that's about?"

"Not really. All I know is that the expenses for that project are actually being logged in the expense records of the UAV contract. From what I can tell, it appears to be a valid research effort in that there is real and verifiable work going on, reports being generated, and progress being made. The two problems I have are first, it doesn't appear to be authorized by the scope of the contracts we have with the Air Force, and second, I can't tell who in this company is responsible for it."

"And this was one of the reasons behind Renley's allegation that the company kept two sets of books on a government contract?" Kenison clarified.

"I'm not a lawyer, but that does appear to be one of the things cited in her complaint," Nichols answered. "There are several other complaints that really amount to nothing as far as I can tell, but that one looks legit."

"Have you been able to track anything down?"

"Every time I asked someone about it, the person I asked ended up dead."

"What?"

"Yeah, I first asked the question of Francine Ketcham since her department was the one directly responsible for the accounting operations on that contract. She never answered me, and I eventually learned that *stonewalling* was one of her favorite tactics."

"She did that often?"

Nichols nodded. "Whenever something I was working on required information from her or her department, she'd either give me inaccurate information or she'd just refuse to answer my questions."

"How would she explain her refusal to answer?" Kenison asked.

Nichols shook his head and leaned forward as he explained himself. "No, no. It wasn't like that. We never had an outright confrontation like that. She'd always be agreeable, face to face, and she'd promise she'd get me an answer. But, she just never responded to my questions, even if I'd ask them over and over again."

"Wow," Kenison prompted.

"In the beginning, I trusted her and operated on a basis of professional and personal trust with her. But once, I made some representations to the president based on facts and figures she provided me, which later turned out to be wrong. When I asked her about it, she pretended she had no idea where I'd gotten my information...I couldn't believe it."

"How did you handle that?"

"I went to her boss about it, but he didn't care either. At the time, that was CFO Day; he basically said that since the president wasn't making an issue of the error, he wasn't either. It was of no concern whatsoever to him that a senior level person on his team was a frickin' liar about professional matters; that was my first hint about Day too, God rest his soul. I hate to speak ill of the dead, but the guy was a bit of a *douche bag*. He pretended to be of truly professional quality, but when you looked underneath the surface, he was really all about his ego."

Nichols chuckled in amusement at a memory that just fired across his synapses as he was speaking. He explained.

"He once hid behind a door to avoid having to speak with someone his underling, Ketcham, had fired. Boy, I got a couple comments about that one on our ethics hotline. My wife was here at that time too and she saw it happen. That very minute, she told me Day was a spineless limp-... well, you get the picture."

Thinking back to his military days, Kenison knew the officer-in-charge was expected to take responsibility for tough decisions that had to be made, not run and hide behind a door to avoid it. Day would never have cut it in the military. "I gotcha," he said, chuckling lightly under his breath.

"So anyway, after Ketcham's lying incident, I started doing every interaction I had with her via email in case I later had to prove what she did or didn't say, or show that I'd asked her repeatedly about something. At that point, she just ignored me completely, and Day was no help either. I'd planned to confront him on the issue the week he died, but I never got the chance."

"And then?"

"Then Ketcham became the CFO. I had no choice but to deal with her again in order to try to get information about this NexChem project. In her usual fashion, she ignored my requests for information. Now she's dead too."

"Remind me, Mr. Nichols, not to ignore you when you ask *me* any questions," Kenison joked. "So you never got any information about Project NexChem?"

"I didn't say that," Nichols clarified. "I never got any information about it from Ketcham or Day. I did learn a bit about it from Dr. Catin. I tricked her to get the information, but I got it."

Kenison wrinkled his brow, tacitly asking how Nichols had tricked Catin into revealing the information.

"I sidelined Catin after an unrelated meeting, and told her Ketcham and I were discussing Project NexChem and that perhaps Ketcham thought Catin would be a better source of information since she was in charge of research."

"That never happened, I take it?"

"What? I didn't lie," Nichols resisted. "I only said *perhaps* Ketcham thought Catin could inform me better. I never said she referred me to Catin or anything like that. I can't be responsible for what people infer."

"Sly, very sly," Kenison commended.

"Forgive me. I don't mean to be rude, but the best way to describe it accurately is to say Catin's a bit of an airhead. She has a Ph.D. but, well, people around here joke that she screwed her dissertation committee to get it. I guess that's my way of saying Catin can be easily led—or mislead."

Both men chuckled.

"So what did she tell you?"

"She didn't have a lot of detail about the program but she told me it was a research program into a chemical that rendered subjects susceptible to suggestion."

"Really?" Kenison asked, thinking this was a joke.

"No, I'm serious."

"Mind control. Truth serum? Really?"

"Well sort of. The best I can tell is that it's a variant of Thiopental, which is commonly referred to as truth serum. The company refers to it internally as NexChem."

"This sounds like a scam—the proverbial *Bridge to Nowhere*. Was this just a way to take money from the government? Are we talking fraud?"

"No, no," Nichols said. "I didn't mean to come across like that. I'm in no position to judge the merits of the undertaking because the government sometimes funds projects that seem crazy to us mere mortals," he joked. "For example, the DoD and CIA spent roughly eleven million on psychics to see if they could foretell terror attacks…The government also spent seven-hundred grand to research how much methane gas cows fart and burp out. A project might sound really stupid if you don't know anything about it, but could still be a valid, authorized research initiative. So, enhanced truth serum wouldn't strike me as obviously pointless. In this case, it appears one of our researchers was working on something related to this, and wanted DoD funding so it could be used in interrogations of terror suspects, criminals, etc. Dr. Catin, as head of research, authorized it."

"Okay, so if you don't judge the merits of these stupid research efforts, why is this one problematic, Mr. Nichols?"

"I didn't really have any concerns about the research itself. There are some protocols they must observe if they're doing human trials, but my concern was the manner in which they apparently accounted for the expenses on that research initiative. The way it appears is that the expenses of the NexChem research were being tacked on to the expenses for the UAV work we're doing for the Air Force."

Nichols shoved a pile of papers across the table at Kenison, and then leaned over to point out the discrepancies he'd mentioned. The compliance officer explained that these documents were reviewed and approved by the CFO, president, and someone on the board at least once a year in preparation to certify the company's annual financial statements. Agent Kenison followed Nichols' pointing finger as it darted around the various pages and listened intently to the accompanying narration. He thought he understood, but would definitely want the agency's forensic accountant to look at it too.

"So in essence, they were mischarging expenses to the Air Force contract?" Kenison summarized.

"Don't know that for sure, because I could never get any information from the folks responsible for the accounting operations, and my review of the papers was inconclusive because relevant documents are missing. What I know is that our original UAV contract with the Air Force doesn't provide for research into chemical compounds."

"Yes, those pesky accounting people were so rude as to up and die before answering your questions," Kenison said, making light of the matter.

"You joke, but this is what Ms. Renley's complaint was partially about," Nichols said.

"And you think Catin is responsible for it?"

"On the books yes, but I don't think she authorized or even knows anything about the accounting operations for these two efforts. Like I said, she's an airhead. More likely, she blindly followed whatever Ketcham told her to do, and didn't give an independent thought about it." Nichols shook his head in disbelief. "That lady has been in charge of five or six different projects, all of which were miserable financial failures for the company. But each time, when the problems came to light, she shut down the failing operation, blamed and fired the people working in them, and then moved on to something else. It's completely lost on her that since she was in charge of them, the programs were her responsibility."

"Why would it have been allowed to go on?"

"Who would stop her? The CFO wouldn't do anything because the actors in the improper accounting activities were his subordinates," Nichols explained. "Making an issue of that would have exposed his own operations, and that would have made him look bad. Of course he wasn't going to do anything about it."

"How did it stay hidden from your president?"

Nichols paused for a moment of contemplation. He hadn't known the president for very long, and really wondered whether he truly knew the man at all. He knew what Mr. Johnston made available for public consumption, but he also knew some things the president probably hadn't intended for anyone, especially a person of color, to know. He recalled a meeting where the company president suggested a white person should handle an internal investigation of race discrimination allegations instead of Nichols because the two complainants were black and Nichols was black. The president was oblivious that his suggestion had betrayed his private belief that a black investigator couldn't be impartial in a racial discrimination complaint because the only factor he'd see was the complainant's race. A white investigator on the other hand could be impartial, regardless of the races of the people involved. This was the same man who sat completely unfazed and unmoved when a retiring executive told him that filling his position was no time to consider a diversity candidate. Thus, Nichols concluded, the president was dull, worn, or deviously deliberative in what he chose to know.

"I think at one point the president was a decent guy at heart, but something has happened to him over the last few years… Even his own senior managers have exchanged private whispers suggesting that he's grown complacent or full of himself. The man isn't stupid, and he can be a skilled liar when he wants to be, and he believes whole-heartedly in the concept of plausible deniability."

"So you think he really knows about this stuff and is just pretending not to?" Kenison asked.

"I think he intentionally avoids anything likely to lead to a conclusion that he knows the truth. Mr. Johnston subscribes to the theory of management-by-crisis, so he'll do nothing about any situation until the shit hits the fan. Once that happens, he'll be all over it and heads will roll."

"As long as it's not his," the agent summarized. Kenison digested these comments for a bit. "I understand he has that tendency, but what does he gain from doing it here?"

"Perhaps he just doesn't want to be bothered."

"Perhaps…but my experience tells me there's something more to it for a person like him. I've talked to Mr. Johnston a few times, and I've read some of his public statements, his dissertation, and a few research papers he published years back. He's obviously not a stupid guy, and I don't think he got where he is by relying on luck."

"Definitely not," Nichols agreed.

"It makes no sense that he'd choose to be ill-informed about the company's defense contracts since they make up so much of the company's revenue. The issues are obvious in the papers you showed me…Operating on the premise that he really does know something about this stuff, I'm guessing Johnston's not likely to do anything to jeopardize his gravy train or diminish his power and influence, even if it's legally and morally required. If things really are how they currently look, this whole situation could do both of those things and more. So there's gotta' be something more to this for him to justify the risk of inaction, or maybe we just don't know some critical missing facts."

"Or maybe both," Nichols said.

* * *

"So, tell me you've made some progress," Lockwood said as he burst through the door into the lab back at the field office. He held his hands in prayer fashion in the air in front of his face, just to dramatize his point.

The loud and unexpected noise startled Ito who'd been enjoying his time working in nearly complete silence while the rest of the team was out working their leads. He jumped, but quickly recovered his composure, hoping Lockwood hadn't noticed his bodily quivering.

"Didn't your mother ever teach you to knock?" Ito asked sarcastically.

"She gave up trying to teach me manners—she learned pretty quickly I was incorrigible."

"Why am I not surprised?" Ito sighed.

He pushed a few more buttons on his keyboard, the last one depressing with his right pointer finger in deliberate exaggeration, and then stood to go greet Lockwood as he wormed his way across the room.

"As a matter of fact, Agent Lockwood, I have made great progress. Wa-la," he said, turning his palm to the ceiling and sweeping it toward the dual computer monitor at his work station.

Lockwood rushed to the monitor and began reading. Ito had broken the security encryption on all the documents on the first flash drive, and had made some progress on several files on the second. He verbally summarized as Lockwood read.

"What you're seeing here are notes, reports, and letters from a private investigator named Kerr. Francine Ketcham hired him to follow her husband and dig up dirt, it looks like. You can see several entries there that show she knew her husband was having an affair with her friend and co-worker, Bette French-Catin."

"Ah, and the plot thickens," Lockwood said.

"Yeah, more than you know," Ito agreed. "Look here," he said, spinning the computer's mouse wheel and flipping through several other documents on the flash drive. After a short time, he found the file he was looking for. "These are PDF files of fully executed copies of a Living Trust and Last Will and Testament of Francine Ketcham, in addition to other random documents. All of them are dated, and have witness signatures and notary seals from the week before she died. These are just electronic files for safe-keeping or reference or something. The real ones are in hard copy."

"Look at this," Lockwood said, peering over Ito's shoulder and pointing to the fine print. "Judging from this language here, it looks like she, at some point, transferred pretty much all her assets into a Living Trust, and her Will gives five grand to the husband and a buck to each of the boys. Everything else is given to *The Sara Buydot Trust*. The language here," he said, pointing, "states that all bequests are void if anyone challenges the Will in court."

"*The Sara Buydot Trust*—who the hell is Sara Buydot?" Ito asked, wrinkling his brow.

Lockwood moved closer and adjusted his glasses to see what Ito was talking about. Peering from the bottom of his lenses, he too wrinkled his brow, more than a little curious about the name they'd not come across anywhere in the investigation so far. "That's just weird—I've never heard of that name before, *Buydot*."

"Me neither," Ito said. "Sounds like a refillable money card or something you buy on the internet."

"It does, doesn't it?" Lockwood agreed.

"Let's see something," Ito said, spinning the mouse wheel again.

He flipped the electronic pages of his monitor until he found the de-encrypted file named *Trust*. He double-clicked the icon and opened the document.

"Pow," he said, celebrating his small victory.

He began scanning the document, but was evidently going too slowly for Lockwood's tastes. The senior agent Lockwood grabbed the mouse wheel for himself, never mind that Ito already had hold of it. He began scrolling down the text of the Trust document, but Ito quickly snatched his hand away, letting the older agent work the device alone.

"I like you, Lockwood, but not like that," he joked.

Lockwood turned his head and looked at his teammate from the corner of his eye. "Shut up, *Idi-Ito*. You wish."

"Hey, hey, wait a second," Ito said, his eye catching something in the text. "Go back a moment." He waited for Lockwood to spin the wheel back a couple times, and then: "There. Look at this," he invited as pointed.

Lockwood squinted to better see the electronic print. "I see."

The preamble of the Trust discussed her husband's extra-marital relationship with her best friend in very damning words and phrases, clearly revealing her anger and hurt about it, indicating the affair was the reason she cut him out of her final arrangements. The language of the Trust document made Francine Ketcham and her son Michael primary co-beneficiaries of the Trust, and her son Dallas a contingent beneficiary, meaning there were certain conditions he had to meet before he could get something from the Trust. They scanned down the page to learn the substantive provisions of the document, but there was one additional page that contained half-sentences, lined-through words, and gibberish statements that looked like amalgamations of incorrectly cut-and-pasted portions, and one completely blank page, and nothing more.

"Looks like this is only part of the Trust document," Ito said. "I'll look around to see if I can find more, but so far I haven't."

"We need to find it. Maybe it'll tell us something juicy. Maybe that's a reason for the hubby to off his wife," Lockwood mused.

"Yeah, maybe so."

"I'm no lawyer, but if I understand this, Ketcham's Will gives the husband five grand, and the boys a dollar each from her estate, and everything else goes to *The Sara Buydot Trust*," Lockwood said.

Ito agreed. "I guess she was pretty pissed when she found out about the affair. Hell hath no fury like the wrath of a woman scorned."

Lockwood laughed. "I know about a woman's fury. I've got three ex-wives."

"Okay, I see why she might want to x-out her cheating husband, but why would she make one boy a primary beneficiary of the trust, and the other one contingent?" Ito mused.

"Everyone says Francine was a Class-A controlling, conniving bitch and the hubby said she tried to rule her sixteen year-old with an iron fist," Lockwood answered. "Maybe mom was still trying to run him over and control his life."

"You think she'd take it all the way to the grave, against her own kid?" Ito asked, shocked.

Lockwood quoted Melville's Ahab. "*From hell's heart, I stab at thee; for hate's sake, I spit my last breath at thee.*"

Ito snickered. "Yeah maybe. I suppose a true bitch-on-wheels just might arrange to get the last word, even from the grave."

Lockwood nodded, but a quizzical expression shot over his face. Ito noticed it as his laughter faded.

"What's the matter?" the younger man asked.

The senior agent gave only a glassy stare as he thought.

"Earth to Lockwood," the technician repeated.

"Control freaks like Ketcham don't do shit without a reason. I get why she'd do all this crap with her Will and the Trust, but why would she name the trust after this Sara lady, when there's no reference to Sara anywhere in the document and no other connection, at least that we know of?"

"Good questions," Ito said. "We'll have to run that to ground."

"Yeah, and something else. My ex number three—Tina—was a crazy old bat with an obsessive compulsive disorder about neatness and orderliness."

"Guess that explains why she divorced your sloppy ass," Ito joked.

"She used to harp on me about *a place for everything and everything in its place.* I remember one of our knock-down drag-out fights started because I put the title to a car we'd just paid off in the file cabinet instead of the fireproof lockbox where she kept all our other important legal documents."

"Yeah, so?"

"So Ketcham stored her Last Will and Testament in a floor safe along with these super-secret flash drives, some purchase agreements, stock certificates, and other things she found important."

"Yeah."

"So where's the Trust document?" Lockwood asked.

"I'm not following," Ito said.

"If Ketcham was anything like my Ex—and I'm betting these two bags were like two peas in a pod," Lockwood said, "so where's the original Living Trust document? People who have OCD about neatness, order, and control are neurotic about keeping shit like that together in one place where they can control and hide it. Ketcham's newly executed Will and other important legal documents were in the floor safe, so why wouldn't she keep the original Trust document there too?"

"Maybe she put it in a bank safety deposit box?"

Lockwood shook his head. "I guess it's worth running that to ground too, but why would she put the Trust document in a safe deposit box, yet keep the Will she made at the same time in her secret home safe? It doesn't make sense."

"Okay, *Dr. Freud*, I guess that makes sense," Ito said, not totally convinced. "So, I guess we need to find that Living Trust document then. Where do we start?"

Lockwood thought for a moment. "Her lawyer or maybe the private-I would be a good step."

"Who's her lawyer?" Ito asked.

"Don't know. We'll have to do some digging," Lockwood said. "The answers are out there. We just have to find them."

# Chapter 6

## Coming into Focus

It had been a few days since the last Powwow, and Tran felt the group was overdue for one. Keeping the whole team informed was both necessary and helpful in keeping it on track for a timely, complete, and quality product. Her team members seemed especially giddy to share today, and Tran knew it had to do with whatever Lockwood had been beating-around-the-bush about the last few days. She'd called an early meeting, and offered Lockwood the first opportunity to present.

"All due respect, Boss, but I think I'd rather go last today if you don't mind." To Ito's and Kenison's accompanying giggles, he brandished the flash drives. "After you see this, we won't be able to talk about anything else," he said.

"As you wish," she said, noting his uncharacteristic delight at his own coyness.

Starr volunteered to speak first. She began by reminding the team her task had been to look into the company's executives as well as the employees reporting to the dead woman.

"I've interviewed every one of the executives and several employees close to them in one fashion or another. Suffice it to say, there is no dearth of people with animus toward Ms. Ketcham, any of whom may have had a sufficiently compelling motive to kill her," Starr said, her inner psychologist quickly surfacing in her word and manner. "I really found it difficult if not impossible to rule out many of them at this point, so I decided to take a different approach. I decided to try to rule-in the most likely of those with possible motive to kill this woman, starting with the long line of fired employees with ruined lives she left in her wake," Starr said.

"Yeah, she did have a reputation as a bitch-on-wheels," Lockwood observed in a manner unique to him.

Lockwood felt Tran's gaze on his face, and heard an unspoken chastisement.

"I'm just saying, boss. I'm just saying."

Tran looked back to Dr. Starr without saying a word.

"One person struck me with particular interest," Starr continued, flipping her notepad to the relevant page. "A former employee named Stan Lauxner, Contract Administration specialist. He's a twice-divorced dad of four, and a former Army Green Beret with service in the First Gulf War, Iraq, and Afghanistan. He's a certified martial arts expert and trainer, and a highly accomplished sniper. His medical file suggests he may have been discharged from active duty following a diagnosis of PTSD or maybe shell-shock following an IED explosion that killed just about everyone in his Humvee."

Starr glanced over the dossier she'd accumulated on him.

"He's highly decorated for his actions during several classified missions—the Distinguished Service Cross with four oak leaf clusters, the Defense Distinguished Service Medal, the Army Distinguished Service Medal with two oak leaf clusters, the Silver Star, the Legion of Merit, two Purple Hearts, and the Joint Service Commendation Medal."

Himself a former Green Beret with combat experience, Kenison opined, "This guy is no freakin' joke."

"He most certainly is not," Tran agreed.

"Sounds like a man's man—the type of guy who'd mix with a ball-buster like Ketcham just like oil and water," Lockwood offered.

*A crude but accurate observation,* Tran thought. "Why did he catch your notice?"

"Three months ago, Ketcham fired him without notice. The guy was a probationary employee—meaning he'd been there less than ninety days—but he'd complained that Ketcham and her subordinate managers above him were abusive, condescending, and oppressive."

"And," Tran prompted.

"And he'd also questioned the way the books were being kept on a couple different contracts, one of which was ERAC's UAV contract with the Air Force. Shortly afterward, they fired him without notice, claiming he simply wasn't a good fit with the organization. He appealed to the company's

HR department for help, saying his PTSD made it difficult for him but he was adjusting and learning the new job well. The HR exec he met with was very close friends with Ketcham, and promised to find him another position in the company, but never did. Lauxner was essentially put out on his ass after being subjected to some pretty intense *management*, as it were."

"Okay," she questioned. "Is that the reason he caught your attention?"

"That and the fact that he told some of his former co-workers that Ketcham would one day find herself laying in a dark alley with a gaping hole in her head if she didn't start treating people with respect."

Tran nodded. "That's pretty convincing. Anyone else jump out at you?"

"I haven't reached any final conclusions about the other executives yet, but I'm not getting any real indicators on this Rick McCool, Executive VP for Eastern Operations. He seems to be generally respected across the board, and keeping his head in his work. Similar story on John Watchman, Executive VP for Worldwide Operations; Dan Williams, Associate Vice President of Public Affairs, and; Keithe Mantix, Chief of Corporate Security. I get no real indicators on the lawyer, Chuck Matos. He seems clean, but it also seems pretty clear they view him as a bastard, red-headed stepchild in the corner, a necessary evil to be tolerated. They roll him out whenever they need a lapdog to do something in his wheelhouse but that's about it. They otherwise leave him alone and he leaves them alone so he can collect his paycheck."

"And the others?"

"Frank Grounds, the Executive VP for Western Operations, seems to have a reputation as autocratic and full-of-himself, but I detect no substantial red flags with him, and this Eilene Reynolds woman, VP of Human Resources, is a go-along-to-get-along type. I think she's just hanging on until she retires, and that's her most important mission in life. She'll do whatever she has to in order to get to that point, including turning a blind eye to improper, even illegal things. She likely has a limit of tolerance, but I don't know what it is."

"So your sense is that everything here revolves around Ketcham, Day, Catin, the president, and this board member?" Tran surmised.

"Yes ma'am," Starr replied. "I reserve the right to change my professional opinion if the facts change, but that's my guestimation at this point."

Tran smiled. "Spoken like a lawyer, Doc. Spoken like a lawyer." She turned to Agent Kenison. "Anything on the financial side?"

"Yeah boss. With the help of our forensic accountants at headquarters, I looked into the financials of all the executives, the dead lady's husband, and the UAV contract. I'm still waiting for some feedback from Washington, but I can say there's *something* amiss here."

"Tell me about the accounting issues on the UAV contract," Tran said, zeroing in on the issues that were clearly federal.

"Sure, boss. It does appear the company had two sets of books being used for this contract. It's not clear whether this was an attempt to defraud the government, or whether it's just a case of incompetence on the part of ERAC. The lady who filed the initial allegations reported in both her written complaint and in my interview of her that Ketcham ordered her to report figures only out of the books Ketcham created, and threatened that she'd be fired if she told anyone about the financial figures from the second set of books. The difference between the two sets of books amounts to about $3.14 million which the Air Force paid."

"So earlier, you indicated there was some missing money?"

"Ketcham restructured the company's accounting practices over the last few years, and in the process took direct control of excess funds from various departments within the company," Kenison began.

"So why isn't that just an indicator of a CFO tightening the company's financial controls?" Tran asked.

"Their budget managers don't understand why Ketcham *nickeled and dimed them to death* on pre-approved expenditures, and ultimately took millions out of their operating budgets. She transferred those funds into accounts for the two UAV contracts to replace money allocated by the government for the projects. To put it in perspective, it seems like a shell game here. Since there weren't corresponding expenses charged to those accounts by the end of the accounting year, we'd expect to see a surplus of funds in these accounts, but there isn't one. The covert accounting records show the money was taken out of the account, but not where it went. The accounting records from which their government reports were made show the expected balances. I suppose one is always guessing when you try to figure out someone's motivations, but I think they tried to mask what they did here by using a lot of unnecessary movement of money and a lot of complex, unusual accounting adjustments and maneuvers. The forensic accountants felt as I did that these actions were either brilliant smokescreens, or just stupid."

"My colleagues in the litigation arena do something similar," Tran said. "Since the trial rules require you to do so when the opposing side makes a proper request for potentially damaging documents, they give the other side the damaging documents, but they also dump a hundred tons of extraneous, pointless paper on them, taking care to bury the damaging evidence somewhere in the middle."

"That's only one reason lawyers have such a slimy reputation," Lockwood volunteered. He enjoyed a little humor at Tran's expense.

She smiled and nodded. "It's a dirty trick but the rules only say you have to give discoverable documents and evidence when properly requested; they don't say you have to point it out for them."

"So what happened to the $3 million?"

Kenison shook his head. "Not sure. It was initially tracked into the UAV accounts, but there were a series of transfers between those accounts and the company's petty cash account. The numbers ultimately don't add up, and neither do the reasons for the transfers. Nobody in Accounting could tell me why this was done. It appears the only one that might be able to shed any light on it is dead."

Tran nodded and then turned to Ito. "What do you have?"

"Of course, Boss," he answered, seemingly nervously pushing his glasses up the bridge of his nose. "I have a couple things. As you suspected, the vases missing from Day's house are the same ones in Ketcham's office. Using the photos you took and a bit of my own personal knowledge, I did a little research. They're authentic 18th century Chinese vases from the Qianlong Dynasty. A larger one from the same era sold for $63 million at auction last year," Ito informed.

Minor gasps filled the air.

"The expert I consulted said these pieces are much smaller and not in as pristine shape as that, but he thought these were worth about $150,000 each," Ito continued. "The Days had them insured under a policy issued by Lloyd's of London. Mr. Day evidently gave them to Ketcham for reasons unknown, and Ketcham used her laptop to shop for a buyer. She found one in New York, just two days before her death. She never had a chance to complete the transaction."

"Mrs. Day didn't know much about the vases," Tran noted. "Did you follow-up with her at all about this information?"

"I did. She didn't know her husband had given them to Ketcham but agreed that's probably what happened. She didn't know the value of the vases, and I didn't tell her."

"You think she was being honest or was she shitting you about not knowing how much the old junk vases were really worth?" Lockwood asked.

"She didn't sign any of the paperwork to purchase or insure them, and the maid and even family friends indicated Marsha Day wasn't into the collections of items in the house. It seems pretty clear that was all her husband's pastime."

"So you believe her?"

Ito shrugged. "Yeah, I guess I do. There's nothing to suggest otherwise."

"How do we know Day gave them to her? How do we know they weren't stolen or something? Maybe even different pieces?" Lockwood asked.

"I found a scanned gift acknowledgment letter on the flash-drives, where Erich Day acknowledges giving the vases as gifts to Ketcham. He declared they had 'nominal' value, but that's inconsistent with what he declared on the forms to insure them with Lloyd's," Ito explained. "The Lloyd's declaration said they were priceless."

"So, unbeknownst to his wife, Day gave highly valuable antique vases to a subordinate with whom he had no familial or other association," Tran summarized. "It's looking more and more reasonable that he was either having an affair with her or being blackmailed by her."

Ito nodded his agreement. "Indeed, and there's more. The flash-drives Lockwood seized from Ketcham's secret safe were encrypted by a very powerful, sophisticated encryption system known to be used by the MOIS."

"The Iranian Ministry of Intelligence and Security," Tran said, footnoting for the benefit of the newer members of her team.

"Yeah," Ito confirmed. "You can't buy this kind of technology from just any old run-of-the-mill big box store at the mall. This particular software is known in tech and intelligence circles as a creation of the Iranian Cyber-Intelligence Bureau, which is part of MOIS. Its sale, trade, use and distribution are restricted by our government and virtually every other western government in the world for security, economic, and diplomatic reasons."

"That's enough to raise a brow or two," Tran said.

"Aside from the illegal thing, it's not a bad security plan on her part," Ito offered, playing devil's advocate.

"What do you mean?" Kenison challenged.

"Think about it. She was probably concerned about her colleagues at the company, common hackers, or maybe her husband, maybe local cops, or other kinds of everyday people finding and exploiting it. None of them would likely be able to break it. It's not readily available in the market for them to lay hands on it, study it, and find a way into it."

"So you're saying you can't do it?" Lockwood poked.

"Not at all, Lockwood, but I'm special," Ito jokingly bragged. "I'm sure our CIA guys, and probably our FBI and military Intel guys have copies of this stuff, but not the everyday person. I've heard about this software and read industry speculation about it, but even I haven't actually gotten hold of it, until now."

"Well how the hell did Ketcham get hold of it?" Tran wondered.

"Not sure."

"Well, there's one easy theory," Lockwood offered.

Tran nodded her agreement.

"Ketcham's laptop was used to access the encrypted files but at least one other computer was used to do so as well. If I had the suspect computer in custody, I could be one-hundred percent sure by checking it for internal indicators, but I need to have the computer to be sure," Ito explained.

"Okay," Tran said. "Anything else?"

"That's it from me, Boss."

Tran turned to Lockwood. "All right, so it looks like we've got some smoke around the allegations pertaining to Ketcham. What have you found on the UAV contract?"

"Nothing overtly," Lockwood answered. "We know Hamidi was very involved with the UAV contract and had a lot of interaction with Ketcham about it, and we know Hamidi is Iranian-born and has ties to radical elements within the Iranian government. But, that's not enough to establish a violation of law because she's now a US citizen. The export control laws don't prohibit transfers of non-classified but controlled technology between US citizens or green-card holders."

"Then could this be illegal corporate espionage?" Kenison asked.

"Not without more evidence," Lockwood said. "Both Ketcham and Hamidi worked for the same company in this context, so they'd both be entitled to know the company's business."

"Okay, I'll check with Agent Sedgwick to see what he's learned on that part...I'll update you all later," Tran said. She turned in her seat to physically orient herself toward Lockwood. "All right, Lockwood. It seems we've come to a point at which you should present your—whatever it is you've been so anxious to tell me," she said.

Lockwood smiled. "Okay Boss. I want to first give a verbal report, but close with a video presentation."

"As you wish," Tran agreed.

"All right. Let's talk about the dead woman's men. I talked to Ketcham's first husband about her, and he wasn't exactly broken up about her death," Lockwood said. "Even after I explained how she died, he said her death was, to use his words, *a bummer dude.*"

"How sweet," Tran quipped.

"Yeah, but I think there was just so damn much choppy water under that bridge, the guy is beyond feeling anything about her except the need to avoid any- and everything about her, with the exception of their son, Dallas. I think he genuinely loves his boy," Lockwood said.

"A motive for murder maybe?" Kenison asked.

"No, her Ex runs a surf shop down the coast a ways, but at the time of the murder, he was in a surf competition at Makaha Beach on Oahu's north shore. It was even televised, and they got great footage of him riding some pretty wicked waves. I also verified his travel and lodging, so I think he's clear on this one."

"And the current husband?"

"Well, he's a little different story. John-Paul Ketcham was in the midst of a two-year affair with his wife's best friend who is also the VP of Research at Earhardt-Roane."

"Dr. Catin?" Tran asked.

"Yeah, they weren't forthcoming about it, of course."

"So why isn't that a motive for the dead woman to kill Catin or perhaps her husband? How does this help us?" Starr asked.

"There's a danger in starting to draw conclusions before you have all the facts," the senior agent corrected the second-most junior agent on the team. "At this point, I'm not saying it's a motive for Catin to kill Francine Ketcham, or vice-versa. We're not quite ready to draw conclusions yet; We're just reporting facts we think we know."

Starr nodded her understanding.

"One thing builds on another, you see. We know from the disks in Ketcham's secret safe that she evidently hired a private detective to spy on her husband, and she knew about his affair with Dr. Catin," Lockwood said. "Shortly after she learned of the affair, she changed her final arrangements to cut out her husband and eldest son. This may not give Catin a motive to kill Ketcham, but given that Francine was her family's primary bread-winner and her estate was worth a few hundred thousand bucks, changing the Will and excluding her husband may give a motive to John-Paul Ketcham to kill her," Lockwood said.

"Yes, but there are still some things that don't make sense to me," Tran added. "Did Ketcham know his wife cut him out of the Will, and even if he did, killing her wouldn't get him the money back into the Will."

"Yeah but it might make him feel a helluva lot better," Lockwood joked.

Tran rolled her eyes. She didn't find divorced man humor as entertaining as Lockwood did.

"But seriously, boss," Lockwood continued, "we found electronic and hard copies of the decedent's new Will, but only an electronic copy of the new Trust she prepared at the same time. Based on personal experience, I know these *Type-A* control freaks."

Tran smiled. "You're talking about Tina?" She recalled the numerous horror stories Lockwood had shared about his life with the third future Ex-Mrs. Lockwood, and wondered if anyone could truly be as awful as he described her. Tran had never even seen a glimpse of the Amazonian blonde Lockwood had so often prattled on about, but she wanted to, just to get a sense what the woman was really like.

"Yeah, that's the little…witch I'm talking about," Lockwood confessed. "Type-A people like her nearly always keep their important papers together in one place where they and only they can get to it, until they say otherwise. I found only a hard copy of the Will, so where is the Trust document?" Lockwood pondered aloud.

"Hey, I was thinking about the Trust too," Ito said. "I ran the name *Sara Buydot* through every database I know, and like we thought, it's not a surname of record anywhere. I can find no mention of that name anywhere or a connection to Francine Ketcham or anyone in her inner circle, such that it was."

Lockwood shook his head. "I'm thinking it doesn't refer to someone's name. It must mean something else," he added. "Like I said, control freaks like Ketcham don't do anything without a reason, so what was the reason here?"

There was a brief silence, and then Lawrence began giggling from the surface of the Ito-pad.

"It's an anagram," she said, smiling.

"What?"

"An anagram," Lawrence repeated. "You know, mixing up the letters in one word to make another," she explained. "I do word puzzles all the time. This one's kind of funny actually. *Sara Buydot* is an anagram for *You Bastard*."

Some people just had a gift for seeing numbers, words, and phrases completely lost to others. Lawrence was evidently one gifted with words and letters, because it didn't take her long to figure it out. But, it made perfect sense…Vindictive control freak Ketcham had just found out about her husband's affair with her best friend when she changed her Will and created *The Sara Buydot Trust*, the two of which essentially cut her cheating husband and a mouthy disrespectful kid out of an estate she worked hard to amass.

"Good call, Viv," Tran said, yet again impressed by Lawrence's far-reaching knowledge and skill.

"I knew that all along," Ito joked. "I was just seeing if you all could get it."

"You Idi-ito," Lockwood snapped. "You probably thought it was a French name…like *bi-dough*," he said, phonetically pronouncing the fictional woman's last name.

The group chuckled at the banter for a moment, and then quickly returned to the business at hand.

"Well if you liked that, you're gonna' love what I got to say next," Lawrence informed.

"Go ahead, Viv," Tran said.

"All right, *Forensics* at Headquarters has confirmed the samples Mrs. Day took from her husband's impounded car had traces of military-grade high incendiary explosives. After coordinating with FBI, they said the explosive signatures have a similar signature to evidence at the scenes of three hate crimes throughout the south and mid-west. It raised some red flags in the FBI's *Domestic Terror* division and the CIA, and our Intel folks suspect there may be some similarities to roadside bombs in Afghanistan and Iran. They've asked for everything we've got related to it."

That was a big one. Tran nodded, making a mental note to follow-up on that with her local FBI counterpart Mark Allen and John Sedgwick, her NSA colleague in New York. She paced the floor in her immediate area as she thought out loud for the team. After several minutes and some incidental back and forth with her agents, she turned back to Lockwood.

"You got anything else?" she eventually asked.

The senior agent smiled. "Yeah, Boss, but not verbally," Lockwood answered. "You need to see this next part."

Rique and Kenison snickered, causing Tran to be alert for something surprising or scary. They were all practical jokers, but not usually during a serious session at work.

"Before we do that," Tran said. "Let me ask, did you ever get around to chatting with Attorney Matos about this case?" Tran asked.

"Yeah I did, but he's a waste," Lockwood announced. "I think your guy Nichols was right about him. He spouts off whatever bullshit he thinks will keep him in good stead with the people paying his salary, or whatever line of crap will make him look good to people he sees as powerful. You really can't rely on anything he has to say, except some shit about attorney-client privilege."

"Does he have any sons?" Kenison asked.

Lockwood wrinkled his brow, puzzled by his teammate's left-field question. "No. He's a fifty year-old divorcee with no kids."

Kenison shook his head approvingly. "It's a good thing then. There's no way a guy like that could teach a boy how to be a man."

"Or how not to fear his own shadow," Ito added, sending the men of the team into a shared snicker.

"It's all right. I didn't expect much out of him, given his role at this company. I figured he'd throw the attorney/client privilege in our face," Tran said.

A trained attorney herself, she fully understood and valued the doctrine of attorney/client privilege. In order to get clients to be completely candid with their lawyers, and thus aid the attorney in assuring the American system of justice worked as it was intended, the laws of every state in the union as well as the federal rules of procedure, require lawyers to keep their clients' confidences under most circumstances. There were exceptions to the rule, several of which Tran thought applied, or knew how to make relevant in this case, but she was resolved not to push the issue unless she had to. At this point, though, she thought she could get what she needed without Matos, or the company's president either for that matter.

"Okay, let's move on. What else you got?" she asked.

"Just the item I wanted you to see for yourself," Lockwood reminded.

Tran chuckled at Lockwood's zeal for his little show-and-tell. "All right then, proceed," she said.

Lockwood in turn nodded at Rique, who immediately toggled the controls on the laptop in front of him, which he then turned around so the entire group could view its large monitor. Lockwood dashed across Tran's office to dim the lights and close the blinds.

"This was on a flash drive taken from a hidden floor safe in Ketcham's home," Lockwood narrated. "Her husband didn't appear to be aware of the safe's existence or its contents..." The laptop finished loading the first of several decrypted audio-visual files stored on the flash drive, and the scene opened with a static shot taken from what appeared to be the ceiling inside a well-appointed office. "I'll just be quiet and let you see for yourself."

For what felt like a small eternity, the video showed a still office, devoid of anything but typical office appointments. Tran was just starting to feel a twinge of boredom suggesting this was a waste of time when suddenly, the office door burst open with great power behind it, as if it had been kicked from the other side by a size-thirteen Brogan. As she watched, Tran saw the force on the door was the backside of a tall thin black man, locked in a passionate embrace with an unidentified white person, the pair passionately locking lips while clumsily stumbling toward a plush leather sofa. It didn't take long for Tran to recognize the black man as the dead CFO Erich Day, but she had to stare a little more closely to ascertain the identity of his paramour. The angle of view didn't allow a clear view of the person's face, but whoever it was, it wasn't the sophisticated, pretty Marsha Day whom she met the prior afternoon. Suddenly, the video showed Day fall to his knees and bury his face between the legs of his mystery lover, now standing before him beside the sofa. His lover's identity at that moment became unmistakable. The tacky toupee atop a head and shoulders much shorter than Day's gave it away—Don Johnston.

The realization momentarily rattled Tran, but she managed to contain her outward reaction. After twenty-plus years as an investigator, she was rarely surprised by anything having to do with human behavior, but candidly, she didn't expect what she'd just seen. She continued to watch as Day performed for Johnston's delight, each and every accompanying sound picked up on audio. The sounds of these two men *in flagrante delicto* were uncomfortable to hear but Tran watched stoically for the entire twenty minute encounter. When they'd finished their business on screen, Johnston zipped his fly, straightened his suit, kissed his partner deeply on the mouth, and departed the office, leaving Day in a crumpled heap on the floor, eagerly cleaning his face with his extended tongue like a dog enjoying the remnants of a meal. The screen suddenly flickered, and the date stamp in the lower right corner changed to a week later. A similar scene played again for another twenty-five minutes, followed by another, and another and another taken over the course of several weeks. Tran had seen enough.

Rique and Lockwood stood in silent anticipation as Tran switched off the monitor, each imperceptibly holding their respective breath, waiting for

Tran's reaction. Unfortunately for them, she didn't oblige. With no expression to betray her thoughts, Tran considered the videos. She turned to face her wide-eyed team members, now gawking, about to completely lose their composure.

"Well," she said after a few lingering moments. "This puts a different light on things."

Her muted reaction was more than some on the team could stand. Like an adolescent boy poking fun at a classmate who was a little "different," Kenison had the most difficulty keeping his laughter and a smart-aleck remark bottled inside. A wisp of snicker escaped his tightly held lips.

"What?" Lockwood asked. "You've never seen a couple dudes in the throes of passion?" he joked.

That was all the prompting needed. Kenison let loose the biggest guffaw he'd had in years.

"Ahhh ha, ha, ha, ha," he laughed, doubling over at the waist and slapping the side of his chair. "OH MY GOD, oh my god," he said. "Who'd a thunk an urgent national security investigation would boil down to a couple old fags getting it on in the office?" he asked.

"A little decorum, Agent Kenison," Tran half-seriously chided.

"Sorry, boss. Sorry," he said, laughing heartily. "I know this isn't right, but neither was that," he said, breaking into a second, deep guttural laugh as he pointed at the now dark monitor.

The others in the room laughed too, almost as loudly as Kenison. Tran stood helplessly watching the professionalism of her team fly out the window, and she shook her head side to side as she tried in vain to hide the smile creasing her face. The more she tried, the stronger grew her own compunction to laugh, and despite her efforts to the contrary, she finally let loose a hearty laugh, joining the unprofessional ruckus. She didn't find anything particularly wrong or funny about same-sex passion, but as Kenison pointed out, it was rather funny that an issue as serious as their mission would come down to this. It was also kind of funny that two stuffy executives who seemed to view themselves as holier than The Man Upstairs were actually living this hidden life, so far divergent from everything they appeared and professed to be.

"All right, all right already," Tran said, trying to regain control of herself and her team. "Is that all we have as far as the videos are concerned?"

"No boss," Lockwood answered, intermittently forcing himself to stop laughing. "Both flash drives contain hundreds of files similar to those," he said, pointing at the darkened monitor. "They have date stamps ranging back five years or so, and show more of that...same kind of activity and even more, if you know what I mean."

"I may or may not know what you mean, Agent Lockwood, so to avoid incorrect assumptions and assure we're all on the same page, why don't you just tell us what you mean, tastefully please," Tran said.

"Well," he began, trying to determine the most appropriate manner of phrasing what to say. "The company president and CFO repeatedly sodomize one another, alternately in the CFO's office, the president's office, the boardroom, the conference room, and the executive washroom over an extensive period of time."

"So Ketcham either somehow rigged the place in order to get leverage on her bosses, or she got her hands on video someone else had," Starr summarized.

Tran uncrossed her legs and leaned forward. "I don't know that we have enough to say she did these things *for the purpose of* getting leverage on these men, but we can certainly say she had compelling fodder for extortion," she explained. "Assuming they knew Ketcham had these videos, it might explain why both Day and Johnston seem to have let her get away with anything she wanted."

"It's been my experience that where there's smoke there's fire," Lockwood said.

"Perhaps. This certainly gives someone a motive to kill Ketcham," Tran said. "The killer may have grown tired of being held over a barrel and thus took matters into his own hands."

"But if this is the motive, the killer still wouldn't have had access to the files," Starr observed. "Wouldn't the killer have wanted to get possession of the video files themselves?"

"That would be ideal," Tran agreed, "but a dead woman couldn't release the video to anyone."

"I guess we can rule Day out of this equation," Kenison suggested.

"Under that theory, the president becomes our primary focus," guessed Starr.

"Not necessarily," Lockwood added. "Catin may yet be in play too. Maybe she wanted Ketcham out of the way so she had a clear path to John-Paul Ketcham."

"I don't think we can rule out Lauxner and other Ketcham victims," Starr added.

"Confirmation biases are often the death of accurate, thorough investigations," Tran warned.

Kenison wrinkled his brow, signaling that he didn't understand Tran's remark.

"Confirmation bias," Dr. Starr repeated. "It's a condition in which proponents only find evidence to support a conclusion they've already reached, and everything else is either dismissed as implausible or it's simply not investigated."

"Let's not start focusing-in on specific people quite yet." Tran said, trying to keep a broader perspective on the matter. "Several different scenarios remain viable to explain what happened here, including several that have nothing to do with the matters of interest to us."

"I'm quite sure there's a psychosis at work in this place," Starr said. "Perhaps I'll call it the *ERAC Paradigm* when I publish ground-breaking findings in *The American Journal of Psychology* based on my study of these people."

The team chuckled.

"All right, let's sum up what we know thus far about the ERAC Paradigm," Tran said. "We've got two murdered CFOs, including one who may have killed the other and whose husband was having a secret affair with her best friend and company colleague."

"We know that Ketcham had hired a private investigator to look into her husband's extra-marital activities, and then changed her Will and created a Living Trust that excluded her husband and older son, right after receiving confirmation of the on-going affair between her husband and friend," Starr added.

"A Trust for which the original document is inexplicably missing, I might add," Lockwood supplemented.

"Right," Tran continued. "We have a homosexual affair between the company's former CFO and its president, both of whom were married to extremely competent, beautiful women. That tryst evidently gave rise to extortion of the lover boys by the recently murdered CFO, who retained incontrovertible proof of their activities on flash drives encoded with a sophisticated encryption system used by the Iranian intelligence service, and which were hidden in a floor safe known only to the decedent. We've got an Iranian-born member of the board who was evidently closely involved with the decedent as well as radical elements in the Middle-East."

Lockwood took over the narration. "We know that, through either affirmative consent or dereliction of duty by the CFO, president, and at least one board member, expenses on their NexChem project were being mischarged to a classified UAV contract, with which both the dead lady and the Iranian board member were involved. We know there were communications by that board member with Iranian citizens with close ties to the Iranian government visiting New York just before the murder."

"We know that within twelve months or so of her murder, Ketcham fired two contract administrators who questioned expenses charged to the UAV contract, and at least one of those former employees has the requisite skill to have carried out an assassination and may have even threatened to do so," Kenison offered, feeling like he needed to get into the conversation.

"And don't forget now, that dead lady got connections to some evil racist-terrorists who mighta' kilt her nigga' boss for her," Vivian said from the electronic screen on Tran's desk. "Them people are treacherous cannibals, and even if they previously plotted together, one a' them wouldn't hesitate to eat his own arm if he thought it had given him the fanga'. Wouldn't be surprised if that's who was running away from the scene in their black clothes. Probably put on black face make-up too, to frame a brother up."

Tran laughed lightly at Lawrence's analogy, but it clearly communicated her very valid point. If a domestic terrorist had reason to suspect Ketcham wasn't meeting her end of some nefarious bargain, violently expressing his displeasure wasn't beyond the realm of likely responses.

"Does that sum up what we've learned so far?" Tran asked of her team.

No one objected or supplemented, so Tran took their silence as agreement.

"Okay. As far as murder goes, the evidence is pretty clear that Day's accident was no accident at all. We still need more evidence to point to the killer, but Ketcham probably looks good for that right now. I think we've got enough clear evidence to suspect something is screwy at Earhardt-Roane, but we've got no compelling evidence of a national security threat. Whatever is going on here seems to revolve around Ketcham and Day, with collateral assists from Johnston and Catin. Are we agreed?"

"Yes Boss," the group answered in turn.

"Okay then… We've got more work to do to get to the next stage of this thing," Tran said. "Let me know if anyone sees it differently, but I think we need to check out Ketcham's connections to possible domestic terrorists in her hometown. We're looking for any evidence that she was behind the murder of Erich Day, as Marsha Day suggested. Kenison, I'm giving you the X on that," she said, assigning him the task.

"Got it," he answered. "I'll also run down the lead on Lauxner while I'm at it."

"Very good. We also need to find the private investigator Ketcham used to spy on her husband. He can probably open our eyes on a few things. Dr. Starr, you have the X on this one. He may not be cooperative, so be prepared to encourage his cooperation about what he knows and what he did for Ketcham. Pull his licenses, criminal and civil records, military records—the works."

"I'm on it, Boss."

"Ito, I need you to work your magic to find out everything you can about Ketcham's flash drives, her computer, and the IT folks that worked on it. Given the right opportunity and motivation, these IT folks can be a rich source of information for us."

Ito nodded. "Yes ma'am."

"I'll dig deeper on the UAV contract and Board member Hamidi, and Lockwood, you stay on the murder. We haven't located the murder weapon yet either. We may never find it, especially in a swamp-ridden seaside town like this, but if we do, that may inextricably tie the murderer to the crime."

"Got it."

"Viv, contact whichever Air Force Program Office is running the UAV contracts. They're the government's best experts on whether things are going according to Hoyle on their own contract, so get them to initiate a full audit of the contract. I wouldn't deal with anyone below the rank of Colonel on this. An O-6 will have bark enough to get this done, get it done right, and get it done quickly. If you need to, you can use my name and credentials…"

"No problem, boss lady."

Lawrence smiled her tactful smile that hid the thought coursing through her mind—*oh honey, that boy best not make me repeat myself or **he'll** be the one looking for help…and if he pisses me off, only God can help him.*

Tran didn't think Lawrence would need anyone else's title, credentials or authority to get this or anything else done. The sheer force of her personality and charm would likely be enough to get the job done, but failing that, Lawrence wouldn't be averse to any of several forms of force she might apply. She was quite skilled in that art.

"...and Viv," Tran called. "This might be a long-shot, but see if you can locate the wreckage of a vehicle previously owned by Venita Renley. It might be in an impound lot or salvage yard somewhere, or it may have been destroyed by now...the accident occurred a while ago. If you find it, have the lab compare it with the findings on the Day vehicle."

"A hunch?" she asked.

"A hunch," Tran confirmed. She was quite skilled in that art.

# Chapter 7

## Picking Up Shards

"Excuse me, Agent Allen," a voice called, its owner approaching from the opposite direction in the hall.

The Supervisory Agent of the Seaside FBI office looked up from the papers in his hand, immediately recognizing Kenison as a member of Tran's team and a temporary tenant in his building. He walked the few additional feet to the door of his office, but paused there waiting for Kenison to reach him.

"Who's asking?" Allen said.

"Hi, Sir. I'm Special Agent Stefan—"

"I know who you are," Allen interrupted. "I'm just giving you a hard time." He smiled.

"I was wondering if I might impose on you for a few minutes of your time."

Allen overtly looked to the stack of papers in his hands. "I was just about to get into these budget reports. It's almost time for our fiscal year planning cycle."

"I'll just be a moment. I just need a little background."

"I don't know," Allen answered. "This is pretty important."

The reality was that while Allen really liked being the agent-in-charge of a field office, he had no taste for the paper-pushing that came along with it. He welcomed anything that smelled even a little like official duty that would also take him away from such matters. Kenison's inquiry was a lifesaver, at least for the moment.

"I just wanted to ask you a question, Sir," Kenison said.

"Well congratulations, kid, you've accomplished your goal, now have a great day," Allen said, stepping through the threshold of his office. He was completely deadpan in his manner.

"No, I mean—"

"Yeah, yeah, yeah, kid, I get it," Allen interrupted, this time with a smile. "I'm just giving you a hard time, dude. Come in. What'd you need?" he asked, motioning to a pair of chairs.

"Sir, I was wondering whether you could tell me anything about a hate group headquartered about thirty miles northwest of here?"

"I'm the agent-in-charge. Of course I can tell you about them."

"We have information possibly linking them to part of our national security case."

"Yes, a recent forensics test sent up some red flags at the interagency coordination committee" Allen informed. "I think your boss got a message about it too."

"Yes, Sir. She did. That's in part why I'm here now."

"She send you over here to talk to me?"

"Uh, no, Sir. She tasked me to follow up on a lead involving this group, and I came to you on my own."

"She tell you to tell me that?"

Kenison was a bit confused. "Sir? Uh, no, Sir."

"She ever tell you about me?"

"Sir, I don't think I understand your questions."

"It's simple English, Kenison. You understand English don't you?"

"Of course, Sir. I guess I mean I don't understand why you're asking me these kinds of—" Something occurred to him. "You're giving me a hard time again, aren't you?"

Allen laughed. "Yeah, I guess maybe I am," he said. Allen sat forward in his chair, took off his suit coat, and then leaned backward and removed his shoes. "You don't mind, do you?" he asked, nodding almost imperceptibly at his shoes on the floor. "I hate shoes and I take every opportunity not to wear them. That's one reason I live in Florida."

"I hear you," Kenison agreed.

"Okay, Kenison," Allen said. "First thing is, you can stop with all the *Sir* shit. I appreciate the props, but I don't need the formality. Just call me *Mark*."

"Yes, Sir," Kenison answered.

They smiled at the irony.

"All right, you're talking about the swampland assholes," Allen said. "That's our little term of endearment. They call themselves the Aryan Supremacy Society, and they hole-up on a little piece of reclaimed swampland just outside Rahain, ergo, swampland ASS-holes."

Kenison laughed. This was his kind of humor.

"Tran vouches for you, so I'm gonna' read you in on our operation up there. I'm sure I don't need to tell you to keep this close to the vest. You can share this with your boss and your team, but nobody else. If you do, you'll put my whole operation in jeopardy, and that shit pisses me off."

"Of course, sir…Mark."

"We've had these ASS-holes under watch for a couple years now," Allen explained. "This is an extremely violent, anti-government, hate-based group with tentacles in a lot of illegal activity ranging from drugs, the human trade, auto theft, smuggling, to common petty crimes. I have someone on the inside who feeds me information. My agent is pretty deep in, and these people are a really suspicious crew, so we don't communicate as much as I'd prefer. When I saw the bulletin, I sent him a message asking what he knew about any possible connection to the car collision that killed your Mr. Day."

Allen stood from his chair and walked to his desk, quickly pulling a file from its side drawer before returning to the chairs where Kenison waited. He withdrew a single page of paper from the file, and stared at it for a moment, before resuming his seat. He tossed the page to the younger agent.

"My agent sent this by secure message."

The paper was a printout of the message Allen's agent sent in response to the inquiry. It read:

> *Can't confirm 4 sure but connex is possible. 1 guy out of camp regular 2 C-side. Former US Army 89D…mental an violent; Preaches death to colored, gay, dike, Jew, and especially ragheds. Durl Hasse… Raised in Rahain, family local, including cousin in C-side. Member of Rahain lodge. Has cell and laptop. Was in C-side 1 day before accident. Also in DC and Mississippi few months ago. Will look further and contact w/ more.*

"Who's your guy?" Kenison asked, looking up from the note.

Allen shook his head. "That's need-to-know only. You can trust that he's reliable." Allen opened the file again, and took out two sheets of paper this time. "I pulled the service jacket of this guy he mentions—Durl Hasse." He handed the pages to Kenison.

Stefan examined the Service Record Summary for Private First Class Durl Hasse. The document wasn't a full record on Hasse's time in the Army, but it gave Kenison a picture of the man with whom they were dealing. Hasse was active duty Army in Afghanistan as a member of EOD— Explosive Ordnance Disposal, which was occupational specialty code 89D. As its name implied, EOD units were intended to attack, defeat, and use all manner of ordnance, explosives, and incendiaries, including weapons of mass destruction. Highly trained specialists, EOD troops were considered preeminent experts in all things that go *boom*. Kenison had worked with many EOD troops as an active duty Green Beret, and he knew Hasse, with his three-year deployment to an intense combat zone, was well-trained, and capable of blowing up a vehicle in a way most civilians would never suspect.

Hasse was ultimately court-martialed for murdering sixty-four people, including women, children, and the elderly. Apparently, he'd taken it upon himself to manufacture his own brand of improvised explosive devices, and deploy them in areas frequented by Afghan civilians. He got caught after the fourth explosion because an Afghan boy had seen him planting one of his devices at the scene, and filmed the whole thing on a cell phone taken off a dead American soldier. An outraged crowd of Afghan civilians formed a mob that chased him down, beat him nearly to death, and then held him for American military police. He justified his actions as self-defense because the savage ragheads lived to kill Americans. *We gotta' kill `em all before they kill us*, he'd screamed in court and on footage that played on the evening news. His actions caused international tensions and great headache for US military brass and top diplomats, all the way to the President of the United States, of whom Hasse was no fan. He was dishonorably discharged and imprisoned at Fort Leavenworth for ten years. He received extensive mental health therapy behind bars, but his discharge evaluation suggested he remain in prison because he still displayed homicidal tendencies, especially against people he thought lesser than himself, which happened to be most people in the world.

"This animal should still be caged," Kenison said as he finished the summary.

"The criminal justice system is far from perfect," Allen said. "Guess who the prosecutor on his case was?" he asked, knowing there was no reason why Kenison would know the answer. "You'll never guess in a million years."

Kenison shrugged.

"Then-Lieutenant Colonel Michael Q. Murphy who is now the presiding judge of the Foreign Intelligence Surveillance Court in Washington."

"That's ironic."

"No shit," Allen agreed. He pointed at Hasse's service summary. "As he was carted away to prison, your boy there spewed out a bunch of ugly words at Colonel Murphy, the jury, the judge, and all the witnesses. He said they were anti-American communist traitors who would one day get theirs."

"So why isn't this guy still behind bars?"

Allen shrugged. "He probably could have gotten the chair, but the country has a hard time executing a soldier for acts committed against people who look like the enemy during wartime. His psych-eval indicated severe trauma and war stress, so maybe the court felt it wasn't all his fault, poor guy," Allen said. "Now he's served his time and the system says he's allowed to walk free among the lambs. He got out late last year, about six months before the CFO's accident."

Kenison shook his head. "I'm starting to think it was no accident."

"You might be right," Allen said, "but don't jump to conclusions. Let the facts lead where they may."

"Of course," Kenison agreed. "You sound just like my boss in that regard."

Allen smiled. "Ironic, isn't it?"

Kenison smiled and nodded his agreement. "Know what else is ironic?"

Allen raised an inquisitive brow.

"Hasse," Kenison said. His name is the German word for *hate*."

Allen shook his head in disbelief. "Here," he said. He tossed the entire Durl Hasse file into Kenison's lap. "Keep it if you want. I have it all electronically." He walked back to his desk. "Let me know if you need anything else."

Kenison stood and walked toward the door, stopping long enough to thank the FBI supervisor for his help.

"Anytime," Allen replied. "I'm happy to give Grace's team whatever it needs."

Kenison paused again. "So…"

Allen looked up. "So?"

"So what's the story with you and Agent Tran anyway?" he asked.

Allen smiled. "I'm not sure that's any of your business, Kenison."

The younger man smiled and nodded. "I'm just asking. It's okay if you don't want to talk about it. We all get shot down by a hot chick sometimes," he chided.

Allen frowned as though he wasn't amused, deep wrinkles creasing his forehead. "I guess you thought I really meant all that *informality* shit, huh?"

For a second, Kenison worried he went too far and let himself get too familiar with a senior-ranking agent who could harm his career, and it showed in his expression. Allen was quick to notice, and smiled.

"Relax man. I'm just giving you a hard time," Allen said, laughing at his junior counterpart. "Oh and I'll be sure to let Grace know you think she's hot."

Kenison laughed, then turned and exited Allen's office. As he walked the hall to the other side of the building, his phone spouted the ugly ringtone he'd set to indicate someone not on his *Friends* or *Family* lists was calling. He recognized the incoming number as one he'd called earlier in the day, and correctly figured this was an important call-back.

"Special Agent Kenison. Good afternoon, Mr. Lauxner."

Judging from the pause, he guessed the caller was surprised at the greeting.

"Um, uh, yes sir," the voice replied. "My roommate gave me the card you left here…He says you had some questions for me, sir?"

"That's right, Mr. Lauxner. Thanks for calling back."

"May I ask what this is about, sir?"

"It's about an opportunity to help your country once more," Kenison said, avoiding an explanation for his visit to Lauxner's home. He preferred to be directly in front of the man before giving up the juicy details.

Despite the fact that he'd been earnestly searching, the war hero and father of four had remained unemployed since Ketcham fired him without cause or warning. Kenison's words sounded like a job opportunity, so his ears were piqued.

"Yes, sir. I'm interested," Lauxner said.

"There's a small neighborhood park four blocks from your house—Veteran's Memorial Park—you know it?"

"Yes, sir. I take my boys there all the time," Lauxner replied.

"Great. Meet me there in ten minutes."

"Uh…yes sir, but could we make it in a half-hour maybe…I just got back from the gym and I need to clean up."

"At ease, Lauxner. I'm interested in what you know, not what you're wearing."

"Yes, sir. I'll head there immediately."

Kenison was surprised by how easily he began to slip back into Army mode when talking to Lauxner, whom he nearly called *Sergeant* in their brief conversation. *It was all Lauxner's fault*, he reasoned. Lauxner's distinctly military bearing was pleasantly familiar and comfortable, even on the phone. He wondered whether Lauxner had behaved that way with Ketcham, and how it had gone over. On one hand, it might have been well-received if Lauxner treated Ketcham as a superior officer of integrity and mettle, but it may have gone over like a ton of bricks if the soldier perceived her as unethical, immoral, and subversive to the laws and Constitution he'd taken an oath to support and defend.

Kenison headed toward the parking lot, stopping long enough to peer into Tran's and Lockwood's offices in turn, but neither was there and their lights were dark. He fired off text messages to them to let them know his plans, then hurried to his designated Chrysler fed-mobile outside. A short time later, he pulled up to Veteran's Memorial Park in north Seaside Beach, where Lauxner patiently awaited him at a picnic table under a pavilion near the swing-set.

Lauxner had no idea what Kenison looked like, but his mind held a specific image of how an NSA agent would appear—fit, muscular, suit and tie, military-style hair, and driving a non-descript government vehicle. For the most part, he was right. The car pulled into a spot beneath a very large old-growth oak tree, and Kenison got out. He removed his coat and tie, and tossed them back in the car, then rolled his sleeves tightly up his arms, ignoring the constriction of rolled sleeves on his bulging forearms and biceps—*guns*, as he called them. The Agent reached in the car for a file, then locked the car and walked with purpose to the table. As he approached, Lauxner stood almost at attention, and waited for Kenison to complete the short journey.

"Hello, sir. I'm Stan Lauxner," he said, extending his hand to shake Kenison's.

"Nice to meet you, Mr. Lauxner," Kenison said. "I appreciate you coming out here at the drop of a hat."

"Oh, yes, sir. No problem sir. You mentioned an opportunity to help my country, and I'm all about that, sir. What do you need?"

Kenison motioned to the table. "Can we sit?"

"Yes, sir, by all means," Lauxner answered.

The pair sat down on opposite sides of the table, and Kenison rested his arms conspicuously on the surface. It accomplished his intended purpose.

Lauxner was quick to note the tattoo on Kenison's arm…The arrowhead with a sword and three transecting lightning bolts was unmistakable.

"You were special forces?" Lauxner asked.

Kenison nodded. "Deployed to the desert seventeen times. Got more confirmed kills than I got notches on my belt," Kenison proudly shared.

"Me too, sir," Lauxner admitted.

"Yes, I know, Sergeant. You did good work and you have a fine reputation. If Bruce Diehl speaks highly of you, you're All right with me. We were in Tikrit and Fallujah together twice, and Kandahar, Kabul, and Jalalabad more times than I can remember."

The Special Forces community was small, all things considered. Major Diehl was Staff Sergeant Lauxner's Commanding Officer at the time of the IED attack that killed Lauxner's entire unit and ended his active duty career. The Major had come to see him in the hospital every day for three months until Lauxner was stable enough to return stateside. He helped Lauxner cope with severe survivor's guilt after everyone else in his Humvee—some of the best men Lauxner had ever known—died horrible deaths.

"Yes, sir. Thank you, sir. Major Diehl is one of the best."

"On that, we are agreed, Sergeant," Kenison said. "He was a mentor to me too."

"Yes, sir. Um, sir, if I may ask, you said something about serving my country again?"

"Yes," Kenison acknowledged. "Before we get started, let me remind you that you're still technically a member of the inactive ready reserves, and you still have an active security clearance. That means you can't share anything we talk about with anyone who doesn't also have clearance. You understand that?"

Lauxner nodded.

"All right then, I'm down from DC looking into a national security issue. I think you may be able to help me in my investigation."

"Yes, sir. Whatever you need. If it helps the country, I'm all over it, sir."

"You were recently employed by Earhardt-Roane Avionics, weren't you?"

"Yes, sir, I was."

"What did you do for them?"

"My title was Senior Contract Analyst. More or less, I processed contracts and related documents on whatever was assigned to me."

"Did that include military contracts?"

"Yes, sir. Some but not exclusively. They did a lot of private R&D work too."

"Your supervisor was a woman named Francine Ketcham?"

"Sort of…my immediate boss was a shrew named Diane Muenster—*the monster*, I called her—but Ms. Ketcham was her boss. I heard what happened."

"I think there's more to the story than you know, and it may have something to do with a report you made about dual record books at the company."

"Really? You think someone killed her to cover that up, sir?"

"We haven't reached any conclusions yet," Kenison said. "Let's start with some basic stuff…Where were you the night she was murdered?"

Lauxner was obviously uncomfortable with the question. He squirmed in his seat. "Sir, am I a suspect in her murder?" he asked, incredulously.

Kenison smiled. "Well, until the perpetrator is caught, everybody's a potential suspect, Sergeant, but I have no reason to think you did this. It's just a standard question we ask people even remotely connected to the issue, so we can rule them out."

"Shouldn't you be reading me my rights or something?"

Kenison chuckled. Lauxner was pretty sharp.

"If we were acting in our military capacities, then yes, I'd have to do that as soon as I asked a question the answer to which might incriminate you. As civilians, it's a little different. I only have to read you your rights if you're in custodial interrogation, like, if I arrest you. But I give you my word as an officer and a fellow Green Beret, Sergeant, I don't think you did this. I do think you have information that can help solve this. I also think you and your boys could be at risk because there's evidence that someone involved in this may have tried to kill another person who knew what you reported."

He paused while Lauxner absorbed what he'd said.

"And I give *you my* word, sir, I had nothing to do with the murder of that woman," Lauxner assured. "She was a venomous, disrespectful bitch who didn't have a shred of decency or integrity in her body, but I didn't kill her. I went to war to protect the freedom of all Americans, and that includes bitches like her."

"So you deny telling people that Ketcham would one day find herself in a dark alley with a hole in her head?"

Lauxner lowered his head, clearly wishing he could take back that statement. "No, sir. I said it, but I just meant that if she didn't start treating people with a little decency and respect, someone would teach her a thing or two. But at the end of the day, people like her always get their comeuppance from Someone much greater than me."

"Okay, so where were you the night of her murder?"

Lauxner thought back to when the news said Ketcham had been killed. "I had my boys that weekend, and I took them, my girl, and her kids to the theme parks in Orlando. We left Friday when school got out, got there around dinner time if I recall. We spent the evening at the pool, and went to bed late—like one or two. Next morning, we got up and hit Disney all day."

"Where did you stay?"

"Room 404, Hilton in Disney."

"You got proof of that?"

"Yes, sir, if you need it. I charged it to my credit card."

"Let me show you something," Kenison said.

He pulled out a couple photos of Ketcham's mutilated face and limp pale, bloody body slumped backward in her desk chair, taken only hours after she departed this world. He laid them on the table in front of Lauxner. Kenison didn't really expect from Lauxner the same kind of shock and horror an average person might display, because as Green Berets often see worse carnage than this. Hell, he knew Lauxner had seen far worse the day he survived the Humvee-IED explosion. Still, he wanted to see Lauxner's reaction. He wasn't disappointed. Lauxner leaned forward and began examining the photos closely, more from a clinical or evidentiary perspective than anything else.

"Hmm, judging from these cuts on her body, the killer used a small double-edged serrated knife," he said, pointing at the pictures, "probably four to six inches long. This is a very unusual blade on this thing. It ain't the blade of professional assassin, least not one who doesn't want to be caught. Could belong to a serial killer who likes taunting the cops, but my guess is this belongs to a collector or a sportsman. You might do okay to check at the knife and gun shops around here, maybe a pawn shop. And the wounds on her face suggest she was hit repeatedly with something that's not sharp, maybe rounded or flat on the end. I don't see any entry wounds in these photos, so I'm guessing firearms weren't used."

He leaned in to stare at the pictures more closely.

"Whoever did this wasn't a professional. All the damage to her face and the extra cuts to the body is gratuitous. None of it was necessary to kill her, so my guess is somebody worked out some anger issues on her face. A professional would've done the job with a single well-placed small caliber shot to the head, center mass in front or back, if he used a weapon at all, and you wouldn't recover any casings. A professional might have killed her with his bare hands. Ketcham was a bitch but she was mostly bark; any bite she had was in her power to fuck with your job, not fuck you up physically. She wouldn't have been a challenge for a normal-sized man alone in the room with her. If I were gonna' kill her, I would've used my gloved hands and would've simply choked her to death. Stun her with a quick lunge and punch to her nose, eyes, or ears, and then quietly strangle her life away...Less equipment to carry, less noise, less blood to get all over you, less chance of leaving something behind that connects you to the crime. Nope, you're not looking for a pro here, but an amateur who's probably a weak, small-framed man or a woman."

"So you had nothing to do with this?" Kenison asked.

Lauxner was visibly irritated that he'd been asked that question again, and by a fellow soldier no less. "I gave you my word, sir, but if that's not good enough, you can check with my girlfriend and our kids. They'll tell you," he barked.

For an enduring moment, Kenison looked at Lauxner's face and then stared deep into his eyes and through to his soul. He saw a sincere patriot doing his best to make it in a society that seemed to have forgotten its veterans, to be a good father to his sons, and to be a contributor to the good of the nation. He saw a man repeatedly decorated for acts of valor in the face of likely death, who put the lives of others ahead of his own many times before, and who'd taken rounds to spare the lives of people he didn't even know. This wasn't someone who'd be moved to murder by the pettiness of a mean, power-hungry pretender. Kenison couldn't explain his gift for accurately sizing people up, but he was certain Lauxner was telling him the truth. It wasn't evidence, but it was enough to make him look elsewhere for Ketcham's killer.

"No need, Sergeant. I believe you completely. I had to get that out of the way, and now that I have, why don't you tell me about a report you made about these two sets of accounting records the company kept on its Air Force contracts."

"All right, sir. If you think it will help. Here's what went down..."

\* \* \*

Rique Ito stepped into a shabby suite in a long-forgotten strip mall and immediately surveyed the place. The pungent odor of dingy, mid-80's carpet and stale, exposed beer, together with the powerful aroma of a rank stogie immediately assaulted his nostrils as he entered the *Data Dump Computer Service*. Ito pressed through a heavy white cloud of billowing cigar smoke, and made his way to the service counter just inside the door. Some distance behind the counter, Ito saw an acne-faced man probably in his mid-30's crumpled into a rickety old chair, his right leg hanging over the armrest. He was consumed by a first-person shooter game that emitted a bevy of ear-piercing gunshots, explosions, and computer-generated death cries from a massive television screen. The disheveled technician wore dirty, haphazardly torn baggy jeans that would have sagged below his butt had he been standing, but the lanky, pale man remained seated, entranced by his mission. With a thick shock of unwashed, matted hair covering much of his face, the man barely looked at Ito, and said even less before returning his attention to the game. Ito tossed an old laptop roughly onto the counter.

"Hey man, I'm looking for some help with this hunk of shit," he said.

For a split-second, the computer tech moved an eye in Ito's direction, and then quickly returned his gaze to the battle. He wanted to assure the enemy didn't outmaneuver him while he was fooling around with the dweeb at the counter.

"Just buy a new one. That thing's a piece of shit," the guy muttered, already re-immersing himself in his game.

"Yeah, *I* told *you* it was a piece of shit," Ito said. "I need you to make it work, man."

Still consumed by his game, the technician defiantly rebuffed Ito. "Yeah, and I told *you* I can't help you with it, man."

"Come on, dude. Just take a look for me," Ito pleaded.

There was no response from the tech, and Ito felt himself growing annoyed.

"Is there a manager I can talk to?" he asked.

Again, there was no response.

"Dude, come on," he pleaded. "I want to talk to your manager."

"I don't know," the tech answered, sarcastically. "We're pretty busy today. Take a number. We'll call you in the order you came in."

Ito looked around the empty room. A number dispenser beamed from the right side of the service counter. The next available number was one-hundred, and the indicator showed they were *Now Serving* customer number two.

"You have the worst customer service I've ever seen," Ito objected.

"File a complaint if you want," the tech said, bobbing his head at the complaint box on the left side of the counter.

Ito looked. The Complaint Box was an inert hand grenade mounted to a wooden box. The "complaint form" was attached to the grenade's pin, and emblazoned at the top of the display were the instructions: *Pull for complaint form. You will have three seconds to complete your form.* Ito wasn't amused.

"Look, I'm just trying to get a little help here. Shall I take my business elsewhere?"

The technician ignored him yet again, preferring instead to fight on in the game.

Ito stormed around the service counter and walked to the wall behind the television screen. In a flash, he grabbed the ends of every electrical cord plugged into the receptacle nearest him and yanked them all out of the wall. The game console, the television, and the surround sound system all fell silent and dark in an instant, thus terminating the technician's quest.

"Mission complete," Ito yelled.

"Oh man, you asshole," the technician yelled, exploding from his seat. "I was just about to conquer level 98. I've worked for weeks to get here and you just screwed me over. Asshole, mother fucker."

The angry technician slowly closed the distance between him and Ito, and began expressing his outrage by jabbing Ito in the chest while berating and insulting him.

"You are such a fuck-ing prick. I can't believe you did that, you ass-wipe. You stupid pussy."

"Now, does it even begin to make sense that I'm a prick and a pussy at the same time?" Ito asked, backing away from the technician's assault. "The probability that someone is born a true hermaphrodite is roughly .0005%, you know."

"You dumb mother fuc—"

"And the human genitalia aren't classified as intelligent life forms in and of themselves, and thus lack the capacity to be intelligent or stupid. There's a saying that we guys sometimes think with the wrong head but—"

The continual jabbing was getting harder now, and it was starting to hurt. Besides, Ito could see he'd soon run out of space to retreat into.

"Please stop that," he asked. "Ok, maybe I shouldn't have unplugged your game. I don't think it would look too good for you to assault one of your customers. Your manager probably wouldn't like that too much."

"You stupid shit. I AM the manager, and the CEO, and the owner, which means I'm your judge, jury, and executioner," the angry tech said.

"Oh, okay," Ito said. "Well I'm afraid I must still insist that you stop poking me. It's starting to hurt, sir."

"You dumb chink-bastard, you ruined my game."

Chink bastard? Ito had had enough. He understood the guy might be upset about his game, but the racial epithets and physical violence was far over the line. Ito had asked nicely to no avail, and now.

In one smooth motion, he snatched the laptop from the service counter and turned it lengthwise. Holding it firmly with both hands, he quickly but forcefully jammed its broad flat side into his assailant's face. The stiff bash across his nose left the technician momentarily dazed, which was more than enough time for Ito to step forward and bring his right elbow forcefully to the technician's chest. The power of Ito's small but toned body flowed up from his legs, through his torso and cocked arm, and then dispersed into the tech's mid-section, instantly launching him backward into the air. He landed with a thud several feet away, atop the robot-thing and knocking computers, spare parts, and peripherals to the ground. Ito leapt across the distance, reached down and grabbed the stunned man by his shirt collar, instantly raising him into the air and turning his body 180 degrees in the opposite direction. He backed the man toward the shop door until his flaccid body leaned over the service counter. Invading his personal space, Ito spoke slowly and deliberately so the technician would understand every word he uttered.

"You just assaulted a federal agent on official duty, man. You'll be going to a very nasty government hotel for the next ten to twenty years unless you start showing a little cooperation, you stupid shit."

He brandished his credentials briefly, and then put them away as he patted his quarry for weapons.

"Anyone else here?" he asked.

The technician shook his head and muttered a muted "no."

"Then I presume you're Randy Wright, proprietor of this fine establishment?"

The man nodded affirmatively.

"Okay, Mr. Wright. I'm gonna' let you up now, but don't make any sudden moves or do anything else stupid. I'm packing heat and I'm an expert marksman. I'll drop you before you ever have a chance to finish the thought running through your feeble brain."

Wright nodded to indicate his understanding and assent. Ito slowly released his grip, and then back-stepped until he was out of Wright's arm's reach.

"I'm, I'm sorry, man," Wright said, wiping the blood from his nostril. "I didn't know you were a cop..."

"Me either," Ito said. "I'm actually something worse. I'm an IT tech, like you. The difference is I have a badge and gun issued by the NSA."

"Well shit man, if you're an IT guy, why the hell don't you fix that piece of crap yourself? Wright asked.

"Primarily because I don't really give a crap about that hunk of junk," Ito said. "What I really want from you is information, and now that I have something to hold over your head, you're gonna' give it to me freely or your life as you know it will be over."

"You didn't have to kick my ass, man," Wright complained. "What the hell do you want to know anyway?"

Ito raised the laptop with which he'd clobbered Wright's face, and then placed it gently on the service counter beside Wright. He carefully observed the technician's face, at once noting the look of recognition.

"You know what this is?" Ito asked.

"Yeah, I built it," Wright acknowledged.

"Tell me about it."

"What's to tell? I built it for this high-brow bitch over at Roane."

"Yeah? Well that high-brow bitch was murdered, and your computer might be part of it."

"I don't know nothing about that, man. Honest."

"Yeah, I'm sure. Look, we're not looking at you as a suspect in anything here, Randy," Ito assured. "We're concerned that whoever killed her is worried about what's on that computer, and everyone knows you were the only person she let touch this computer. They may come after you and do to you what they did to her. If you want my help in keeping you on *this* side of the grass, you better start talking dude."

"Anything, anything. Just tell me what you want to know. I got nuthin' to hide."

"Okay," Ito said. "Let's begin with why you worked on Ketcham's computers."

"Yeah, man. Yeah, I can tell you that, uh, she came to me a few years back, flashing around a lot of money. This private-I guy I know around town brought her in here a few years ago."

"Does he have a name?"

"Yeah, his name is James Kerr, but he goes by "Slim Jim." He's a local badass around here who used to be into all kinds of shit when he was younger."

"Like what?" Ito pressed.

"Various business enterprises you don't want to piss off, if you know what I mean."

"How about you spell it out for me, man?"

"You know, people, powder, guns, coercion, stuff obtained through five-finger discount—that stuff. Now he's turned legit. He just does his private-I shit."

"And you knew him how?"

"First met him years ago when he got locked up in the county pen for roughing up some dude. It just so happened to be the same time I was there for DWW—driving while wasted, you know," he said, snickering at his attempted humor. "I spent a very uncomfortable night in a small cell with that giant dude. He came to me years later with that Ketcham lady, asking me to do some computer work for them."

"And I take it you did?"

"Look at me," Wright pleaded. "I'm a little dude with no back-up, you know. Kerr's a big burly dude with a bad temper. He says he's all legitimate now, but he's got a nasty past, and I'm not one to believe a leopard can truly change its spots, you know. Anyway, he wasn't asking me for anything illegal so he subcontracted me to help him diversify his services, so to speak."

"Okay, and what kind of computer work did they want you to do?" Ito pressed.

"She wanted me to create video surveillance systems for her computer and a couple remote devices she could put in someone's room so she could watch what went on when she wasn't around, you know."

"Did you?"

"Hell yeah. I figured she wanted to spy on her kid, babysitter, or maybe see if her husband was looking at internet porn or something like that, but what the hell, didn't bother me none. Besides, she was offering a lot of money to do some pretty easy shit. She told me if I worked for her and remained absolutely loyal, she'd take really good care of me. Plus, I could continue working my own business. She promised to help me out there as well. But, she also said if I ever told anyone about anything she asked me to do, I'd be a dead man."

"You believed her?"

Wright grinned. "She's rich and snooty and she had Kerr as her dog. I wasn't going to take a chance on not believing her. Hell man, she owns this whole damn strip mall," he said, motioning all around him. "I haven't paid one cent in rent since I started doing her work."

Some of Wright's information would be easy enough to check out, so Ito didn't press him on those issues.

"Did she ever ask you to do anything else for her?"

Wright thought for a moment. "Yeah, early on, she asked me to put some additional security measures on her personal computer, and also make sure some security software already on her computer was invisible from the root directory. She also wanted me to be on stand-by if her computers needed maintenance or had problems talking to the computers at that big company she worked for."

"Didn't you find it odd that she'd ask you to fix issues between her computer and the network at her office? I mean, Roane is a huge corporation with a huge IT department full of really smart, highly educated highly computer techs for that sort of thing," Ito pressed.

He could see Wright was a little insulted. Wright didn't have an advanced technology degree from any institution, much less an Ivy League school, but he'd been well-educated in the school of hard knocks. He said he could do anything with computers from hacking to software design to building systems and running sophisticated networks, anything really. He passionately argued that dumb Ivy league IT ass-wipes were no better than a skilled IT artist who knew what the hell he was doing, only the latter didn't waste $400,000 to get a piece of paper that told them so. Ito enjoyed pushing Wright's buttons, but knew it was an unproductive use of time that didn't advance his purpose. So, he redirected Wright to the subject at hand.

"No offense, man," Ito said, "but if they had a stable of smart guys with fancy IT degrees to do precisely this kind of thing, didn't you wonder why you'd be asked to do it?"

Wright shrugged his shoulders. "I just figured she wanted to make sure no one ever saw what she had on her computer. Rich people can be pretty paranoid, you know."

"Did she have reason to be?"

"What do you mean?"

"Did you find evidence that anyone was hacking her computer or stealing information from her?"

"You kiddin' me? I designed a security system for her that was so good, nobody could get past it. And let me tell you, what I designed is a thousand light-years beyond that secure encryption shit on her computer."

"You mean the security software already on her computer when she brought it to you?"

"Yeah, man. The stuff she wanted me to make invisible."

Ito knew Wright's type very well. In addition to his past issues with DWW, Wright had had a little trouble with federal authorities. As a kid, he'd unsuccessfully tried to hack into Pentagon computers after watching a movie about a kid his same age who did so in order to play a war game. Ito knew of the movie that had inspired Wright, but wondered why Wright, even as a stupid, adolescent punk, would have been inspired by it. The kid in the movie nearly started a thermo-nuclear war between the two biggest superpowers in the world at that time. Ito guessed he'd answered his own question—because Wright was a stupid, adolescent punk. But Ito was a techie himself, and like Wright himself had said, leopards didn't usually change their spots. When someone tells a techie something he didn't design was impenetrable, it's like waving a red flag in a bull's face. Ito would feel drawn to beat it, and he suspected Wright did too.

"So, did you break it—her impenetrable security software?"

Wright's face crinkled and he stammered as he denied the question. Ito broached the subject in six different ways and each time Wright pretended he'd not done what Ito was certain he did. Maybe Wright failed to actually breach the security algorithm but Ito was beyond all doubt he tried. Under relentless hounding, Wright eventually started to crack.

"Even a no-good, talentless IT artist would try to hack an impenetrable security lock on something over which he had complete control and unlimited time."

"Why, why would I do that?" Wright asked. "It wasn't none of my business. Long as I was gettin' paid, I didn't really give a crap what was on her computer."

"Right," Ito sarcastically goaded. "Then admit it, dude. You were incapable of breaking the security."

"I didn't try. Like I said, it wasn't any of my business."

Ito smiled and then laughed. "It's okay, man. I did it, but very few people are as good as I am."

"You broke the encryption?" Wright asked.

"Both yours and the other, but what do I know? I'm just a dumb Ivy-league ass-wipe." He laughed at Wright. "I guess the fancy degree makes a difference after all."

"Bullshit." Wright objected, exploding from his seat. "I got into it too, probably quicker than you did."

"Ah," Ito said, almost melodically. "So you did try to penetrate her secure software?"

"*Try* my ass," Wright yelled. "I got through that bitch in record time."

"So what was she trying to protect?"

Wright smiled and laughed aloud, but he didn't answer the question.

"Ms. Ketcham's killer most certainly knows you've had access to her computer and all its files. Maybe he'll pay you a visit too," Ito pressed. "Too bad you won't have anybody to keep the boogey man away."

Wright contemplated the situation. He really didn't care about what Ketcham was trying to hide, and she was dead. She couldn't do shit to him anymore, he reasoned. And the little Asian dude made a strong point. The killer could come after him. He chuckled once more.

"Aren't you supposed to offer me witness protection or something like that?" he asked.

"Depends," Ito answered.

"On what?"

"On what you have to tell and how much you cooperate, among other things." Ito waited a few seconds. Then, he heightened the incentive. "One thing's for sure: if you don't answer my questions, you won't get shit from us except a pair of tight silver bracelets and some time in a maximum security federal hotel."

Wright squirmed at the thought.

"The woman was a freak, okay," he finally said. "She had a butt-load of video files of two old dudes doing all kinds of nasty sex shit to each other, and…"

"And what?"

"And a bunch of files with dates and numbers."

"Dates and numbers of what?"

"Hellifiknow," Wright said, making one word of four.

"You're so full of crap your eyes are turning brown. You know more than what you're telling me, Wright, and that makes you more than a target. It makes you an accessory to murder," Ito said, bullshitting the frightened witness.

"I don't know anything else."

"Liar."

"I'm telling you man, I don't know anything."

"I'm done wasting time with you, asshole. Stand up and turn around," Ito ordered, reaching for a pair of zip cuffs in his pocket, thus exposing his weapon.

"All right, all right," the man screamed. "The only other thing I know is some saved emails."

"Emails about what? From whom to whom?"

"There are emails to and from some dude named Erich Day, "Slim Jim" Kerr, and some guy called…Hassel or something like that. The scariest ones were between Ketcham and Donald Johnston and Iriyana Hamidi."

"And why are those so scary?"

Wright was sweating bullets. He wiped his brow and sighed deeply. "Oh man, I really, really, really don't want to get in the middle of this, whatever it is. I don't know who the hell most of those people are, but I know Johnston and Hamidi. They're two of the biggest names around here. They got more money than God but they ain't as forgiving, especially if you sin against them. Crushing peons is sport to them, and I'm even less than a peon. I'm like a crap-on, a gnat on their show-dogs' asses. I cross them and I'm in real trouble."

"You should be more worried about crossing me right now," Ito said. "Tell me about the emails."

"I don't know. It was like Ketcham put them all in one place for safekeeping. They talked about all kinds of stuff. The ones between Ketcham, Johnston, Day, and Hamidi dealt mostly with money, a couple talked about some collectible porcelain one of them gave another of them, and some dealt with contracts. The other ones, I'm not really sure but I know one told the Hassel dude where he could pick up money after he completed something she wanted done."

"What?"

"The job?" he asked. "I don't know what it was. Apparently, they'd talked about it face-to-face at some point, and the email was just a follow-up. She specifically told him not to mention the job in any further emails or other kind of written means, and told him to burn his computer. She said she'd get him a new one."

"Why does that email stand out for you?"

He looked a bit sheepish as he answered the question, clearly ashamed to voice his thinking. "I, I was thinking about getting there first to lift the money before the guy got it."

"And did you?"

"Hell no. The money was gonna' be put in some out-of-the-way tree up in the damn swamps north of here. I hate that place. The little town near there is home to some real rough dudes that don't like outsiders very much. I ain't anything other than pure white, but I don't think those guys would like a geek as weird as me anymore than they'd like a black, brown, yellow or red guy or a Jew or a fag. They're equal opportunity haters, you might say. They'd just as soon skin you as look at you. Every time I go up that way, I hear dueling banjos in the back of my mind, so I generally try to stay away from there."

Even Ito thought that was funny. The reference to a scene from the movie *Deliverance* made most every man cringe and clearly conveyed the depth of his concern for his physical safety in that neck of the woods, or more accurately, swamp. Nonetheless, Ito stifled his laugh and masked the humor he found in the description.

"I have her computer. What's the file name? I'll look at it myself."

"You can't. It's not on her computer anymore."

"What are you babbling about?" Ito asked.

"She deleted them from the computer before the last time I worked on her computer. I looked for them but didn't see them no more. Then she asked me to wipe her hard drive."

"Did you?"

"She paid me, didn't she?"

He paused for a moment as he obviously contemplated whether to say anything more. Ito sat in silence as he observed Wright for a few minutes. Then, finally, Wright spoke.

"I copied everything on her computer to a few disks. I still have them."

"Did you know?" Ito said, not truly surprised. "Why and where are the copies?"

"If there's one thing I learned from that conniving bitch, it's that sometimes you have to be a sneaky bastard when you're dealing with a conniving bitch. I made the copies in case she ever turned on me. Then I'd have something to hold over her head. Didn't figure any of it would get me killed—must be something there I don't know I have."

"Yes, must be." Ito stood. "Mr. Wright, you've been very helpful today. If you'll go and get me those disks, I think I'll have what I need for the time being."

"Oh, sure," Wright said, motioning toward the back of the shop and tacitly asking permission to go in that direction.

Ito nodded his approval, and Wright gingerly maneuvered his way around him, rushing to a small cluttered office in the back of the cluttered shop. As he went, Ito unsnapped the loop on the holster holding the Glock in the small of his back and then smoothly took the weapon's safety off, all the while keeping a close eye on Wright. Once he reached the messy office, Wright began sifting through volumes of junk stuffed into ratty sticking drawers on a natty old metal desk.

Watching him through the glass partition separating the office from the rest of the shop, Ito spoke out loud enough that Wright could hear him from the front of the store.

"Don't leave town without notifying me first okay? I'll leave you my card if you need to reach me. If anyone comes around asking questions about Ketcham or her computer, tell them nothing and call me right away. You got that?"

Wright returned to the front of the store where Ito was waiting and nodded his understanding. He handed over four flash drives that supposedly contained copies of everything that had been on Ketcham's laptop since Wright began working for her.

"One last thing before I go," Ito said. "You ever hear about any lawyer she saw or hired?"

Wright thought for a moment. "No. Never saw anything on her computers and never heard her say anything about a lawyer. Sorry."

Ito nodded. "All right. If you think of anything else or if you need anything, give me a call at that number," he said, motioning to his card.

Will do, sir. Thank you," Wright said, happy he wasn't being carted out in cuffs.

Ito backed out of the store, ready to draw the moment he sensed anything wrong. Fortunately, that didn't happen. Sitting comfortable in the driver's seat of the late-model Crown Victoria, he felt satisfied, and a bit eager to see what was on this second set of Ketcham flash drives. If it's what

Wright had promised, he'd have solid evidence to advance the team's mission. He sent out a few text messages to his teammates.

\* \* \*

James "Slim Jim" Kerr walked into the door of the Seashell Café, paused long enough to shove a wad of beef jerky into his mouth, and then pulled roughly on the worn brass handle to open the heavy glass door. He stepped up from the sidewalk into the restaurant, and immediately began searching for the woman he was there to meet. The establishment's morning rush usually ended by 5 a.m. when the fishermen and tour captains went out to their boats, so there weren't many people in the place by ten. Besides, he figured a guy who got paid to find things others might prefer he not know shouldn't have any trouble spotting a lady tourist who sounded on the phone like big northern money in fine Parisian garb.

The moment his eyes adjusted to the restaurant's lesser indoor light, he saw Mrs. Starr sitting in a booth facing the door about twenty feet away. She looked to be reading messages on her phone or perhaps playing a game of some sort as she awaited him. There were five other people in the place, but they sat at three different locations, one at the counter and four others at two tables in the rear, near the restrooms. His potential new client was a tall, thin white woman whom he figured to be in her late thirties or early forties. Her high-style garb, meticulously made-up but otherwise pale skin, and general bearing suggested she lived a pampered indoor life, probably as the wife of some highfalutin Ivy-league corporate type who was down here cheating with his secretary, Kerr guessed. She seemed prim and proper, and very retiring in nature—the type who'd be a good socialite for fundraisers, tea parties, and nights at the opera, the type a thrill-hunting husband facing the reality of his lost youth would have no trouble foolin' around on.

Agent Starr saw Kerr long before he entered the café. She recognized his rusted brown 1980 Pontiac Grand Prix when he parked it across the street, and got out to wobble over to the café. Standing about 6'5" and weighing roughly four-hundred pounds, Kerr was hard to miss, in a crowd or otherwise. Starr found it more than a little funny that a man as large and rotund as he would sport a nickname suggesting thinness, but she guessed his associates might have given him out of ironic humor. But, as she poked around for information to build a profile on him, she learned he'd gotten the name from the fact that he habitually consumed beef jerky treats like some

166

people chain-smoked. She glanced once more at his picture, scanned through the historical summary about him, returned his dossier to the leather bag on the seat beside her, and then patiently awaited his arrival. She locked eyes with him as soon as he entered, watching his face for any sign he was looking for someone. He gave it as he walked directly toward her.

"You must be Mr. Kerr," she said as she stood, displayed a polite smile, and extended her delicate hand.

He gulped down the remains of the jerky in his mouth and extended his hand. "Yeah dat's me," he said, grasping her hand as firmly as he would any man on the street.

"Thank you so much for meeting me," Starr said.

"Don't thank me yet, lady. You ain't heard my fee yet. I ain't cheap and I don't make no promises 'cept do my best to find whoever it is you're lookin' for."

"That's quite fine, Mr. Kerr," Starr replied. "Please sit down. May I buy you a cup of coffee?"

Starr neatly pressed her skirt against her leg to avoid wrinkling it as she gently resumed her seat and waited for her guest to situate himself.

"If you say so, lady," Kerr said.

The private investigator unceremoniously plopped into the booth, his round belly barely fitting into the space between the Formica table and the vinyl seat back. He pushed at the table's edge, but it didn't budge—he'd just have to deal with the tight fit. He usually ate at the counter when he came to the Seashell, so this was a bit different for him. That was okay though, because the nature of a first meeting with a new client sometimes required more privacy than the counter could offer. Besides what he'd already noted in their initial phone call ninety minutes earlier, he really didn't have much more to say. A sit-down really wasn't necessary, but the chance for a free breakfast was too much to resist, especially when a hot broad was paying.

A gaunt, well-worn waitress approached the table, smiling widely as she came. Her nametag read, *Bitsy*.

"Mornin' huns," she greeted in a long, drawn-out, high-pitched tone. "Can I get da' two a yoots sump'in da' drank?"

"Miss, I'll have decaffeinated black coffee please," Starr answered. She pointed to her guest. "Mr. Kerr?"

"Yeah, I'll have that too, 'cept I'll have mine leaded, wit cream an' sugar, an' two flapjacks, the steak an' cheese omelet, white toast with butta an' jelly, some grits wit butta an' a touch a maple syrup, an' a cheese Danish...oh, an' bring me a coke with breakfast," he said. "Better make it a diet coke—I gotta' cut down a little."

Both the waitress and Starr looked at Kerr, hunting for signs he was joking, but they found none. The two women shared a telling glance and smile, tacitly communicating with one another as only daughters of Eve could.

"Yeeah, whateva floats yer boat, hun," Bitsy finally answered.

She grinned, turned, and walked quickly from the table. Absent even a hint of tact, Kerr leaned into the aisle to ogle her backside as she waltzed toward the swinging door separating the kitchen from the dining room.

"Mmm, mmm, good," Kerr exclaimed, devoid of all couth and any regard for the woman across the table from him. "All right, lady. Here's the deal: I can find whoever it is you're looking for, even if he don't wanna' be found. But as I said, I ain't cheap. I charge $800 a day plus expenses, includin' gas, mileage, meals, cell, faxes, and hotel, and I'll need a $5,600 retainer up front before I even lift a finger."

"That's fine, Mr. Kerr," Starr answered.

Not realizing his voice betrayed his surprise, Kerr repeated her words. "It's fine?"

"Yes, Mr. Kerr. I'm not deterred by your fee."

Quite satisfied and perhaps a bit smug, Kerr relaxed into the seat. "Okay then...You said on da' phone you wanted me ta' find somebody for ya?"

"Yes precisely. We've had no contact in weeks and law enforcement...well, let's just say the police have a lot of priorities other than mine."

"Figures," Kerr said. "Them guys are a bunch of regimented asshole losers that can't think outside da box if their life depended on it," he said. "Dat's why I do what I do, ta really help good folks like you wit da problems da cops just can't handle, you know."

Kerr's comments masked the fact that he'd attempted several times to join the ranks of various law enforcement agencies in his forty-eight years on Earth, but each time had been rejected as *UNFIT, DISQUALIFIED,* or *SUBSTANDARD.* He'd not been a successful law enforcement officer who retired and decided to enter the private-eye business where he could pick and choose his cases, and charge fees that reflected the value he brought. Instead, becoming a private detective was the path of least resistance that got him the right to carry a gun and badge—it was as close to being a police officer as he could get. The prerequisites for a PI license and a concealed weapons permit were minimal, and the costs of this credibility were pretty cheap, all things considered. Besides, people who hired him merely from the *Private Detective* sign on his door would know nothing of his background.

"I'm so glad," Starr replied. "I'm not sure what I'd do without your help…"

"All right, you got his cell number?"

"I beg your pardon?" Starr asked. "Do you plan to simply call and just ask where the person is?"

"No, Miss Smartie-pants," Kerr barked. "Wit his cell numba, I can get his call and text records from the carriya—that's usually a good place ta start 'cause it gives me his last locations before he disappeared and tells me who he's been associatin' wit."

"Mobile carriers don't give that information to just anybody who asks," Starr challenged. "You must either be a law enforcement officer or have a court order to get their cooperation."

"Everybody's an expert," Kerr objected. "Amma' professional at dis, ya' know. I been doin' this for ye'ahs. If I go there and flash my private-eye badge real quick, an' just act like a cop, they don't tend ta challenge the 'sumption. They give me whateva I ask for. I'll get the records, don't you worry none."

"And how do you proceed if people don't cooperate with you, Mr. Kerr?" she asked.

He looked at her to assess why she was asking. Perhaps she wasn't sure he could handle the job. Or, perhaps a woman like that, married to a man who'd cheat on her probably wanted confidence and strength in her white knight, so Kerr resolved to give it to her.

"Don't you worry your pretty little head, sweetheart. I been known to do a little physical persuasion of witnesses if I have to," he said, balling his right fist and solidly punching his left palm to mimic striking someone's face.

Starr shook her head and yielded a very slight smile. "Okay, I'll trust you," she said, taking her checkbook from her bag. "Do you need anything else from me?"

"Yeah, a photo of the person you want me to find, and where was the last place you saw him? I also want to see his room or office, and look at his recent mail, all his latest phone bills… That's enough to me started."

"Okay," Starr replied, opening her bag.

She withdrew a large tattered brown envelop into which were stuffed more papers than it could reasonably hold. She carefully flipped through its contents and hunted meticulously for the most appropriate photograph for her purposes at the moment. Finally, she selected one and gingerly placed it on the table. Kerr's expression showed his familiarity with the subject.

"Who, who is this?" Kerr asked, after several long glances between the face on the photo and Starr. He withdrew a package of beef jerky from his breast pocket and began chewing feverishly.

"You know who this is, Mr. Kerr," Starr said.

"I never seen this woman before," Kerr resisted.

"Are you telling me you don't know her?"

"No I don't know her," Kerr insisted.

Starr withdrew a photograph of Erich Day from her bag and placed it on the table beside Ketcham's.

"How about this man? Do you know him?" Starr asked.

"Never seen him before in my life," Kerr replied.

"Are you sure you don't know them?"

"I'm sure. Who did you say they were?"

"*Were?*" Starr asked? "Interesting you would use a past-tense term for these people."

"So what?"

"The *so what* is this: both of these folks were murdered recently. It's curious you would use the term *were* for them and not *are*—it's almost like you knew they were dead, but that's not possible because you said you didn't know them."

"I didn't catch who you said they are, or were," Kerr repeated.

"That's because I didn't say, Mr. Kerr, but I believe you already know who they were," Starr said. "After all, the woman was your client."

There was a notable shift in Kerr's demeanor and in his perception of Starr.

"What are you talking about?" he asked, clearly agitated.

"I'm talking about Francine Ketcham. She hired you to follow her husband."

"That's privileged client information, lady. And who the hell are you to be askin' anyways?"

Kerr intended to get up from the table and indignantly slam his napkin to the ground, but he was too tightly wedged into his seat to stand, indignantly or otherwise. Starr simply observed him as he struggled.

"So you do know her?" Starr pressed.

"I didn't say that."

"Sure you did, Mr. Kerr. You indicated you couldn't tell me about your work on her behalf because it's privileged client information. If she wasn't your client, you could tell me about your interactions with her, but if she's your client, you'd be prohibited from doing so, isn't that right?"

"Whateva. I'm outta' here, lady."

"Mr. Kerr, I think you should remain seated and simply tell me about Ms. Ketcham," Starr invited.

"You got a load a shit between your ears, lady? I told you it was confidential information."

"So you did. Let me ask you another question...Would it still be confidential for $500,000?"

That commanded Kerr's attention. He stopped trying to un-wedge himself and relaxed back into the seat, staring dead pan at Starr.

"You serious?" he asked.

"I have a major interest in this," Starr said.

"Yeah? So what's your interest in this and what exactly is *this*?" Kerr pressed.

"Why don't we start with what you know about her," Starr said.

"I'll tell you what I know if we're still talkin' about the 500 G's you was offerin'," Kerr agreed.

"I'm so sorry," Starr said. "Perhaps I was a bit too exuberant when I said $500,000...How about you just tell me what you know in exchange for this breakfast I'm buying you?"

At that point, Bitsy returned to the table carrying a tray with the several platters of food Kerr ordered, plus two cups of coffee and a diet coke. The pair fell silent as the waitress organized Kerr's meal in a semi-circle around him, and served up Starr's coffee.

"Can I get the two a' yoots anythin' else?" she asked, smiling widely.

"Naw" Kerr said.

"No thank you, Miss. We're just fine for now," Starr replied.

They waited for Bitsy to withdraw and then Starr re-asked her question.

"You were about to tell me what you know of Ms. Ketcham," she prompted.

"No I wasn't," Kerr objected. "We was about to discuss the 500 G's you're payin' me, *that's* what we was discussin'."

"My bad. I thought we dispensed with that idea," Starr said. "I'm not paying you $500,000 for the information. I just want you to tell me what you know about her to help me out here."

"And people in hell want ice water. Doesn't mean they're gonna' get it."

"What will it take to gain your kind cooperation, Mr. Kerr?"

"Five-hundred G's."

"I'm sorry but that's just not going to happen."

"All right then, a hundred G's."

"That's not happening either," Starr insisted. She shook her head and sighed deeply. "Perhaps I'm approaching this in the wrong way," she said, really to herself. "Let's try it another way."

Starr dug into her purse and removed her badge and credentials, flashing the wallet open for Kerr to see. She pulled two more photos from the envelope in her bag. The first was a close-up of Ketcham's dead body behind the desk in her office. The second was a broader shot of the blood-splattered walls and floors at the crime scene. Starr placed them on the table, and then sat silently as the man unsuccessfully tried to resist the urge to gawk at what he saw.

"At this particular moment, we don't think you're in any way responsible for the murder of Francine Ketcham, Mr. Kerr. But that may certainly change based on your cooperation right here, right now," Starr said, manipulating the man. "You can help yourself a great deal by answering my questions."

Kerr hesitated a moment more. Finally, he seemed to change tactics.

"I would if I could, but like I told you, lady, that's privileged client information. I'd lose my license if I share it with you."

"Sir, in the last ten minutes, you've confessed to impersonating a police officer to coerce information from cell phone carriers, to roughing up people who don't cooperate with you, and to your willingness to sell your client's personal information. I'm informed you have a history of involvement in unsavory activities in this area, and based on what my colleague tells me, you may very well be party to violating this state's Computer Crime Act...Maybe I'm wrong, but I believe all those things are illegal under the rules regulating private investigators in this state. What interesting facts do you suppose I might find about you if I bother to look, even a little?" Starr gently threatened.

She paused for a moment while it sunk in, but Kerr apparently wasn't convinced. She reached into the bag at her side and withdrew another file. It was the dossier on Kerr, his name emblazoned across the middle of the file in large, clearly legible red letters. She put it on the table so Kerr could see it easily, but she didn't reveal anything of its contents. Again, she sat quietly, allowing the magic of silence to work Kerr's nerves and insecurities.

"That supposed to scare me?" Kerr challenged. He pulled a pack of beef jerky from his pocket and nervously fidgeted with it as he tried to open it.

"Does it scare you, Mr. Kerr?" the psychologist asked.

"There ain't nothin' about you that scares me, lady," he said, shoving two pieces of beef in his maw. "I've handled far meaner and definitely a lot uglier than you," Kerr barked.

He grew suddenly angrier to outward appearances, but Starr recognized his reaction as one designed to mask his fear. She could tell she was beginning to permeate his outer layers, but he needed to feel more pressure.

"Obviously you ain't looking to hire me, so I'm not lis'ning to this crap no more."

Kerr pushed and pressed at the table in earnest, as he wiggled his way sideways out of the booth. He grunted as he finally got to his feet, then crumpled his napkin and threw it into an abundant puddle of syrup in which his pancakes were floating like islands in a vast sea.

Starr stood too, much more quickly and nimbly than her guest. "I kindly suggest you sit your fat ass back in that seat, Mr. Kerr," Starr said, more forcefully than she'd presented at any point in their interaction to date.

She waited but he didn't resume his seat. He didn't leave either, so Starr knew something was keeping him there.

"Sit down, Mr. Kerr," Starr said, sternly.

It was clear she wasn't really asking, and Kerr was hesitant about pressing her. She might have been bluffing, but he simply didn't have a good read on what this small-framed woman would do, or could do. Clearly, she wasn't intimidated by his size or by his thinly veiled aggression, and as much as he didn't want to admit it, even to himself, he was afraid to find out. Slowly, he sank down and wedged himself back into the booth. Starr gingerly folded her skirt beneath her, delicately folded her legs, and resumed both her seat and discussion.

"I'm trying very, very hard to help you here, but you're making it very difficult," she began. "If you don't start telling me what I need to know, I'll see to it you get new opportunities to again deal with those mean, ugly people you mentioned, but this time from the same side of the bars behind which you helped put a few of them."

"If I did put any a 'dem behind bars, it was 'cause I was doin' my job. You can't arrest me for doing my job, lady. The most you got is something that could get my license suspended. It's been suspended before an' I got it back, an' lemme' assure you, I'll just get it back again."

Starr opened the file sitting on the table and pulled a set of phone records from within.

"You see, Mr. Kerr, I *do* have a badge, and I *can* get phone records—lawfully, I might add," Starr said. "These just happen to be yours."

"That ain't my phone," the private detective objected.

"You didn't even look at these papers, Mr. Kerr. How do you know this isn't your bill?" Starr asked. "Please, take a look."

Kerr leaned closer and glanced briefly at the bill. He looked so quickly, he couldn't possibly have seen anything on it, but that didn't stop Starr. She continued.

"Do you see this number here," she asked, pointing.

Kerr looked at the number from the side of his face while trying to pretend he wasn't looking. He recognized the number to which she was pointing, but said nothing.

"This number goes to a house in a little swamp town called Rahain—obviously you've heard of it. It's owned by one Kevin Duke Russ, leader of a militia group called the Aryan Supremacy Society, suspected of involvement in a number of hate crimes in this region recently."

"Yeah, so what?"

"So, we have reason to believe this group recently carried out the execution of a man whose death financially benefitted your client, Ms. Ketcham. As you can see, that number appears on this bill several times prior to the accident that killed Mr. Day, and once the day afterward. I don't know about you, Mr. Kerr, but I'm not a big believer in coincidence when it comes to human behavior."

"That's all fine and dandy, lady, but it's got nothin' to do with me. I told you, that ain't my phone bill, so those calls didn't come from me."

Starr sat erect as she lowered the bills to the table.

"Yes, you did tell me that. Perhaps you think this burner phone can't be traced back to you, especially since you paid cash for it and never used a credit card to add air time to it, and because you disposed of the burner phone somewhere?" Starr asked.

Kerr had no reaction, but Starr wasn't done. She smiled as warmly as she could.

"The problem for you, Mr. Kerr, is that you used a credit card to purchase the air time card with which you refilled the minutes on the burner phone. We don't need the phone itself, although I'm sure it will turn up somewhere eventually."

She waited but still Kerr didn't crack.

"Mr. Kerr, have you ever heard that old joke about two friends walking in the woods and happen across a huge mamma grizzly?"

He gave no response.

"They start running from the bear as fast as their feet will carry them. As they go, one friend breathlessly tells the other, *wait a second. We can't outrun a bear.* The other one answered, *I don't have to outrun the bear; I just have to outrun you.*"

She paused to let it sink in for a second.

"You see, we're visiting with your friends in Rahain any minute now, Mr. Kerr. Who's going to outrun whom in this case? We may offer a deal in this case, but we'll only offer one. Will you be the one, or perhaps one of your friends in Rahain will make the deal."

Kerr remained stoic as he sat there squirming, his eyes darting around the inside of the café. Starr could see he was deep in internal debate, and decided to *help* him.

"Even if you left here right now without making a deal, Mr. Kerr, you're smart enough to know we'll be monitoring your movements and all your communications now that we're on to you. We'll know of any effort you make to contact your friends and warn them of anything as well as anything you discuss with them."

Starr paused for a moment, again smiling widely at Kerr. Just in case the man felt backed into a corner, she moved her hand to the butt of her weapon inside her suit jacket, making sure the private detective detected her not-so-covert action.

"Of course, they may not be so eager to share anything with you if they strike a deal with us first. I guess that would leave you the one running behind, closest to the bear."

Silence hung awkwardly in the air for a few lingering seconds as Starr and Kerr locked eyes with one another. If Kerr was thinking of doing something, Starr was ready for it at a split-second notice.

"All right, all right," Kerr finally capitulated. "I admit it. I did make those calls, but I didn't kill nobody."

"What did you do?" Starr asked.

"All I did was put my client in touch with my cousin and his friend."

"Your cousin?"

Kerr seemed a little exasperated, perhaps a little embarrassed as he rubbed his hands over his stubbly cheeks, up the sides of his head, over his ears, to the top of his head where he lightly scratched his scalp as though it would help detangle the thoughts running through his mind. He grimaced as he inhaled and exhaled deeply, running his hands down the back of his head and finally dropped his arms back on the table.

"Yeah, ma' cousin Durl got brainwashed by Russ's crap a few years back, an' `aventually joined that lame-ass gang Russ runs up there. I hear Durl's now some kinda' rising star wit dem folks. He's my step-cousin really. His mom married my best uncle `bout twenty-five years ago or so. They weren't together long but by the time they split, the damage was done. My kid brother an' me, we got pretty close to Durl an' we all three used ta' hang out all da' time, getting' inta' all kinds a' stupid shit. We had a fallin' out after Durl started hangin' `round Kevin Duke Russ an' his gang—they're a strange bunch, them. You ain't one a' dem, dey don't like you much, an' Durl started actin' just like 'em after while. I ain't really talked to Durl since then."

"So you don't have any relationship with cousin Durl—what's his last name?"

"Hasse, an' no. I ain't talked to him."

"How did you put them in touch with one another?"

"I gave her da' number to call up there."

"Oh but you did more than that, didn't you, Mr. Kerr? Otherwise, Kevin Duke Russ's telephone number wouldn't appear on your bill."

"Oh yeah, well, I think she mighta' made da' call from my office."

"You mean from the burner phone which was, at the time, in your office?"

"Yeah, from that phone while sittin' in my office."

"So you heard Ms. Ketcham's conversation with Mr. Russ?"

"I ain't said that."

"I know you didn't. I did, because I've seen your office and it's not that big. I presume you heard their conversation."

"I didn't hear nothin' they talked about," the man insisted.

"You were being deceitful when you said this wasn't your phone number," Starr said, pointing to the phone bill on the table, "and so perhaps you're being deceitful when you pretend not to know anything about the murders?"

"Whoa, whoa, whoa there, Nelly. I din't say nuthin' 'bout no murders. All I did was put my client in touch wit ma' cousin. I din't do nuthin' wit no murders," Kerr protested.

"Why did you put Ms. Ketcham in touch with your cousin and Kevin Duke Russ?"

Again, Kerr fidgeted in his seat as he struggled to fabricate a reason for the contact that wouldn't simultaneously implicate him in anything bad.

"She was looking for someone to do some things for her."

"Some things like what?" Starr pressed.

"Things I don't do."

"Like what?"

"I don't know."

Starr paused for a second as she—and he—considered his response. "Right. You don't know what it was she wanted done, but whatever it was, you knew it was something that went against your personal standards of acceptable conduct?" Starr asked, illustrating the absurdity of Kerr's reasoning.

Reluctantly, Kerr finally answered. "She wanted to have them pay someone a little visit, you know."

"No, I don't know. Perhaps you can enlighten me. What did she want done during this little visit?"

"I don't know."

"You don't strike me as the type of guy who'd be hesitant to merely go *visit* someone on behalf of a client who was paying you really good money," Starr pressed. "So, what did she want done during this visit?" she asked more sternly.

"Look…I guess she really just wanted to scare this guy a little."

"All right. So it was a male she wanted to scare. Who?"

"I don't know."

"Uh-huh," Starr said, doubtingly. "Why did she want to scare this guy whose identity you say you don't know?"

"I don't know."

"So, let me see if I understand. You're asking me to believe that you, a man who has no trouble roughing up people who don't cooperate with you, were reluctant to merely go *visit* and *scare* some guy on behalf of a wealthy client who was paying you $800 a day plus expenses?"

Starr sat back in her seat and let her comments resonate for a moment.

Kerr's reply was short and simple. "Yeah."

"And so for this reason, you put your client in touch with your step-cousin whom you haven't seen or spoken to in years, and who is a member of a violent hate-based militia headquartered close by, but you have no idea why your client would need such people…no idea at all?" Starr pressed.

Kerr said nothing, but instead simply sat there with a blank expression on his face. After several seconds of resounding silence, Starr began collecting her papers and folding her files. Kerr watched tacitly, wondering what to make of her actions.

"You really aren't making much sense, Mr. Kerr, which leads me to believe you've been lying through your teeth for much if not all of our conversation," she said. "I hate it when people lie and treat me like I'm a perfect idiot, so I'm done with you."

"But," he protested.

Starr didn't let him speak, but instead, spoke over his pitiful utterance.

"I was hoping to give you a chance to save yourself a lot of grief, but frankly, I'm beyond caring what happens to you. Most likely, you'll go down for the murders of Erich Day and Francine Ketcham, two very prominent Seaside citizens whose murders could win you the death penalty. If you're *extremely* lucky, Mr. Kerr, and I mean *ex-tremely lucky*, you'll simply rot your life away in a maximum security facility with a big African or Hispanic tough-guy named *Bubba* for your BFF, while Kevin Duke Russ and your dear old cousin live out their happy miserable little lives."

Nimbly, Starr stood from the table, tossed down a twenty dollar bill, and headed for the door out of the Seashell Café.

"Wait," Kerr finally turned and said as her hand grasped the door handle. "Wait a minute. Please come back an' sit down, please," he begged. "I'll tell you what I know."

Starr stopped in her tracks and slowly turned around. She stood there, staring at Kerr.

He lowered his head and spoke softly. "I didn't know exactly what she wanted done until after it was done. I delivered a bag of cash to the nigga tree in the swamp outside Rahain," Kerr admitted.

"The nigga tree?" Starr asked.

"Yeah, it's a tree they used to hang blacks from after da' civil war all the way up to da' 50's. She told me ta' take it there an' not ta' open da' package but I did anyway."

"All right, Mr. Kerr," she said.

Dr. Starr returned to the booth and seated herself. She pointed her finger at him and spoke very sternly.

"You have my attention for now, but the moment you lie to me, I'm done and the possibility of any deal will be gone. Do you hear me?"

"Loud an' clear," he answered.

"Let's start with what you know about your client's lawyer," Starr said.

* * *

Lockwood had remained in the office all day, while his teammates were out and about running various leads to ground. They were doing real field work while he sat inside looking at stuff rather than talking to people. He much preferred the former, but he'd put off this part of his task for too long now. Besides, something in the video surveillance just might be a key piece of evidence.

He'd poured over every frame of video and hadn't seen anything particularly useful except the frame of the likely perpetrator's backside as he or she fled the scene on the night of the murder. Ito's computer analysis of the person based on his or her size relative to other items in the video suggested this person was probably a Caucasian male, about six feet tall and one-hundred ninety pounds. Given the agility with which the person moved in the video, and the odd contortions of movement the person would have to make to avoid getting his face on the video monitors throughout the building, the person was likely younger than thirty. While not definitive, this could certainly start narrowing the list of possibilities, at least in terms of this person's identity. Given the time the video was recorded relative to the murder, that person was either the killer or had information that could lead to the killer, which may or may not be relevant to the NSA investigation. Still, Lockwood grew tired of looking at the stuff. He needed a break, and sometimes, that was the best technique for breaking an intellectual jam. Brief distance often helped one's clarity.

He went outside the small office building for some fresh air. In the old days, he'd have lit up a cigarette, but thanks to Ex Number Two, he'd given up the habit—as he told it, she'd wanted him to be healthier and live longer so she'd have more time to torture him. As vile as the wife turned out to be, getting him to quit smoking was the one good thing that came from their relationship. Nonetheless, Lockwood found himself standing in the parking lot where current smokers had obviously been taking their breaks. He could smell the smoke and nicotine all around him, and see discarded cigarette butts scattered about the area near the disposal.

"Damn smokers," he muttered.

Lockwood looked over to his car, and decided to go for a ride. That should help clear his head a bit, and hit his reset button. Joy riding wasn't generally an acceptable use of government-owned vehicles, but following up on leads was. He decided to drive past the headquarters building of Eardhardt-Roane just to take a daytime look at the place. Perhaps something would occur to him.

After a ten minute drive across the small beach town, he saw the corporate crime scene looming a short distance away. The building was definitely the most ornate structure around, clearly intended to make a bold statement to all who'd see it. Lockwood took in the view, mentally sizing up the distance from the penthouse offices down to the main floor, and assessing how a determined assailant could quickly descend the stairs and exit the building, all while avoiding the notice of the security guard in the lobby. He pulled the fed-mobile into the parking lot of a small strip mall across the street from the building, parked and got outside. Leaning against the side of the car, he canvassed the entire area for about a half-mile in either direction. That's when it hit him.

There were two banks near the Earhardt-Roane building, one immediately adjacent to it, across a small access road on the same side of the main thoroughfare, and the other across the main thoroughfare in the strip mall. Both had outside ATMs that faced the Earhardt-Roane headquarters. Lockwood got back in the car, and drove the few hundred feet to the nearest bank, parked, and bounded inside. Flashing his credentials, he asked to speak with the manager.

"I'm Josh Patel," a young dark-skinned man said, emerging from the rear of the bank.

"Hi, Mr. Patel, I'm Special Agent Ian Lockwood, NSA. I'm conducting a national security investigation. I need to see all surveillance footage recorded by any camera you have that points in the general direction of that building across the street," he said, pointing through the glass, metal, and bricks that made up the bank's façade to the Earhardt-Roane headquarters.

Patel examined Lockwood's credentials, and quickly canvassed his body. He'd been trained to spot concealed weapons, and Lockwood's Glock commanded Patel's eye.

Certainly, Agent Lockwood. I'll need Security to assist you," he explained, reaching for his cell phone. "Won't you come this way, please?" he said, walking toward his office, away from the lobby.

After a few minutes, an older armed guard in a police-like uniform appeared in Patel's doorway, carrying a silver rectangular metal briefcase. He stepped into the branch manager's office, nearly oblivious to the manager's presence. Two additional guards appeared a few feet behind him, but stood in silence as the evidently senior officer spoke.

"How do you do?" he asked, looking askance at Lockwood. "I'm Officer Donlan."

Lockwood observed the man carefully and quickly, noticing immediately that the safety strap over his holster was unattached, and the safety on his weapon had been deactivated. Lockwood smiled his most friendly, forthcoming smile and slowly moved his hands up and away from his body.

"I'm well, thanks, Officer Donlan. My name is Ian Lockwood. I'm a special agent for the National Security Agency. I have my badge and credentials in my breast pocket, and I'm going to get them out for you now," he explained.

Donlan nodded his assent and stood by while Lockwood did as he indicated. He inspected the Agent's credentials and evidently found them satisfactory. He nodded to the other officers behind him, and they turned and walked away from the office, presumably returning to their perches in the main lobby. Donlan placed the briefcase on the branch manager's desk and opened it.

"I'm so sorry, Agent," Patel said.

"I hope you understand," Donlan added. "We don't often get visits from the NSA so I thought it was a little weird."

"No apologies necessary, gentlemen," Lockwood said. "I used to be a cop so I know how it is. Can't be too careful these days."

Donlan chuckled. "Yeah, and I'm a month away from retirement," he said. "I don't want to be one of those guys who dies in the line of duty just barely shy of retirement."

"No worries here, Chief," Lockwood said.

"All right, if you'd like to view the video here, I have this here mobile unit that lets you watch the video you asked about. If you just want to take it with you, I can download whatever you need to a disk or upload it to the net and send by email."

"How about we do both," Lockwood said. "Let's just take a look-see at the video and narrow down the timeframes I want in the email."

"All righty then," Donlan said.

The old man activated the device and then programmed into the computer the dates and times Lockwood had asked about. The small screen flickered to life, showing a series of bank customers approaching the machines and conducting their business, several of them making goonie faces, waving, and mouthing *Hi Mom* as they stared directly into the ATM camera, and two of them dug for gold nuggets in their noses, clearly oblivious to the fact that they were being recorded.

"This is video from our ATMs at the front door there," he said pointing in the general direction. "Which one is this...oh, this is number 124—the one on the right as you face the building."

Most of the video was grainy, dark and not at all helpful. They watched on, speeding up the playback to get through it as quickly as possible without missing anything of importance. It took ninety minutes to go through all the surveillance from the designated period, and it had been a complete wash as far as anything helpful to Lockwood's investigation. They won the same results for the second ATM.

Lockwood leaned backward in exasperation and rubbed his hands over his face. He sighed deeply and shook his head, annoyed that his hunch hadn't so far brought anything worthwhile. His eye caught sight of the teller bay out in the main lobby. Above the tellers' head-level, there were a series of interior cameras designed to capture video of patrons who came inside and conducted business with the tellers from the lobby. But, two of the cameras in the middle of the bay were positioned directly across from the ERAC building, and directly in front of the glass doors leading into the bank.

"How 'bout those inside cameras?" he suggested.

The old security man was surprised at the comment. He'd not considered the possibility those cameras could be useful for this purpose, and thus hadn't mentioned them. Still, it couldn't hurt to check every plausible source.

"They're really angled for lobby coverage, but we can look."

He left the manager's office for a few minutes and returned a short time later, another flash drive in hand.

"Let's try this one," he said.

He inserted the drive, and in moments, the trio was back into video-viewing mode. They stopped after twenty minutes.

"There," Lockwood yelled, pointing. "What's that?"

The three peered closer. The top portion of the footage seemed to show part of a distant dark spot moving on the right side of the Roane building around the time of the murder. It first appeared near an auxiliary door west of the main lobby, skirted the building a short distance, and then moved into an area outside the camera's purview. In all, the shadow spent about four minutes on camera.

"Can you rewind and enhance frames nineteen through twenty-five?"

"I can rewind no problem, but enhancing—that's beyond our capability here. Remember, this system was designed to pick up images in our lobby. That's a prime coverage range of about a hundred fifty feet. I'm not a good judge of distance, but I know that's far less than the distance from our front door, across the parking lot, six lanes of traffic, a median, the yard between the street and their parking lot, and then up to the building."

"Is that the best you can do?"

"That's it, Agent. Sorry."

"No, no, Officer. You've given me a real good break here. I'll take this flash drive, and I'd appreciate it if you could email me this file as well."

"We're happy to help law enforcement at any time, Agent Lockwood. We're proud to be good patriotic citizens and a partner with our government," Patel added.

"Yeah, thanks a bunch, Mr. Patel," Lockwood said. "Here's my card...the email address is right there on it. When can I expect you'll send that to me?"

"I'll get right on it. You'll have it before you get back to your office." The security guard noticed the Washington DC address on Lockwood's card. "...or your hotel. Where you staying?"

"Near the airport, but we're working out of the local FBI office. Email is fine though. I appreciate your help."

After a few hours at the first bank, Lockwood departed and headed to the second bank. It was much closer to the Roane building and on the same side of the road. Thus, he was hopeful their cameras might have captured a better view of the dark shadow. In five minutes, he was entering the lobby of the second bank, flashing his credentials, and requesting to speak with the branch manager. He spent nearly four hours at that institution, but when he left at the end of the day, he toted in his pocket precisely what he'd hoped to find. If the first bank had been a lucky hit for him, the second was almost a jackpot. He still couldn't discern a face or other specific information about the shadow, but he'd gotten a much more complete screen capture of the shadow, and he could tell it moved off toward the airport after leaving the Earhardt-Roane building. These were things he could work with. Now, he just needed to get these flash drives back to Ito, the miracle worker. If there was anything to be found, Ito would find it. He lifted his phone and punched a button from his Favorites list.

"What the hell do *you* want?" a voice playfully demanded a second later.

"Can it, Ito. Don't have time to bullshit with you right now," Lockwood said. "Where are you?"

"Just finished talking to the dead lady's computer chump. I'm gonna' drop some stuff off at the office, and then back to the Fly-Inn for a swim, a hot tub, a shower, and some dinner."

"Hate to ask this, junior, but can we meet back at the office, like now? I'm about ten or fifteen minutes out, but I need your expertise right away. I've got some stuff too."

Ito had worked many long days and late nights since coming to Seaside Beach, and that was usually par for the course when the team was deployed. Ito was probably the most demanding person of himself when it came to work, but he tried every now and then to force himself to do something beneficial for himself. Rigorous exercise, a decent meal, and good quality night of sleep were occasional treats about which he didn't need to feel guilty when he partook, but it didn't appear he'd being doing so tonight. *Oh well*, he thought, *there'll be other nights.*

"It sounds like a party," Ito said, sighing and resigning himself to an all-nighter.

"Two don't make a party," Lockwood said. "You better get Kenison too."

"Oh joy. We'll see you shortly."

A slightly guilty Lockwood aimed to ease the sting of his request. "I'll stop for burgers and beer."

# Chapter 8

## The Eye of Providence

Grace Tran was sitting in her borrowed office reading the reports from the lab, following up on the evidence collected by the ERT—Evidence Recovery Team—at the crime scene. She'd placed them into the electronic case file so everyone could review them, but she'd not had time to review it herself, until now. Nothing thus far seemed to contradict the preliminary conclusions offered by their initial reports, which was good news. That meant they didn't need to redo any parts of the investigation done so far in reliance on the early information available to them. She was interrupted by a call from a New York telephone number to her cell.

"Tran," she said, answering the phone.

"Hey, Grace. John Sedgwick here," a voice greeted.

"Hey, John. How are things in the Big Apple treating you?"

"Good, good, thanks. Busy as hell, but I guess that's par for the course."

"No doubt," Tran agreed. "Please tell me you're calling with good news for me?"

Sedgwick laughed. "I don't know that it's good or bad. It just is."

"Well, lay it on me, dude."

"My team has been looking at possible connections between your board member, Iriyana Hamidi, and the Iranian delegation during the latter's UN visit a few months ago."

"Uh-huh," Tran prompted.

"We still haven't found any direct connections between Hamidi, and the Iranian government," Sedgwick informed. "We did, however, uncover contacts between Hamidi and an Iranian national who works as a secretary in the Iranian Interests section of the Pakistani Embassy. Ties between the

Hamidi and Sorosh families go way back, it seems. They've been working a scheme to direct US dollars back to revolutionaries in Iran."

"That's not illegal or anything, is it?" Tran sarcastically quipped.

"Yeah, apparently, these two families are quite active in promoting political reform back home in Iran. They want to replace the current religious government with a western style government based on capitalist principles."

Tran didn't necessarily have a problem with the idea of promoting regime change in Iran—that was, after all, the official policy of the US government. She did, however, have a big issue with the fact that private individuals would seek to effect this change on their own initiatives. That was contrary to US export control laws which prohibited essentially all forms of trade with and investment in Iran for reasons the Congress and the President of the United States deemed compelling. But, the general consensus among employees of Earhardt-Roane, who spoke on condition of anonymity, was that the Hamidis had little regard for rules and regulations that restricted what they wanted. Sedgwick's discovery was certainly consistent with that view, Tran thought.

"Nothing showing tech transfers or funding of terrorist groups?"

"Well, sort of."

"Don't keep me in suspense, man," Tran prompted.

"Okay, I gotta' give this to you in two parts," Sedgwick said. "The first part is this: CIA thinks Sorosh is an Iranian double-agent. Her family does go way back with the Hamidi family, but Sorosh seems to be a rogue member of her clan, and is loyal to the clerics and Iatollahs running the government. Curiously, Iranian authorities have arrested many of the benefactors of their political reform scheme. The Agency thinks the Iranian government has intercepted the funds intended for them, and used it to fund Iraqi and Afghan extremists."

"That's pretty damn bad," Tran said. "And Part Two?"

"This encryption program your subject used...the name of it translates from Farsi to something close to *Deepest Secret*. It was created by the Iranian intelligence ministry as a way to prevent outsiders—in particular the United States and her allies—from accessing their classified documents. Unfortunately for them, we broke it before it was ever even deployed, and fortunately for us, they don't even know we've done so. In any case, there's no reason your subject should've had it—it's not available for sale or purchase anywhere in the western world. In fact, the only place someone can get it is from the Iranian government or from someone with inside connections to someone in that government."

"I'll run it by the US Attorney to be sure, but that seems like pretty conclusive evidence to me," Tran said.

"Yeah, to me too," Sedgwick agreed.

"I've assembled a pretty detailed file with the findings of my investigation, and I'll send it to you via encrypted agency mail. We'll run every continuing lead to its end, and keep you posted as things develop."

"Great. Send me what you have. I think things are starting to gel down here."

"Okay, check's in the mail, as they say," Sedgwick said.

"Thanks, John. Appreciate it."

Tran disconnected the line and leaned backward in her chair. Lockwood didn't like the man very much, but Sedgwick didn't seem so bad. He carried himself with a confidence that might easily be mistaken for arrogance, and she was painfully aware that some folks had made this misjudgment of her. After all, Sedgwick had come through for her on this one, and she didn't have to pull teeth for him to do so. His information was helpful—it didn't reveal the kind of crimes she worried it might, but what he found was troubling enough to her, and it would be even more so to Hamidi.

Tran looked for the lab report she'd been reviewing before Sedgwick's call to resume where she'd left off. As her eyes settled onto the last few words she'd read before the interruption, her cell phone rang again. She didn't even have a chance to utter a greeting or her name before the voice on the other end started talking.

"Hey, girl, have I got some news for you."

After doing some leg work with the Air Force Procurement Office at Wright-Patterson Air Force Base in Ohio, Vivian Lawrence was excited to call her boss. She was an excellent support for the team, and she often provided invaluable assistance with their arrangements, but she absolutely delighted in the chance to contribute substantively to an investigation. This would be one of those great opportunities.

"Hey, Viv. How are things in the beltway?" Tran asked, staring at the call phone.

"Same ole' same ole, you know. Got delayed for an hour on I-295 this morning...some asshole tried to pass on the shoulder, and another asshole thought he'd use his car to prevent him from doing it. Their stupid little game of chicken caused a hellacious crash that snarled traffic all damn morning."

"That's why I like the metro," Tran quipped.

187

"That's for you impatient folk," Lawrence replied. "Besides, since I got my baby back from the shop, I'm driving her like there ain't no tomarra."

Lawrence had saved her money over the years and finally bought her dream-car, a 1988 high-output V-8 Porsche 928 S in champagne—it was almost exactly like the one in a Cruise movie where he played a teenage boy who accidentally dumped his dad's car in a Chicago lake. It had been out of commission for forty days while she awaited the arrival of new replacement parts. Now that Betty, as she called it, was back in service, Lawrence drove it as though the DC freeways were part of the Autobahn. Her friends joked that her car had two speeds—park and 150 mph. The police didn't frequently find it funny at all, but in more than twelve occasions being pulled over, she'd always managed to sweet-talk her way out of a ticket. She feared that the thirteenth time might be her unlucky number, and thus wasn't anxious to push her luck.

Tran chuckled. "So what's got you all excited, Viv?"

"I talked to this Colonel at Wright-Pat about our little issue, and it was a real eye opener. Colonel Blunt reviewed the information I sent him, and said that there is definitely something out-of-order with the submissions ERAC sent in. First of all, the numbers don't match what was reported. If that's intentional, that's fraud, according to him. Their JAG lawyer said unless there's a smokin' gun, it's usually pretty hard to prove fraud by a contractor because of the number of people involved and the high standard. He's gonna' have his Defense Finance and Accounting Service go through everything submitted not only on this contract, but on all ERAC contracts the Air Force is running, and he's going to call his counterparts at Army and Navy and suggest they do likewise."

"Well that's pretty much what we expected, isn't it?"

"Yeah but that ain't all, girl," Viv continued.

"Do tell?"

"Yeah, he said the research results Earhardt reported differs substantially from the data in the documents we sent."

"So the report was doctored somewhere along the way?" Tran clarified.

"Yeah looks like."

"What's the nature of the discrepancy?" Tran asked.

"There were a couple areas of variance," Lawrence explained. "The first one was the accounting figures for expenses and charges against the contract."

"Just as former employees Renley and Lauxner had said."

"Looks like it," Lawrence agreed. "But he was also concerned about the fail rate on something called the neuronetic linkage array."

"Why?"

"Well, it seems this linkage array thing fails at forty-two percent according to the raw data, but the rate reported by the company was .02%."

"That's a big difference," Tran noted, "but can you help me out here, Viv? What does all this mean in the real world?"

"I don't know, boss, but that wasn't all."

"What else?"

"The Colonel also seemed pretty aggravated about something the researchers called *collateral adversities* on the Phantom and Casper platforms."

"Did you say Phantom *and* Casper?" Tran asked.

"Yeah, that's what he said."

This was surprising to Tran. "You sure?"

"Positive—what are you thinking, boss lady?"

"From the documents I read, Air Force was aware of the reliability issues on the Casper prototype, but they had no such issues with the Phantom. That's already deployed fairly widely, if I'm not mistaken."

"I'm pretty sure that's what he said," Lawrence assured.

"All right," Tran conceded. "Text me his number please. I need to talk to him."

"Damn," Lawrence exclaimed. "I don't know this techno-crap like you young-folk do. I'll have to figure that out and get back to you," she said.

Tran wasn't the least deterred. Lawrence was one of the sharpest minds she'd ever met, and there wasn't a single task that was beyond her. For whatever reason, Lawrence delighted in misleading people into thinking she didn't know how to do things, but she always came through in the end. Perhaps under-promising and over-delivering was the name of her game.

"You'll figure it out," Tran assured.

"Got it," Lawrence exclaimed after a few seconds. "It's coming to ya' now."

Moments later, the number appeared on her phone, and Tran toggled the minute controls on her handheld to dial the Colonel's direct number.

"Colonel Blunt," a gruff voiced answered.

"Good afternoon, Colonel Blunt. This is Special Agent Grace Tran with the NSA. You spoke earlier with my associate, Vivian Lawrence, about issues related to Earhardt-Roane's UAV contract your office is administering."

"*Administering?*" Blunt repeated. "*Administering* is a bit of an understatement Agent. I'm the designated Procurement Official for the UAV project, which means this is my baby. I've honchoed it since it was barely more than an idea in an adolescent engineer's wet dream. We're not done with our official inquiry into this thing, but I can tell you I'm more than a little concerned about this one."

"I understand, sir. I assure you, you'll have the NSA's best work on this."

"I'm sure I will," the Colonel said. "Your Ms. Lawrence said the two of you used to bleed Air Force blue, eh?"

"Yes sir. Nine years in OSI. She was my admin assistant almost from day one."

"Office of Special Investigations? You were the guys nobody wanted to see coming through the door."

"No sir, *that* was the Judge Advocate. We were the ones nobody knew were there until after we left," Tran joked.

"Well, that Vivian Lawrence is a real piece of work—in a good way. I'm not sure how the hell we let her get away from us, but you better hold on to that one or I might steal her back. She's a real pit bull, that one—in a good way."

"Yes sir, she is. That's why I've held on to her my whole career."

"You're a smart one, I see, Agent."

"Thank you, sir. Viv told me that you said this whole thing made you want to *ball-up on somebody*? I was hoping you could give me some more detail on this."

"Damn straight I can."

"Maybe you can start with your overall assessment, Colonel."

"Maybe I can," Blunt repeated. "Based on the information you initially sent us, I had my contract administration team and the number-crunchers from DCAA crawl up Earhardt's ass with a microscope, so to speak. I nearly shit a brick when my senior program manager briefed me on their initial findings."

"What did they find?"

"He reported significant issues in four main areas: variances in the expenses and charges incurred against the contract, unauthorized expansion of the scope of work under the contract, misreporting of the fail rate stats on the neuronetic linkage system, and misreporting of the frequency and severity of collateral adversities on two UAV platforms."

"I take it these are material and substantial differences?"

"Ehh, the number-crunchers in DCAA will have a cow about the accounting variances, but—"

The Colonel didn't dismiss the concerns of his colleagues in the Defense Contract Audit Agency, but he was more concerned about the other aspects of the issue. He thought about what he'd learned in the last few days, and Tran could hear him getting choked up as he began to finish his thoughts.

"It's just that, well, I don't know how else to say it other than to say, I wanna' kick some ass and take some scalps over the other issues. When money-grubbing contractors lie and cheat about shit like this, our boys and girls in harm's way die. There are few things worse than some limp-dick, greedy corporate assholes putting their profits ahead of our folks in uniform."

Tran got the impression Colonel Blunt was an older, somewhat thick, cigar-smoking, rough-around-the edges soldier's soldier who was no stranger to people who'd have taken pleasure in blowing him out of the sky, and maybe even had been a resident of a POW camp or two. He may have had impressive rank on his shoulders, but he took seriously the responsibility that went with it. This was a leader imbued with true concern for those he led. This was a man who lived up to his name and deserved the respect that went with his uniform and position.

"Sir, I'm sure I'm showing my ignorance here, but I wonder if you could explain just why the last two categories are so upsetting to you."

"Listen, Agent," Blunt clarified. "Don't get me wrong. In this day and age, when the Pentagon brass and the muckety-muck politicians nickel and dime all the services over every little program, fudging the numbers is pretty damn serious. Hell, the Phantom is already deployed to the field, so pulling it back is gonna' be several hundred million dollars if it's a penny," he guessed. "But the money isn't the worst of it. These other things—they lie about how reliable their little toys really are, and redirect money into bogus research efforts instead of what we asked them to do. That puts the lives of hundreds of thousands of people at risk. Can you imagine if one of those UAVs goes down with a nuclear payload on board?"

"I can only imagine."

"Yeah, and even if the payload didn't detonate, we'd have classified technology in the hands of unfriendlies in the very best scenario. But even if everything went right with the missions, the shit with the collateral adversities means our pilots get screwed no matter what. That's some shit I can't let happen."

"Okay, I get the risk of the aircraft crashing in hostile territory, Colonel, but I'm still not following you on the *unauthorized expansion* and *collateral adversities* issues," Tran pressed.

"Here's the deal: the unauthorized expansion basically revolves around work they're apparently doing in chemical research."

"This is the truth serum thing?" Tran asked.

Blunt nodded over the phone. "Yeah, apparently, they call it NexChem. This isn't part of the contract, so they shouldn't be spending a single dime of our money on it, at least not on this contract."

"Is it possible they could argue the NexChem research is a natural extension of the authorized work they're doing?"

Blunt laughed, telegraphing his view of that possible explanation. "Those damn knuckleheads can argue anything they want, but it would be pure bullshit. There might be some government contracts under which research into chemical compounds is appropriate—maybe some Defense contracts, even—but this UAV contract is for unmanned aerial vehicle hardware, software, and anything closely related. *Truth serum*," he mocked, "is nowhere in the same realm."

"All right, I get that. What about this *collateral adversities* thing?"

"And one other thing. If they thought this was a legitimate thing under the UAV contract, why wouldn't they have included this information in their routine progress reports? I had my people scour every report Earhardt sent us since we first funded this contract. Not once did they ever mention a single thing about NexChem or any chemical research of any kind."

"That's pretty persuasive," Tran agreed.

"Now, collateral adversities—that's a fancy term the researchers use to mean bad side effects." He paused momentarily. "Do you know what the neuronetic linkage array is, Agent Tran?"

"Yes sir, I think so. It's a pioneering technology that lets pilots control the aircraft remotely from great distances using what is essentially thought-power."

"Yeah, that's right for the most part. Well, they've under-reported the rate at which the technology fails—that's the fail rate issue. But they've also under-reported the collateral harm it inflicts on our pilots who use the device."

"What kind of harm, sir?"

"Brain damage, Agent Tran. Brain damage."

"Oh my God," Tran involuntarily said.

"Yeah," the Colonel agreed. "We cross-referenced our findings with medical conditions reported to Air Force Medical Command by our pilots assigned to our particular UAV squadrons. There's a fifty-three percent increase in neurological complaints by this subgroup. The incidents range from headaches, migraines, and mini-strokes in pilots who've used the technology less than three years, to dementia, major strokes, and early onset Alzheimer's in pilots who've used it six years or more."

"And Earhardt-Roane knew this?" Tran thought aloud.

"That's what it looks like. I can think of no other reason why they'd bury these results. We're talking a huge jump in the number of occurrences compared to the general population. They had to have known, unless they're complete idiots."

"Colonel, forgive me for what I'm about to suggest, but I need to cover all the bases here," Tran prefaced.

"Why do I get the feeling you're about to piss me off, Agent Tran?" he asked. "Go ahead, give it to me straight."

"Is there any reason the Air Force didn't recognize these problems?"

Unseen to Tran, Blunt sighed and shook his head as he often did when bureaucratic foibles impacted his mission. "The Air Force is a big organization, Agent Tran. Sometimes it takes a little time for the right hand to learn what the left is doing. Air Force Medical had been collecting and analyzing data on this very thing, but this is a big program, financially, politically, strategically, and a whole bunch of other ways. Nobody wants to sound the alarm about a highly visible, high-value initiative like this unless they're damn sure there's a significant problem, and then some of them would still wet their pants about having to do it. Know what I mean?"

Though he couldn't see her across the seven hundred miles separating them, Tran nodded her head in the affirmative at his question. "Yes sir, sure do," she said aloud. "How much money is there on the UAV contracts anyway?"

The Colonel considered the question for a moment. "Lots of contingencies and permutations on this whole thing, but all in all, under the most favorable circumstances, it's worth about $2 billion over the first ten years of the effort."

"Follow the money," Tran said softly under her breath as she remembered Vivian Lawrence's advice in the Powwow.

"Based on what we know to date, I've already suspended all non-essential work on every contract they have with us while we finish looking into this," Blunt informed. "Now I got a few more I's to dot and T's to cross, but I plan to initiate some pretty stiff action against Earhardt-Roane if this keeps going the direction it seems to be going. Their past successes and reputation have them in pretty good regard with a lot of Pentagon and Congressional big-wigs, but this is way over the edge. I guess all of us—myself included—forgot that old adage, *all that glitters isn't gold.* These folks have grown way too complacent with themselves and sloppy about their work, and we let it happen."

"Thank you, Colonel. I appreciate your help. I hope I can call you if we need additional information," Tran said.

"I'd be pissed if you didn't, Agent Tran. I appreciate that you're chasing this down. If these bastards are screwing over our fighting men and women and our law enforcement community trying to protect this great nation, as well as the taxpayers, we need to run them down, beat them down, and make an example of them. I'm all over that, so you just go ahead and call me for whatever you need."

"Thank you, sir, and likewise if we can do anything for you."

Tran disconnected the line, stood, and stretched. She'd been sitting in the chair with her ear glued to the phone for a long time now. She felt all sensation departing her buttocks, and thus needed to stretch her legs.

\* \* \*

"I need to know what the hell's going on people," the president barked, pounding on the conference table, his toupee sliding toward his reddened face.

Don Johnston sat in his well-appointed, wife-decorated office sweating bullets alongside corporate general counsel Chuck Matos, Acting CFO Lydia Mann, and Chief Compliance Officer Matt Nichols. Since the federal agents arrived following the murder of the CFO, the company's once-abundant Department of Defense revenue seemed to be coming to a slowing trickle, and it was starting to affect their likely quarterly results. Additionally, the company's once-cozy relationships with high government officials seemed to be growing more and more uncomfortable, as Johnston's calls to them went routinely unreturned, and his requests for assistance or information went unheeded. It was likewise for other company officials who frequently worked with government officials. To make matters worse, as news, rumor, and innuendo of the federal investigation leaked to relevant corners, Earhardt-

Roane's stock value began a precipitous drop. Board members were breathing fire down Johnston's neck daily, demanding answers about what was happening, but Johnston had nothing to tell them. He needed something and needed it badly.

"Lydia, what do you know about this double bookkeeping crap we're hearing from the feds?"

"I have a little information on that, sir," Mann replied.

"Well don't just sit there, damn-it. Tell me," the president growled.

Lydia Mann was a quiet, middle-aged woman who lived an unremarkable but steady life. Having finished at the top of her MBA class at Wharton, she'd served successfully as Chief Financial Officer and Controller for three different companies, but found the internal politics and backstabbing seemingly innate to those positions repugnant to her devout Catholic upbringing. The accounting department manager position at Earhardt-Roane presented her the opportunity to simply come to work and quietly do a good job for a few more years, until she and her husband could comfortably move out-of-state to semi-retire closer to their daughters and six grandkids.

Mann was immensely proud of her gentle unassuming presence in the world, and she was religious about showing kindness, manners, and deference to others. Impressed by the fact that the Son of God was a simple carpenter who lived a simple life, she believed humility was among the most important virtues a person could model. Her flashiest possession was the Saint Jude—Patron of Lost Causes—medallion around her neck, which had been handed down to her by her mother and grandmother. The unfortunate turnover in Earhardt-Roane's business and finance division had forced her into unsought promotions, first to Director of Business and Finance, and then to Acting CFO while the company did a national search for a successor to Ketcham, herself the recent successor to Day. Though she was promised it would only be for a short time, Mann was regretfully aware it would be longer—*after all, she reasoned, who the hell wanted to be CFO at a company where the two predecessors died, one by brutal murder in the very office the new CFO would occupy*. It all had a very bad juju that could make the job very difficult to fill.

"Yes, sir," she replied. "The federal agents initially came in here because of the murder as we know, but we've also learned that one of our former employees, Venita Renley, made a Fraud, Waste, and Abuse complaint, alleging we were giving false information to the Air Force program office and keeping two sets of books on our UAV contract: the right ones and the ones from which we reported."

"Well why the hell wouldn't she just tell us about it instead going outside to report it to the feds?" Johnston barked.

"She did, sir," the Chief Compliance Officer said.

"And?"

"...And we fired her," Nichols answered.

"What?" the president angrily asked.

"We fired her," Matos repeated. "She has a wrongful termination suit pending against us right now."

"How does this shit happen, damn-it, Chuck," Johnston snapped.

The general counsel and the Chief Compliance Officer traded glances, but nobody offered an answer. Nichols full-well knew the reason but he also knew the president wasn't truly seeking answers to fix a problem or address an issue, but was instead venting, perhaps talking just to hear himself talk. He didn't want to hear that the corporate managers and leaders responsible for the contract were in fact responsible for this issue, and any fallout related to it.

Mann knew the precise question the president was asking, but she purposely interpreted it a bit differently, and then continued what she had to say.

"I've been through Francine's records, and there's simply nothing to explain how or why this happened, or what she did in the recordkeeping. She evidently didn't involve her staff in anything she was doing, so there's no one to consult about it."

"We can just plead *mistake* right? I mean, there's no smoking gun here is there?" the president asked. "There's no evidence to prove we did anything intentional right?"

The lawyer leaned forward. "So far sir, there's nothing we know of to show that, but I have to caution that we don't currently know what the government has. They've been keeping us informed about the investigation, but that's focused primarily on the murder investigation..."

Johnston leaned forward and pointed his finger at Matos. "Look, I don't give a single damn about the murder thing, except to the extent it impacts us. I'm sorry for Franny and I hope they catch the bastard who killed her, but my concern," he said, stabbing his finger in the air, "is the financial health of this company. That's all you care about too, Counselor."

"Yes, sir," Matos replied. "I, I'm just saying we probably shouldn't volunteer anything about this to anyone at the moment, because we could dig ourselves in further. My advice is that we work with these folks and show them we're being open and cooperative in getting to the bottom of whatever they're concerned about."

"I'm quite skilled at working these things, Chuck," Johnston lectured. "I know how these government bureaucrats think."

"Sir, we need to be very careful about how we proceed in this matter," Matos argued. "We tried playing hardball with them once already, and in addition to the NSA folks we had poking through our business at the start of all this, they suspended our contracts and brought the Defense Contract Audit Agency and Program audit officials down here to help poke through our business. They can make us hurt if they want. Playing games with them is asking for trouble."

Johnston scoffed. "I admit we got some problems right now, but this'll blow over sooner or later. I'd just rather it be sooner than later. We have some very wealthy, politically connected board members, and some very powerful friends in Congress who'll surely be happy to rain some heat down on these folks if we ask."

"Forgive me sir, but I just don't think that's a good strategy," the lawyer continued, shaking his head. "Politicians are usually happy to intercede on behalf of major donor-constituents, but this is an election year when voters are regularly tossing incumbents of both parties out on their asses. Depending on what happens with it, this whole investigation thing has the potential for huge media coverage. Our political friends will be a lot less willing to do anything that might remotely connect them to scandal or wrongdoing by one of their corporate *friends*. If they smell even a hint of it on us, we're in this thing all alone. We may even be seeing some of that already."

The president vehemently resisted the lawyer's logical arguments. He couldn't deny they were in some kind of straits, but he didn't think it was anything they couldn't handle with a little swift footwork. It was only temporary—after all, they'd been in pinches before and came out of them just fine.

"Chuck, Chuck," he said, smiling. "You're being overly cautious in your analysis. Given the volume of work we do for them and the investment they've made in our very promising technologies, the truth of the matter is, we're too big to fail," the president confidently gloated. "They need us as much as we need them, if not more. We just need to do some damage control, give them a little song and dance, and razzle-dazzle them real good, and they won't see anything but the sequins in their eyes."

Matos hoped the president meant they could warmly invite the government officials in, and wine and dine them as the company fully cooperated with the federal investigations. But, the man's remarks struck him as an odd way to phrase it, and it started to give him pause to question.

"Are you aware of any reason we may want to hide anything, sir?" Matos asked.

Johnston didn't answer his lawyer's question, but instead gave him the death stare of all time. Matos didn't know how to interpret it, except that he'd hit some kind of nerve. Maybe Johnston was aware of some wrongdoing, or maybe he just didn't want to face the fact that the company's dirty laundry was about to be washed in public. For the next three minutes, which felt to everyone but the president like the next three hours, silence filled the air in the president's office. Finally, Nichols spoke. Since bad news was already out there, he wanted to pull the band aid off quickly and completely, so to speak—just get it all on the table at once.

"Correct me if I'm wrong, Lydia, but I think the incorrect information in our federal reporting on the contracts makes our IRS filings a problem too," he said.

The president looked at Mann, tacitly daring her to say something he didn't want to hear. Still, a direct question was asked and in Mann's view, it demanded a direct answer.

"Yes that's right," Mann replied. "We used that information in compiling our federal information returns, so a substantial error in the accounting on that contract will cause a substantial error in our federal tax filings."

"Again, we can just say we made a mistake," the president suggested. "File an amended return—no harm no foul."

"It won't be that simple, sir," Mann said, pressing her luck.

"What now, Lydia?" Johnston howled.

The Acting CFO sighed heavily. "Sorry to say, but there could be another issue here…These discrepancies were previously noted in a pre-planned self-audit we did some time ago. Internal Audit included it in their draft report for the year, but the final report doesn't reflect this issue."

"How the hell did that happen?"

"The draft audit report was edited internally before it went final, and it appears these issues were edited out of the report."

"Great, great," Johnston said. "What idiot did that?"

Now *that* was really a question nobody wanted to answer. The truth would be really uncomfortable to say, and might really hurt anyone who did. Mann sat back in her chair.

"Uh, I'm not sure…Counselor?" she asked.

The lawyer at once grew red-in-the-face, more from anger the buck had been passed to him—again—rather than embarrassment. He stammered for what to say, and finally settled on a slightly watered down version of the truth.

"Looks like it was edited somewhere in the president's office as well as on the committee."

"By whom?" Johnston demanded.

Reluctantly, the lawyer answered the president's question, only because the president was staring at him when he asked it. "You, sir, and the audit committee chair."

*Boom.* There it was, out in the open. Nobody wanted to explain to the president at this point that these facts would make it appear to a jury that the failure to disclose the right information was an intentional decision made by the president of the company and/or the chairman of its audit committee, and maybe by the board itself. Alternatively, they could press forward with a *mistake* defense, and look to employees, shareholders, Pentagon officials, customers and potential customers, the general public, and possible future employers like a bunch of ignorant buffoons merely playing a game of big business. Another awkward silence hung in the room, and yet again Nichols broke the ice.

"The numbers aren't the only concern," he said. "The NSA agent, Kenison, indicated there were problems on the UAV contracts."

Johnston sat stone-faced as he stared at Nichols. "Go on."

"First," Nichols explained, "He indicated something about out-of-scope work for which charges were made against the contract, and second, there was some variation between our progress reports to the Air Force and what they found when they audited us."

"What the hell does that mean?"

"The first comment goes to whether we went beyond what we were chartered to do under the contract."

"English please, Mr. Chief Compliance Officer," the president admonished.

This time, the lawyer jumped into the exchange.

"Based on what I've read and my interactions with them, they're indicating we exceeded the scope of our authority to conduct research on

NexChem, a new chemical compound that essentially renders an interrogated suspect unable to deceive."

"Truth serum?" Johnston suggested.

"Essentially, yes," Nichols replied. "Their second contention on the UAV contract is that we told them two different things about the status of our R&D efforts on the Phantom and Casper programs."

"Good fucking grief," the president groaned. "There's a problem with our research reports now? Get Dr. Catin in here," he yelled out to the anteroom.

The president's secretary shuttled into the room, whereupon he instructed her to interrupt whatever Dr. Catin was doing and get her into his office at once. Meanwhile, Nichols reviewed his notes.

"While we're waiting for Dr. Catin," he said. "Let me just summarize the last of these issues."

"I can't wait to hear this," Johnston quipped.

"The research issues revolve around the fail rate statistics on the neuronetic linkage system used to control the UAVs remotely, and the frequency and severity of what we're calling collateral adversities."

The president seemed very agitated by Nichols' complete explanation.

"Matt, everybody knows you're a smart guy. You don't have to be so precise in your explanations. Just give me the hundred-thousand-foot view."

Both Matos and Nichols were surprised by their chief executive's commentary. After all, the devil of any issue was in the detail. Tending to the excruciating minutia and detail of an issue could be determinative in whether an organization succeeded or failed at a given initiative, and it was what legal and compliance experts got paid big salaries to do. The president was asking for a drive-by, dime-store version.

"Um…uh, yes sir," he said, nearly imperceptibly shaking his head in disbelief. "They're suggesting our equipment doesn't work the way we said, and that we lied to cover it up."

"Oh, okay, I understand that," Johnston said.

Catin came rushing into the president's office at that point.

"Hey, Don, what's going on?" she asked, nonchalantly.

"What's going on is, things are going to hell in a hand-basket on our UAV contract. I need someone to explain to me what that's about," the president grumbled.

"What do you mean?"

Mann, Matos, and Nichols explained the situation in as much detail as Catin needed to understand the president's question. They explained it once, twice, three times in different ways, and by the fifth time, Catin began to grasp the significance of what she was being asked. Like a deer in the headlights, she stared wide-eyed and silent for a moment as she mentally grasped for ideas on how to respond.

"I don't know, Don," she finally said. "Legal had this issue for months and simply didn't act on it. That's why we've got this problem now."

As general counsel, Matos was responsible for the Legal department and its operations. Catin's suggestion that Legal was at fault for the issues associated with the execution of any research contract was a red herring. It annoyed Matos not only because it was wrong, but also because Catin only said it to throw him—or anyone other than herself really—under the bus in an effort to avoid being responsible for what she was responsible. Matos spoke in his own defense and that of the staff reporting to him.

"That's not a plausible answer to the question, Betty. Legal doesn't conduct research on *any* research contracts—that's not our role. We review written documents for legal sufficiency before they go out, but the problem here isn't that the reports didn't get to the Program Office on time, which I believe they did. The problem is that what was written in the reports is substantively wrong, and some of the work for which we charged against the contract shouldn't have been done under this contract. That means someone in one of your areas performed the work improperly, drafted the reports improperly, or some combination of both."

"Well, I'm not the one who does the research," Catin said. "That's the researchers' issues. If there's something wrong then it's their fault, not mine."

"Excuse me," Matos countered, "but doesn't all research report up through you, Madam Vice President for Research?" he challenged, holding back a long-stifled angry outburst.

Then Nichols chimed in. "And as Vice President of Research, don't you approve or disapprove the research reports before they go out?"

"Oh," Catin answered, surprised. "Well I, uh, uh, I probably signed off on whatever I was told to sign, so the Director of Business and CFO would have been the ones who told me to sign the reports."

This was why Mann hadn't wanted the positions into which she'd been thrust. "I didn't have anything to do with authoring or approving research reports," she said, trying to avoid looking like a willing participant in *the he said, she said* game playing out in the president's office.

*Aha. This is a good way to tactfully move away from who's at fault,* Catin thought. "Well, Erich and Francine aren't here to tell us what they did," she said in reference to the two dead former CFOs.

Matos pressed. "Your signature is on the bottom of the reports, Betty. Do you make a habit of simply signing whatever someone puts in your face, Dr. Catin? Don't you read what you're attesting to?"

"Look, goddamn-it," Johnston interrupted. "I need some answers and I need a strategy for reigning in this catastrophe that seems to be spreading like a tilted bucket of horseshit. You people had better get together and figure a way to throw some water on this thing 'til it blows over. Come back and present me with some plausible alternatives. And I don't want to hear any crap about admitting wrongdoing. Even if we did it, we didn't do it, if you get me. Now get out."

Johnston didn't know exactly where this whole matter would end, but his finely tuned intuition from years as a corporate climber and survivalist was telling him that a sacrifice would be necessary. His first priority was assuring that he wouldn't be a contender for that particular honor. As his three vice presidents and the acting CFO filed out of his office, he'd already begun fashioning a plan. When he was satisfied they'd gone, he yelled for his secretary.

"Yes, sir?" she asked, hurrying to his side.

"Get Eilene Reynolds up here STAT."

"Right away, sir."

The secretary walked briskly back to her desk, and raised her phone. She knew the direct dial number for the Vice President of Human Resources by heart.

* * *

"Good morning, everyone," Tran said, closing the door and walking back to the conference table in her office. "I know this is way before the normal show-time for most of you, but maybe this will take the edge off," she said, taking the seat at the head of the table.

The rest of Field Team Six was already assembled at the table, and trying to look alive, alert, awake, and enthusiastic, while awaiting the start of the impromptu meeting the boss had called late last night. She'd indicated she wanted a Powwow, but there was something different about the lead-in for this one. Tran pulled coffee and Danishes for everyone from a Star-Doe's bag, and passed them around the table. It was a consolation prize for having to come in early, but Vivian on the Ito-pad would have to settle for hearing the *mmms* and *yums* her teammates would utter as they partook.

"Sorry, Viv," Tran said. "I'll eat some extra for you."

"Don't bother me none," Viv said. "You know what they say…a moment on the lips, a lifetime on the hips," she chided. "Girl, I don't need no help there, that's for damn sure."

Tran and Starr got a good laugh from Lawrence's remark, but the humor seemed lost on the men in the group. Tran waited a few moments for people to get their bounty and settle themselves. When they had, she began.

"I've been going over the bits and pieces of information you've all been sharing with me by email, text, voicemail, and phone conversation in the last couple weeks…Thanks to your hard work, there's been quite a bit of development on various parts of this case. I believe we're ready to move beyond evidence-gathering and analysis to telling the narrative…in a more formal, perhaps forceful way."

"Here, here," Lockwood cheered.

"I'll start with an update on board member Hamidi's potential connections to nationals of her native country," Tran said. "From early on, we knew the dead woman encrypted her flash drives and her laptop with security software created by MOIS, the Iranian Ministry of Intelligence and Security. CIA says this software, called *Deepest Secret*, is used exclusively by the Iranian government and its allies, arguably to protect their classified information from the west. According to classified CIA information, we cracked this encryption algorithm two years ago, long before the Iranian's ever deployed it. The long and short of it is, acquisition, distribution, trade, and use of that commodity is, by itself, a violation of US law."

"How?"

"Our best guess at this point is Ketcham got it through Hamidi, who in turn got it through her contacts in Iran, namely this woman named Meera Sorosh, an Iranian-born naturalized citizen of Pakistan who serves as a secretary in the Iranian Interests section of the Pakistani Embassy in DC. The Hamidi and Sorosh families have long-standing business and political ties."

"So the board member is working her husband's family connections?" Kenison asked.

Tran nodded. "That was the thought, anyway. They supposedly shared the goal of effecting political reform in Iran, and were directing funds through an off-shore account via several different organizations, and eventually to an organization in Pakistan dedicated to doing just that."

Ito interrupted. "And I can tell you that the money transferred to the off-shore account that ultimately went to that Pakistani front came from the same ERAC accounts designated for UAV contract work, at least according to Ketcham's secret transaction record. I cracked the encrypted flash drives her IT guy gave me, which he copied from her computer. They contain a butt-load of transactions, several of which show multiple transfers to these different accounts."

"You mean to tell me that Ketcham woman was dumb enough to write this shit down?" Lawrence asked.

"Apparently so," Kenison said. "She didn't learn one of the key lessons of the Watergate Scandal. If you want something to stay secret, don't record it. She made a record of all her transactions. "

Starr added, "She was probably getting to the point where there were just too many lies to keep straight in her head."

"I'll say," Kenison agreed. "She sent the money through multiple agreements, contracts, and arrangements with several different foundations, non-profits, and private companies, including a few run by Hamidi's husband. This was clearly an effort to put space between Earhardt-Roane and the transfer of the money, and it would have been enough to throw off the average guy. She just didn't count on me chasing her down. I'm just too good."

"I told you, follow the money," Lawrence exclaimed. "Always follow the money."

"Man, this is several different kinds of illegal, no matter how you look at it," Lockwood noted.

"It's a lot worse than that," Tran said. "CIA believes Meera Sorosh is most likely an Iranian double-agent. Her family did go way back politically with the family of Hamidi's husband, but this woman is kind of a rogue member of her family. The Iranian authorities have arrested many of the people who were benefactors in Iran of this Pakistani organization, and the Agency believes the money being funneled into these political reformist groups in Iran is actually being used by the Iranian government to fund religious extremist groups in Iraq and Afghanistan," Tran said.

"Shit," Kenison barked. "These bastards are funding the terrorists trying to kill our men and women in uniform."

"This is probably enough to arrest Hamidi right now, but there needs to be a little more digging to see who else is involved. That's beyond our scope, so we'll pack up our files on this matter and hand it off to our friends at the Bureau, the US Attorney, and the Department of Justice. We have the evidence and several ABC agencies have eyes on Hamidi, so she won't go anywhere the government doesn't let her."

"Bam," Lawrence yelled, clenching her fist in the air and pulling downward as though pulling a cord from above her head. "Guess we're gonna' take that bitch down a few pegs."

"I think a little more than a few," Tran said. "Moving on…"

"Boss, before we move on, can we go back to the flash drives I got from the IT guy?" Ito asked.

"By all means, Rique. The floor is yours," Tran offered.

"I interrogated Ketcham's IT guy yesterday and got a wealth of information from him, although I don't think he even knows how much he gave me. He kept copies of all the files on Ketcham's computers from shortly after he started working on them."

"He did this surreptitiously or with Ketcham's consent?" someone asked.

"Covertly. This guy was afraid of Ketcham and her connections, and he broke into her files merely for the challenge of doing it. He ended up copying the files once he saw what was in them in case he ever needed to hold something over Ketcham's head."

"Such trusting work relationships," Starr observed.

"He had a good teacher," Ito said. "He told me Ketcham tasked him to install video monitoring surveillance on her computer and in two remote devices."

"Obviously the means for acquiring the video tapes of Johnston and Day in flagrante delicto," Kenison said.

"Yes, but it communicated an important lesson to him as far as dealing with this woman was concerned. He saw what she valued and then used it against her," Starr said. "Her behavior was instructive for teaching him how best to deal with her."

Ito continued. "Among the more interesting emails were those between Ketcham and a guy named Durl Hasse."

Kenison supplemented the group's knowledge of this new name in the group conversation. "Hasse's an ASS-hole—it's a term of endearment the local Bureau boys use for members of the Aryan Supremacy Society who hole-up on a farm in Rahain," he advised. "He's former Army explosives ordnance division, and thus has a great deal of explosives expertise…"

"Hey, boss lady," Lawrence called from the screen of the Ito-pad.

"Viv?"

"Remember you asked me to locate the wreckage from the Renley lady if I could?"

"Uh-huh," Tran said.

"Well this is as good a time as any to tell you I did it," Lawrence gloated. "I had it tested like you asked, and guess what?" She didn't wait for an answer. "The results matched the chemical traces found in the Day crash."

"So, both Day's and Renley's deaths were murder," Kenison said.

"Looks that way," Lockwood said. "And by the same boogie man."

"Hasse definitely has the skills to do it," Kenison continued. "The bomb signature in the Day accident, and now presumably the Renley accident, matches that of IEDs used in the same part of Afghanistan where Hasse was stationed. Hasse was court-martialed and sent to Leavenworth for ten years for setting IEDs that killed sixty-four Afghan civilians, including women, children, and the elderly whom he called *ragheads and camel jockeys*. After getting bounced from the Army, he returned last year to his hometown of Rahain. He's very bitter toward the Army, the US government, the President, and anyone of color. This guy's final discharge evaluation suggests he's capable of violence, especially against anyone he deems a lesser person."

"The emails?" Tran prompted.

"Oh yeah," Ito said. He hadn't really forgotten but just hadn't figured a way to jump back into the flow. "According to her emails, Ketcham gave Hasse a list of do's and don'ts, including never contact her directly, never show up anywhere she was, and never talk about the job in writing. She told him to get a pre-paid phone with which to contact her, and gave him a number to use with which to contact her. She said there could be no traceable connections between them. Emails tell him where to meet her, where to pick up a package, which I believe to be a cash payment for *the job* they referred to several times."

"This is good stuff," Lockwood opined.

"One of her transaction records shows she made a $50,000 cash payment to him and a guy named Kevin Duke Russ around the same time as the emails."

"Russ is the big ASS hole-up in Rahain. He owns the land where they live and train, and they all take their orders from him," Kenison footnoted.

"And my guy, Ketcham's private detective, connects Ketcham to both of them, along with the cash payment. He says his cousin, Durl Hasse, gloated about getting Ketcham a promotion for which she'd be indebted to him for life."

Tran nodded. "Okay. That perhaps addresses the murders of Day and Renley, but where are we on the Ketcham murder?" she asked, turning to Lockwood.

"I think we can rule out Lauxner as a suspect," Kenison chimed. "I interviewed the guy and I've seen into his soul. I'm convinced he didn't have anything to do with it."

"Sounds like you've got a little bromance going on there," Lockwood joked.

"The guy's an honest, genuine war hero, smartie-pants. Besides, his alibi checks out solid," Kenison retorted.

Lockwood laughed. He enjoyed poking fun at Kenison, but he really respected Kenison and anyone else who served in the US armed forces. He nodded slightly to indicate his true agreement with Kenison's assessment.

"And boss," Kenison added, "Lauxner is an out-of-work war hero trying to take care of his little boys on his own. He's pretty sharp in tactical observation and analysis. If there's a place for him somewhere in the agency or somewhere else you know of, I'd vouch for him."

"You feel that strongly about him after having met with him once?" Tran asked.

Kenison nodded. "I only met with him once, but like I said, I looked into the man's soul. Besides, I feel like I know this dude. I reviewed every Army record made about this dude from his first day of enlistment, and talked to a few people who knew him, including a Major I personally know and respect immensely. Everybody says the same thing about him—he's a really good guy, the kind you want on your team."

Tran nodded. "All right, Stefan. If you feel that strongly, I'll look around and find something for him, but that'll have to wait until we're done with this case. Deal?"

"Deal," Kenison said. "And thanks."

Tran nodded.

"I have a little pearl to add too," Lockwood announced. "About our potential suspect, following a hunch, I got surveillance footage from the banks across from the Earhardt-Roane building. With the kind assistance of *Boy Wonder* over there," he said, bobbing his head at Ito, "we isolated a shadow we think could be the murderer. Cameras caught the shadow moving around outside the building at approximately the same time of the murder, and there's no reason for anyone to be there at that hour."

"Are you sure you didn't just capture a trick of light, maybe shadows from passing cars?" Tran asked.

"Quite sure," Ito answered. "I applied an analytic algorithm I developed to the footage Lockwood gave me. We had to work around interference from trees, landscaping, cars, and road signs, but eliminating as much of the video *noise* as possible, we came up with some basic biometrics on the shadow. We still couldn't get a clear picture of the face, but we think the shadow is a male under thirty, probably Caucasian based on light levels and distribution, and probably about 6'2" tall and one-hundred eighty pounds or so, with a shoulder span of roughly sixteen inches. I can show you if you like."

Despite the excitement in his voice, Tran deferred on that opportunity, but nonetheless considered the new information. "So where does this lead you?" she asked.

"I'm glad you asked," Lockwood said. "With this information, I went back over the entire case file and something jumped out at me."

"What's that?"

"If you recall, at the original scene inspection, there was a soda can on the floor, which contained a fingerprint belonging to the victim's son. We initially didn't consider him because if that can came from her home, it would be logical for his fingerprint to be on the coke can."

"Where are you going with this?" Kenison asked, a twinge of excitement in his voice.

"Hold your horses, junior," Lockwood said. "I'm getting there... Anyway, before I was so rudely interrupted, I said we didn't consider the son a suspect, but Ito's new information made me rethink our assumptions about who might or might not be a suspect. The son occurred to me because of the soda can. I looked up his info in his JROTC file, and it just so happens, the boy is a close physical match to the biometrics Ito told us about."

"Shit," Kenison said.

Tran leaned forward in her chair. "Shit indeed."

"That would be a huge leap with deep psychological underpinnings," Starr said. "It wouldn't be unheard of but—" She inhaled and exhaled deliberatively as she shook her head side to side at the possibility.

"I agree," Lockwood said. "So I did a little further looking at something...When I was out at their house talking to the husband, I noticed a supply of soda there. It didn't really mean anything to me until I started rethinking about the soda can on the floor of Ketcham's office. The soda at their house is the Diet Cola Blast brand, not Star Cola. I paid a little visit overnight to Earhardt-Roane. As it turns out, the batch numbers on the Star Cola can found at the scene match the batch numbers of the Star Cola cans sold in the corporate Vending Room."

"So the son's print on the can at the scene means he was in the office at some point recently," Lawrence said.

"Yeah. The security guy at Roane said the vending machines in that building were restocked by the outside supplier the day before the murder," Lockwood said. "So it stands to reason the print got onto the can sometime between midday Thursday and 4:00 a.m. Saturday morning. We can further narrow the time by a few hours, because if it was the son, I found out from the school that he was in JROTC drill team practice on Thursday until 7:30 p.m. Now we're looking at a window between say 8:00 p.m. Thursday to 7:20 a.m. Friday when he was back in school, and another window between 7:30 p.m. Friday when he left drill practice again, and 4:00 a.m. Saturday when the murder occurred. That's roughly a seventeen-hour window in which he might have gotten his fingerprint on that bottle of Star Cola in his mother's office."

"It's possible the victim bought the can at work, took it home during that seventeen hour period, where her son applied his print, and then she returned it to her office next time she went," Tran thought aloud. "That's a bit distorted, but a crafty defense lawyer could make some hay of it."

"Those damn shysters will try to make hay out of anything," Lockwood objected. "That's okay though because I also asked the lab to specifically type the skin cells from the dandruff ERT recovered from the backrest on the chair at the crime scene to see. If they're a match, it means the kid was inside the office. They'll have to reckon with that too."

"Won't they just argue the son had been in the office before and that's why the skin cells were there?" Kenison asked.

"The executive offices have maid service every night after hours. Ketcham's office would have been cleaned and dusted down the evening before the early morning murder. But like I said, shyster lawyers will say anything to get what they want—look at Matos. He cowers and babbles to keep his highfalutin Earhardt job, and any lawyer defending this kid will do likewise. The long and short of it is, they damn well might argue that, but all the little pieces of evidence combine together to paint a pretty damning picture for a jury."

"Look, I'm not saying we don't move forward with this, but we'll need to consider the possibility of counter arguments the other side will make," Tran said, pausing to think about the next steps in the process.

"Well, I plan to go talk to the kid at his school. I put in a call to his principal an hour ago to arrange it. I just want to see what he has to say. Dr. Starr, I'd appreciate it if you'd come with me whenever we finalize a time. I think that'll point me one way or the other for sure on this, but I'm feeling something here. I'll keep you posted," Lockwood said.

"Very well," Tran agreed, shifting focus. "As you all know, our real purpose here is evaluating the national security threat this situation may pose...We've covered the potential links to foreign nationals, but let me brief you about the UAV contract."

"Please tell me you found something," Lockwood said.

"Yes, I'm real interested in that too," Kenison agreed.

"We have found something. We got the Air Force program office responsible for the UAV contract to help sort through the contract issues involved here. The principal program official is a Colonel named Blunt. He told me Earhardt-Roane is performing unauthorized research into something called NexChem, a new and improved sort of truth serum evidently. He also said there was serious misreporting, and probably fraudulent reporting, on the reliability of some aspects of the UAV contract. Blunt says there's a national security risk here because the correct data shows the UAVs are much more likely to fail than anyone at the Pentagon thought. If deployed with weapons payloads or intelligence equipment onboard, a failed UAV could place vital US property and information in the hands of hostiles."

"Then it seems our work here is done," Lockwood said.

Tran nodded. "Partially, but there may be more left to uncover. The agency wants to know who's involved and how deep this runs," she informed. "They wouldn't tell me as much, but I also think they'll want to use this as an opportunity for counter-intelligence... that's what I'd do if I was running that show."

"So you think they're not ready to move on this?" Kenison asked.

"No, I don't."

"That sucks," he exclaimed. "These rats are putting our troops in harm's way every day this goes unaddressed."

"I understand your feelings, Stefan," Tran said. "But the right people are aware of the situation and can thus mitigate any harm to our troops. Plus, we now know what's going on here, and can stop them from exploiting the government. None of the people involved are going anywhere, and if they tried, we can get them wherever and whenever we want. On the other hand, the potential gain by not reeling everyone in immediately may become a treasure trove for our covert Intel operations."

She could see Kenison really wanted to just go arrest all the bad guys right away, humiliate them on the nightly news, and ruin their lives for their treachery. She didn't blame him—in many ways, she felt the same. But, at the top of the chain, she had to take the long view. As he matured professionally, Kenison would come to see that as well.

"All right," Tran said, apparently coming to some conclusions. "So the transaction records and emails link Ketcham to the private investigator, who in turn links Ketcham to Russ and Hasse. We've got pretty solid evidence to pin the murders of Melvin Renley and Erich Day, and the attempted murder of Venita Renley to Russ and Hasse in a murder-for-hire scheme initiated by Ketcham so she could get a promotion," Tran summarized.

"That's about the size of it," Lockwood agreed.

"We also have solid evidence on illegal transfer and trade in Iranian technology by Ketcham, and we think it was through Hamidi and Sorosh, the latter of whom may be an intelligence double agent for Iran. We have funding of middle-east terror groups, albeit inadvertently, by Ketcham and Hamidi using ERAC funds which were redirected from a US government contract, all under the nose of the company President."

"And that's about the size of that," Lockwood said.

Tran sat in momentary silence as she considered the strength of the evidence they'd gathered. She wasn't the US Attorney who'd prosecute the case, but she was a legally trained professional who knew her job well. She made a command decision.

"Very well. I think it's time to invite Mr. Russ and Mr. Hasse to spend a little time in our chateau. Saddle up, people. We have work to do."

# Chapter 9

# Up the Ante

Like former Green Beret Stefan Kenison, Tran would have liked to strapped-on her weapon and body armor, and then driven over to take Russ and Hasse by surprise, using shock and awe, and overwhelming firepower as the tactic of choice. It would have been a great machismo moment that appealed to Field Team Six's cowboy instincts, but doing so without coordinating with Agent Allen might have compromised the Bureau's ongoing investigation of the Aryan Supremacy Society. It might have also caused more bloodshed than necessary because the ASS-holes weren't shy about their disdain for any government agency or anyone who worked for them. They had plenty of arms and munitions, and a deeply ingrained survivalist mentality, and the government didn't want another Ruby Ridge or Waco on its hands. Besides, Field Team Six's forte' was much more stealth in nature than anything else. That started with meticulous advanced planning, something at which Tran was particularly skilled.

The FBI believed it could fashion a limited operation to arrest Russ and Hasse without permanently damaging its long-term surveillance of the group and anyone allied with it. They couldn't launch an all-out armed assault because the ASS-holes would resist, thus forcing the team to either abandon the effort altogether, or engage with overwhelming firepower. That could generate a great deal of press coverage just like Ruby Ridge and Waco did, and in addition to dealing with the political and PR fallout from such an assault, their surveillance operation would be disrupted for a very long while, if not forever. In the aftermath of such an action, the ASS couldn't continue its normal activities and other militias and hate groups allied with them would be wary of anything associated with the ASS. This particular intelligence-gathering operation would be done. So, arresting Russ and Hasse while leaving the ASS otherwise intact would require a surgical covert operation in which the other members of the ASS and their allies didn't know the two were arrested. Agent Allen and Agent Tran had worked long and hard into the wee hours of night every day for the past week to create such a plan in which a 9-member assault force divided into two teams would get in and get out of the house with their targets as quietly as possible rather than a bullet-blazing firefight that left the scene littered with bodies. Having fully vetted it for potential oversights, errors, screw-ups and downfalls, a combined NSA-FBI assault team was now poised to execute the ops plan.

In the pre-dawn hours the day of the raid, the team flew into Rahain on ultra-quiet Pave Hawk helicopters out of Patrick Air Force Base. The stealthy choppers came in inches above the tree line, and then dropped to a foot above the middle of a swamp two-hundred yards southwest of the ASS headquarters. Dressed entirely in black and toting advanced weapons, they jumped from the chopper into the water, and hurried to the shore. Once there, they quickly organized themselves and then dispersed into the woods, moving fast and silent like modern Ninjas until they were positioned around the ASS farm. Allen's inside man had pinned chemical tracking beacons to the necks of Kevin Duke Russ and Durl Hasse without them even knowing. All it took was a friendly clap on the back of their necks during a greeting and the tracker was set. They'd be detectable by assault team's scanners for thirty-six hours after which they'd become inert and wash away with water or sweat.

The team had been in position one-hundred fifty feet from the house for roughly two hours, carefully watching the farm on several different types of scanners, in addition to using more traditional methods like binoculars and bare-eyed observation. Except for the one night guard whom Allen's deep-cover agent said would be on watch, there was essentially no movement or activity in the house. Allen hoped his agent would have been successful in getting assigned to watch duty for the night, but the first time he saw the guard come out of the house and light up a cigarette, he knew it wasn't his agent. Still, the single sentry ventured onto the front porch every thirty minutes or so, smoked a cigarette for roughly ten minutes, walked the perimeter of the house, and then returned to the front room where he continued flipping channels on the TV. Except for perhaps Allen's insider, everyone else in the house was asleep, secure in the knowledge that a brother-in-arms kept watch with an automatic rifle and vigilant eyes. Besides, it had been several weeks since they'd done anything that might have caused anyone to seek their heads on a platter. Hasse was in the downstairs bedroom at the back of the house, along with three bunk mates sleeping nearby. Russ and apparently a smaller-framed partner of the fairer sex occupied an upstairs bedroom at the top of the stairs in the front of the house. Eight others were in the two remaining upper bedrooms, all with weapons nearby.

The teams would enter the house through the front door, locate and render the targets unconscious, and then egress the entry point with targets in tow. Once clear of the house, the teams, their cargo, Ito, and his FBI protector would fall back to the swamp a hundred feet southwest of the duck blind. They'd wade through the swamp and hook-on to evacuation lines from the Pave Hawks that would be in hover mode, awaiting their return to the drop zone. Hoping to avoid any need for firearms, the teams were equipped with an impressive array of silent, non-lethal weapons, but if anything went wrong, they were also equipped with a plethora of lethal options. Allen staunchly reminded them about his deep cover agent inside whom he didn't want harmed. *Tango, Tango 123* was Logan Noel's ID phrase, and the team had clear instructions not to harm anyone uttering it. Tran had detailed Lockwood, Starr, and two FBI agents to grab Hasse, while she, Kenison, and Allen went after the big ASS-hole upstairs. Ito and an FBI agent to cover his flank remained in their makeshift command post in the woods, camouflaged by darkness, heavy thicket, and a duck blind. There, they'd monitor surveillance equipment and the team's vital signs and helmet cameras, and manage the team's communications. After a final review of the ops plan, it was time for the team to move.

"Systems check," Tran whispered into her air-mic.

"Team One, check," those on Lockwood's team whispered in turn.

"Team Two, check," Kenison and Allen said.

"Alpha check," Tran said.

Listening carefully to the exchange and watching the monitors, Ito gave a thumbs up and a nod.

"All right, goggles on and start mission timers now. Let's move out."

The agents lowered their night vision eyewear, poured smoothly from the command post, and fanned into the woods. Moisture wafting from the swamp wet the ground and muffled the noise of twigs and brush crushing under the team's feet as they quickly and quietly closed on the house. The lone sentry stepped outside just as they reached its front porch, but since his pupils hadn't yet adjusted to the nighttime light outside, he didn't see the black-clad agents only ten feet away, and he didn't know anything was wrong until he felt a sharp pain in his neck. Thinking he'd been stung by a bee or wasp, he fell first to his knees and then nearly face-planted on the porch, save for a quick catch by Kenison, who hoped to prevent the man from making a thud when he fell. Enriched ketamine delivered by blow dart into his right carotid artery spread quickly through his body, sending him into an immediate slumber. Meanwhile, Starr rounded the side, careful to avoid stepping into the line of sight from the windows, and made her way to the house's air compressor. Even at this time of year in Florida, residential air conditioners ran nearly 24-7 to keep homes habitable by contemporary Americans. She jabbed the pointed end of a gas canister into the return-air line and then rejoined the team as its contents filtered into the air going back inside.

Up front, the team kept low in the bushes, shadows, and other out-of-sight places while they waited for the fast-acting gas to saturate the ventilation system and circulate. It was the longest seven minutes any of them could remember in a while, but when it was done, they donned masks that covered only their mouths with a small extension to their noses, and breached the front door, one guarding the advance of the other. From the entryway, they could tell the place was a pig-sty. Empty, half-crushed cans of beer, empty or half-empty bottles of whiskey and vodka, fast-food wrappers, and other refuse lay strewn about the rooms visible from the entryway, and to the right of the door was the lamp-lit living room with an older-style tube television playing re-runs of shows from the 1970's, the canned laugh tracks echoing through the house. The team members double-checked to assure their scanners hadn't missed a random person loitering or sleeping in either of the rooms at the front of the house, and once satisfied, began to split into their separate parts of this mission. Lockwood's team pushed deeper into the rear of the house, while Tran's group ascended the stairs.

Allen moved in quickly and planted himself at the foot of the stairs while Kenison went up first, followed by Tran. Then, Allen followed and advanced to the lead position while Tran covered him on the right and Kenison the left. They moved a few feet to the door of the master bedroom on the left side of the hall and took position on either side of it. Allen went to the far side, and kept watch to assure no one surprised them from down the hall or from down the stairs. Tran reached for the doorknob, but Kenison suddenly slapped her hand away lightly, and whispered into his microphone.

"Movement inside," he said, pointing at the door and forcing each whispered word around the air supply steadily streaming into his mouth.

Tran alerted and checked the motion sensor strapped to her weapon. By the metrics displayed on the scanner, it appeared Russ's companion hadn't succumbed to the gases leaching into her love chamber, but Tran didn't quite understand why. She quickly had to determine how she'd eliminate this secondary target as a threat to the objective, and decided a Ketamine dart would suffice for her too. She toggled her weapon and prepared to fire as Kenison made ready to open the door, giving his boss a clear shot at the target. A voice softly cracked over the speaker in every team member's ears.

"Tango, Tango 1-2-3," the voice called. "I'm moving toward the hall door of the master bedroom. Nobody shoot me."

It was Allen's inside man, or woman, in this case. Tran and Kenison snapped their gazes to Allen, who after recognizing the code and tone of voice, nodded and thumbs-upped his confirmation.

"Target One is under," Noel said. "I say again, Target One is under and the room is clear. You can come in to retrieve him without resistance. I'm opening the master bedroom door in three, two, one," she signaled.

The door opened slowly, revealing a woman wearing an oxygen mask similar to those worn by team members. She held both her hands above her head, with her palms facing the agents she knew would be on the other side of the door, waiting in the dark with weapons that could maim or kill her. She wore a black wife-beater T-shirt that did little to hide her plentiful breasts which were obviously unrestrained by a bra, and holey, green camouflage pants that tapered into a pair of dingy black combat boots. Her arms were decorated with skeleton and snake tattoos that matched the double ring piercings on her lower left lip, and a spiked chain lay atop her boney clavicle. A heavy silver chain hung on her waist, as did empty holsters for a handgun and a large knife of some sort. Her unkempt blonde hair hung lackadaisically at her neck, easily capturing the scarce light in the darkened room. She reeked of several different kinds of booze mixed with fetid remnants of cigars, cigarettes, and pot.

"Tango, Tango 1-2-3," she repeated. "Don't shoot."

Tran, Kenison, and Allen had trained their weapons center mass on the door, just in case this was some sort of ruse. As the woman slowly advanced, Tran quickly snatched her out of the room and tossed her to Allen, immediately retraining her weapon into the dark room…just in case. Allen caught his agent and quickly looked her over. She appeared okay.

"You All right?" he asked.

"It's all good, boss," she answered. "He was passed out drunk and high before you got here."

Allen caught Tran's eye, gave her a thumb in the air to confirm his agent's identity once more, and then helped Noel back to her feet. Tran and Kenison rushed into the room, taking care to check behind the door as well as any shadows and recesses along the wall before finally reaching the bedside of the unconscious Kevin Duke Russ. Looking down at the pallid, scruffy, oddly shaped lump in the bed, they accurately guessed he'd once been a thin guy who drank too much and did too many drugs that adversely affected his body. Kenison leaned over and in one fell swoop, hiked Russ onto his shoulder, and turned for the door. Tran called over the mic to let everyone know they'd secured Target One, and then led him out of the room and down the stairs. Allen and Noel fell in behind them and hurried to the assembly point near the front porch. Moments later, they heard Team Two inform their Target was also secure, and then watched them exit the house with Hasse's rear bobbing alongside Lockwood's head. They all removed the masks from their faces and took deep breaths of fresh swamp air.

"Proceed to the rendezvous and load the cargo. We'll be right behind you," Tran directed the porters.

Lockwood and Kenison didn't verbally respond, but instead hot-footed back toward the command post. After instructing Starr to retrieve the empty gas canister from the farm's A/C unit, Tran turned, climbed the porch stairs, and walked back inside the house to Allen and his deep cover agent.

"Agent Noel, this was a smooth operation largely due to your efforts. I hope you didn't have to do anything too distasteful to make this happen," Tran said.

At first, Noel didn't realize what the NSA boss was talking about. When she considered where they'd found her and what state they'd found her in, she knew at once.

"Oh, no," she said. "I poured liquor all over myself and gargled with it to maintain appearances. It would be very dangerous for a woman to lose control of her faculties around these pukes," she said, nodding at the unconscious hater on the ground. "And the big ASS-hole—like I said, he was self-medicated before you got here tonight. I just helped him go down a road he was already traveling." She laughed lightly under her breath and shook her head as she thought about Russ, the big ASS-hole. "That disgusting pig has been pawing at me for a while now, but tonight was just the latest in a continuous string of nights he hasn't gotten lucky, at least with me."

"How have you kept him off you," Allen playfully asked, admiring her garb.

"Easy. I told him he and I bat for the same team."

"You're a piece of work, as they said," Allen quipped, shaking his head.

"Sometimes I think he sees it as a challenge," Noel replied.

"Well whatever you did, you did it well. Thank you very much, Agent Noel," Tran said.

"Any time," she answered. "Anything to promote interagency cooperation."

She smiled, and then turned and rushed into the living room, where she grabbed several half-empty bottles of liquor. She opened them and poured their contents all over the sentry's clothing, and just enough to taste into his mouth.

"Russ chewed him a new asshole the other day for drinking too much and too often, so this will focus attention on him when the others realize those two are missing…Okay, I gotta' get back up there before your magic starts wearing off, and you need to get the hell outta' here. Take these…" She handed a set of keys to Allen, whom took them and immediately passed them to Agent Thorsten, one of his other agents.

"Stay safe," Allen whispered, loud enough for her to hear as she retreated into the house and closed the door behind her.

"Let's go," Tran barked.

Except for Thorsten, the remaining team members beat a hasty retreat to the command post where they met up with Ito and helped him disassemble the duck blind. Precisely ninety-two seconds later, leaving no trace of the command post, the team struck out for the swamp. The Pave Hawks quietly awaited them 20 feet above the murky water, a sound like the thud of one's fist lightly striking his own chest and some strong rotor-wash the only signs of the black aircrafts' presence. In ten minutes, they'd be back at the FBI field office, where Russ and Hasse would be attended by an FBI medic in *Detention*. Allen's last remaining agent, who happened to be about the same build and hair color as Kevin Duke Russ, walked a few paces to the latter's old pick-up and fired its engine. He'd enjoy a leisurely forty minute drive along the main highway through town and back to Seaside Beach. It was still early and a bit dark, but he'd leave the truck parked in the lot at the Farmer's Market, one of Russ's favorite places when he wasn't playing *rogue commando*.

\* \* \*

A single, loud, piercing knock at the door announced someone's presence, but the people inside the conference room could only assume who it was.

"Come in," Mrs. Short replied to the sound.

The door opened to reveal a tall thin young man dressed in the unmistakable uniform of a United States Marine. His brown short-sleeve shirt had perfect creases ironed into them from the top of his shoulder down to his elbow, a bevy of training ribbons and patches neatly adorning the left side of his chest above the pocket, and his nametag on the right. The button line of his shirt flowed smoothly in line with a highly shined belt buckle and the zipper of his perfectly pressed blue trousers. The pockets of his pants were sewn shut to enhance the appearance of neatness and the unmarred alignment of his body from top to bottom. His knit cap was neatly folded and wedged between his belt and pants on his right side, and his feet were covered by high-gloss black shoes that reflected the school's standard institutional lighting. The young man entered the room and walked in straight lines and ninety-degree angles to within a few feet of the principal's seat on one side of conference table.

"Cadet Gunnery Sergeant Dallas O'Brien reporting as ordered, ma'am," he said, standing at attention and staring straight ahead, above the principal's eye-level.

Never having been around anyone or anything military, the middle-aged principal had never quite adjusted to the military behavior of the junior ROTC students that attended her school. She simply pretended not to notice it and treated them as she would any other student.

"Uh, yes, Dallas. I'd like to introduce you to Special Agents Starr and Lockwood," she said motioning toward the visitors. "They're visiting today because they have some questions for you."

Lockwood and Starr stood to greet the high school student, whose military bearing was surprisingly disciplined for someone of any age, let alone his. O'Brien relaxed from the position of *Attention* into *Parade Rest*, and then stepped back one step before turning to the two adults who'd come to see him. He extended his hand to them in turn, offering them a *Sir* and *Ma'am*, respectively, as he bobbed his head in a shallow pseudo-bow to acknowledge them.

"Please sit down everyone," Short invited and she motioned to the chairs around the table. She waited for everyone else to seat themselves first, and then took her own chair, carefully folding her skirt under as she did so.

219

"Special Agents Starr and Lockwood are with the National Security Agency, Mr. O'Brien. They have some questions around the, uh, recent events," she explained.

"You mean the death of my mother?" O'Brien asked.

"I'm afraid so," Lockwood said.

"Do you feel comfortable about this?" Starr asked. "Something like this is a very traumatic experience, and it's quite okay if you're having a hard time with it and would rather not talk to us."

The young man looked into his lap for a moment, and then returned his quickly steeled gaze to meet Starr's eyes.

"Ma'am, we've got soldiers deployed to the sand, where every day someone gets shot, or gets their legs blown off by IEDs. We had 3,000 civilians get incinerated in the World Trade Center, or they jumped twenty stories their deaths, or had a billion tons of steel and glass smash the life out of them. Those are traumatic experiences. This is just a conversation between a few people in a stateside air conditioned office," he said.

*Well*, Starr thought. *Guess I've been told.*

"Your step-dad apparently isn't answering his home, office, or cell phones, Mr. O'Brien, but I did reach your father," Principal Short explained. "I informed him the agents wanted to talk to you and asked whether he had any issues with that, or whether he wanted to be here for this. He said the two of you have talked about this matter at some depth on several occasions and that you had nothing to hide. He said it's your call, though—if you want to speak with the agents you may do so, but if you didn't want to, then he'd support that decision."

Cadet O'Brien responded immediately. "I'm not afraid to talk to you."

"We're not suggesting you're afraid to talk to us," Starr said. "You may simply feel uncomfortable or you may want some parental guidance in doing so. There's nothing wrong with that."

"Ma'am, with all due respect, my mother is dead. She can't help me with anything. She never did anyway. She only told me what to do all the time. My dad has never really guided me with things other than surfing, and John-Paul, well he's useless, with all due respect. He only did what my mom let him do anyway, and without her, he probably can't find his way out of a paper sack. I can do for myself. I am a Marine, you know—at least I will be."

"Okay then," Lockwood said, chiming into the conversation. "First, let me say I'm sorry about what happened to your mom. I know that has to be hard."

"It is what it is," O'Brien said, shrugging his shoulders and looking at the ground. "Everyone dies—it's the great circle of life."

"So how do you feel about—" Starr began.

Lockwood spoke over her as he lightly pressed her wrist under the table. He wanted to get to the heart of his questions, and besides, this wasn't a therapy session. That was someone else's job.

"Dallas, do you know what lawyer your mother or your mom and step-dad may have used on a regular basis?" Lockwood asked.

"I don't know of any lawyer they used. I know she kicked some people out of one of her rental properties before, but she did it herself. She didn't hire a lawyer for that."

"And you never heard her talk about using a lawyer, or talk about anyone she knows who is a lawyer?"

"No. Sorry, sir."

"It's okay. Let me change subjects here a bit, Dallas. Have you ever seen a knife like this?" Lockwood asked, holding the artist's rendering for the boy to see.

The young man looked at it for a brief second. "Not really."

"Not really? Does that mean you've seen *something* like it?"

"My step-dad has a fishing knife that might be something like that. Don't they all look alike?"

"I don't think so," Lockwood said. "I mean, the blade on this thing's pretty radical isn't it?"

"I guess," O'Brien replied. "A blade's a blade."

"If you had to bet a million bucks on it, would you say your step-dad's knife is like this or not?" he brandished the picture again.

The young man stared at it again. "Yeah I guess so."

"Okay, cool. Let me ask a random question. What kind of pop did your mom drink?"

The boy wrinkled his brow, quizzically pondering Lockwood's question. *What does that have to do with the price of tea in China?* he wondered.

"She was Nazi about Diet Cola Blast," he quickly answered. "If we brought any other kind into our house, she'd have a cow. She insisted that if we were going to drink soda, it had to be Diet Cola Blast because it contained no calories, no fat, and no high fructose corn syrup."

"What kind do you like best?"

"Star Cola or root beer," Dallas answered.

"You didn't like Diet Cola Blast?

221

"No sir, it tastes like shit."

After a few seconds, he seemed to realize he'd let his military bearing slip, and in front of civilians, no less. "Sorry ma'am, ma'am, sir," he said, looking at and nodding to Short, Starr, and Lockwood in turn.

"No worries, son," Lockwood said. "I heard a lot worse when I was in 'Nam."

"You served, sir?" O'Brien asked.

"Drafted at eighteen, and saw action at nineteen," he said. "Got a Purple Heart at twenty for taking three rounds in the left shoulder. I got real bad blood poisoning from it. I was sick for seven months, and thought I was gonna' die or at least lose the arm."

The adults could tell the young man was awed by Lockwood's war story, something Lockwood didn't really like to talk about. That he did so with this young man was telling to Starr, and she could also tell he didn't want to dwell on it. He quickly redirected the momentum to the business at hand.

"Uh, your mom—she was health conscious, I take it?"

"Only where everyone else was concerned. She never said crap about the calories and fat and unhealthy stuff in all the mixed drinks and wine she guzzled like water, but she acted like she was pure as the driven snow," O'Brien replied. "She was one of those *do as I say not as I do* kind of people who didn't understand that leaders have to lead from the point."

"Your mom didn't walk the walk?"

O'Brien scoffed. "No, sir. Francine barked orders at everybody better than any drill sergeant I ever saw, but it was all to keep people from seeing what a fake she was." He paused as he thought for a moment, his eyes cast to the floor.

"Seems like you were angry at her," Starr said.

After a moment, Dallas continued. "She was an overbearing manipulator who tried to make everyone think she was better than she really was by making their lives as miserable as possible. She did it to my dad, she did it to my little brother and me, she did it to people at her work, and she did it to our neighbors. She even did it to her husband—I don't know how he could stand to touch her unless—"

"Unless what?" Starr prompted.

He shook his head—in exasperation, frustration, or disgust, Starr couldn't tell.

"I don't know—nothing, I guess," he said, still staring at the floor.

The room fell silent for a few moments. They were very uncomfortable moments for Mrs. Short in particular who was wondering whether this was getting a little too heavy for a school conversation. Starr could see she was approaching some sort of breaking point and wanted to avoid that if possible.

"Dallas, these seem like some pretty harsh things to say about your mother. Maybe you should talk to someone about your feelings and everything you've been going through. Maybe you can talk to your dad, or the school's counselor, or I can refer you to someone who can help walk through your feelings."

O'Brien sat up straight and looked her dead in the eye. "I don't need to talk to anyone about this or anything else, ma'am," he objected. "Marines don't wallow in sorrow and we don't talk to shrinks about feeling sorry for anything. We don't blow sunshine up people's—" He stopped to rephrase. "We don't sugarcoat things either. We deal with things as they are whatever they are. Francine's dead and that's that. Nothing I say or do will bring her back, even if I wanted to."

"You deal with your mother issues by running away, don't you?" Lockwood asked.

"What are you talking about, sir?" O'Brien challenged.

"I heard you ran away from home a few times. Was that to get away from her?"

"I didn't run from anything, sir," the boy resisted. "I made a tactical retreat so I could regroup and come back to the fight again another way, another day."

"You were fighting with your mom all the times you retreated?"

"We always fought. She expected me to capitulate to her like I was a scared little boy or something, but I'm a Marine, through and through. I don't frighten easily, and I don't back down from a fight. I adapt and overcome by any means possible. We're the first ones to take on the bullies of the world, and we win."

"So your mom was a bully?" Starr asked.

O'Brien tried to restrain the cold glare he felt rushing out of him. He found it annoying that the woman kept repeating things he said, and wondered whether she was dense or something. Still, he forced himself to maintain his composure.

"Yes, ma'am," he calmly answered. "Even my kid brother, her sweet baby, thought so, and I'm sure we had a lot of company in that."

"I heard your mom wanted you to be a businessman—she must have cared about your future, don't you think?"

O'Brien stared blankly for a moment as he tried to fashion an answer to a question, the subject of which pissed him off more than almost anything.

"Francine didn't want me to be a businessman because she cared about my future, sir. She wanted me to be a businessman because that would make her feel like something special and feel proud, not of me but of herself. My becoming a businessman in her mind would tell the world and all her snooty friends that she was successful, especially if I became rich and ran one of this big multinational companies or something. The point is, it wasn't about what I wanted; it was about what she wanted—like always, like with everything and everyone."

"You didn't want success and a lot of money?" Starr asked.

"Ma'am, I wanted to be a Marine. I'm gonna' be a Marine. Francine couldn't handle the fact that I'm the one who controls my future, not her. Marines don't need a lot of money to be successful. We need duty, honor, and country. We need victory. That's what drives me, ma'am," he explained.

"You didn't like your mother's focus on business," Starr paraphrased.

"No ma'am. I didn't. That's what I've been saying for the last ten minutes. I don't give a care in the world what Francine wants—or wanted."

The uncomfortable silence returned to Mrs. Short's office for a few seconds that felt more like an hour.

"You seem pretty mature and pretty knowledgeable about the world for such a young soldier," Lockwood finally said. "Any idea who might want your mom dead?"

Short put her hand to her left brow, as though trying to beat back a migraine.

O'Brien paused for an inordinate time. Finally, he spoke. "I'd look at the people at her work who hated her guts, sir," he answered. "Somebody would call the house and just breath in the phone, or hang up as soon as she'd answer, and I overheard her on her cell phone talking in whispers to someone a couple times, after which she'd be pretty upset and say stuff like *so-and-so is gonna' be the death of me,* or she was gonna' kill someone."

"Any names, by chance?"

He shook his head.

"All right, Cadet. You've been a great help today," Lockwood said as though he was preparing to end their conversation. He stood and began gathering his papers, but then suddenly stopped short. "Oh, just one more thing so I can check this box off my list—where were you the night your mother was killed?"

"I was home with my brother. We were watching a movie on-demand."

"What did you watch?"

"*Star Trek Nemesis.*"

Lockwood laughed lightly. "Yeah, that's one of my favorites—I'm a trek nerd too."

"*Trekkie*, sir."

"Excuse me?" Lockwood asked.

"*Trekkie*—the proper term for someone who's really a Star Trek fan is *Trekkie.*"

The agent laughed again and nodded his understanding. "You're right," he agreed. "Trekkie. When was the last time you were up at your mom's office?"

"I don't know—a long time ago," O'Brien answered.

"A day ago, a week, a month, six months?"

"I don't know, at least a year or something," he said. "I didn't like being around her at home, so why would I want to go see her during the day?"

"You got a point," Lockwood said. "I was hoping you could help me solve something confusing about a soda can on her floor. Remember you said your mom liked that Diet Blast stuff?"

"Yes, sir."

"And you have nothing but Diet Blast in your house right?"

"Right."

"So your mom wouldn't have brought Star Cola into your house right?"

"Yes. I told you she was a Nazi about it."

"So how do you think a can of Star Cola happened to get on her floor in her office?"

He shrugged his shoulders. "Maybe someone at her work left it there…Maybe the killer herself."

"You think a woman killed your mom?"

Again he shrugged. "Maybe. They're all a bunch of sharks in that place, so maybe one of them offed her to get a shot at her job. It happens, you know."

Lockwood nodded. "Yeah maybe, just like that one Reman guy in *Nemesis* wanted to off the Captain and take his place."

"I'm serious," the cadet said.

"Okay, Cadet O'Brien, I appreciate your time. You've been a great help," Lockwood said again. "I think we're done here, and unless Mrs. Short has any objection, you're dismissed."

All eyes turned to the principal sitting on the same side of the table as O'Brien. She didn't speak, but shook her head side to side. With that, O'Brien stood from his seat and gently pushed it back under the table. He put his body in the position of Attention and requested permission to withdraw from the room. Short told him he was excused, and Lockwood repeated that he was *dismissed*. They waited a sufficient time for him to leave the outer office and put distance between him and the door. The principal stood.

"Mr. Lockwood, it seems you had an agenda in mind. Do you folks suspect that boy in the murder of his mother? I thought you were here on a national security issue anyway," she asked. "I feel like he should have had a lawyer present for some of your questioning."

"We are here for national security purposes, Mrs. Short, just as I said. We're just following up on every lead. The prosecution of the murderer of his mother isn't our primary focus."

"But it is a focus of your activity here, isn't it?" Short pressed. "You know, Columbine was committed by some very disturbed young students at a high school. If I have one on my hands, I need to take precautions to protect my other students and my employees."

Dr. Starr chimed in. "Speaking as a psychologist, based on what I saw here today, I think that young man has some deep issues to work out over his relationship with his mother and her brutal, untimely death. But, I don't see in him or his comments substantial indicators of generalized anger or emotional disorders that would make a mass incident likely. Of course, you should review this whole matter with your school psychologist and get his or her opinion on what to do—that's what you pay them for."

"It's always the quiet ones, isn't it, Dr. Starr?" the principal asked, or stated.

\* \* \*

Since the medic advised the suspects would be out for three to four hours after ingesting the gas, Tran had taken the time to clean up and change out of her commando garb. Once back in her normal office attire, she sat in her office reviewing the electronic case file on these two *gentlemen*, so to speak. She didn't really think they were gentlemen in the classic sense of the word.

They were far from it. She thought these two were as close to the bottom of the barrel as human beings could get because they were narrow-minded fools who peddled in hate and violence, and preyed on the fears of weak, frightened fools who suffered a scarcity mentality. In that sense, they were cannibals, and they had virtually limitless access to weapons, chemicals, equipment, and information on what they could do with it. Combined with the willingness to act, a generous portion of intolerance, a lack of empathy for others, and a touch of charismatic leadership skill, this was a recipe for disaster. The disaster-in-chief, Kevin Duke Russ, was still under due to his drug and alcohol stupor prior to the arrest raid, but Durl Hasse had awakened from his assisted slumber ninety minutes beforehand. He'd been read his rights, and given a second medical check and something to eat and drink, and now, it was time for Tran to meet him in person. An entry in the file reflected information reported by Logan Noel. She indicated there was tension inside the ASS, with several members challenging one another for positions of prominence within the organization. Russ wasn't immune from the tussles either. He'd publicly dressed down a few of the members for operational gaffs, stupidity, and laziness in the last several weeks prior to the report. That was something Tran could use to her advantage.

The detention rooms were on the far side of the half-used building, closer to the offices used by the local FBI. They were designed to hold people the Bureau wanted to question and not for long-term detention of prisoners, but they'd do fine for the interrogation the NSA wanted to do with these guys. If a greater need later presented, there were federal prisons an hour in each direction, or the city lock-up and county jail right down the street. The latter options would prompt a need for explanations Tran wasn't yet ready to give, so they really weren't viable. She hoped the need wouldn't present.

Tran grabbed the dossier on Hasse, which seemed to have grown much thicker in the last few days, and browsed its contents as she traveled the hall, rethinking whether the interrogation method they'd settled on was the best way to question this suspect-witness, whom she was fairly certain had committed several capital crimes. Although the ASS would have no reservations about waging war on the US government, Tran didn't think measures like sleep deprivation, environmental manipulation, and torture were appropriate in this case, even for this kind of *douchebag*, as her nephew would say. Russ, Hasse and those of their ilk were repulsive beyond measure, but they were Americans, and America proclaimed fairness, equity, equal opportunity, and the rule of law. That wasn't something Tran took lightly.

More acceptable measures like yelling, loud music, and induced stress weren't her normal style either, but she knew she'd have to make final decisions based on the facts as they presented, when they presented. Her objective was to get information from Hasse to determine whether he represented a national security threat or whether he could yield any information about anyone or anything else that might pose such risks. Secondarily, she wanted to know what his involvement was in the murders of Day, Renley, and perhaps even Ketcham, and who else was connected to them.

Tran rounded the corner to find Lockwood and Starr standing near the FBI medic, chatting about the patient-suspect, and heard only the last bit of their conversation but not enough to understand the entire context.

"Did I miss anything important?" she asked.

"Hello, Agent Tran," the medic greeted. "I was just telling Agents Starr and Lockwood that, medically speaking, this suspect is fine for interrogation. He's very agitated, vulgar, and intimates violence. It's a good thing he's chained down."

Tran peered through the small window in the locked door from the hall, but couldn't see anything except the darkened, empty observation area where interested parties could watch an interrogation in progress without being seen by the interrogatee. She saw light shining from a large window at the far end of the hall. She keyed her access code into the keypad on the wall beside the door, and a clicking sound told her its lock had disengaged.

"Care to watch?" she asked, holding the door for the trio.

They nodded and stepped through the doorway, and Tran closed the door firmly behind them. She turned and walked several paces further down the hall to another corridor with another keypad, this one giving access to the front of the interrogation rooms. An elaborate surveillance system covered all locations in the hall, as did a computer-controlled gas system that could flood the area with the same fast-acting gas the team had used at Russ's house. It was an added safety measure in the event a suspect escaped the interrogation room. He could be rendered unconscious quickly with little confrontation before he could get into the main building or out onto the public streets. Tran keyed her passcode again, and stepped inside the hall, smiling for the camera as she sometimes did at the ATM. As she approached the particular room at the end of the hall where Hasse was being held, she could hear his vitriolic rants spewing from inside.

"You mother fuckers got no right to kidnap people, you bastards," he yelled at no one in particular. "I got Constitutional rights. I'll kick your asses back to whatever hell you crawled out of."

Tran found it funny in an ironic way that a man who belonged to a group that decried the United States and the things it stood for, and that advocated the violent overthrow of the government would have the unmitigated gall to cite the very Constitutional he fought against as some form of protection for him. But she knew hypocrisy was a common characteristic of people of lesser ilk.

As she reached the door, Tran steeled herself for what might happen next, and anything could. These sessions could be smooth, easy events like the arrest raid had been, or they could turn into catastrophes like one she'd witnessed as a junior agent. She and every other agent in the building at the time had drawn their weapons and taken cover when a foreign national detained while trying to enter the US escaped a less-sophisticated interrogation room and snatched a pocket knife in an effort to escape. Although the guy only had a small, rather dull, boy-scout blade, he stabbed two surprised agents, and slashed the face of a random secretary in the hall. That situation ended with the detainee taking a round in the leg and one in his knife-wielding hand, and the responsible agent took a quick demotion and transfer to another station. It was an ugly scene that stuck in Tran's mind ever since. She checked the video monitor outside the interrogation room to assure her detainee was alone, zip-cuffed, and shackled to the floor with heavy gauge chain. Satisfied, she opened the door and stepped inside.

"Oh great, a black chink bitch," he said, looking her over. "You gonna' *luv me long time, honey*? You *make it real special*?" he asked, trying to speak with the accent of one of the Saigon prostitutes he remembered from the Vietnam war movies he so revered. "Well I ain't looking for no damn whore right now, honey, but come back later and maybe I'll light-up your sorry life a little."

*Racist to the bone*, Tran thought as she looked at him. She shook her head and firmly closed the door behind her, hearing it click and lock tight.

"Good morning, Mr. Hasse. I'm Special Agent Grace Tran, and I'm the agent-in-charge of your—"

"I don't give a flying fuck, bitch. As far as I'm concerned, your name is *Bitch*, you fuckin' bitch. If you didn't have these chains on me, I got a little sump'n-sump'n for you," he said, grabbing at his crotch.

Tran didn't let him finish the vulgar insult he thought would unnerve or frighten her. She exploded the few remaining paces across the room and

229

tossed the file in her hand at his head. It struck him center-mass in the forehead and fell to the floor with a loud thwack.

"...And I don't give a flying fuck about you either, you fucking piece of shit," she said, venomous spit flying generously from her mouth.

The brown object flying at his head, Tran's quick, unexpected movement, and her thunderous yell caught Hasse off-guard. He shuttered and instinctively lurched backward away from the threat. Tran fell immediately quiet as she slowly circled him, looking him up and down without saying a word. Then, she overtly stared at the wall-mounted camera above the door, and went to it. Reaching up, she snapped a wire running to it, and the small red light beside the lens faded from view. She was fully aware four other cameras trained on the room would catch the goings-on of the interrogation.

"You think the chains are there to protect me from you?" she asked, laughing. "You're even dumber than you look, asshole." She paused. "You're obviously no Rhoades Scholar so I'll spell it out for you...Those damn chains are there for your protection, dumb-shit. You see, if they weren't there, you'd be stupid enough to try to get out of that chair and make a run at me, and if you did that, I'd get to kill your fucking ass."

"You ain't got no gun and no other kind of weapon," Hasse said, suggestively looking her over once more.

"I don't need a weapon to take your sorry ass out," Tran scoffed. "Don't you know, we black chink bitches are born knowing all kinds of martial arts shit that can turn your asshole inside out and wrap it around your head and tie it off with your own intestine as you choke on your own shit."

Hasse was silent for a moment. "Yeah? Well you're full of shit, bitch, 'cause I know you cops can't lay a hand on me."

Tran withdrew her badge and slammed it to the table in front of Hasse. "You see that?" she asked. "What's that say, or can't you read?"

Hasse looked at the imposing brass badge. National Security Agency, Joint Investigations Task Force, he said aloud.

"Oh, I'm surprised you can read," she said. "That's right Einstein—National Security Agency. That means I'm not a cop. Since my job is protecting this country you and your gang hate so much, I don't have the same rules as the cops. So you may want to reconsider what you think you know about my limits."

"Why the fuck did you bring me here anyway, bitch? I didn't do nuthin."

"Nobody would give much of a shit if I offed you in here," Tran pressed. "They're going to kill you anyway. I'd probably get a medal for saving them a lot of damn time, money, and the hassle of putting you through a trial."

"What the fuck are you talking about, bitch? Why the hell am I here?"

"It's rather imbecilic for you to think I'd be motivated to do anything you want after you've spoken to me like that."

"You better fucking tell me what's—"

Tran shook her head and laughed as she sat down in the only other chair in the room, across the table from Hasse. "I see why Kevin thinks you're an idiot."

"What does Russ have to do with this?"

"We brought him in at the same time we took you," Tran informed. "We have him in a room just like this. And you'd be surprised what people will say and who they'll give up when they want to get their asses out of a sling."

"Look, lady, we—"

"Oh, so I'm a lady now? Not a *black chink bitch*?"

"Whatever," Hasse said.

"Whatever?" Tran repeated.

"Yeah, whatever," Hasse barked. "You don't scare me. I been in jail before."

"Yes I know all about your escapades in the sand, Hasse, and your little firecrackers."

"Firecrackers? Firecrackers, bitch?"

"...your time in Leavenworth."

"My firecrackers took out sixty-five of them damn raghead terrorists."

"You think you're some kind of hero?" Tran laughed.

"I'm more of a patriot than you'll ever be, bitch," Hasse screamed, straining violently at his cuffs and chains as though he might break them. "I took action to protect this country of yours while panty-waste like you knitted socks and fucked your sorry-ass lives away spitting out little bastard nappy-headed bugaboos. Then the US government shit on me for doing it, so fuck it, fuck them, and fuck you too, bitch."

Hasse tugged, pulled and strained, visibly seething with anger. Tran laughed aloud some more as she sat there watching him struggle to no end.

"Yeah, come on over here. I hope you get loose—I'd be arrested if I just shot you, but if you get loose and come after me, well that's a different story. I need a little exercise, and it'll be a lot of fun putting you down like a dog."

"Bitch, I'm a fuckin' war hero."

231

"Yeah, what a hero you are. You killed sixty-five women, children, and a bunch of old people who weren't gonna' hurt anyone or anything," she yelled. "You're pathetic. The world will be a much better place after you're gassed."

"What the hell are you talking about? I paid my dues for that shit already, bitch. You can't gas me for it now."

Tran relaxed back into her chair. "You must really think I'm dumb, eh? Guess that shows who's dumber, you or me. See, you think I don't know about the shit you've done since you got back to town, but that's really dumb. I told you, we have Russ in another room. We know about the car bombs, your cousin, and his client. We know about the forty grand, the nigga tree, Day and Renley. We know it all already. I don't need a single thing from you...I just wanted to get a look at you because I've never looked a racist murderer in the eye before. I just wanted to do it now, so I can tell stories about looking a monster in the eye before it was executed. Double-murder, and an act of domestic terror too—that's surely enough to get you the chair or the gas chamber."

"Yeah right. We know how you people work, trying to play one against the other. We won't fall for it."

"Oh, I'm sure *you* won't," Tran said. "And I'm kind of hoping you don't talk because that would be the only way the government might *not* kill you. But you're too committed to your cause and that line of bullshit they fed you to do that. Kevin knew you would be, but he's not."

"It ain't working, bitch."

"What?"

"You're trying to get me to say something."

Tran shook her head, smiled a little, and sighed. "Have you heard me ask you anything, dipshit? In case you missed it, I haven't asked you a damn thing because I don't give a rat's ass about anything you have to say. See, I was in the sand too—as your superior ranking officer I might add. Soldiers like you make me sick. You're a blight on the rest of us, and your dumbass antics drove thousands of Arab and Islamic boys into the terrorist camps where they learned to kill decent Americans. So, it would do me a world of good for you to just keep your fucking mouth shut and not tell us anything. We already know you killed Day and Renley with your signature IED, just like Afghanistan. Kevin's testimony gives us all we need, and it gives you a death sentence."

Tran stood and moved slowly to the side of the table, not taking her eyes off the prisoner. She leaned over slightly and used her low-rise heel to scoot the file across the floor, away from Hasse and closer to her. When it was a sufficient distance from the vile prisoner, she bent over and picked it up.

"I'm outta' here. I'll send someone to transport you, then I don't have to deal with your stupid ass anymore. My business with you is done. I have a witness to prepare."

"Wait. Wait. You talking about Russ?"

"Goodbye, and good riddance," she said, over her shoulder.

She stopped long enough to restore the camera above the door to operating condition, and then blocked Hasse's view of the security keypad with her body. She entered her access code to unlock the door, and then stepped into the hall, closing the door firmly behind her without uttering another word to her potentially condemned prisoner. She walked to the main corridor and entered her key code again. When she stepped into the hall, Lockwood and Starr awaited her.

"You've got him," Lockwood said.

"The anger, inflated sense of self, callousness, lack of empathy and remorse—these are all signs of a deep sociopathic disorder, but I think you've whet his whistle with frightened curiosity about what will happen to him now," Starr informed. "He seems to be developing concern that his comrade has betrayed him and that people might think he's stupid. I'd play that up," she advised.

"And that's where you come in," Tran said, turning to Lockwood.

"My pleasure," he answered.

With that, Lockwood entered his passcode into the keypad, and stepped inside the hall leading to the interrogation rooms. Tran and Starr went to the observation area to watch the *good cop* take a run at Hasse.

Lockwood stepped into the holding area as Hasse sat slumped over, leaning on the table as comfortably as he could while wearing cuffs and chains. He sat up when Lockwood entered the room.

"What, the black bitch couldn't get anything so they sent in a competent white man?" he asked.

"I don't know what you're talking about, Mister," Lockwood answered. "I'm just here to transport you."

"Where?"

"Look, make this easy on yourself as we do this okay because we don't play around with prisoner transport. I don't want to kill you, and you don't want to die today, do you, man?" Lockwood said.

"Where are you taking me?"

"Enemy combatants are housed at Guantanamo until disposal. That could be trial that leads to your freedom or it could lead you to the chair, depending."

"Depending on what, asshole?"

"Depending on a number of things that probably don't apply in your case, man," Lockwood said.

"What the hell are you saying, you fuck? I don't recognize your authority to put me on trial. You're just a bunch of un-American asshole communist bastards."

Lockwood shook his head, but purposely avoided laughing at the prisoner. "Look, I know this sucks for you, but I'm just doing my job, man—I sure as hell don't want to piss off that ballbreaker of a boss of mine, so she says prep you for transport, I gotta' prep you for transport..." He paused a moment before continuing to set the pick, appearing to be deep in thought. Then: "I'm not a big believer in the death penalty, to be honest. But your screaming, yelling and name-calling, and protesting the government's authority—none of it means a damn thing now. Your buddy's information will serve you up on a silver platter, and if they get their way, you'll never see the outside of Guantanamo again after you get there. Your buddy on the other hand will probably go into witness protection and end up on a beach somewhere, getting a stipend from the government for the rest of his life."

"You saying Russ is talking?" Hasse asked.

"The sedative we administered wears off of different people at different rates. Your buddy woke up a lot earlier than you did, so we've had a little more time with him... How do you think we know about all the stuff we know already?"

"Son of a bitch," he said sharply.

"Don't feel bad. Whenever people get into something together, one of them always turns on the other when the fire gets hot. You just happened to be the loyal one this time, and he was the smart one."

"Don't nobody play me for a fool."

Lockwood shook his head. "Looks like Kevin Duke Russ did. Something about superior intelligence."

"Mother fucker."

"We understand you planned and executed the bombings of Day's and Renley's cars because you wanted to impress that Ketcham lady."

"That's bullshit, man."

Lockwood shook his head again. "Look, I can't get into this with you, man. I gotta' get you ready to go. Stand up please," he said.

Hasse sat there looking down at the table, anger burning in his eyes. He didn't move, not even a muscle other than those in his jaw as it clenched and unclenched.

"Come on, Mr. Hasse. This is what I was talking about...just make it easy on yourself and cooperate. I'm not your enemy here. I'm just following orders to prep you for transport just like you're following Russ's orders to keep your mouth shut."

"That bastard don't give me no orders," Hasse yelled. "And he ain't my boss."

"Really? Because the information we have is that he runs that little Aryan boy-band you belong to, and the rest of you are his minions."

"What the hell are you talkin' about?" Hasse resisted. "I ain't no damn vegetable."

"I said *minion*," Lockwood said, laughing lightly as he spoke. "A *minion* is a servile underling and an onion is a pungent vegetable, Mr. Hasse."

"Whatever, I don't really give a shit bout your damn English lesson, you tool. Russ is a bigger fuckin' idiot than you an' I ain't his *service underling*," Hasse blurted, mocking the words Lockwood had used.

"He made you do the Day and Renley bombings, so it looks like you are his underling."

"He tell you that?" Hasse barked. "Yeah, I took out the nigger with the fancy car, All right, but not because Russ made me do it. I wanted the money my fuckin' self 'stead of sharin' it with that re-tard, so I did it on my own...He thinks he so damn smart, but he didn't knowed it was done 'til it was done."

"Hmmp," Lockwood said, nodding his head. "I admit it, I'm a little curious about something... I'm sure you know from the news that the Ketcham woman's dead...why were you so sure she'd honor her end of the deal? How did you know she and Russ wouldn't try to set you up or something? From everything I can tell, she was a real backstabber."

Hasse smiled as devious a smile as he could muster. Then, proudly, he said, "Let's just say I took me out a little insurance policy."

"What do you mean?" Lockwood asked.

"I mean I recorded our conversations about the jobs she wanted done. From the very first one right up through the one when I confirmed I picked up her money out the tree. Neither of them even suspected it, so I'd have some company if either one of `em tried to send me up the river."

"So what happened? Did she get wind of it so you decided to take her out?"

"What?" he asked, wrinkling his face. "Hell no. We didn't have nuthin' to do with killing that bitch."

"Yeah," Lockwood answered, "why should I believe you? If you did it, you wouldn't tell me."

"I take pride in my work, man. If I'd have done her, I'd claim it, 'specially because that shithead Russ already told you what we done. If we'd a done it, we'd a hit her somewhere besides her office—too many cameras 'round there, and too exposed. We'd a gotten her on a county road or at her house or somethin' easy."

"So maybe that's why Russ made you do the dirty work…He'd still get a cut of the money, but he could keep his hands clean if you guys got caught."

"That stupid fuck didn't tell me to do it and he sure as hell didn't *make* me." he continued. "Renley was Russ's handiwork, but he fucked it up, so I did the second one myself—how a real pro does it."

"He would have gotten away with it if we didn't happen onto it by luck, so maybe he's not as stupid as you thought?"

"That stupid ass missed the intended target, and he burned my arm building the damn bomb. And he lectured us about being lazy and sloppy? Who the fuck he think he is?"

"Maybe he thinks he's the head of the Aryan Supremacy Society. It's his ranch you're living on, his equipment you're using, and the group was his idea."

"I don't giva shit about that neither. I shoulda' been runnin' this operation. We'd be bigger an' better if I was. We'd do some other stuff that could make us some cash you know. He tell you about the score on the bitch in Washington?"

Lockwood didn't say anything, mostly because he didn't know what the man was talking about. He knew most people were very uncomfortable with silence in a conversation, and usually sought to fill it with something. So, he simply stared at Hasse.

"That Ketcham woman paid me to follow some bitch to DC and fuck her up good."

"What are you talking about?"

"Some blonde bitch she worked with who was screwing her husband. She wanted me to make her pay for it bad. She was specific about fucking up her face especially. She wanted to make a point."

"Oh yeah, I forgot," Lockwood said, trying to fake as though he knew this already. "The VP of Research at the company—Ketcham learned about that from your cousin. Maybe that just got buried in all the shit Russ told us."

Hasse's expression contorted into one of disgust. "Russ is a small time idiot that don't know shit about commanding troops, but I been trained, you know. I been through ranger and explosives training. Your file tell you that?"

Lockwood admitted he'd read about Hasse's military record, and it seemed to trigger something in the latter's mind. Hasse realized Lockwood was sitting in the chair across from him, listening but not preparing him for movement anywhere.

"Hey, man," Hasse said. "You in here acting like you understand me and bein' all sympathetic or something but you're just trying to get information outta' me just like that chink bitch boss of yours. What kinda man are you, takin' orders from a woman, 'specially a black chink bitch?"

"I'm just following orders, and I was told to get you ready."

"Then why ain't you doing it?" Hasse challenged. "Well I got news for you, boy. You didn't read me my rights when you came in here so none of that shit I said is admittable in your pathetic courts no-way. I know my rights, dumbass."

Lockwood shook his head, in simultaneous pity and delight. He knew the suspects had been read their rights by other personnel at the station at least twice already, but even if he'd not been so informed, Hasse demonstrated he already knew and understood his rights. Under those facts, a court wouldn't likely invalidate the admissibility of his statements. Rarely was Lockwood presented with so fine an opportunity to apply one of his favorite quotes. He'd not waste it. *"A little learning is a dangerous thing,"* he said aloud. *"Drink deep, or taste not the Pierian Spring. There, shallow draughts intoxicate the brain and drinking largely sobers us again."*

"What the hell you babbling about?" Hasse snapped, a perplexed expression distorting his face. "You stupid or what?"

Lockwood smiled and then left the room. As he exited the hallway, he saw the other detainee locked down at the table in Interrogation Room One at the other end the corridor. He paused a moment, and then walked the rest of the way to the main hallway outside of interrogation. Immediately, he went to Observation One, where his colleagues greeted him in whispers, congratulating him on his winning performance. They didn't celebrate for long. The medic assured the group of Russ's satisfactory medical status, and like his colleague, he'd been read his rights, informed of his status, and given just enough food and drink to prevent distraction.

Tran went in to speak with him first. Based on her interaction with Hasse, she had low expectations of this encounter, and mentally prepared herself for another round of combat.

"Good afternoon, Mr. Russ," she began, stepping inside and closing the door behind her. "I reviewed your file, so I know you've been read your rights already. I'm Special Agent Grace Tran, agent-in-charge of this case."

"Good afternoon, Miss Tran," he greeted. "And just what in the heck do you think you got against me such that violating my private property and kidnappin' me is the right and Godly thing to do?"

Kevin Duke Russ was a pale, unkempt forty-six year-old Caucasian whose physique and overall condition made him look more like sixty. He closely resembled the stereotype of an 11th-grade dropout who'd had a difficult time in life, bumping around between a series of no-skill jobs, eating hand-to-mouth, paycheck-to-paycheck and never quite getting off the ground. His lack of education and worldly exposure had fostered a strong xenophobic bent in him, and his lack of opportunity further ingrained and radicalized it. His black-and-white constructs of the world made it inconceivable in his mind that someone could disagree with him and still merit respect, and his overly simplistic views rendered him incapable of drawing parallels between his own circumstances and those of the *ragheads, sand niggers, and wetbacks* he so often railed against. His *us-or-them* and *they're-taking-our-jobs* speeches and segregationist views showed a scarcity mentality that might have been pitiable if fewer Americans secretly shared them, and worse, acted on them. Unlike Russ and his crew, many of those types had long-ago shelved their white, pointy hoods, and had instead gone underground to use more covert, pernicious tactics like voter-exclusion schemes, educational repression, health care disparities, and financial servitude, while smiling and pretending they didn't. This type was much more dangerous and destabilizing because they were harder to see. Russ and his crew weren't this more cunning breed, but had instead opted to be openly defiant, hostile, active, and vocal. For that reason alone, Tran was surprised by the decidedly civil tone with which Russ had initially addressed her.

"That's quite a different tone from the one your boss used with me."

"A'scuse me," Russ said, raising his brow. "My boss?"

"Yes, Durl Hasse. He seems like the angry violent type. He addressed me as a *black chink bitch*. You sure he won't take it out on you for being courteous to me?"

"I'm sorry 'bout that, Miss Tran" Russ offered. "We clearly have different...interests shall we say, but there ain't no need for personal animalosity 'atween us."

Tran stared incredulously at him for a moment as she took the seat opposite him. "I quite agree there's no need for *animosity between* us, Mr. Russ. I must admit my curiosity about something, though. Do you suggest it's okay to insult, threaten, and be violent to a whole group of people but not to one of them individually?

"No, Miss Tran. I mean the things we do serve a greater purpose but it don't serve no purpose for me to be insultin' to you in this here little room," he explained. "Your kind and mine, we're just different. You need to go stay with your people back home in Africa where you came from, and we'll keep to ourselfs here in America where we're from," he said.

"But it's more than that, isn't it, Mr. Russ? You think you're better than women and people of color, don't you?"

Russ shrugged his shoulders in resigned acceptance. "Can't help that's how God made things, Miss Tran. White people are s'pose to be the superior race see, and mens are s'pose to run their women. That's why God made white men dominant over all other races and the fairer sex."

Tran stared at the man with absolute disbelief. She could discern no objective criteria by which a guy like Russ could think himself inherently better than anyone else, and that was particularly poignant in individual comparisons. Education, wealth, physical prowess, IQ, constructive contributions...by all such measures, and likely any others, Russ couldn't hold a candle to her or anyone she knew.

"And if you think about it, it's much more humane and fair to your kind because then y'all don't have to compete in stuff you can't really do. Why give your people false hope, especially to them little black, brown, yellow, and A-rab kids? Don't make 'em aware of what they can't do; just let 'em be happy where they are. Why would a woman want to distract herseff from her womanly duties to worry 'bout runnin' anything other than her house and kids...and maybe her man, behind closed doors?"

He giggled slightly as he delighted in his own humor, and Tran continued to look upon him, nearly dumbstruck by the depth of his ignorance. By most calendars, it was the 21st century, yet centuries-old notions still sputtered in the heads of people like Russ.

"And by the way, he ain't my boss. If anything, I'm his."

Tran knew the real story, but she was in the midst of a thespian performance. She looked at pages of hand-written notes on Hasse's comments, and knew they didn't say exactly what she was pretending they did.

"Sorry, but I wrote it down when he said it. He's in-charge of the Aryan Supremacy Society—you only felt your oats once in a while. You're telling me it's not actually him?"

Russ said nothing in reply. He simply sat there staring at Tran for a full minute of silence. Finally, he spoke.

"He—ain't—my—boss."

"Apparently you two need to get your facts straight because he says otherwise. Wanna know what he said?"

Russ again said nothing.

"He said you were, and I quote, *a fucking idiot* and a *retard.*"

"It ain't working, Miss Tran," Russ resisted.

"He told us you planted the explosives in Renley's car, and that you, quote, fucked that up too. Said you killed the wrong person, that you actually meant to kill the dead guy's wife, but said you were a total fuck-up."

"It ain't working, Miss Tran," Russ repeated.

"He said he recorded your conversation with the woman who hired you to kill those gentlemen because he thought you and Ketcham might try to backstab him—then he'd have a little insurance policy, he said."

"It ain't working, Miss Tran."

"Durl said the Aryan Supremacy Society would be bigger and better-known under his leadership because you're a small-time idiot who doesn't know a damn thing about commanding troops."

"It ain't working."

"Yes, so you keep saying, Mr. Russ. Why is that?"

Russ laughed in a way intended to show overt condescension. "We know a lot about your interrogation tactics," Russ said. "Divide and conquer—play one against the other. Well it won't work. I ain't saying nothing and none of my people will either. We've trained extensively to resist your interrogations, Miss Tran."

It was Tran's turn to laugh condescendingly. "In the words of the inimitable boxer, Mike Tyson, *everybody has a plan until they get punched in the face,*"

240

she said, shaking her head in feigned pity. "Well, you've been punched in the face, Mr. Russ. You'd be surprised what people will say and who they'll give up to save their own asses, your training notwithstanding. Despite your mantra, your people talked and talked freely. They'd rather cut a deal for themselves and hang you out to dry."

Russ silently stared daggers at Tran, and Tran picked them out and threw them back.

"There's really no need for you to say anything to me, Mr. Russ. Your colleague, your boss, your employer, whatever he is to you, Hasse has already given us everything we need to sentence you. We know about the car bombs, Mr. Hasse's cousin and his client, and the forty grand in the *nigga tree* to pay you when it was done."

"Then why are you here talking ta' me?" he asked. "See, I think you're in here 'cause you want to get some intelligence information out of me about what we got and what we're up to."

Tran chuckled. "Yes, Mr. Russ. I'd love to hear some intelligence out of you, but I'm only here because SOP requires it," she explained. "My higher-ups apparently think prisoners should have a chance to report agent brutality or impropriety before being transported. Where you're going though, I don't think it'll matter much."

Russ again sat silently staring at Tran, sizing her up and trying to determine her end-game. He didn't want to believe any of his folks had broken their code of silence when it came to cops and feds, but then again, he knew the brain capacities of his brothers-in-arms, and apparently, Hasse was singing like a bird. Now, he had a choice: fall on the sword and stick to his principles, or bail on them and cut the best deal he could for himself before his comrades used up all the bargaining chips, leaving him holding the bag and bearing the brunt of negative fallout. He fell back to one of the tactics they'd learned—use the enemy's rules and regulations against them.

"Your laws require you to tell me the charges against me," he said.

Tran nodded, and then opened the hard copy file.

"That's been done once already, Mr. Russ, but if it makes you happy, I can do it again… You've been arrested for conspiracy to use a weapon of mass destruction, use of a weapon of mass destruction, murder, and conspiracy to commit murder in connection with the deaths of Erich Day and Marcus Renley. To be fair, I should also say that by the time your case is ready for trial, the US Attorney could draw up some other charges against you too."

"Who are those people you mentioned?" he asked.

Tran smiled. "We'll just establish for the record that you pretended not to know who these people were or that you had nothing to do with it okay, so you needn't go through the motions…We also have information that you may be connected to the murder of your employer in this scheme as well—Francine Ketcham." She stretched the truth a bit, but that was okay—a little pressure would be good for Russ.

"All I know is you folks trespassed onto private American property in the middle of the night, kidnapped me, and brought me here against my will."

Tran faked a cringe at the use of such a harsh description of her team's overnight action. "I wouldn't quite use the word *kidnapped*, Mr. Russ. We arrested you in connection with a lawful order of the US Foreign Intelligence and Security court in Washington…"

"I don't recognize the authority of your courts over me."

"Be that as it may, Mr. Russ, you're under arrest by authority of those very courts acting on the laws of the United States of America. Anything else you care to know before we send you off?"

"Send me off?" he repeated. "Where are you sending me?" he asked.

"Enemy combatants are held at the Guantanamo facility, Mr. Russ."

There it was…a slight sneer on Russ's face. Tran could tell he was trying to conceal his reaction, but she saw it nonetheless. The idea of being shipped to Guantanamo was evidently what coaxed the reaction, and she assumed the company he'd keep there was what bothered him the most. Russ couldn't figure out how to object to being housed with middle-east terrorists without also showing the federal idiots holding him that they'd hit a nerve. They'd certainly hold it over his head.

"You have no authority to do that, Miss," he said. "It's illegal."

"It may surprise you to know you're not the first one to make that argument, Mr. Russ, but until the President tells me otherwise, enemy combatants will be held at Guantanamo."

"You can't do that."

"Sure we can. The Aryan Supremacy Society isn't a recognized nation by the UN or any legitimate government, and you're not a party to the convention on the treatment of prisoners of war. At the same time, you've declared that you're not bound by US law while you occupy land within the sovereign territory of the United States. Since you've also advocated the violent overthrow of the recognized US government, you've committed an act of war under international law. So, you present an interesting conundrum.

242

We really don't know what to do with you, to be honest. That's way above my pay grade, and until the Attorney General determines exactly how you're to be held, tried, and executed, you go to Guantanamo."

She waited a moment.

"Listen, Mr. Russ," she continued. "I won't insult your intelligence by pretending what I'm about to say is anything other than what it is, so here it is…If you want to fully cooperate with federal authorities, I'll convey your offer to the US Attorney. I can make no promises other than convey your offer, but she may be willing to make a deal with you that keeps you out of Guantanamo and may even keep you from the death penalty. It may be inconsistent with your ideology, but you can take heart that you'll have company. Maybe you and Mr. Hasse can plan your futures together. Or, let him cut a deal by himself and take over your group, your farm, and your girl."

For the umpteenth time in a very short span, Kevin Duke Russ sat in silence, staring hard at Special Agent Tran. She had him trapped up a tree just like a `coon, and he was slowly coming to see it. He had the option of a bad choice or another bad choice, and if he thought about it very carefully, he could probably come up with another bad choice.

# Chapter 10

# Quilting

"Yes sir. We've completed our investigation and we're about ready to wrap it up here," Tran said in reply to her superior's query.

"Give it to me in a nutshell, Tran," General Sharp said.

"In a nutshell, sir, there are significant issues here, not just with the particular matter that brought us down here, but also in who these people are. They may look good and smell good on the outside, but on the inside, things are rotten. They say the right stuff and maybe they even mean it when the words roll from their lips onto the pages, but they're too weak and unprincipled to carry it into reality."

"Sounds like you've got some philosophical differences with them, Tran," the General summarized.

"I do, but it's more than that, sir." She shook her head in disgust as she mentally reviewed the situation. "Their integrity has been overwhelmed by their individual desires for money, power, and influence, and that dynamic has adversely affected the projects they're doing for us. Without a doubt, it has resulted in severe compromises to two UAV programs and has elevated the risk profile for our troops, national security objectives, and diplomatic initiatives."

"You're sure of this?" Sharp asked.

"Absolutely, sir."

There was a slight pause on the Fort Meade end of the call as General Ken Sharp, Director of the National Security Agency, considered Tran's report and the next plausible steps. This would be a big decision and a bold move, with consequences that hit the national budget priorities and maybe even garner the unwanted attention of a sharply divided, deeply partisan, and increasingly biting Congress. Worse, it would force the Secretary to reevaluate resource allocations he'd advocated to the President in supporting the defense posture of the United States. But, it was better to deal with bad news head-on and right away rather than waiting for a crisis to surface before taking corrective action.

"All right, Tran," he finally said. "I trust you implicitly, the Secretary trusts you, and the President himself is fast-becoming a personal fan of yours. In the words of one of my favorite pop icons, *make it so.*"

"Yes, sir," Tran said, smiling. "Thank you very much. I'll brief you again afterward."

Tran disconnected the line to Fort Meade, and then sat back in her chair, already contemplating how the next few steps would unfold. In the week since Field Team Six wrapped up its investigation and transmitted its report to Headquarters, the Director of National Security had reviewed and approved it, and circulated it among the Pentagon brass and DC power-players that needed to be involved. Given the value of the contract and the potential impact on military operations, national security, and international relations, the investigation had visibility all the way to the White House, and General Sharp's call was the culmination of thoughts, opinions, and concurrences of a plethora of senior government officials. Considering the size of the federal bureaucracy and the varying agendas of the people involved, it was remarkable that decisions of this magnitude had been made and approving nods given so quickly, but that was par for the course when the President of the United States took a personal interest in an issue. With the *go-ahead* from the Director of National Security, Tran would now move to the penultimate phase of her work in Seaside Beach. But first, she had to activate the coordination plan she and Special Agent Allen had worked out, and brief the local authorities about the status of the investigation.

Earhardt-Roane's top brass, as well as the city's mayor, police chief, and head detective had in the last few weeks repeatedly pressed for information about Tran's investigation. Indeed, they routinely badgered Tran and her team members, called Air Force and Defense Department officials, intimated legal filings, and threatened to involve their Congressional representatives in an effort to move the issue to closure sooner rather than later. As they explained, they were eager to put this issue behind them and return to business as usual. In addition to the anxiety fomented by lacking information and an inability to manipulate a desired outcome, the company's stock price, revenues, and good will continued to take a beating as speculation mounted about what was happening with its federal contracts. They were thus very receptive when

Vivian Lawrence contacted them to arrange a short-notice meeting. Tran took her whole team, save Lawrence, and drove out to the magnificent corporate facility to deliver the briefing. The clear, blue, sunny skies made for a beautiful morning drive, but the dark clouds on the horizon promised a menacing afternoon. *Perhaps that was an appropriate omen for the folks with whom she was meeting,* Tran thought.

Between the inspection of the initial scene and several visits in follow-up, this was Grace Tran's fifth time in Earhardt-Roane's corporate headquarters. As the quintet journeyed through the well-groomed gardens of the parking lot into the ornate main lobby and then upstairs through deep burl wood hallways to the corporate boardroom in the penthouse, Tran marveled at the meticulous appearance the company had obviously gone to great lengths to create. The facility truly projected the image of a professional organization dedicated to its employees, its shareholders, and its stated mission of public service. ERAC relied on it in great measure to curry the favor of well-positioned people who decided matters that affected its bottom-line, so the importance of appearance couldn't be emphasized enough in the mind of its president and in the executive wing. It was also part and parcel of the Earhardt-Roane Avionics corporate culture. The facts evinced through the investigation seemed to suggest that substance, quality, and character occupied very prominent positions in the rearmost flanks of their secondary afterthoughts.

Tran's group arrived roughly ten minutes early for the meeting, and as they walked toward the boardroom, they could hear the low din of pre-meeting strategizing, pondering, and general discussion. As the president's secretary escorted them into the room, all talking among the people assembled there stopped at once. Tran walked with purpose to the center chair on one side of the table and seated herself as her team members took seats to her right and left. The locals were all seated on the opposite side of the table.

"Good morning, ladies and gentlemen," Tran began. "You may remember Special Agents Lockwood, Starr, Ito, and Kenison," she said, motioning to them respectively, "and I'm the Agent-in-Charge Grace Tran."

"Yes, of course, Ms. Tran," the lawyer greeted. "And just to refresh your recollections, this is."

Attorney Matos began to reintroduce the attendees, but it was unnecessary. As she quickly surveyed the room, she saw the faces of all the key players in this drama—Earhardt-Roane Corporation President Don

Johnston, Executive VPs Rick McCool, Frank Grounds, and John Watchman; VP & General Counsel Chuck Matos; VP for Research Betty French-Catin, VP & Chief Compliance Officer Matt Nichols; VP of Human Resources Eilene Reynolds; VP of Public Affairs Dan Williams, and; Chief of Corporate Security Keithe Mantix.

From the town, Mayor Dean Cuthbert, Seaside Beach Police Chief Bill Lazlow, Chief of Detectives John Wardley, and Public Information Officer Datillo were all present. There was one additional face she did not recognize, seated immediately beside the company president. He was a very tan, older Caucasian man dressed in a fine blue blazer, a nice unbuttoned polo shirt and tan cotton pants, and he wore three diamond rings on his fingers and a large imposing Rolex on his arm.

"Um, thank you, Mr. Matos. I believe we know most everyone here," Tran said, "except, I haven't had the pleasure of making your acquaintance," she said, walking around the table and extending her hand to the unknown older gentleman.

The president spoke. "This is Mr. Richie Whiteman, Chairman of the Board of Directors. He and I were out on the course when your call came in that you wanted to have this little soiree, so I invited him to attend," Johnston said.

"Pleasure to meet you, Mr. Whiteman," Tran said. "I generally like to meet people under better circumstances, but it is what it is, isn't it?"

"Whatyagonna' do?" the man asked politely, smiling and shaking Tran's hand.

Tran returned to the chair she'd selected for herself in the middle of the opposite side of the conference table. She adjusted herself, her notes, a pad of paper, and her pen, and then officially launched the debriefing. "Thanks for making this time available on short notice… I know you've been anxious about the status of our investigation, and at this point, I can formally brief you about it."

"Are we still obligated to keep this information confidential, Agent Tran?" the lawyer asked.

"We've coordinated this briefing with the US Attorney and the Department of Justice, and for reasons that will become clear shortly, much of what I'll tell you this afternoon will become public knowledge shortly. So at this point, what you choose to say about this matter is really up to you and your people. Are there any questions?"

Tran paused for a moment but there were no questions.

"Very well…Let me begin with the murder of Francine Ketcham…"

She nodded at Lockwood and Starr, who in turn handed sealed envelopes to selected attendees. Lockwood slid to the president of Earhardt-Roane one large brownish-orange document-sized envelope and one standard white legal-size envelope, the outside of which read, *Eyes Only, Don T. Johnston—Personal and Confidential.* To Chief Lazlow and Detective Wardley, Starr passed two separate envelopes like the large one given to Johnston.

"These envelops contain our investigation documents, forensics reports, and a summary report on the murder of your CFO. The hard evidence will be delivered by the FBI crime lab to Detective Wardley, unless you desire otherwise, Chief Lazlow."

"Cut to the chase—what did you find in your investigation?" the mayor asked.

"We have a suspect in the murder of Francine Ketcham, but we aren't making an arrest," Tran advised. "As I said at the start of this, our main purpose here wasn't solving the murder of your CFO, but was instead to determine whether there was a national security risk here that merited action by the government."

"I *told* you this should've been our case, Agent Tran," Chief Lazlow blurted, triumphantly. "I told you."

"And at this point," Tran continued, not acknowledging the Chief's outburst, "we're releasing that matter to you."

"Great," Wardley groaned. "We've been shut out of the investigation for weeks, and now you want us to pick it up, handicapped by an inability to examine a fresh crime scene and conduct our own investigation."

"I think you'll find the work of the FBI's Evidence Recovery Team more than sufficient to do whatever you need to do, Detective Wardley. The ERT set the standard for modern criminal investigations so much of what your department would do is precisely the same as what ERT did here. I don't believe you'll be handicapped by anything."

"No of course not. You just want to blow into town, stir things up, and drop this in our lap," Wardley complained.

"The murder of your CFO doesn't appear linked to a national security risk, and since murder is a crime under state law, not a federal offense, we thought you'd have a greater interest in prosecuting the case, Detective. After all, you do have responsibilities to the citizens of Seaside Beach," she said, repeating words Wardley had previously said to her.

The Detective said nothing in response. His boss stepped in to relieve the awkward moment.

"We'll certainly look at what you've provided. Do you have a point of contact if we need to follow-up on anything?"

Tran turned to the former police officer and former FBI agent beside her. "Agent Lockwood will assist you with anything you may need."

"So then that's it, right?" the president suddenly interjected. "I mean, if you've determined there were no national security implications, then your business here is done and we can get back to what we do best, right?"

"Regrettably, Mr. Johnston, that's incorrect," Tran informed. "We—"

The obviously annoyed president spoke over Tran.

"Goddamnit. I have a business to run here, Agent Tran. I don't need you people screwing with our ability to operate because of your bureaucratic baloney. My patience is wearing thin, and by God, we do have some options here, you know," Johnston screamed, his frustration bubbling over.

His staff cringed at his outburst, and even the local officials seemed taken aback. This wasn't the poker-faced, non-confrontational approach they'd discussed in their pre-meeting about this debriefing, and all of them knew—with the exception of Johnston it seemed, it wasn't constructive. It might even make things worse. The attorney tried to smooth over his president's rant, but Johnston continued, yelling over him.

"Don't think that because you people print your own money and buy ink by the barrel that Earhardt-Roane is powerless to do something about this in court. We've got a bunch of big box lawyers in DC who'll tie you up in court for as long as we want."

The room fell silent as everyone waited on edge for Tran's response. She too remained silent as she quickly considered how best to respond to Johnston's rude, misguided reaction. The law and facts of the case were both on Tran's side, and that's what would ultimately determine the outcome of all issues involved, regardless of Johnston's posturing and threats. Johnston was clearly trying to manage this situation with the same underhanded, bullying, intimidating tactics he normally used to address Earhardt-Roane's problems, but this was a new kind of situation, one he couldn't see beyond the ego in his way. Worse, he was incapable of accepting the sage advice of others who perhaps saw things more clearly. In a way, Tran pitied him because he didn't realize the light at the end of his tunnel was really a train that would destroy him if he didn't handle it appropriately. His legacy at Earhardt-Roane wouldn't be one that gave him the public adoration and regard he coveted, or the favor of his Creator whom he claimed to love. But those were demons with which he alone would have to struggle. Tran quickly decided not to respond in kind, but would instead continue in a calm, measured tone.

"I guess you'll do what you will, Mr. Johnston, but I suggest you take stock of your acts and omissions that brought us all to this table at this time for this reason," she said. "I believe the necessity of that will be abundantly clear by the time I finish here today…if not to you, then to others in this room."

"I'm sure we'll very carefully consider everything you tell us, Agent Tran," the lawyer said, trying to end that particular line of discussion.

Tran nodded. "So we'll leave it to local authorities to follow-up and take action on the murder of your CFO, but there's a lot more here," Tran informed. "We've discovered that Ketcham isn't the only murdered Earhardt-Roane employee."

She paused to accommodate the gasps that greeted her revelation.

"Your prior CFO, Erich Day, and the husband of one of your former employees were also murdered for reasons associated with this company. It appears Francine Ketcham hired two members of a local militia called the Aryan Supremacy Society to kill Mr. Day because he was an impediment to her advancement to the CFO position…"

"That's nonsense," Johnston barked. "We have a close-knit team here that models our values every day in every way. I wouldn't tolerate anything less."

Amazed at the bold inaccuracy of Johnston's assertion, Tran forced herself to stifle a laugh. She hadn't been around Earhardt-Roane very long, but in the short time she had been, she could easily see significant incongruity between the president's views and those of his line employees. *It's a case of corporate Quadrant Two syndrome*, Tran thought, recalling the Johari Window she first studied in freshman Psych. Either Johnston was lying about the nature of his organizational culture or he was oblivious to an insidious reality others around him knew well. Neither was good for any organization, its people, or its mission. She wondered how much better the company could be and what great things it could really achieve if it truly meant what it claimed in its PR materials.

Tran shrugged in resignation or perhaps dismissal. "It's not my place to tell you how to run your company, Mr. Johnston, but the generally accepted view amongst many of your employees and even some of their spouses appears to be that the environment here is cutthroat and that your corporate executives would do anything to enhance their money, power, and ego, including murder."

"That's preposterous," Johnston resisted. "Our annual environment surveys prove that we live our value statements, Agent Tran."

Tran felt a bit of shame that she found Johnston's discomfort humorous, but she couldn't deny this instance had an entertaining quality. She pressed forward.

"Mr. Johnston, have you ever been in Francine Ketcham's office?" Tran asked.

The president wrinkled his brow, tacitly wondering about the point of Tran's innane question. "What? Of course I've been in her office."

"So you'll recall a pair of blue and white porcelain Chinese vases?"

Johnston paused, still not seeing the connection to anything of relevance. "Yeah maybe."

"Those vases belonged to Erich Day. The evidence shows Francine Ketcham extorted them from Mr. Day or accepted them as payment."

"Or he gave them to her as a gift," Matos interjected. "If that happened at all, you can't possibly know their motivations."

"Have you ever given $300,000 out of your own pocket to a subordinate, Mr. Matos? These vases are authentic 18th century Qianlong Dynasty pieces valued at $150,000 each," Tran said. "Why would Day give such a gift to Ketcham when they weren't long-term friends? They'd only known each other a few years, and outside of work, they had no interaction with one another at all."

Matos didn't quite know what to say about that information. "I just have a hard time believing what you're saying here, Ms. Tran."

"One of the video files found in Ketcham's home safe shows a meeting between her and Day in which he indicated he couldn't give her the raise she demanded without raising suspicion that would get them both into trouble. He specifically said your VP of HR would ask too many questions about the raise, especially without a corresponding increase in responsibilities. This would have come on the heels of an enormous raise she received six months earlier. Day pleaded that the rare vases he gave were more than adequate to cover the difference, and he'd take care of the salary adjustment next year."

Matos shook his head. "I knew Francine very well. We talked all the time. We lunched together regularly. I just find this too incredible to believe."

"So, you'd be surprised to learn that Francine Ketcham hired a private investigator to gather dirt on her colleagues?" she asked. "She had peoples' affairs, trysts, encounters and social foibles carefully documented and, Mr. Johnston, maybe you'd be surprised to learn she even had some of this on video."

"She just wasn't that kind of person," Matos resisted.

Tran turned her attention to the VP for Research. "Dr. Catin, I understand you had some difficulty during a trip to Washington, DC a short time ago?" Tran said.

Catin froze when she heard her name called in a serious forum like this, but immediately relaxed when she realized she could reply with just a minimal response. "Yes," she said.

"Well, I'm sorry to inform you that it was orchestrated by Francine Ketcham."

Gasps wafted through the room.

"I can't believe that," Matos said.

"One of the men we took into custody confessed to the crime, and the evidence corroborates his story…He was on the same flight as you to Washington, Dr. Catin, and he stayed at the same hotel, just down the hall as a matter of fact. He clocked your movements while you were there, and when the time was right, he attacked you with orders from Ketcham to mess up your face and make you hurt."

"This is absurd. Why would Francine Ketcham want to do that to Dr. Catin?" Detective Wardley asked.

"Yes, they were friends," Matos added.

Tran hesitated before offering a verbal response, and instead looked to Dr. Catin. Although she didn't realize it at the time, Catin knew at least one reason Ketcham might have harbored such animosity for her. Whether she'd share it with her colleagues was a question awaiting an answer.

"Perhaps that's a question you should ask Dr. Catin," Tran suggested.

As everyone turned to Catin for an explanation, she turned several shades of red and the corners of her eyes began to well with tears. After a few uncomfortable seconds, she quickly stood and rushed from the room. The eyes turned back to Tran for answers, but she didn't offer one, at least not directly.

"Okay, what the hell's going on here? Wardley demanded. "There's clearly some backchannel communication taking place, and you should quit playing games and just tell us what you're talking about."

Tran nodded. "There are underlying motivations for a lot of what has happened here, some of them intensely personal. I believe these facts will be extremely embarrassing to people when they come out, and I'm not prepared to go there right now," Tran said.

"That's bullshit." Wardley barked.

Tran continued, undaunted. "More than a few Earhardt-Roane employees identified significant motives to get back at Francine Ketcham, either for themselves or on behalf of others. Several opined that managers here routinely hunt for information they can use to extort their colleagues. Describing the environment as a *viper's nest*, they testified that lots of your managers are *out to get* each another. Shortly before his death, Erich Day even expressed this sentiment to his wife. My point is, there's an underlying current in this company that is conducive to very bad outcomes."

"So some things are a little weird here, but in a big organization like this, there'll always be a few bad apples in the bunch," the mayor bellowed. "That doesn't diminish the fact that Earhardt-Roane and its employees are good citizens and community partners. They take care of their own."

"Marsha Day would disagree," Tran countered. "She filed a complaint with the Civil Rights office alleging that local law enforcement refused to investigate her husband's death, despite her seventy-eight calls and visits. When she got nowhere, she made several calls to you, Mr. Johnston, asking you to persuade the Chief here to look into the matter. She told me you wouldn't return her calls or meet with her."

The police chief scoffed. "If you've worked in law enforcement for any amount of time, Ms. Tran, you'd know surviving spouses are often forlorn and often see conspiracies in every shadow and behind every curtain. We can't open expensive, time-consuming, disruptive investigations every time someone cries foul, especially when the facts clearly indicate a car accident," Lazlow protested.

Tran stoically listened to the Chief justify his department's action, or more aptly, its inaction. When he finished, she declined the opportunity to let him off the hook.

"Having done investigations for over twenty years, I know that reaching conclusions without getting all the relevant facts and giving them a full, unbiased review generally leads to bad results. When that's done by people in positions of high responsibility, with power over the lives of others, it often creates a miscarriage of justice."

"How dare you accuse me," Lazlow challenged.

Tran arched her brow but otherwise sat expressionless. "I don't believe I accused you of anything, Chief."

Silence hung poignantly in the air.

"And I don't have time to meet with just anyone who wants to see me," Johnston protested. "I'm CEO of a major corporation. Everybody wants to see me."

"I'm sure many people want time on your schedule, Mr. Johnston, but not all of them are the wife of one of your senior executives and closest advisors who was murdered in the preceding weeks."

"We didn't know he was murdered 'til just now," Johnston rebutted.

"Perhaps," Tran agreed, "But in light of your special relationship with Mr. Day, I might have thought you'd be the first to comfort his widow simply because he passed away."

Johnston momentarily froze in place, wondering why Tran had used those words— *special relationship*. As his stomach muscles constricted, he carefully examined her face for any tells she might give. It didn't take long for him to pick up on her subtle glances at the white envelope sitting unopened on the table in front of him. Slowly, he moved his hand to the envelope and inconspicuously slid it into his lap. Without opening it, his fingers groped whatever was sealed inside. The hard plastic shape was easily recognizable as a computer flash drive. He couldn't know what was on the device without sticking it into a computer, but the totality of the circumstances made him very nervous, scared really. Johnston was clearly agitated before, but in a matter of seconds, his disposition transformed from anger into something completely different, something so far from the confident pretension of wealth and privilege. He lost his usual swagger, and Tran wondered whether it was as obvious to others in the room as it was to her. She leaned into her backrest, once again mustering all her self-discipline to suppress a smile as she watched Johnston's face grow ashen.

His mind racing wildly, the president stammered. "Uh, uh, of course we were concerned," he said. "But sometimes we just get too busy to remember what's important. Families, marriages, wives—they're the most important things to protect, and help." He shrank into the fine leather of his chair.

Tran nodded her agreement. "In any event, the evidence shows Ms. Ketcham hired two men from Rahain to kill Erich Day and a former employee named Venita Renley. They planted explosives in their vehicles, which killed through concussion, toxic fumes, and flames. They missed Mrs. Renley because her husband took her car that particular day instead of his own. We have these men in custody, and they've both confessed."

"Why would Ketcham want to kill one of her subordinates?" Johnston asked.

"Because Renley filed a whistleblower complaint about misreporting of accounting numbers," Nichols said, thinking out loud. "This is what I was trying to tell you about."

"I DON'T THINK the agent is here to hear our dirty laundry, Matt," the lawyer said, speaking loudly enough to drown out the Compliance Officer and signal this wasn't a topic for discussion in mixed company.

Tran chuckled at the lawyer's effort to hide something she already knew, but she understood it was his role to protect his client. She also understood it was damn near impossible for a lawyer to protect a client too smart to know he needed protecting and too stupid to accept good advice when given.

"Mr. Nichols is right," Tran said. "Renley was cooperating in the military's initial inquiry arising from the Whistleblower Complaint she filed on one your contracts."

"And you're taking the word of a couple low-lifes on something like this?" Wardley challenged.

"Hardly," Lockwood said, glancing at Tran for approval for him to respond. She nodded. "Their statements are consistent with an audio recording of Ketcham talking to the triggermen about the crimes. Voiceprint analyses prove a match between the voice on the recording and the voice greetings on Ketcham's cell and office phones, which we know were recorded by her. In addition, the transaction records on Ketcham's hidden flash drives also support this."

"I just don't accept that any of my executives are capable of such stuff," Johnston barked.

"Perhaps that's a reason why they are," Tran said.

She was actually quite befuddled by Johnston's remark. If Ketcham was capable of blackmailing him and Day over their special relationship, then it stood to reason she could and would undertake other heinous activities to get what she wanted. Tran figured Johnston evidently liked swimming in a river in Egypt because his comment suggested he was deep in denial.

"This is just too easy," Matos said. "Feels like a set-up. If she was as cunning and manipulative as you suggest, why would she create incriminating evidence and leave it where someone could find it? It just doesn't make any sense."

"Most liars are caught because they can't remember the details of all the lies they tell over time," Lockwood said. "I think she created the records to help keep her stories and actions straight in her own mind. She used a lot of odd transactions, dummy corporations, and accounting tricks to hide what she did—who could possibly remember all that lying?"

"That's a lot of disrespectful talk there," Wardley objected. "We don't know—"

"Well we do," Tran sharply interrupted.

She hadn't come to debate the evidence with these people. She'd come to inform them of her investigative findings insofar as they needed to know. The locals would soon have an opportunity to act on the investigation, but this wasn't the time. Based on what she'd seen of Earhardt-Roane's actual corporate culture and values, and the company's mutually adoring, co-dependent relationship with officials who should otherwise keep them in check, Tran doubted whether any of them would follow-up on these ugly revelations, but she knew things like this had a habit of finding the light—they always did. Tran hadn't yet gotten to some of the most important information from the investigation and thus needed to move her briefing along.

"Sometimes the truth hurts, and it's better to just rip the bandage off all at once," she said.

She nodded at Lockwood and he continued as though he'd not been interrupted.

"And Ketcham didn't keep the flash drives where anyone could find them," Lockwood explained. "She kept the records on multiply-encrypted flash drives which she stored in a secret floor safe in her home."

Tran added, "The flash drives contained a lot of files, including video recordings of various events, meetings, and rendezvous, some that even took place in the executive offices here at corporate headquarters," she said, staring directly at Johnston.

"What's on these flash drives? Matos asked, probing what he might eventually have to defend against.

"Most of what we're discussing is contained in the envelopes we provided for you, and all of the evidence in this case can be obtained through the US Attorney during the discovery process."

*Discovery*, Matos repeated in his head. *Sounds like they're moving ahead with legal action.*

"Everything?" Johnston asked.

"Yes, Mr. Johnston…everything will be revealed in discovery," Tran said.

"Who will get it?" he asked.

"Your lawyer can make a discovery request to get it, Mr. Johnston," Tran answered. She furled her brow. "Excuse me for saying so, Mr. Johnston, but you don't look well. Are you okay?"

Everyone turned to the president. He did look ill, but he waved off the question, indicating she should continue.

"Okay then," Tran said, shifting her presentation. "This leads us to more important issues…We found several connections between Earhardt-Roane, your deceased CFO, and foreign entities that are, at best, troublesome. Ketcham diverted money from your Air Force contracts to pay several domestic companies and their off-shore affiliates, and then later replaced that money with funds impounded from your operational cost centers. This complex money-moving process was part of the reason Ms. Renley thought something was wrong, which led her to file the fraud complaint."

"I don't think that's right," Matos argued. "Someone correct me if I'm wrong," he asked of his colleagues, "but the year-end financials show the accounts were all in proper order. If there was anything funny there, the annual audit would have caught it."

"That's how it's supposed to work, but it didn't in this case," Kenison said, taking Lockwood's lead in jumping into the briefing. "After Ketcham doctored the books, her work was approved by the chairman of your internal audit committee, Ms. Hamidi. The accounting irregularities were further swept under the rug by your outside accountants, perhaps thinking it would never become a real problem. But it did, and it doesn't help that the owner of your outside accounting firm is the spouse of one of Ms. Hamidi's employees—which may make him unlikely to find and report anything Ms. Hamidi didn't like for fear of his wife's job."

"Listen," the mayor said, standing abruptly from his seat. He waved his finger in the air as he spoke. "The Hamidis are upstanding members of this community. They do a lot of good for people around here. You don't just come in here and start throwing accusations like that around."

"I understand that Ms. Hamidi is amongst your biggest political donors and that the family name graces a lot of buildings around here, Mr. Mayor, now please sit down… There's more to discuss," Tran said.

She waited a moment for the mayor to resume his seat, realizing he'd be completely within his rights to remain standing from sheer intractability if he so desired. His Honor wasn't a criminal suspect, and this wasn't a custodial interrogation where SOP required suspects to remain seated and chained.

Nonetheless, the older gentleman reseated himself after a brief but awkward stare-eyes contest between him and Agent Tran.

"We're not in the business of merely throwing around accusations, Mr. Mayor. We follow the evidence…What it shows in this case is that the chairman of the audit committee signed-off on materially deficient financial disclosures filed with the federal government."

"You have a big burden to prove criminal intent, Agent Tran, which is far greater than showing Ms. Hamidi merely made a mistake in judgment," Matos countered.

"This wasn't a mistake in judgment," Kenison retorted, feeling his own work was being challenged. "Your own internal auditor, Sue Jackman, detected these irregularities in your last year-end audit and noted them in her draft report. Sometime between her draft and the final report, all mention of the irregularities was omitted from the text…Ms. Jackman would only say she didn't remove the findings and that the report was sent up the chain before it went final. But like any good auditor, she made a CYA memo which we found in her personal notes and papers. It shows the audit committee chair directed Mr. Johnston and CFO Day to remove those findings from the final report, over the auditor's objection. I think that proves intent," Kenison crowed.

"The reality is," Tran said, intervening to address the lawyer's point. "…I don't have to prove anything, Mr. Matos. That's for the US Attorney and she seems satisfied with the strength of the evidence," she explained. "We might be having a different discussion if we were only talking about an incorrect financial certification, but it's bigger than that. Your CFO's transaction records and an inquiry by the Office of Foreign Asset Control show the money diverted from your Air Force contract was ultimately transferred to a Pakistani group, the mission of which is political reform in Iran."

"So that's consistent with U.S. policy," Cuthbert noted.

"Yes it is, Mr. Mayor, but it's illegal for private citizens to take such action—that's reserved to the White House, State Department, and Congress. It's also illegal to use government funds for purposes other than officially approved purposes and then lie about it. That seems to be what happened here."

Tran didn't tell them the money was delivered to an Iranian double-agent who passed it to the Iranian government which eventually used it to buy IEDs and fund terrorists fighting our troops in Afghanistan and Iraq. She wanted very badly to illustrate in as humbling a way possible the far-reaching and potentially disastrous things that might come from their bumbling idiocy, from playing at being grown-ups, and thinking they knew what they were doing. But that would only serve her desire to stick it to a group of people she'd come to see as rich in greed and unbridled ambition but devoid of integrity and good character. The sad thing was they probably wouldn't even care about the butterfly effects of their behavior until it hurt their egos or wallets. That would soon happen too. But the most compelling reason Tran didn't follow her desire was that the CIA brass planned to capitalize on the counter-intelligence coup her team had just handed them. Paraphrasing her favorite sci-fi character, *the needs of the many outweigh the needs of the one.*

"I object to this characterization of Earhardt-Roane's actions in this matter," Johnston said. "If it's true what you're saying about our CFO, we didn't know anything about that."

"Perhaps you didn't, Mr. Johnston, but you should have," Tran scolded.

"Like I said, Ms. Tran," Matos interjected, "there's a difference between intent to commit a crime and negligence."

"Call it what you like, Counselor, but Earhardt-Roane knew or should have known the statements in its federal filings were materially false. In my book, that's a crime. Ultimately, you can tell it to the judge."

She paused for a moment as she reviewed her notes, checking off items she wanted to cover. Suddenly, the door to the president's conference room opened, spewing forth a recomposed Dr. Catin. She'd taken a few moments to get herself under control, but the puffy eyes told that she'd continued her breakdown outside the room. Sheepishly, she returned to her spot at the table, offering no explanation or apology for fleeing the room earlier.

"We done arguing about this?" Tran asked.

Nobody offered a verbal response, but attorney Matos nodded affirmatively.

"All right then, there's one more item."

Johnston sighed. "Oh what now?"

"You know that our investigation prompted the Air Force contracting office at Wright-Patterson Air Force Base to audit the contracts in question here. They'll send you a more thorough letter of explanation, but the program procurement officer— Colonel Blunt—has authorized me to summarize his determinations. To that end, the Air Force has formally concluded your reports are materially fraudulent in four areas…Contract Charges, Scope of Work, Fail-Rate Statistics, and Collateral Repercussions of technology failure."

The expression on the lawyer's face suggested he knew nothing of the issues Tran mentioned. Clearly, his client hadn't fully prepared him to defend them, but Tran couldn't tell whether it was by lie or omission. No lawyer liked going into battle unarmed, but it was a hundred times worse when his own client disarmed him in the process. Matos, and everyone else, turned to Betty French-Catin to offer an explanation.

Pensively, Catin began speaking as though she was unsure of her right to be present or speak. "Um, what makes you think our disclosures in those reports are inaccurate?" she asked, her voice quivering noticeably.

"Auditing officials physically inspected your records and interviewed the employees working the contracts in question. In comparing what they found here to the final reports sent by you, Dr. Catin, they noted significant disparities in reported fail rates and collateral effects, as well as unauthorized chemical research work—something you call NexChem, which the Air Force says is not authorized under your contract."

"Wait, what's this NexChem thing?" Catin asked.

Kenison was very surprised by her question. He quickly thumbed through the accordion file he'd brought with him, and withdrew a paper relevant to the NexChem research project.

"According to an email to you from a researcher named…" He squinted at the paper as though it would help wring clarity from its surface. "…*Something- I-can't-Pronounce* Shinkoda, NexChem is a new chemical compound that renders subjects susceptible to heightened suggestibility."

Catin paused in thought for a moment, overtly casting her eyes upward.

"Oh," she finally said. "That's not a result of intentional conduct by the company, Ms. Tran. We discovered the two researchers working on the project went rogue and started doing things on their own, but that's not our fault, and I fired them over this."

The lawyer's face immediately turned pallid, and the president snapped his head toward Catin. Obviously, they'd not been privy to the decision to fire the researchers and didn't know it until that very moment. Lockwood withdrew his smartphone under the table, and sent a text to Vivian Lawrence. Now out of ERAC's influence, those researchers could be valuable witnesses for further investigation or trial.

For the second time in as many minutes, Kenison was utterly surprised, and again, he jumped foot-first into the conversation. He crinkled his face and engaged the *stupid teenage boy* voice his mother used on him when he said something ridiculous as an adolescent.

"Doh!" He lightly slapped his forehead with his palm. "The email from Dr. Shinkoda and your reply to it shows you knew about the chemical research months before at least one of your periodic reports to the program office."

"Well, I only signed-off on what the CFO and Business Director told me to, so they're responsible for that—Day and Ketcham."

Though he tried not to do so, Matos rolled his eyes at Catin's standard *play-stupid-and-blame-someone-else* defense tactic, and then shot an exasperated glance at Nichols.

Kenison sighed, shook his head, and pounced on her once more. "Let me point out that these are *emails* between you and Dr. Shinkoda, not reports you had to sign and send out, Dr. Catin."

The woman started to speak in further self-defense, but across the table, Tran held her hand in the air, effectively silencing the confused Ph.D.

"Please, Dr. Catin," Tran said. "You're not on trial at this point, and we're not asking you to defend yourself. I will say, however, Mr. Day and Ms. Ketcham aren't here to say what happened, and whether your subordinates did this at your direction or did it on their own, Earhardt-Roane is responsible. When you're in charge, Dr. Catin, you're in charge. You can delegate duties but not responsibility."

Feeling like a chastised child in the corner, Catin fell quiet, hoping Tran would quickly move to the next thing on her agenda. She'd spoken too much and brought too much attention to what she'd done and not done, and that wasn't something she enjoyed.

"The chemical research was a natural by-product of the work we were doing," Johnston explained. "It was an added benefit we produced for the Air Force."

Tran lifted her pen. "So you knew of this?" she asked.

"Of course," the president assured. "This was something we're proud to offer our men and women in uniform."

"If this was something you knew and thought was authorized under the contract, why was it omitted from all your periodic progress reports?" Tran asked. "There was a contract requirement to fully disclose all significant developments and material set-backs at the earliest possible time."

Johnston drew a blank as he tried to fashion a reply. Matos gently grasped his arm to encourage him not to speak further on the subject.

"We'll have to look into that and get back to you, Agent Tran," Matos said.

She half-smiled and shook her head. "Yes, I'm sure you will."

Tran checked her notes once more, and then looked to her teammates, tacitly asking whether there were any other points they thought should be covered. With them offering no indications to the contrary, she moved to conclude her briefing.

"All right then. I believe we're nearly done here. You can read additional details in the envelopes we gave you. I've already told you we arrested two suspects in the murders of Erich Day and Melvin Renley, and the attempted murder of Venita Renley, and at this point, I will tell you federal agents are en route to detain your board member, Iriyana Hamidi. Dr. Catin, two agents will be awaiting you outside the door when we finish. My last order of business at this point is to leave you with these."

Tran stood and slid two sets of documents across the table, one to Don Johnston and the other to corporate lawyer Matos. They opened their packets immediately, their eyes at once growing wide as they darted over the papers inside. The first document was a court order for the seizure of all remaining records, books, papers, computers, items and devices relating to federal contracts and grants involving Earhardt-Roane Avionics. The second was a court order prohibiting Earhardt-Roane or anyone working for it from doing anything else on any federal contract or grant, or making further use of federally funded materials. It also ordered the company to deliver all work in progress, and related data and papers to a location determined by the government contracting officer. The final document was an order suspending the security clearances of Earhardt-Roane Avionics and all its directors and employees pending further action by the Department of Defense and National Security Agency.

"These actions are effective immediately. Federal agents will be entering your facility, perhaps as we speak, to execute these orders. Please ask your employees to cooperate so we can avoid any unnecessary unpleasantness."

She turned to the Mayor and Police Chief. "The murder investigations are now yours as of this moment, gentlemen. The federal government still has an interest in Hasse and Russ, but please contact Special Agent Mark Allen of the local FBI office to make arrangements for the transfer of custody…With the completion of my report and the conclusion of this meeting, my team's work here is done. We'll be closing our files and turning the federal management of the case over to the US Attorney. I'm told she'll hold a press conference about this case at 6 p.m. tomorrow. You should contact her directly if you have any questions or concerns. Any final matters for me?"

The stunned group asked nothing more.

"Very well," Tran said. "We'll see ourselves out."

With that, the members of NSA Field Team Six stood and walked for the door, pausing to look once more at the distinguished group of people around the conference table. Tran ushered her team to the door, and was about to exit the room herself when she heard an excited utterance behind her.

"You gotta' be shittin' me, Agent Tran," someone yelled.

"I beg your pardon, Detective Wardley?" she asked.

"Your prime suspect in the murder of Francine Ketcham is her sixteen-year-old son?"

Tran nodded. "If the shoe fits."

# Chapter 11

# Fallout

With the federal investigators withdrawn from the room, Johnston did his best to keep from blowing his lid in front of the locals. He was angry that he'd been put in this position, and that it had all come out in front of the Chairman of the Board was even worse. Based on the Board's great financial generosity to him over the years, Johnston knew the stoic man was usually one of his biggest cheerleaders, but the things Tran announced in her post-investigation briefing would have severe financial consequences for the company and for its Board members. That meant, it would have severe financial and perhaps other consequences for him personally. Inside, he was frightened that his cushy lifestyle was now under threat, and he was mentally scrambling to determine the best way to minimize the damage.

"How the hell does all this happen right under our noses?" Johnston bellowed.

A few of the corporate executives assembled around the table—Dr. Catin chief among them—were actually at a loss for knowledge as to how the situation had deteriorated to their current straits, but the more insightful and informed among them knew such things happened because in one fashion or another, through intentional conduct, ignorance, or dereliction of their duties, they let them happen. But, none of them offered a reply, despite the enduring silence hanging in the air as the president canvassed the faces of his top advisors. The only one he didn't look at was the Chairman at whom he was loathe to glance.

"Damn it, people," Johnston barked, slamming his fist on the table. "What that goddamn civil service worker just did to us is gonna' screw us over and we don't even know how the hell this happened?"

Again, silence met the president's rage. The Board Chairman watched intently for a few moments, and then stood from the table, no expression on his face. He carefully pushed his seat into place, and began maneuvering himself in a doddering old-man style around the table behind the president.

"Donnie," he said softly, patting the president firmly on the shoulder. "...I'm more interested in what the hell you're gonna' do about this. Not only did you get the company screwed hard, but you're pulling your board into the whorehouse with you. Our ball and chains won't like this very much, and I don't mean wives."

"Richie, we can deal with the shareholders," Johnston explained. "We just need to—"

"I'm not talking about shareholders, Donnie," Whiteman gruffly interrupted. "I'm talking about what really matters here, money. We're going to lose a bunch of it because you and your team screwed-up. All your damn policies and procedures, your silly titles and corner offices, these stupid meetings you hold. All of it is pointed at one damn thing, and you people didn't keep your eyes focused on it."

"We can't panic, Richie," the president advised. "This is a bigger bump in the road than normal, but it's a bump nonetheless. We'll come through this with flying colors."

"At my age, you spend a lot of time going to doctors," the chairman began, "...so I'm pretty good at knowing when one is needed." He paused and bobbed his chin at Johnston. "Sounds like you need an optometrist and an audiologist, Donnie."

He pointed his finger at the president and jabbed it in the air a few times for emphasis, and then dragged it back and forth above the faces of the vice presidents.

"You people had better get this fixed, and I mean quick. I don't need the details."

He turned to the mayor and police chief. "And don't think you people are off the hook on this...We put a lot of money in your campaigns and community development funds, and you boys can bet your asses that'll come to a quick halt if we start losing money, you hear?"

Whiteman stopped talking but held his icy gaze on the two public officials for a few seconds, and then abruptly turned for the door. Remarkably spry for an old arthritic man, he stepped into the hall a split-second later, letting the door slam shut behind him to underscore his current disposition. Immediately, he withdrew the phone from his breast pocket. There was

265

nothing he could do for Iryana Hamidi, but he and the other members of the board could certainly start planning their next steps.

Inside the conference room, Johnston struggled not to show he was unnerved by the chairman's uncharacteristic severity. Nonetheless, he raged internally that Whiteman, whom Johnston truthfully thought an intellectual midget, had dressed him down, and in a way, spanked his bare ass in front of all these people, including his subordinates. But despite Johnston's true feelings about the chairman, Whiteman had substantially more wealth than Johnston, in addition to the capacity to adversely affect Johnston's power and comfy lifestyle. For that reason, despite any pretense to the contrary, Johnston knew he would do whatever Whiteman said, when and how the man told him to do it. If that meant puckering up for some amorous gluteal activity, then Johnston would do it with a smile. He didn't, however, have to give such deference to his staff or the public employees. He turned to the mayor and police chief.

"I'll be in touch with you gentlemen later," the president told them.

"Of course, Don," the mayor said on behalf of the group, knowing they'd been tacitly asked to leave.

They quickly stood, and bolted from the room, while trying to look as though their exit was casual. As they filed out, the tension amongst the Earhardt-Roane employees escalated beyond measure. Everyone knew something unpleasant was coming down the pike. When the conference room door closed behind the last police officer, Johnston lowered his gaze to survey his executive staff.

"So you're really going to sit there like bumps on a log, people? I asked a question and I expect a fucking answer," he screamed, again pounding the table. "How the fuck does this shit happen right under your noses?"

Resounding silence hung heavy in the air, no one quite sure what the president truly wanted. Was he seeking real answers to his questions, or was he seeking a scapegoat? Was he looking to hold the proper people accountable for their actions, or was he looking for plausible deniability? Lydia Mann didn't know for sure, but she was an insightful, experienced professional manager whose mind offered an immediate answer. But the part of her dedicated purely to self-preservation quickly rose up, scolded her, and fought to obliterate those potentially harmful thoughts from Mann's mind. Her silent voices argued vehemently with one another, firing pros and cons, costs and benefits, risks and rewards at one another in a fight measured in billionths of a second. But in the midst of it all, she suddenly remembered

Micah—the Book of Micah, Chapter Six, Verses Six through Eight to be exact. Her pastor had delivered a powerful sermon about it in church a few days earlier. In nearly an hour-long homily about the Lord's expectations of man, he counseled the congregation that God wanted people to do justice, love kindness, and walk humbly with God. Particularly in the circumstances in which she'd found herself of late, the message took deep root in Mann. She wasn't a biblical scholar and thus wasn't one-hundred percent sure what it meant for her day-to-day life, but she'd grown more and more certain it meant she couldn't continue as she had. For too long, people in the company walked on eggshells afraid to say the things that needed to be said and pretending things were all right when they weren't. For too long, people stood idly by while others were mistreated because a manager didn't like their shoes or thought they dressed too nicely, or because doing their jobs uncovered unpleasant realities, or because their failure to sufficiently genuflect in the hall grossly offended some executive's majestic pretense. It was a sickening display, and Mann was ashamed that she'd been one of those people for as long as she had. Perhaps the pastor's pointed message at that particular time meant it was time for her to change.

It became all the more apparent after she'd been involuntarily inducted into the executive ranks, albeit temporarily, especially because people were coming to her with serious work-related problems and expecting her to do something about them. But she couldn't. She didn't have the clout to change anything about the company's operational practices, and she knew the president didn't care about it, provided he maintained the lifestyle he'd come to enjoy. Figuring it wouldn't be long before she pissed-off one of her new executive colleagues merely by doing the job the company asked her to do, Mann and her husband had taken the last few weeks to throw together some contingency plans in the event she suddenly found herself involuntarily removed from the company—that was the Earhardt-Roane custom when members of the company's elite didn't like someone. She took advantage of the momentary silence to quickly review it in her head. Though she planned to work a few more years before moving closer to her grandkids, if worse came to worse, this could become an opportunity to make it happen early. Her momma's voice spoke in her heart, quietly reminding that *God sometimes makes you uncomfortable where you are to get you to move to where He wants you.* As her mother's voice fell silent for the moment, Mann reasoned this was perhaps one such occasion, and decided to step out on faith. God would take care of her because He wouldn't have lifted her up just to let her down. Besides, she imagined that whatever resulted from what she was about to do would be better than cowering under a constant threat at work. She cleared her throat and braved an answer.

"Mr. Johnston, I, uh, I'm not exactly sure what you want someone to say, and I think I may be risking my job here, but are you really asking for input on how this happened?"

There was a collective suck of air in the room as the vice presidents awaited the president's reaction. The lowest level manager in the room was the only fool to voluntarily step into the peculiar morass born of Johnston's ego and anger. He didn't say anything, but instead merely stared at Mann, in equal parts annoyance, disbelief, and curiosity. This last part overwhelmed the others, and compelled the president to follow this line of discussion to its termination.

"I asked didn't I, Lydia?" he said, a dare secreted in his tone and manner.

Mann sat more erect and scooted closer to the table as she nervously fidgeted with her notepad. "I don't mean to offend anyone or point fingers, but we as a management team have an opportunity to learn from our mistakes and improve on things we've not maybe done so well in the past…"

"Just get to it, Lydia," Johnston interrupted.

"…Of course, sir…In my experience, these things have occurred through intent, ignorance, inattention, or a combination of the three."

Johnston nearly imperceptibly sucked in his lower lip. "Really…And just who has been intentional, ignorant, or inattentive enough to cause this mess?" he pressed.

In less guarded moments, Johnston had publicly boasted that, as a southern gentleman, he could charm someone and smile in their face while concurrently plotting their undoing behind their back, so Mann knew he was baiting her. Even so, something welled in her gut and compelled her to press forward just as forcefully as Johnston challenged. The ERAC-indoctrinated part of her pleaded for her to soft-peddle her response and back away from the precipice onto which she'd stepped, but if she had any hope of accomplishing what she wanted to achieve in starting down this path, her reply had to be honest, even if brutally so. At her core, she knew it was an uphill battle but the medallion of St. Jude on her neck and in her mind gave her great inspiration. *Here goes*, she told herself.

"Everyone in management who has overlooked some of the bad things that have gone on here, sir, and everyone who's turned a deaf ear to the reports of our line employees, or been afraid to tell you or any vice president or director the truth for fear of losing their jobs, and any one of us who has allowed this to continue. Ms. Tran pegged it when she said *if you're in charge, then you're in charge. You can delegate duties but not responsibility."*

Zing. There it was, again. For the second time in as many weeks, someone had laid it out naked on the table, the cold hard ugly truth.

"Do you mean me?" Johnston calmly asked.

Mann almost wished the president had screamed and yelled, because she would have been prepared for that, but his calm, measured response was unnerving. His southern gentleman was undoubtedly showing itself, she thought. "Yes sir—you, me, and everyone in this room," Mann answered.

Again, a heavy pall hung in the air as everyone stared at one another. Finally, a second brave soul stepped forth.

"I'd have to echo Ms. Mann's statements, sir," Matt Nichols offered. "In my role as compliance officer, I've seen a number of things that we've not done according to Hoyle. We seem to have chosen expedience over doing things properly."

"So why didn't you prevent that from happening, Mr. Chief Compliance Officer?" Johnston asked.

"Sir?" Nichols said in disbelief.

He wondered whether the president had forgotten the multiple occasions he'd tried to talk to him about things that weren't quite right, and urged various other executives to retool their operations to be compliant with federal and state laws and regulations, as well as with best industry practices. Nichols had made compelling cases and persuasive arguments to support his theories about what was going wrong in the company and what they could do to fix things, but most of the other execs responded as though Nichols had invaded their sandboxes. Rather than focusing on a particular problem he'd identified in her area, the VP of Human Resources had even asked him, "*Who asked you to look at that anyway?*" One had tried to get Nichols' staff members reassigned when she identified problems in his area, and still others had simply ignored preventive advice. The General Counsel had shared similar stories with him on multiple occasions, so Nichols surmised the problem wasn't just him.

"If you're the compliance officer, it's your job to prevent things like what's happened here, isn't it?" Johnston said.

"Yes, sir, it is part of my role to identify those problems, as I have on multiple occasions. However, I don't have the authority to address problems in areas that don't report to me. That's the province of my fellow executives, and ultimately you, sir," Nichols said in self-defense.

"And how about you, Counselor? Are you going to deny your role in this too?" the president asked.

"Excuse me, sir?" Matos asked.

"There's no excuse to offer, Chuck. You're the General Counsel. You should have kept us out of this mess."

"I, I didn't have a role in any of this, sir," Matos protested. "My job is to advise on legal matters, but I'm not a decision maker."

"So where was your lawyerly advice in all of this? This is what we pay you for…and you too," Johnston said at Matos and Nichols. "Your charge was to keep us out of trouble, and it hardly looks like either of you have done a very good damn job of it."

The men looked at one another, not certain what to say or how to respond to the president's berating.

"Sir, I understand you're upset," Matos began. "But I think."

"Chuck, I don't give a single shit what you think," Johnston said, "so you can just stop talking. I've got no further use for you, so get out of my sight. Go clean out your desk. Eilene," Johnston prompted.

The vice president of human resources stood from her spot at the table and handed Matos a large envelope.

"This is your severance package, Chuck. As long as you go quietly and agree not to discuss anything about Earhardt-Roane, we're providing you with six months of pay to help your transition."

"I don't believe this," Matos said. "As hard as I've worked for this company, you're dismissing me just like that because of things I didn't cause, things I tried to warn you about and help you resolve?"

Johnston turned his seat sideways so he was staring out the penthouse window, making sure to avoid the lawyer's gaze. He said nothing, but instead allowed his HR-VP to speak for him.

"I'm sorry, Chuck. I consider us buddies, but the board has made its decision…" she said, lying to cover her boss.

Reynolds resembled a decent person down inside, but she was too close to retirement to risk it all by doing anything other than exactly what anyone with more influence than she told her to do, and the president was certainly one of them. Thus, her opinion on any given subject was whatever his opinion was, and his wishes were her boundless pleasures to service. She'd made it an art form to be effusive in her praise and ratification of each and every one of his decisions. She'd done so with respect to this decision, as well as for the other envelopes she held.

"Security will escort you to your office to get your personal things and take your pass cards, ID, and corporate credit card. They're waiting for you outside the door." She nodded to the ornate double doors leading into the conference room.

Matos stood from his seat, incredulous at the burden heaped on him for matters far outside his control and knowledge.

"Can we talk about this, sir?" Matos asked. When the president ignored him, he turned to Reynolds. "Eilene?"

"There's really nothing to discuss, Chuck. I'm sorry." She waited for a moment for Matos to make his exit, but he seemed too stunned to move. So, she spoke to incentivize him. "Please don't make them call the police."

Matos shook his head and threw the envelope Reynolds had given him to the table with force.

"You won't talk to me, Don?" he asked to the back of the president's head. "Yeah ok. That's fine. I'm a lawyer, you know. I have ways of making you talk to me, you bastard."

With that, Matos stormed out of the conference room, slamming the door behind him. The president rotated his chair just enough to nod at Reynolds. A split second later, Reynolds withdrew the second envelope from her stack of papers and handed it the Vice President and Chief Compliance Officer.

Matt Nichols stood from the table, resigned at his fate as far as Earhardt-Roane was concerned. He gracefully took the envelope held out to him by his now-former colleague, opened his briefcase, and placed it inside. In the same motion, he withdrew three envelopes of his own, offering one to Reynolds and tossing another to the table in front of the president's spot. The third one was for the company's lawyer, but since the president had taken Matos out of play, Nichols kept it to himself.

"It's okay, Don. You don't need to talk to me right now," Nichols said. He turned to Reynolds. "This is a Records Preservation letter asking you to retain certain records, documents, and other items of evidence in the event they're needed in imminent litigation, which I think they will be. And in case you had any doubt, I do already have this information documented in my CYA file somewhere other than in this building. Now since you're aware of the potential for litigation in this case, if you dispose of these items I've given you notice about, you'll have to answer for it in court. I suppose you might

271

have gotten some legal advice from your General Counsel had you not just fired him, but I guess that's not really my problem any longer."

With that, Nichols exited the conference room and the building. He'd sensed things were coming to a head in the last several weeks and had already removed most of his personal belongings from his office. What was left were things he didn't really care about—certificates of appreciation from the Earhardt-Roane Corporation, photographs of him and various corporate officials, mementos from various corporate events, and the like. When he walked out the door, he didn't wish to take any memories of the corporate pit with him, except for material he'd already taken—that was fodder for the book he planned to write.

"We have one of those envelopes for you too, Dan," Johnston bellowed.

"Sir?" Williams pleaded in voice and manner. He stood from his seat and immediately fell to his knees at the side of Johnston's chair, cupping his hands in prayer fashion. "I'm begging you, please don't do this, please, please, please, sir."

"You're the friggin' public information officer. How the hell does our stock take such a beating on the market and our reputation get so tarnished in the media? It's your job to stop that shit from happening, but you're useless."

"Sir, you know I live to serve you, sir, and I'll take care of this, but I need a little time. I didn't cause this, but I can fix it if you let me. Please, please don't fire me."

"Out, out, out," Johnston barked in successively greater volume while pointing to the door.

Williams stood and immediately broke down as he babbled unintelligibly. He slowly walked toward the door, trying to stop the tears from flooding out his vision. He nearly neglected to retrieve his severance envelope, but Reynolds quickly tucked it under his arm as he passed. The remaining members of the group watched as the public information officer departed the room for the last time, and then sat completely still and quiet in the room. Johnston turned to his next target.

"And I'd like to know how the hell those feds got into our business without us knowing about it in advance," he demanded, staring daggers through his chief of security.

"We don't exactly know how they became aware of the murder and got to the building before we did, but once they did, our policy is for our security personnel to cooperate with law enforcement officials and notify me as soon as possible."

"Guess that worked real well," Johnston said.

"It worked as we intended, sir. Our guys can't refuse to cooperate with law enforcement…"

"Why the hell not?" the president barked. "This is our damn building and our damn property…we can do what we want, damnit."

Mantix was shocked. He understood the president was under a great deal of stress at this time, especially after his boss's earlier display, but the man just wasn't being realistic about this matter. It was almost as if Johnston were drunk and beyond reason, but so far as Mantix could tell, the president hadn't taken even a sip of alcohol. But given the president's current distemper, Mantix didn't feel in any position to dispute the man much further.

"Well, sir, uh…"

"Save your breath. Take an envelope and get the hell out of here," Johnston said, staring through Mantix.

The Chief of Security sat motionless for a moment, thinking of how he ought to play this issue out. He'd devoted nearly thirty years to Earhardt-Roane, and he didn't believe the president really meant to do what he was doing, but the facts clearly spoke for themselves. Now, Mantix would be escorted off the premises by his own former subordinates—*how humiliating*, he thought. He hoped for some measure of loyalty from his own employees, but he knew the economic reality of the situation was that they'd do whatever they had to do in order to keep their jobs, even if it was a little wrong. He also knew the concept of economic slavery was one Earhardt-Roane used to its full advantage when dealing with its employees. Mantix stood from his seat and departed the room without question or comment. As he approached the door, he saw shame in the eyes of the security officers awaiting him, one of them who now wore a *Chief of Security* badge offering a low verbal apology.

The conference room was cold and silent after the public terminations of four high-level company officials. No one dared say a word, but Johnston wasn't quite finished. He hadn't anticipated getting rid of Mann today, but he was displeased with her earlier finger-pointing.

"We hadn't prepared an envelope for you, Lydia, but you can clear your desk too."

Mann stood from the table, nodding her head in acceptance and smiling the same genuinely warm smile she'd had for every one of her coworkers. "I truly wish you the best of luck, Mr. Johnston and the rest of you too—I think you'll need it. The Bible says a prayer of faith will save those who are sick, and the Lord will raise them up. If they've committed sins, they will be forgiven, so I say a prayer of faith for you all. I think you'll need that even more."

With that, Mann pushed her chair neatly into place and walked gingerly from the conference room. She felt marvelous. Again, the air in the room was awkward and thick, with none of the remaining executives daring to move or make eye contact with anyone for fear they might be the next convenient target. The old-fashioned ring of the cell phone in Johnston's pocket cracked the silence, causing several attendees to jump slightly in their seats. Johnston withdrew it from his slacks and answered, pressing a button and raising it to his ear. Before he could say a word, the surly voice of Chief Lazlow started speaking. Johnston waved his audience out of the room and then rotated his seat to put his back to them.

"Yeah, Don," Lazlow began. "I just got off the horn with my mouthpiece, and in respect of our years of friendship, I gotta' tell you, I'm not so sure this thing can be contained on my end."

"What do you mean, Bill?" Johnston asked.

"I mean we're going to have to move on the evidence they gave us. We're bringing in your gal's kid for her murder and those low-lifes for their crimes, and we're going to work with the feds to prosecute every crime involved in this mess."

"That'll bring all kinds of bad press on me over here, Bill. We don't need that."

"Look, I hear you on that, Don, but that bitch investigator put a pretty clear shot across our bow. We don't move on this and the Justice Department will probably crawl up our asses like they did yours. I don't know exactly what the hell they can do to us, but I know it ain't good and I know we don't want any part of it. It makes me shit my pants a little because this is an election year, you know."

Johnston banged the phone against the table as he listened to his long-time ally explain why he couldn't help contain the fallout from the recent events involving Earhardt-Roane. "Are you listening?" Johnston asked. "All we gotta' do is maintain a unified front against the feds' involvement in this local issue, and we'll all be okay. I just fired half my executive team up here. We can serve them up to the feds and the media and smooth this thing over."

"My legal types tell me otherwise, Don. They say this could blow up in my face six ways from Sunday if I don't step right here. Besides, the prosecutor wants to move on it."

"You're screwing me here, Bill. I don't give a crap about any of these people involved, so do what you want with them, but I need time before you do. If you don't give me that, I got bad press on my hands, and that means bad business. My Chairman is already piss-faced about this, and that'll just put a nail in my fucking coffin."

"Sorry Donnie old boy. I'll bring flowers but you're on your own."

The police chief hung up the phone abruptly and immediately called the mayor to let him know it was done. He felt badly about doing what he'd just done, but as the mayor had said, trapped animals are known to chew off their own arms to get free.

\* \* \*

Though it was three in the morning, Tran sat in the puffy chair in her hotel room flipping through the late-night television broadcasts, but despite the hundreds of cable channels at her fingertips, nothing captured her interest. She hit the *mute* button and cast the remote to the bed, leaving the faces on the screen miming their reports, at least to Tran. She thought to try to sleep, but knew her mind was still too active to settle down. She reflected on the last several weeks. Between wrapping up odds and ends of the Earhardt investigation and packing her things for the trip home to DC, she hadn't really had time to enjoy her final night in Seaside Beach. Since she arrived, her schedule hadn't allowed time for that dinner she promised to her old flame, or a visit to the actual Seaside Beach. The area offered little in terms of art, theater, or other traditional forms of culture, but it did boast several historical and Native American sites of interest, as well as Li'l Sheila's Barbeque, a small, minority-owned dive that purportedly made the best barbeque east of the Mississippi. She'd been urged to try the ribs which were *so good, they'd make you slap yo' momma*, someone had told her. Alas, she hadn't taken time to do any of it while here. Though she constantly swore it was a habit she'd one day change, it was par for the course when she was deployed for field assignments. With everything now done and ready to load up, this was the first moment she'd found to sit down and really do nothing.

She saw something slide beneath the door into the hall. Instinctively, she visually located her weapon and then silently moved closer to the door to investigate whether she needed to grab the firearm at the moment. She relaxed when she discerned the objects on the floor beneath the door were the hotel's courtesy copy of the Seaside Beach Times and a flat paper bearing the hotel name and logo. The staff was making its morning rounds evidently.

Tran moseyed to the door and lifted the documents from the floor. She first surveyed the bill from the hotel and found herself pleasantly surprised how inexpensive the cost of her lodging had been for the extended period she was there. In DC, she'd have been looking at a hotel bill larger than her monthly mortgage payment, but this was Seaside beach in not-quite-yet the tourist season, and the fact that they'd gotten a government rate didn't hurt either. Tran quickly scanned the itemized charges to assure the hotel didn't accidentally or otherwise include charges for things she didn't order, and then noted that the invoice was being direct-billed to the NSA. She then turned her attention to the newspaper, unfolded it, and turned to walk back to her puffy chair as she scanned the headlines.

***Crash and Burn: Federal Probe Sends Local Employer Down in Flames***, the title read. The US Attorney's press conference the previous night was the local media's equivalent of a fisherman chumming the water. With print reporters creating substantive articles about Earhardt-Roane as well as articles about coverage of the story by television reporters and vice-versa, the local media had evidently gone wild over salacious tales of sex, lies, and videotape, and of course, money, power, and corruption. She'd heard from one of the Assistant US Attorneys that they'd received numerous Freedom of Information Act requests from network researchers in Chicago, New York, and Washington, so she presumed the story might soon gain national press as well. As she began to read the lead story, she was pleased the article didn't mention her name or her team, and could only hope they'd be gone before any reporter made his or her way around to ask her questions she'd have to tactfully dodge. She'd given her standard response many times over the years, but she truly hated saying "no comment" or any of the other iterations of it in response to valid probative questions. As pesky as members of the press could be at times, she really respected the fourth branch of government for its awesome power to educate the public, keep people honest, and punish those who weren't.

As she plopped into the chair, a knock at the door startled her. She jumped from the chair, grabbed her weapon, and gingerly made her way to the door for the second time in as many minutes. She squinted with one eye and closed the other to get a clearer look through the peephole, only to see Lockwood's bulging, veiny, red eye staring back at her and a goofy grin on his face. She shook her head, unlocked the door, and pulled it open, and in the same motion turned to walk back to her chair. Lockwood stepped inside, and followed behind her.

"I should've shot you for coming over here at this hour and peeping in my eyehole like that," she said, flipping the safety back on her firearm.

"Scare you?" Lockwood asked, his grin having now matured into a full-blown giggle.

"Seeing your mug at my door at this hour, damn right it's scary. What the hell, Lockwood?" she asked.

"I didn't think you'd be asleep anyway," he snickered. "You see this?" he asked, holding up the newspaper.

Tran nodded. "Yeah, I was just starting to take a look."

"The locals arrested Dallas O'Brien in connection with the murder of his mother," he said. "The article says he confessed, stating his mother had hurt so many people and that true Marines were duty bound to protect Americans from all threats, foreign and domestic."

"Color me surprised, on all levels." Tran didn't know whether the Seaside PD would arrest the boy based on her team's investigation, and she figured if they did at all, it wouldn't be for a very long time, after they completed their own investigation from square one. That they had done it this fast meant they'd relied on some or all of the investigation by Field Team Six. "What else?"

Lockwood held the front page open and scanned the article. "They talk about the murders of Ketcham, Day, and Renley, and the attempted murder of Mrs. Renley, and speculate whether it was a hired hit. Here's some stuff about Hasse and Russ, and the FBI...and something about the Aryan Supremacy Society being a terrorist group linked to Earhardt-Roane and the Hamidi family."

Tran chuckled, not because she found something humorous, but more from amazement. "The multitude of possible juicy connections of one thing to another in this thing will keep them busy for weeks," she said.

"They've got a bunch of so-called experts talking about the company's business and economics. The market-watchers expect ERAC's stock to tank as soon as the markets open this morning—they're predicting a ninety-six percent devaluation from this time last year and they're saying the NYSE will probably temporarily suspend them on the floor." Lockwood's eyes grew wider. "Oh my God. There's another little piece here about a wholesale house-cleaning going on there."

"Yeah, Matt Nichols told me the president fired a bunch of the executives en masse a couple days ago," Tran said. "They're all becoming government witnesses and informants now."

"No, no," Lockwood said. "I knew about that, but this says the president and CEO is getting the ole' foot-in-the ass."

Tran nearly leapt from her seat and snatched up her copy of the paper. She quickly scanned the various articles until one in particular caught her eye: *A Clean Sweep-Directors Move Boldly to Save Company*. As she read, she learned the Chairman of the Board had met with federal authorities throughout the night and agreed to full cooperation in the continuing investigation and prosecution of any wrongdoings that may have occurred in the course of the company's performance of defense contracts.

At that point, Tran caught sight of Chairman Whiteman talking to a microphone on the silent television screen. She quickly found the remote and unmuted the device.

"...suffering from exhaustion, so we've placed him on leave while we search for a permanent replacement," the Chairman explained as the sound resumed.

"And is that with or without pay, Mr. Chairman?" the reporter interrupted.

Whiteman ignored her question, and continued with what was obviously a prepared and rehearsed statement. "We've appointed Vice President Rick McCool as Interim President & CEO and we're fully confident he'll quickly rebuild the ethical and operational foundations of Earhardt-Roane and begin restoring public confidence. He's already appointed Mr. Matt Nichols to an expanded role as Senior Vice President for Operational Compliance, and he'll report to both the President and the Chairman of the Board. Likewise, he's elevated Ms. Sue Jackman to Senior Vice President of Internal Audit. Both of these talented, highly-competent executives will have sweeping powers to detect and prevent greed, corruption, and nonfeasance anywhere in the company, and together with the Board and President McCool, we'll assure Earhardt-Roane returns as quickly as possible to making important valuable contributions to the defense and security of the United States and protecting its heroes in uniform."

The reporter turned to the camera as Richie Whiteman walked off-camera and got into a stately new Bentley Flying Spur. It would whisk him to

278

the private hangar at the airport, where he'd head to Washington for meetings with executive branch officials and members of Congress.

"...And there you have it, ladies and gentlemen," the reporter transitioned "The Chairman of Earhardt-Roane Avionics announcing early this morning that the Board has replaced long-time president Don Johnston in the wake of serious scandals at the company that rival the likes of the Enron, Arthur Andersen, and Tailhook."

"Wow," Lockwood said, staring at the television screen. "What goes around comes around."

"Live by the sword, die by the sword," Tran offered.

# Chapter 12

## The Truth Will Out

Six months after leaving Seaside Beach, Grace Tran reviewed a file on her team's new assignment. She was scheduled to board a plane in ninety minutes to jet off for some recon on its current assignment, but a sealed envelope was just delivered to her by an armed military courier from the White House. She figured she'd better take a look immediately, and she was glad she did. The orders had come directly from the President of the United States, and though he phrased it in the form of a polite request which he said she was free to decline, Tran wasn't keen on telling the President she'd not take a legitimate assignment he'd personally asked her to handle. The President was bothered by a disturbing report he'd received and wanted her to look into it. She didn't yet know all the details, but it looked like she and her team, including its newest member, would be going on a little trip. For now, though, she had to get to the airport or miss her flight. The doorman had already called twice to tell her a driver was awaiting her downstairs.

Tran packed the communique into her briefcase, slung it over her shoulder, grabbed her roller board suitcase, and headed for the door. She made sure she had her keys, cell phone, and everything else she needed for the trip, and then opened the door. She was startled to find a handsome young boy standing at the door. She didn't recognize him as a child connected to any of her neighbors, and wondered whose he was and why they'd left him unattended.

"Whoa there, young man," she greeted. "You startled me."

He didn't respond, but instead merely stood there smiling at her.

"What's your name?" Tran asked, subconsciously raising her tone of voice a few octaves.

She smiled and crouched down to put her eyes on the same level as his. She'd learned this was instinctive adult behavior when approaching the young of the species so the larger, more imposing adult wouldn't come across as threatening, thus putting the child in fear. Studies had found this behavioral pattern absent in a large population of child predators, but it was normative for typical adults. The blonde-haired, fair-skinned child was about nine or ten years old and somewhat frail compared to Tran's nephews, the source of her only real and personal experience with children so far. He wore a plain blue T-shirt under a light *Devils* team jacket, jeans, a Rolex watch, and oddly, flesh-toned silicone gloves. Viewing him close-up, the boy looked a little familiar, but Tran couldn't quite place him. His large blue eyes stared playfully back at her, exuding an enticing warmth and innocence.

"You needn't speak to me like I'm a baby, Agent Tran," the boy said, matter-of-factly.

His eyes at once lost their vulnerability, and instead took on a cold blankness, menacing and unnerving in a child so small. In her line of work, Tran had seen that look before but in vastly different settings—mostly having to do with criminal sociopaths. Taken aback by her juvenile visitor, she quickly stood to her feet, staring down at the boy. He pressed on before she was fully settled with her thoughts.

"You obviously don't recognize me, so allow me to introduce myself. My name is Michael Ketcham," he said, pausing to observe Tran's face for her reaction.

A millisecond later, he saw that she'd mentally connected the dots, and then proceeded to push past her, walking deeper into her apartment. He removed his backpack, lowered it to the floor at his feet, and then hopped up onto her sofa. Scooting his bum into the back cushions, his legs dangled over the side but didn't quite reach the floor. He looked curiously at his baffled, surprised host still standing at the open door, and then patted the cushion beside him, inviting her over to the couch. Tran stuck her head in the hall and searched right and left for whoever had brought the child all the way from Florida, but she didn't see anyone except Old Lady Reece at the far end, pulling a grocery cart into her apartment.

"Did someone bring you here?" she asked, closing the door and lowering her suitcases to the ground.

"May I call you Grace?" Michael asked.

Tran paused and looked askance at her surprise visitor. "I think it's more appropriate that you stick with *Agent Tran*," she answered.

"Okay, Grace," the boy slowly replied, staring her dead in the eye. "Of course someone brought me here…They're called pilots and cabbies."

Tran found no humor in the kid's multi-faceted, smart-aleck reply. Michael noticed it, but he didn't care. He seemed to love that he irritated her, and Tran immediately took note.

"I assume you recognize my name from one of the case files you no doubt put together about Francine's murder," he said.

"How did you get my address?" she asked, knowing she'd been careful to keep her name and home address off of all publicly accessible documents.

"I might have thought a super-secret agent like you would be more careful about such things, but it was pretty simple really…I waited for you to come out of your office and then I followed you home. I got past your doorman by tagging along with that lady on the 9th floor who has all the kids. He probably thought I was one of hers I guess, or maybe he thought I was her nephew or a babysit-ee or something."

Making a mental note to recheck her security arrangements, Tran nodded her understanding, a little impressed by this kid's resourcefulness. She was curious to see where all of this was leading. "Okay, Michael," she said. "What can I do for you?"

She walked over and sat beside the boy on the sofa.

"You seem like the kind of woman who enjoys solving difficult puzzles and riddles, and other intellectual challenges."

Tran shrugged and nodded slightly. "And?"

"The cops back home arrested my brother for Francine's murder, and he confessed to the crime," the boy said.

"Yes I know," Tran said.

"Well two days ago, he was sentenced to ten years in a juvenile mental health facility."

"I know that too," Tran said.

"I suppose that was largely due to your investigative handiwork."

Again looking at the silicone gloves on the boy's hands and noting his bizarre tone and manner, Tran grew concerned that something very unpleasant was about to happen. Perhaps the boy was angry his brother had been arrested or maybe he held Tran responsible for everything that had happened to him in the last several months and was looking for revenge. She knew she could grab, aim, and fire the Glock under her jacket in two seconds flat and that she could physically incapacitate the child in any one of a hundred different ways equally as quickly. But, she really didn't want to hurt or kill a child any more than Lockwood had wanted to kill that kid who aimed a nine millimeter semiautomatic at him all those years ago.

"I'm sorry for what's happened to you, Michael. Losing your mother and now your brother…it must be very difficult. But for his own reasons, your brother chose to commit this terrible crime, and he has to take responsibility for what he did. I'm not psychologist or anything, but I understand confronting one's criminal actions is the only way he stands a chance of getting healthy enough to rejoin society one day."

Tran suddenly felt very uncomfortable again and fidgeted in her seat. "Is your dad here with you?" she asked. "How did you get here?"

"JOHN-PAUL," Michael began, raising his voice over Tran's, "…is drunk more than he is sober, and when he's not shitting, eating, or passed out, he spends most of his time with that whore, Betty Catin."

Tran's heart fell in her chest. The poor boy had lost his mother to crime, his brother to the criminal justice system, and his father to the bottom of a bottle and the arms of someone he clearly didn't like. She wished there was something she could do for him, but her mind knew there were so many things wrong with even his presence in her apartment, unaccompanied and hundreds of miles away from home.

"I'm sorry you have to deal with all that, Michael," she offered.

"Why? I'm not," the boy calmly replied. "Keeps him out of my way. I can do what I want and buy all kinds of things with his credit cards, like trips for an unaccompanied minor to DC."

"I see," Tran said.

"I knew you would," Michael replied. "You're a pretty smart cookie."

Being condescended to by anyone was quite repugnant to Tran, but the fact that it was being done to her by a child was a really strange sensation. She didn't enjoy it.

"I have my moments," Tran said, again waiting to see where this discussion was headed.

"Looks like you were having one of those moments when you unraveled Francine's murder."

"Looks that way."

"But as they say, looks can be deceiving," Michael advised.

That was an ironic statement coming from him, Tran thought. She wanted to move this encounter along. "I'm sorry, Michael. I don't mean to be rude, but I need to be somewhere else right now and I don't have time for whatever game you're playing. Are you going somewhere with all of this?" Tran pressed.

"You were right," he answered.

"Excuse me?"

"You were right about Francine's murder, but only partially," he said.

Tran wrinkled her brow. "What do you mean?"

"I mean that my brother is guilty. He's the one who bashed Francine's face in and cut the shit out of her because she was an overbearing, controlling bitch."

"You came all the way to DC to tell me what he's already confessed, the evidence supports, and the court has ratified?"

Michael didn't offer a verbal response, but instead, he withdrew a small brown vial from his pocket, tossing it in Tran's lap. She picked up the tube and read the label affixed to its side: *NexChem 86, Sample #06-66 SCMB*.

Michael stood from the sofa, pulled his backpack onto his shoulder, and started for the door.

"Why did you give me this, Michael?" Tran called after him, walking to the door.

"It works," Michael said.

Tran knew what NexChem was, but she didn't yet see its relevance to Michael Ketcham or the case.

"Look through the internal reports the company *forgot* to send the feds. I saw it when I went in Francine's study one night. She'd put something new into her secret floor safe, and I wanted to see what it was. The reports on her desk caught my eye too, so I read them."

He bobbed his chin toward the vial in Tran's hand.

"That shit's engineered to render people highly susceptible to suggestion and I thought, *hmmm, that could someday be very useful to me*," Michael explained. "A year later, it was. Frankly, I'm doubtful it would work on sophisticated intellects like mine and yours, but it works really well on the simple-minded."

"What are you suggesting?" Tran asked.

"I'm more than *suggesting*, Grace. I'm outright telling you the NexChem formula works. Big brother is a big dummy with a big heart. He's certainly got the physical prowess to kill Francine like he did, and he's certainly got a history of trouble with the law and skirmishes with Francine that make him a good suspect, but he doesn't have it in him to hatch a plan to do something like this to anyone, especially his own mommy, even if she was a raving bitch." He shook his head for emphasis. "No, Dallas was just a flunkie, a puppet of a mastermind behind a very complicated plot."

Tran didn't believe Michael, but she had to admit to herself she was eager to hear the boy out.

"The evidence is pretty clear that Dallas committed the crime," she said "Cameras captured video of him leaving ERAC headquarters at the precise timeframe of the murder, and a search of your brother's belongings uncovered the murder weapon, gloves and clothes with your mother's blood on them, dirt from his shoes matched dirt outside Earhardt's building, and the footprint collected there matched his shoe," Tran explained.

"Yes as I said, my brother did the bashing and slashing of Mommy Dearest, but someone was pulling his strings."

"You're telling me some mastermind administered this NexChem compound to your brother and brainwashed him into killing your mother?" Tran asked, incredulous.

Michael nodded affirmatively. "Exactly."

"And who is this mastermind?"

Michael merely smiled. He lowered his backpack to the floor, leaned over and got something out of it. It was a partly folded but mostly crumpled document, which he promptly handed to Tran.

"What's this?" she asked.

"This is just a copy. My lawyer filed the original in court a few weeks ago."

Tran unfolded the paper. It was the original version of *The Sara Buydot Trust*. Its preamble discussed her husband's extra-marital relationship with her best friend in very damning words and phrases, clearly revealing her anger and hurt about it, indicating it was a reason she cut him out her final arrangements. The text of the document directed the Trustee to hold $200,000 for her oldest son until he reached forty years old, provided he met certain conditions. First, he had to earn a business degree with high honors from one of several schools Ketcham identified as appropriate; Second, he had to have a successful career in business management for a Fortune 500 company or operate his own successful business, and; finally, he could have no criminal convictions, no drug use, and no out-of-wedlock babies or same-sex romantic involvements. If he met these conditions, the money was his. But, the moment he violated any of those provisions, his entitlement to the money would be voided and his share would be paid over to her other son, described as the good one. Dallas would then only receive one dollar of her money. Everything else would be held until Michael turned eighteen, at which time the Trustee was to give everything, including the proceeds of Ketcham's life insurance, to Michael outright. He would become a very wealthy eighteen year-old with unrestrained ambition.

Michael waited as Tran read the document. When she finished and her eyes fixed on him again, he smiled widely.

"The truth is, there was no way in hell my idiot brother could ever meet Mommy Dearest's controlling terms and conditions, so it was appropriate that we just acknowledge it and get it out of the way now. One thing I've realized in my old age is that I'm not at all a patient person, and I don't particularly like sharing," Michael said. "But you know, if Dallas plays his cards right after he gets out, I'll throw him a little something now and then, as long as he does what I tell him, when I tell him, and how I tell him."

The boy paused for a moment of thought. Then, he continued.

"I'm fully aware that the Trustee stands between me and my money, legally, but I think he and I will get along just fine. He'll ask *how high* when I tell him to jump…you people aren't the only ones with hidden flash drives, you know."

Tran looked back at the document to see who the Trustee was—Chuck Matos. Her mouth hit the floor as she shook her head in disbelief. Despite her years of experience with people acting badly, she couldn't fathom how anyone, much less a child so young and otherwise innocent could be so vile. It was almost too fantastic, too far-out, too wild to believe. The fact that Michael's young brain could conjure such sinister thoughts and hatch such a gruesome plan was truly frightening.

"So why are you telling me all this?" Tran asked. "If it's true, why wouldn't I just go tell the authorities and unravel your grand scheme?"

Michael laughed. "You don't even believe all of this yourself, Grace. You really think those backward dumbasses where I live will believe a word of what you say or even care? Just think about it: I'm the victim in all of this—a cute, innocent, local white boy with blonde hair and blue eyes who'll play really well on TV, and you—an Afro-Asian, Yankee trouble-maker who invaded our sandbox, stirred up a bunch of trouble, and brought down one of the biggest companies in town. At risk of being rude, they use some very colorful epithets when referring to you behind closed doors, you know." He shook his head side to side and again laughed aloud. "Your name is *Shit* where I come from."

Tran did think about it for a moment. Sadly, the kid was probably more right than she wanted to admit. Tran was sure she could find some corroborating evidence to prove Michael's involvement in the fantastic story she'd have to tell, like proving his use of his father's credit cards and his visit to her in DC, and perhaps she could find evidence that the NexChem compound was used on Dallas O'Brien. Michael had evidently taken care to assure his fingerprints didn't get on the NexChem vial, and had probably taken other steps to cover his tracks, but she was sure she could find something. Nonetheless, Tran shook her head at the prospects for success in further pursuing the issue. Even to satisfy herself there was any truth at all to Michael Ketcham's assertions, she'd have to start a new investigation and chase down a bunch of new facts that really weren't related to a national security issue. Assuming she did that, she'd then have to put her career on the line to persuade a lot of people that might not even give a crap to take action on the incredibly demented fantasy told by a sweet, innocent ten year-old who might be having mental health issues adjusting to the loss of his mother to a brutal murder at the hands of his big brother. It was a bigger mountain to climb than Everest, and Tran knew it. Even worse, Michael knew it.

"How does someone so young get so distorted by unbridled greed and ambition?" she asked, almost rhetorically.

Michael smiled. "I had an excellent teacher."

With that, Michael Ketcham opened Tran's door and stepped into the hallway. "Good day, Grace," he said. "And have a nice life. I sure will."

**--The End--**

**Vincit Omnia Veritas**

Sujata Massey - The Salary Man's
Wife